THE CHRONOMANCER AND THE
Crimson Invasion

Destiny of the Void Triangle: Book two

By Jason Jay Harrington

Narrated by Mason Jesse Hamilton

Cover Art by Ankur Juneja

Other works by Jason Harrington:

Destiny of the Void Triangle: 1 The Chronomancer and the Book of Worms

For updates, content, and more please visit Jason's storyworks, or tik-tok @iroaris for Jason Harrington, and @mashonmiltonx for Narrator Mason Hamilton

For Matt Forsythe and all my friends and coworkers at Autoliv Brigham City, for cheering me on and reawakening the passion for this storyline.

And for Mason and Ankur, together we are an awesome dream team at challenging the odds.

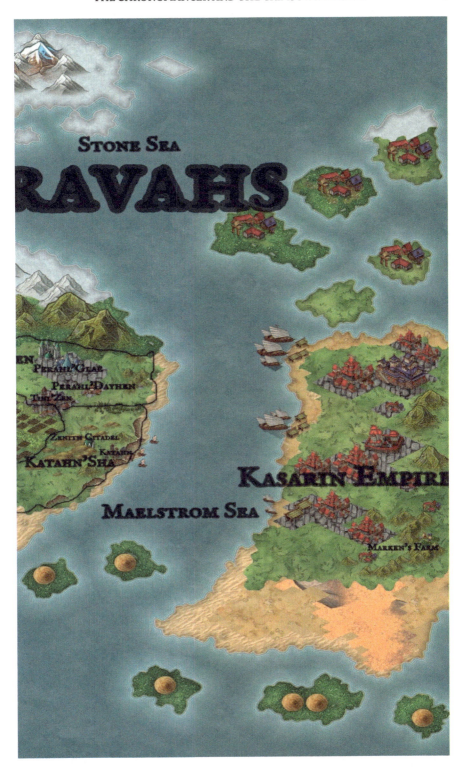

-1-

Time was an anomaly for the Book of Worms as it sat inside the exposed hull of the Wave's Gift. Its only attendants, now, were the obedient reanimated worms of its namesake. The devourers, the blood drinkers...all were exterminated in the burst of white-hot light and spirit. Now, they were more trapped than when they were in the dirt. They were stuck in a derelict ship that was stabbed into a decimated city. The barrier that surrounded everything seemed to laugh at them and mock them. Perhaps it did too, they mused. The souls of the magi were fused together in the imprisoning energy.

Two thousand years, a perfect unification, and they still made an over-estimation like the one that cost them the world. They knew, as they did then, that their power was far too overwhelming for any group of sorcerers to stand against them.

Just as back then, those who were not students of the Children of Nothing held an answer against their power. Then, it was the boy Magus-King, and his giant crystal sword. Now, they discovered a way to unite-in sacrifice- to stop them.

Disgust seeped into them for the irony of it all. Self-sacrifice to put a vengeful end to everything, and self-sacrifice to stop their progress.

The Book took consolation in the destruction they caused. They felt the wreckage of the city around them. There were great piles of corpses and sea-faring debris washed against the shattered harbor. It was all trapped within the confines of the spirit barrier. The spirits of the Book were grateful they held no mortal senses, because the stench of sulfuric hellfire and rotting soaked flesh was also trapped in the barrier. If summer heat could penetrate the barrier, it would be worse.

Mounds of broken stone and spikes of charred wood stretched to the top of the rise, at the city's edge.

The ruins were a satisfying testament. Most of the world that passed around the Book, in the last two thousand years, did so with the belief that the Order of the Void Triangle was a myth. The fear remained in the people, and that was pleasing; but other than that, it was as if their near total conquest of the world did not exist.

A levelled city was a token comparison of what they achieved millennia ago, but now Stratia would remember the Void Triangle.

Seagulls and fish died as they attempted to pass through the barrier. The barrier was not made of solid material. It was an abundant form of shimmering spirit energy. Anything living would be overwhelmed by the infusion of so much raw force.

This imprisonment was no defeat. They waited in the earth for two millennia. The Book was made of hundreds of Void Disciples that escaped capture by offering their bodies and souls to create the book. It commandeered various slaves and gained control of a ship to travel thousands of miles. At the end of it all, the Book destroyed an entire city.

The Book of Worms had come a long way to achieve their goal. Only a little patience was needed now. As bleak as things seemed, the Book was still smug and certain. Everything that transpired was a part of an era of prophecy. Fate was on their side now. Nothing in their way could change that.

As if in answer, there was a new presence inside the barrier. How much time passed before this intrusion? It could not know for sure. Time, outside of decades and centuries, was irrelevant.

The Book narrowed its focus on the individual. It was a dark moonless night, appropriate for the encounter the Book was waiting for.

The Book of Worms waited as the Crayaht' En approached, the Chosen One, the Champion of the Void. The Book of Worms had risen for this purpose.

Creation's End approached the interior of the Wave's Gift, bold and fearless while walking among the writhing worm slaves. He was a shadowy presence, radiating darkness in waves, like a contradiction to the sun.

Even in their state of mindless servitude, the worms felt something of Crayaht' En, and they parted before him.

He walked down the stairs and the narrow hallway. The Book of Worms flared with the cold blue light of the fragmented souls of the disciples. The room filled with the light and a low-clinging layer of mist.

At last, we may begin.

The Temporal Projection behaved in a way Rylin did not expect. Rylin had pushed into the past, hundreds of times. He was accustomed to an emerald cast that gave way to a cold blue pressure as he pressed deeper into history. The Temporal Current always attempted to correct oddities in its stream, but not this time.

The layers of time parted easily for Rylin. History seemed to pull him further and further back. He watched dust and decay fade, revealing rooms and buildings while they were new. He watched a reversed progression of Katahn, as a new city, just before its blocks and timber peeled away from their foundations. He watched the elderly become young adults, then children.

All the while, there was no emerald or blue hue to the world. Time only invited Rylin to go deep into the past. Years, decades, and centuries moved backwards in a blurring parade of events.

When the blur began to slow and steady itself, Rylin gaped in amazement.

The world around him was darker than night. The skies boiled with oily black clouds that burst with wicked arcs of lightning. The ground was gouged with smoking bloody trenches and craters. Sickening bits of flesh and mangled limbs littered the soaked landscape of carnage, fused into steaming patches of glassy black sand.

There was a foul twin reek: one like rotten eggs, the other a sharp acrid smell of burned meat. The intensity stung in Rylin's nostrils and throat, compelling him to vomit.

Rylin looked to the east, on the top of the rise. The copied personality of Yaekrim, the younger student who would one day become the last leader of the Mage Clans, shrieked in delighted recognition. Rylin shielded his eyes. Every wall, parapet, and tower radiated a brilliant white light. The wall was giant; three times the width of the Zenith Citadel. Inside the wall there were three buildings circled by six spires that pierced the dark skies. The combined light of the structures pushed against the besieging dark storm. The two forces embodied the clash of light and darkness.

Then the blood-soaked rise erupted into chaos. Rylin fought the impulse to cringe down and cover his head. He reminded himself that he was just a witness to this event. He had no actual presence in this time. No one would see him.

From the direction of the compound of light, several hundred white-robed men and women charged into the dark. They held ivory, polished staffs that gleamed like pearls and radiated white light. Their faces showed no fury, only a calm resolve.

When Rylin looked to the east, he wished his eyes did not turn from the light.

There was a mixed horde of thousands of people at the front. Robed figures, farmers, merchants, kings, soldiers, men, women, children; there appeared to be nothing in common. Only on closer inspection did Rylin realize what similarity brought them together in an unruly mass. Throats were torn. Torsos were opened wide with most of the innards gone. Their eyes were white and expressionless. Their only sounds were tortured moans and animal hisses.

All of them were dead, and somehow brought back in this 'condition' to fight.

Behind these walking corpses, the scene was far more horrifying.

There were hundreds of creatures covered in slime, scales, or mottled leathery skin. Glowing eyes of green, red, and blue filled their ranks with unleashed hatred and blood lust. Some of them stood two stories tall, and wide enough to fill a city street. Others were smaller, naked, with barely feminine shapes and leathery wings where their arms should be. There were some with long, curved, pointed horns, while some were covered with sharp studs and spikes. Among all of them were disembodied shadows that slithered along the ground, as smooth as liquid, pausing long enough to rise and glare with baleful red eyes.

Behind these monsters, Rylin saw over a thousand of the unmistakable architects of this nightmare siege.

They floated, their black-booted feet pointed down, a full body length over the ground. They were clothed in such blackness that they did not blend into the darkness at their backs. They were men and women in shape, wearing loose pants, long sleeved tunics, and gloves. Their long billowing cloaks were deep-hooded, making them seem faceless in shadows. They all held semi-transparent black staffs.

Everything about the wraith-like figures was so tell-tale

that Rylin had no trouble identifying them.

All at once, the familiarity of the attack on Katahn, the dream from so long ago, all of it came together. These dark figures- the Void Hands-were behind all of it. Rylin thought they were a myth. He knew everyone thought they were. But, even with the strangely easy Temporal Projection, Rylin knew he was not dreaming.

Rylin forced himself to watch as several hundred white-robed magi bravely charged into battle against the greatest force of nightmares, ever. He had to honor their courage by baring unwavering witness.

The magi halted. The Endless Current created a roaring wave of fury. They hurled white spheres of light into the advancing dark army. The spheres blossomed into grand explosions of white fire and energy, disintegrating anything caught within. The series of explosions pushed the darkness back further, drowning out the howls and shrieks of the oncoming nightmares.

The lightning from the storms was forcefully redirected at the winged demons in the skies. Electric assaults illuminated them, briefly, before dropping their ashes to the ground.

The Void Hands retorted with bands of rainbow fire, as wide and tall as several men combined. The flames were so hot they created wide deep trenches of red-hot molten glass in their passing.

That was the last certainty Rylin needed. These trenches were the same as the gouges cut through Katahn.

Rylin was about to turn away, to return to his waiting body in the present, when the Yaekrim presence in his mind insisted he stay a moment more. It was more than two years since she last insisted on anything. The structure of light was her home, fashioned by the hands of his predecessors. It was the temple of the Supreme Radiance. The Supreme Radiance were the leaders of the Mage Clans.

Rylin was taken aback when one woman strode forward from the Supreme Radiance, alone. She was tall, with her long brown-blonde hair tied behind her neck. She was wiry, almost lanky, and her blue eyes surveyed the coming onslaught with calm detachment, and hard resolve. Her clothes and staff were no different from her clansmen; but she radiated such command that the army of evil hesitated before her.

The sheer force of the Endless Current flowing to her was far beyond anything Rylin felt from any other magus. With a wave of her hand, blinding white energy enveloped hundreds of corpses and demons. When those lights vanished, nothing remained.

She pointed her staff at the coming bands of fire. White light and crystalline water met and dissolved the flames.

The Yaekrim in Rylin's mind watched with fascination. He knew he was watching Yaekrim as an adult, and the last Supreme Magus. Now Rylin knew why she was the last. This was the catastrophic war that wiped out the four remaining Mage Clans.

So, this was the day Yaekrim died. No matter how well they appeared to defend themselves, their fate would not change. The Void Hands would win.

A sad pang of sympathy struck Rylin. Everything she struggled and studied for would die, that day. She would die. Her brother and sister clansmen would die. Her home would be ground into dust. Only books would remain. There were no graves or monuments for any of them.

Worse still: history had forgotten the sacrifice they made. This battle never happened.

Rylin returned to the present, despite Yaekrim's protests. Watching the end of everything she knew would be cruel and horrifying.

Rylin stood up from the golden circle, the image of outside the Citadel still fresh in his mind. It was all he needed to shape such a short Fold Step. In an instant, he stood on the grassy slopes that led down to the ruins of Katahn.

Further investigation into the attack on Katahn was breaking a promise. He justified this with the knowledge that he was looking into something far more ancient.

It was late…several hours past midnight. The winter air was bitter cold, seeping through Rylin's gray robe and clothes. He shivered, rubbing his arms before hiding them deep in his sleeves.

The darkness was also an issue for Rylin. The entire oceanside was obscured by total moonless night. Rylin fought with the cold a moment more before holding out his hand, palm up, and conjuring a Torch Sphere.

It was not easy for him to create at first. While elements were becoming easier, his first attempts to creatively infuse and combine were clumsy and exhausting. Had it not been for the efforts of a well-known Pyromancer from northern Malkanor, and her patient lessons, he might not have learned it. It was several months of practice and Temporal Projection before he gained a greater proficiency.

The Torch Sphere hovered in the air while he knelt. In Malkanor, at this time of year, he would need to push aside the frost-biting snow first; but he extracted a rusty, neglected knife, and slashed furrows into the hard soil. When the dirt was loosened to his satisfaction, he scooped up a handful. He stood up, sheathing the crude blade, and opened himself to the Endless Current. His hand weaved circles over the handful of dirt. His mumbled words were lost in the roar of the ocean waves and the winter winds, as he spoke in the ancient language of the Fabricators.

"Ann an gras na talmhainn tha mi 'sireadh meorachadh air iomadachadh." (I seek my reflection multiplied in the grace of earth)

Rylin hurled the dirt forward, and the particles split and danced in the air. The dust gained momentum and force, pulling up soil and dry grass to join them. In moments, several clouds of swirling dust and debris danced, side by side. They began to take definitive shape, changing into contained arms and legs. The dust swirled faster, accelerating into a blur.

The swirling clouds began to form flesh and clothes. The process ignored blood and bones, allowing for incompletion. In seconds more, they began to appear the same as Rylin.

They were Dust Mimics. They were a lesser imitation in Fabrication. A perfect copy would be excessive, a lengthy process to create so many, and it would tax Rylin more than he wanted. He only needed his eyes, mind, and magic spread all over the rise.

Rylin and the Mimics nodded and dispersed in a simultaneous Fold Step. Their magic spread out, searching deep into the earth as they looked at the landscape. Each one was assisted by their conjured Torch Sphere. They would scour every inch before dawn.

Rylin walked a steady pace, his hands open, facing forward at his sides. His magic reached into the earth with incorporeal waves. Soil and wet grasses pushed against the skin of his palms. The cold grainy moisture of the dirt sifted between his fingers. The vibration of the Endless Current hummed. It was an amplified sensation in his searching magic.

Rylin and his Dust Mimics scoured the east face of the rise. If any one of the Mimics found what he was looking for, their Torch Sphere would glow noticeably brighter, and the other mimics would vanish as the remaining Mimic stood still.

When one of his Mimics did find something, it was far to the south after three quarters of an hour of searching. The other Torch Spheres winked out into the dark, their wielders returned to the Current and the earth.

Rylin Fold Stepped. The Mimic stood in, what looked

like, an old dried-up riverbed. The Mimic vanished as Rylin approached, his magic already fixated on the object he was looking for. He pushed into the ground with raw, invisible force; like the one he used to strike at Amorlic, so long ago. His magic grasped a head sized chunk of transparent dark stone. It was buried more than thirty feet in the ground. The location came as no surprise. Time would have buried it.

The riverbed was not evidence enough. The only thing that ran through this ground was an incinerating blast of fire. But if this were enough evidence, history would already tell everyone more.

Chunks of the frozen ground split, overturning grass as soft earth pushed upward. A three-foot mound looked like it was boiling as the stone crested the surface. Rylin's magic pulled it upward until the stone rolled down the mound toward him. Inside the stone was a single claw, attached to a long scaly finger. Its tip was sharp, and the scales were blackened with slick patches that told of melting. The fire was not enough to reduce this to ashes. It did not belong to any creature in the world. The burns were more likely caused by lightning.

Rylin would have been horrified or revolted if he didn't know to expect it. It was a single piece of evidence that was not scoured away millennia ago. It would have been impossible to remove every piece of evidence of a battle that massive.

Rylin held up the fossilized demon claw, looking at it, scrutinizing it. A Solas Geomancer would be able to feel the energies of the ancient glass. If there were an Ard Solas, they would be able to detail a history from those energies. Not that it was needed. One preserved demon claw would reveal a great deal of lost events.

Rylin appraised the stone a moment more, his eyes lost in the dark transparency. His mother's words filled his mind, then. Their truth was before his gaze.

"The earth remembers when everyone forgets," Rylin quietly recited.

-2-

Ishell stood several feet away from a particularly sheer drop. The cliff descended almost a hundred feet to the churning crushing waves of the Maelstrom Sea below. The rain poured down in thick sheets from dark gray clouds, drenching the grass around her. Even with the hood of her gray robe pulled up, her long, coarse, dark blonde hair clung to her face in a wet frame. Her calloused hands were raised into the cold, late autumn air, her magic extended far and strong, all around her.

Ten feet above, in a twenty-foot circle all around her, dozens of varied gray jagged rocks swirled and floated in a threatening vortex. Unformed energies danced around her fingertips, an invisible force that waited for her command to take shape and strike. Meanwhile, she maintained an upward force of air, cautiously keeping back a measure of the rain.

"Are we done yet?" the comically sharp nosed Borvis Len complained. He sat in the lee of a rocky outcropping, beneath the canopy of a leafless birch tree. It was not enough to keep his lanky shape from being thoroughly drenched.

Borvis's stick thin arms strained under constant pressure while his hands were raised in front of him. The swirling stones were his magic. His role was to strike Ishell, at random, and gather more stones to keep her guessing.

"I am a Polymancer, not a Geomancer," Borvis reminded in a grumpy whine.

"Quit your belly-aching. It is minor geokinesis. It's not like I am forcing you to move a mountain." It was a harsh dismissal. Stepping away from a Light's expertise might be required, at times, but that made it no less difficult.

But she enjoyed pushing hard work onto Light Borvis. His complaining made for interesting banter. She looked forward to it.

"Of all days, you had to choose a cold wet day, at the end of winter, at the edge of a cliff. You couldn't choose to train in doors?"

"Adversity creates the greatest blades," Ishell quoted her father. "Anyway, it would take much longer for you to transmute the stone from raw Current, and if you took stone from the Citadel, it would be an ugly mess."

Borvis grumbled under his breath and sent three of the stones flying at her in irritation.

The shift in the circling rocks was evident long before they moved. The energies at her fingertips coalesced into three violet-colored jagged lances of electricity. The lightning shattered the stones into tiny pieces after only an inch out of their orbit.

"Fates, that is aggravating! Couldn't you at least let me think I can hit you?"

Even annoyed, his irritation made her smile with amusement. It was much more entertaining than Rylin's unquestioning compliance to help in whatever way he could. The only moments he rewarded her with conflict was when he felt the need to defend any one of his explosive choices.

It was one of those catastrophic choices that was so aggravating now. Rylin couldn't take her advice, even for that once, and leave the Katahn matter alone. He found another way to scratch one of his absurd itches in his fool brain. In doing so, he uprooted history, gave every scribe and lore keeper ten times more work; and put the entire Zenith Citadel in an uproar.

Training from teacher to student had come to a halt, leaving Lights to train alone, as she did.

Borvis raised an eyebrow, and Ishell knew the beak-faced Torch was up to mischief. He always seemed to know how to tune into her thoughts.

"The emissary to Perahl'Sen returned yesterday." Borvis sent five more stones from random trajectories at her. Ishell was not as distracted as he hoped. Her violet lightning struck down the stones in a swift instant. Borvis snapped his fingers in frustration.

After Rylin gathered evidence of who really attacked Katahn, several Solas were dispatched to inform the kings of the discovery. The rulers would be advised to cease investigating the Kasarin Empire.

So far, half of Malkanor complied. Teril and Vodess agreed with the suggestion, even if they didn't believe the council. Katahn'Sha, Perahl'Sen, and even various lords of Nerinmor chose to ignore the accusation.

"And?" Ishell asked as annoyance thinned the flow of Current.

"Lycendrik believes our council is too inexperienced to give him facts without delusions born of grief."

Ishell ground her teeth and was struck by a stone to the left side of her hip for it. It stung more than she wanted to admit; and she glared at Borvis for it.

"Truly? Of all places to strike, in my distraction, you choose there?"

Borvis smiled, impishly. "You ordered me to make sure it hurts enough to remember. I doubt you'll forget the added shame."

Ishell shrugged. When Borvis wasn't complaining, or being over-pragmatic to the point of pessimistic, he could be a little lecherous. He was not afraid to show her subtle attentions, at least when the time was right. Someday, she might even humor him a little. She would see if she could enjoy it as much as he thought he did. She fantasized at sharing an intimate moment with a Polymancer. It was enough to make her blush for imagining it.

"Regardless, he has decided to increase the presence of informants in the Empire. He also wants to get closer to the Crimson Throne."

There went her entire concentration. She didn't so much as flinch when the stones assaulted her arms and legs, all at once.

"Fates, girl! Did I even hurt you? You're made of iron."

Ishell ignored his exclaimed observation. "They'll be found out. He will start a war, for certain. Did that blundering horse even look at the claw?"

Borvis shook his head. "We told him Void Hands did it, Light Ishell. We told him a children's ghost story destroyed our harbor city. Fates! I can't even believe it, and I saw the stone. Void Hands are real? The same that we scare grown men and children with around a night fire? How can we expect anyone to believe something that sounds so ludicrous, especially with the state our order is in?"

Ishell observed how adamant and vehement Borvis was about it. He was this way on a tirade he felt so strongly that he was right about. It took her back to the days of listening to her father complain as he hammered away at the forge.

Ishell relaxed and turned to look at Borvis. The exercise was pretty much done, anyway.

"What do you think this council will do if this becomes a war with the Empire?" Ishell asked.

"They are fairly new in their role. There are maybe three Ard Solas, in all. There is no battle experience to be found among them. I think they will avoid conflict. They will declare that Perahl'Sen were the ones to begin this, they can be the ones to end it."

A wave of Endless Current, accompanied by a metallic bloody smell, intruded on their conversation. Ishell ground her teeth in anger. In front of Ishell, a Meld Walk produced two Torches she least wanted anything to do with.

The yellow-blonde, and the dark-haired twin girls were commonly nicknamed the Blood Scathe Twins. They reveled in their name as much as their gruesome reputation.

They stood slightly shorter than Ishell, with far less muscle on their wiry frames. They were a few years older than her. The more curvaceous of the two allowed her long blonde hair to fall in tangled snarls that coupled well with her blood shot, steel blue eyes. Her face reflected a hint of barely contained madness. Her gray robe was tattered and cut, as well as stained with her own blood. She was Layrienn, and she favored a grisly, nearly forbidden form of magic called Sanguimancy, blood manipulation. She could often be found experimenting on herself, only to quickly mend her wounds.

The other, Kaysienn, was the rigid iron fist of the two, which was appropriate as she favored a form of Polymancy that favored using the iron content of blood. Her steel blue eyes were less blood shot but shone with cold contempt. Her hair was far less tangled, tied behind the nape of her neck. With a little more physical exertion, she would have been an equal to Ishell. It was rumored that she had a hidden sadistic side. It was also said she had a fondness for poisons, and studied them, frequently. This chilled Ishell as it reminded her of the rumors of Maesellen Moarenroak, Queen of Malkanor.

"Sitting on our hands, during wartime, would be a tragic waste of our talents. Don't you agree, Light Ishell?" Layrienn cooed, playfully.

"If you want your talents to go to war, simply join the Empire's Havoc Guilds," Ishell suggested, her smile dripping with sarcasm.

Layrienn hissed, putting a hand to her chest. "Oh, you wound me, Light Ishell. I merely wish to defend the good people of Stratia."

Ishell wanted to say more, but Borvis cut in. "Is there something we can help you with?"

"We felt a lot of Current this way. We thought we would investigate," Kaysienn explained.

"Imagine anything but the demon claw holding your attention," Ishell quipped in a murmur.

Both the twins snapped a glare on Ishell and she feigned a wan smile. It was commonly known they hated Rylin for his discovery. It was a bone, so close to the Citadel, and they never felt it. The bigger insult was that they were with the Order for five years before the arrival of those discovered during the Malkanor Inquiry.

"For a boy who is so quiet, he seems to shake the world with a breath. Don't you find it annoying, Light Ishell?"

It was a jab as sensitive as the comment she gave them. It was why frustration brought Ishell to this cliff. Those who live in glass palaces, she supposed.

"Are you all going to continue to pretend I am not here, shivering in the rain?" Borvis interjected.

"Quiet, weasel nose," Kaysienn snapped.

Borvis gathered a trickle of Endless Current, shaping it at Kaysienn. He smiled a wide toothy grin when her nose lengthened. She looked at the long protrusion on her face with cross eyes before she glared at him.

"Truly?" Kaysienn's voice whined around her awkward nose.

Kaysienn corrected the alteration, more annoyed at being forced to use common transmutation than the actual prank. She sighed.

"I guess I should expect such childishness from boys who will never become men."

Borvis held his wide smile. "Any change I wish, my dearest heart. Any change I wish."

"We don't have time to toy with a man child. We came to inform you of what you already suspect." The smile Kaysienn gave Ishell was cold and mocking. "The council has declared inaction for the inevitable outcome with the Kasarin Empire."

-3-

Kera slouched back in her armchair and sighed with exhaustion. The light blue velvet chair was one of the few guilty pleasures the Solas Evoker allowed herself. Right now, she could not be more grateful for its presence in her reading den.

Not only was the chair a great comfort, but it was also a marked difference between her office and Ard Solas Matisia's. The roof was only several feet taller than herself. The room was modestly small and square. Shelves were lined full of books, or decorated with glowing, steel, throwing daggers and vials filled with fire and contained lightning.

At the four corners of the room, there were tall, bronze candlestands. These held white candles that burned three times brighter than normal. Beneath it all was a Kasarin maroon rug, embroidered with silver swirls. A window to the north overlooked a rolling decline that gradually descended to the waves of the Maelstrom Sea. The tall window was open to allow the late winter ocean breezes to waft in.

Kera allowed her head to fall back against the soft velvet. Her long, white-blonde hair draped the chair while her sleepy brown eyes stared upward at the ceiling.

The loss of Light Matisia was a very deep wound, but she was never allowed the time to fully grieve for her. The Ard Solas Evoker was an icon. Kera spent much of her time, even while she was a child in northern Vodess, admiring Matisia's legendary exploits. When Aeromancers and the Order's only Pyromancer were sizing up her future, Kera craved the versatility of an Evoker like Matisia.

Matisia was so grand, powerful, and fearless; standing with abrupt elemental fury to halt the quaking of the earth, or the blasting of volcanoes. The Grand Illumination always fell back on her wisdom. She was Kera's role model and mentor. After two years, her death was as unreal to her as it was unthinkable.

Kera still remembered looking out the windows in the halls, facing east, when the thick blackness swallowed Katahn. No matter what the Solas present said, Kera sided with Light Rylin: in the darkness, there was a great battle. No one felt anything from an opposing force, but the huge bursts of Endless Current, and the massive explosions that followed, were from the Ard Solas. It was a clear sign of an intense struggle.

A long flash of blinding white light followed an enormous surge of Endless Current, at the end of the struggle. After that, the power of all the beloved Ard Solas dispersed into the air.

That was an overwhelming blow, but she had to take it head on. Her student, Ishell, needed to gather her own strength from watching a Solas square her shoulders to the hard times ahead.

A moment of gratitude washed over Kera. Matisia discovered the promising young Evoker. Of any Light Kera ever encountered, Ishell's intuitive and reflexive abilities were, by far, the most fluid. She achieved her Elemental Potency in a matter of a few months. Her Elemental Affinity was far stronger than any Kera had ever heard of. She was already able to feel the formation of raw elements from over a mile and a half away, even when they were shaped with the expert hands of an Elementalist.

If anyone could ever reach beyond Elemental Potency, and into the final and lethal skill level, Ishell might be the one to do it.

No Evoker or Elementalist ever survived the tier of Elemental Incarnation. Becoming the element, while maintaining the Light's personal sentience was a test that killed all who attempted it. Becoming fire meant you could die out as your flames waned. Becoming earth meant you could be forever turned to stone.

But there were times that Kera trained her student, and certain oddities appeared and widened her eyes. Ishell would channel fire into a furnace, only to have her right arm change into pure orange flames and back to flesh in a blink of an eye.

Beyond that, Ishell was not just direct to the point of bullheaded, as so many Evokers and a few Elementalists tended to be. There was a practical level of forethought to the girl, as well.

Kera admitted that she could be a bit of a hot head, herself, from time to time. It was enough for her opponents to exploit. Light Yelisian knew this about Kera. Not only was it the reason she was never tested for the level of Ard Solas; but it was why she was left behind to guard the Citadel. She could not fault his decision. He was right, and it was too much of a danger to bring to such a battlefield.

Kera sighed, frustrated, as she thought on the future battles that the Order might be absent for. After two years, Maloric's wisdom during the ceremony was regarded only to a degree. The other kings did not start a war with the Kasarin Empire outright, but Lycendrik Derin, King of Perahl'Sen, was not so easily swayed by conventional wisdom.

The King of the ivory nation sent a growing number of informants and spies into the Crimson Empire, and Perahl'Sen was not a nation known for military or espionage greatness.

So far, Lycendrik failed to gain any evidence of Kasarin involvement with the attack on Katahn. If he had found anything, he might have convinced Delkit Mayzeneth, King of Katahn'Sha, to unite and strike the juggernaut empire. Talic Cenis, King of Teril, might have supplied provisions for such a campaign. Kellman Forzen, King of Vodess, was too much of an opium addict to go against Lycendrik's manipulations.

The Enlightened Sun, meanwhile, procrastinated on selecting new leadership for more than a year, when they finally chose Ard Solas Geomancer, Martenen Delak, to assume the mantle. So far, that was one of the worst choices made. Martenen was too slow, preferring to debate for hours before action was taken on anything. There was a standstill on recruiting, training, and testing that was threatening to stagnate the Order. He had a dozen equally bureaucratic Council Solas, with only three Ard Solas to put any progress for the Order into a bog.

So far, the Council showed no signs or rushing to Stratia's aid if war broke out between the Kasarin Empire and the six nations. They were allowing Lycendrik to blunder and antagonize the Kasarin Empire.

The military and nobility of the Kasarin Empire could be violent and volatile. Their peace and commerce with Stratia could be tenuous, at best. The Empire knew it held military superiority. Their Havoc Guilds, a branch of Magus Guilds that specialized in war and conquest, numbered thousands of the most sadistic men and women. They were destructive, cruel, and preferred torturing and killing, discovering new ways to inflict agony on their enemies.

The Emperor of the Crimson Throne made it clear centuries ago: Stratia would remain unharmed while there were no unwelcome intrusions.

If Lycendrik's blunderers were discovered, motives would become irrelevant, and war would become inevitable.

What would Stratia do to defend itself against several thousand homicidal Magi and tens of thousands of armed brutal soldiers? Kera believed Stratia would be overwhelmed, or worse.

If these unpleasantries were not enough, Light Rylin uncovered a piece of evidence that would require every history tome be rewritten.

That boy was full of one earth-shattering surprise after

another. To this day, Kera did not recover from his surprise revelation of increasing his power and skill by levels that were beyond imagination. She felt, first-hand, his skill as a Chronomancer from the beginning; but he held a glaring weakness in elemental spell-shaping for the first two years of his training. After his display, just after his mentor's death, that was no longer the case. He could now fuse different forms of sorcery together on a level that bordered masterful.

Rylin's growth, even without a teacher, was terrifying.

When he was first discovered, his power was already frightening enough. Almost overnight, during the Malkanor Inquiry, it became slightly subdued, as though it was cut down.

Kera could not account for and explain the sudden loss in magnitude in Rylin, any more than she could explain several of his more recent leaps in overall ability.

Rylin was a colossal enigma. He was not even aware that his raw power caused so great a fear in the Solas. None of them wanted to train him, and some of the new council thought he should be exiled from the Order.

Kera believed that decision would be a grave mistake.

So, Kera stood before this new council, earlier in the day, arguing on Rylin's behalf. She had to redirect their attention away from his level of raw power to look at the training he was completing on his own. Rylin took an alarming initiative in moving forward without a Spark, showing the entire Order that Yelisian left him with enough to finish what he started.

More importantly, Rylin was not just studying spell-shape after spell-shape. (Kera admitted that she would have done that if she were given such freedom when she was his age). He studied risks, dangers, philosophies, spell structure; all before he ever tried to cast them for the first time.

Everyone wanted to know how Light Rylin's power was growing so quickly. Until now, Kera knew little about the Chronomancers, only footnotes placed randomly in the open histories. She knew they were powerful and versatile; but that was the extent of it. She asked Rylin if she could borrow some of his study tomes. He politely obliged. He could be very pleasant that way.

So, in her lap, Kera held a book of Basic Chronomancy, while a book of their history sat on the floor beside her chair.

Kera read the Temporal Projection meditation for the tenth time in a week. She attempted to perform it a month after Rylin's shocking display; but it left her curled up in a ball, on the floor, with the worst headache she ever experienced.

The new council wanted her to attempt it again, soon. Kera preferred the safety of studying and scrutinizing it. Either way, between the histories and the book of magic, she could not understand how Chronomancers became so strong with that skill, alone. If it was a simple test of endurance, shouldn't every wielder of elemental sorcery grow stronger by resisting an opposing element?

Kera read the last passage of the meditation before closing the book. She shaped a gust of wind that snuffed out the four candles, and she sat, relaxing in the tranquility of the night. She inhaled the ocean wind, at length, savoring its fresh cool scent.

The world she had always known was changing. The brittle façade of certainty in the world crumbled away. History was more terrifying than she imagined. The Order was led by what could become failure. War was likely. After two years, Stratia needed to recover, to heal.

Martenen turned his attention away from dozens of impoverished merchants and farmers every week. Hydromancer Healers were no longer scouring the six nations for those who needed them. Advisors did not return to the rulers and nobles to help counsel them. Waste heaps were growing without the presence of Domestic Polymancers, leading to an increase in disease and packs of feral vermin.

There were hard times at play. Kera wondered if the Order

would simply sleep as everything shattered around it.

-4-

Tihl'Zen was a commerce town set at the borders of Teril, Katahn'Sha and Perahl'Sen. It was large, spreading thirty-five miles in each direction from the conjoining border center. Each direction seemed a reflection of each nation. From the center, into the northeast, ivory white polished stone shone brightly in the noon sun. The residents were engaged in poetry and contemplation, while painters created wondrous scenescapes on canvas and easels. Pale pastel colors were favored for the clothing here. Often, residents could be found wearing cool, almost gauzy robes that caught the wind in fluttering drapes.

Southeast Tihl'Zen was made of dark gray stone, donning colors as bright and lively as the clothes of its residents. Here, there could be found various shops, cafes, and inns. It was a perfect reflection for their lost jewel city of Katahn. Though talk of the Enlightened Sun and the effect of their lost harbor was common here, people still hurried about, and coin still exchanged, frequently. The industry of Katahn'Sha's Tihl'Zen would thrive for a while yet.

To the west, owning much of the central hub city, were the many plain brown homes belonging to the farmers of Teril. Their orchards, vineyards, pastures, and fields stretched far into the western horizon. Tool sheds and carts lined the flat dirt streets. It wasn't that the farmers of Teril could not afford the paved streets of its neighbors. They never felt it practical to have them.

Tihl'Zen was close enough to the eastern shores and the warmer south that they enjoyed green seasons, year around. Snows were a rarity. A winter rain passed, some days before, and the sun left the streets only pleasantly cool. A few wispy white clouds passed, slow and lazy, further adding to the relaxed contentment for the people of Tihl'Zen.

So, it came as a startling surprise when a strange sorcerer, not of the Enlightened Sun, appeared from a Meld Walk in the middle of the Perahl'Sen circle.

He was a tall, imposingly muscled figure, his height placing his vision far over the heads of the residents. His dark skin was covered with swirling, sharp, black tattoos. The top of his bald head was marked with three scars that ran from his forehead to the back of his neck. These were deep enough to proclaim that their cause passed beyond his skull. His brown eyes glared with unveiled contempt for the people who now parted around him. He wore a long, sleeveless, burgundy vest coat, open to reveal his bulging muscles. He wore baggy black trousers. His thick forearms were covered with black leather bracers covered in sharp brass spikes. He wore shining black boots that came up to the middle of his shins.

A short, balding, paint splattered artisan made the mistake of closing within arms-reach of the imposing sorcerer. With unbelievable speed, the sorcerer whipped one hand all the way around the painter's throat. He struggled for air, as well as freedom, in a grip that wouldn't budge. The sorcerer narrowed his eyes, with murderous hatred, as tendrils of crimson lightning snaked around his arm, concentrating into his fingertips, and invading his victim's body. The artist thrashed and convulsed, his mouth foaming, while his eyes rolled back, smoked, and then melted out of their sockets.

The artisans of the Perahl'Sen part of Tihl'Zen screamed and fled as the sorcerer flung aside the corpse like an empty water skin.

Then a sorceress, as dark skinned, and only slightly less intimidating as the sorcerer, appeared. She unleashed a wide horizontal wave of blood red fire that ignited dozens of residents. They ran, screaming and burning, trying to flee from the flames that devoured them.

In seconds, dozens more of the red-garbed mages appeared, unleashing killing magic on the citizens of Tihl'Zen. Hundreds of people died screaming in minutes. Homes and shops burned, the air filling with choking clouds of black smoke.

In a little over an hour, all Tihl'Zen burned. There were some who fled into hiding in cellars, and they were trapped and burned alive. Every building was devoured by infernos determined to consume them to the foundations.

Women and children fled into the fields beyond the city, thinking to find cover in the orchards. All of them were found. Their heads were cleaved by arcs of thin red energy. Not even the trees could hide them well enough. The attackers appeared to possess a sixth sense of their presence.

In the end, all the corpses were hauled back into the burning city center to be burned in unceremonious heaps.

In half a day, the city was quiet, except for the crackle of the burning buildings and the roar of the endless inferno.

By nightfall, the flames died down to embers. The charred skeletons of the foundation of homes waited to fall and rest in heaps of ashes.

It was only when the last ember died in the cold midnight that the burgundy mages Meld Walked out of the city. It was their custom to leave a razed city only when the last sign of life was extinguished.

After all, the mages were members of the Crimson Throne's Havoc Guilds. The Emperor of the Crimson Empire sent them ahead as an advance wave for a force that would exterminate all Stratians.

Whenever the Havoc Guilds were called on to invade

and destroy, their tradition was to obliterate every farm stead, village, and city, leaving nothing alive in their wake.

-5-

"Do not allow your concentration to waver or you will burn, Light Teranen."

Teranen was a tall woman, with long coarse brown hair tied behind her neck. Her dark brown eyes locked with intensity on her down-turned hands, and the waist-high flames that crackled beneath them. The sleeves of her gray robe were rolled up, revealing thin pale arms marked with frost-burn scars.

Her mentor, Solas Barahn, was a short round pyromaster, much more agile than he appeared. His gray, ash-stained robe was open, unable to completely wrap around his weighted body. Polymancers had offered to alter the size of his robe, many times. He turned them down with glowering disgust. He also wore a shirt underneath that appeared to cling uncomfortable and tight.

Teranen and the Solas were an odd pair in the Zenith Citadel. The Solas present during his boyhood believed he should be a Domestic Polymancer. He let them know, with much profanity, that he despised their shallow view of his potential. It was Ard Solas Derra and Ard Solas Matisia who first read deeper into the boy's retaliation and temper. They advocated that he should study the ways of the Pyromancers. Barahn liked the sound of it, without understanding what they meant at the time.

Teranen was a few years more than middle-aged. The new council believed that she would make and ideal healer, or Hydromancer.

Much of the required nurturing side for a healer was absent in Teranen though. She lost them on the day she lost her husband and son, eleven years ago.

They were foraging in the woods, north of Malkanor's northernmost barony. The snows were thick. They could barely make out details twenty feet ahead. Her son, Kaedin, was only eleven years old, and the push through the waist-deep snows taxed his already hunger stricken stamina. When frost bite and fever claimed him, Teranen and her husband, Borik, had no will left to press on. They were already lost, and even if they knew the way, what was the point?

Teranan assumed, at the time, that she would die first. That was alright with her. She didn't want to carry on without the two loves of her life.

The Fates would not be so kind to her.

A burly wagon driver from western Teril chanced upon her on a journey to southern Vodess. By then, the snows had already claimed her husband, freezing away his life and then burying him deep. The wagon driver only found Teranen by a lock of her brown hair laying on the surface of a snow drift. She was at the edge of death. To her dismay, the kind old bear nursed her back to health.

For the next year after, Teranen was catatonic. She spent her days sitting alone in the empty hut that belonged to her family. Glimpses of the world passed in flashes around her. There was evidence that her neighbors were feeding and cleaning her. She wished they would let her join Borik and Kaedin in the grave.

Winter came again. When it did, Teranen was forced to rejoin the world around her. A powerful white blizzard swept through much of Malkanor. The merciless snows crushed many of the weaker homes, forcing the families to unite and survive.

When the snows came to Teranen's home, tiny flakes drifted through the open windows to land on her face and arms. They brought with them the cruel memory of that day, the day she wished she died. The pain and the cold slammed into her awareness with ruthless disregard.

Teranen blinked several times. She filled the quiet winter storm with a scream of heartache and rage that echoed for a mile.

It was then that something changed within her. She hated the cold. It wasn't the simple dislike people often feel that makes them seek blankets and a warm fire. Teranen hated it in a personal way that is reserved for a mortal enemy.

In that moment, Teranen stood and walked out of the hut in northern Malkanor for the last time. She walked south, into the killing snow. Her head was numb and feverish. The world shifted lethargically with each step. Warmth seeped into her legs as she walked. Raw fire burned in her throat and chest as her breathing labored.

Yet, these pains were welcome to her now. These pains were heat, they were fire, and they burned the cold that took everything from her.

When Teranen first heard the wind through the open window, she heard a mocking taunt to the sound. The cold laughed at her loss, tormented her for not being strong enough to face it.

In her aimless walk, the wind groaned and howled with agony. Teranen reveled in it, burning her enemy. Each wailing gust filled her with hot ecstasy and growing determination. In fiery hate, Teranen's mind returned. She was no longer the nurturing mother, or the loving wife. Teranen was reborn as a vengeful fire.

Then Teranen came upon a village, several days later. She was hungry and tired from walking day and night. She was thirsty. Her throat was dry and scratchy. The light of crude torch posts and tiny hovel hearths reached out to her from a cloudless cold night. More than any other need, Teranen was drawn to that wonderful orange glow of fire. Her mind fell into a lulling trance as blood pumped, laboriously, in her veins. Everything in her mind fell away, like autumn leaves, and she was drawn along.

A single torch post blazed at the end of the road leading into the village. Its light flooded Teranen's awareness from over a hundred yards away. Its radiance was like perfection. Its warmth, even so far away, was as soothing as the embrace of Borik. The crackle of flame was a perfect melody, a siren song calling to her, enticing her with promises of endless heat. All these attributes of the fire permeated deep into her spirit.

Within arm's reach of the torch, the true surprise of her new nature was revealed. Tiny sparks and bits of fire, as big as the tip of a candle, abandoned the wood and pitch. The flames floated in a swirling rhythmic dance, approaching, and surrounding her.

In response, the blood in her veins rushed hot. A vivid joy coursed through her and made her light-headed. Fire continued to come and dance around her. It started to float from further sources, from torches, hearth fires, and candles from all over the village. A swirling, playing whirlwind of heat and orange light surrounded her. She closed her eyes, raised her arms high and laughed, reveling as the flames melted a wide circle in the snows around her. The night was alive as the villagers left their homes to investigate the commotion. She was reborn with a renewed sense of purpose she missed for more than a year.

"I said concentrate, Wench Teranen," shouted Barahn, breaking her reminiscence.

Teranen cupped her right hand and scooped flame as easily as a handful of rice. She hurled a crackling wad of fire at her mentor's face.

"Call me 'wench' again, Spark Ball. See where that goes."

Barahn caught the fireball and threw it upward behind his back in an artful flourish. Truthfully, Teranen was constantly caught off-guard by her mentor's graceful displays. He juggled the fire and whistled a tune he must have heard in one rowdy tavern or other.

Barahn was the only Solas looked at with revulsion by his peers. Not only did he remain in an overweight shape his fellows disdained, but the Pyromaster from Teril favored two things that made him an oddity. He loved tavern brawls and rum so hot it would burn away everyone's sense of taste.

Many nights, he would return to the Citadel drunk and bruised, with no sense of shame.

"I apologize. I cannot take threats seriously when they come from silly old biddies," Barahn grinned.

"I didn't think a little king's jester could take anything seriously," Teranen countered.

Barahn gripped his chest and gasped with sarcasm. "Careful, such wit is fatal in one's dotage."

Ishell walked the halls in the Citadel basement when she was stopped by a gathering of Torches and Candles outside the furnace room. The gray and brown robed boys and girls listened in nervous silence as shouts sounded from the other side of the tall iron door. The walls shook with loud booming explosions. Clouds of smoke escaped from under the door.

Some of the Torches snickered and whispered to each other.

Ishell rolled her eyes and sighed in exasperation. "Yes, Lights, the Flame Witch of Dunell and Solas Barahn are having it out again," Ishell shouted for the eavesdroppers to hear.

A younger red-haired Candle turned to her. "This makes the second hour, today."

"They're Pyromancers, Light Kellen. They're supposed to be insane."

Ishell's observation drew a mutual laugh from the Torches before everyone walked away.

Teranan resisted the impulse to smile with impish delight after the exchange of fists, fire, and verbal insults with her mentor. It was all in agreement with Barahn's unorthodox training, of course.

When Barahn discovered Teranen in the remote northern village of Dunell, he loudly made his obvious claim on her as a teacher. (He threatened to punch any Light in the face that tried to take her from him.) He had watched her hold a ball of fire in her hand, that rainy Inquiry night. She walked about Dunell, lighting hooded torches along the road.

Since that day, Teranen's training was both simple and complicated. On the one hand, she spent no time reading spells or gathering Endless Current.

On the other, her training as a Pyromancer held one thing in common with every other Elementalist: she had to embody her favored element to exclusion and on a personal level. Her relationship with fire had become almost intimate under Barahn's instruction.

Furnace fire streamed into her palm from five feet away. Her other hand braced against her aching back. The fire soaked into her skin and created an orange glow in her body as it travelled into her. She gasped with relief as the fire soothed and healed torn muscles.

"Hah!" Barahn laughed, massaging his jaw, and spitting out blood and a loose tooth. "You have a pretty good hook for an old crone."

"Watch the age quips, or you will be gumming your next meal," Teranen threatened.

Barahn was about to start another brawl when a rush of Endless Current filled the furnace room. Solas Kera finished her Meld Walk, standing between the teacher and student.

The little Evoker gave Barahn a look of disgust, then gave Teranen a measuring scan before rolling her eyes. "This is why there are few Pyromancers in our Order."

Barahn gave a bloody and wide grin. "You can't have too much of a good thing can you, Light Kera?"

Kera closed her eyes and pinched the bridge of her nose. "Mend yourself before you make faces, Light Barahn," Kera groaned. "You'll frighten small children."

Barahn continued to smile without gathering Endless Current or fire.

Kera sighed and rolled her eyes, again. "Then I'll get to the point. All Solas are to gather in the council chamber, at once."

Barahn's grin ceased, and his brow furrowed. "Any idea what they're about? New council or old, you know I ever trusted only two of them."

"If I knew, I would tell you and save them the displeasure of your company."

Before Barahn could retort, there was a sudden gigantic burst of strange Current that sucked the air out of his lungs.

"Fates! That is anything but subtle!" Barahn exclaimed as he struggled to catch his breath.

-6-

Rylin's Fold Step ended in the center of the gold circle in the floor of his Temporal Study. He held a leather knapsack in hand. Its contents rustled as he moved to a wall to the right. He traced a series of runes into the white marble with his right index finger. When he was finished, the traced runes flared with yellow light, and a section of wall dissolved, revealing another room beyond.

The room was well-lit by six Current Spheres, each one bolstered with Simulacrum Runes that would constantly recast the Spheres before they faded.

There were several red oak tables with bottles, vials, and tubes. Colorful liquids passed through the tubes to mingle and mix in the bottles and vials. The concoctions bubbled, loudly.

There was a bookshelf to the left that held several ceramic vases and glass jars. These held herbs and flowers, either whole or ground down into powder.

Before Rylin discovered the demon claw, he created this additional room to study alchemical medicine. He knew Aemreen Tahkaer, his lover, would already have many means of following her dream of healing the people of Malkanor. He wanted to help her any way he could.

Aemreen was the only child of Malkanor's noble house of Tahkaer. She was also involuntarily betrothed to King Maloric's violent tyrant son, Amorlic. She was unlike any noble girl in

Malkanor. She was strong, intelligent, caring, fair-minded, and she was also the most beautiful girl Rylin ever met.

Thinking about Aemreen made Rylin want to see her soon.

Not yet, Rylin thought to himself. *The gift is not ready, yet. I need to finish it before my next Fold Step into Malkanor.*

Rylin set the knapsack down on one of the tables. He took off a long, concealing travel cloak he favored on his larger Fold Steps. He smoothed his long, raven black hair out of his luminescent, deep blue eyes before he began to extract the contents.

Some of these were herbs Rylin already had; but their potency was greater. He took some risks in procuring them from merchants in the Kasarin Empire and its outlying protectorates. He sat in Temporal Projection long before each Fold Step, searching for burgundy clad soldiers while he kept his presence concealed from the Havoc Guilds.

For the moment Rylin's task was easy. Neither soldier or guildsmen patrolled the markets and streets. He would have thought about their absence on most other occasions, but he was grateful for the opportunity to conduct his sought-after trades.

Desert Frankincense, Island Irises, all difficult to find in Stratia, especially with Katahn in ruins.

Then Rylin extracted the one item he searched months for. It was a glittering emerald, its edges rough and raw, covered in dust and marked with particles of smooth obsidian. He wandered the world, in Temporal Projection, when he found its secret home on an island far east of the Kasarin Empire. The island was a tropical place, formed from volcanic undersea bursts only seventeen thousand years ago. A series of barely noticeable quakes gradually shifted the volcanic masses upward over millennia. They were so new that they were not yet mapped by explorers.

Coming from such a raw, young, untamed land, the gem

held a potency that would be excellent for many of his purposes. It made a home in a cavern filled with glittering crystals that caught and refracted a rainbow of faint illumination. It was a place where earth energies and Endless Current created a powerful mix, shaping a wondrous place of natural beauty.

Rylin was about to set himself to working on his gift for Aemreen when he felt a series of pulses in the Endless Current. His skin tingled, and the hairs on his arms lifted. His Temporal Study was outside of the world, created from a future that didn't exist anymore. The Endless Current shouldn't have been felt with such ease from where he stood. He was told that his fellow Lights could feel his work, clearly, but he never understood how that could happen when he never felt their training.

This would have to be strong in a colossal way.

Rylin returned to the white granite corridors of the Zenith Citadel. He would investigate.

A dozen other Lights were present to the left and right of Rylin. Most of them wore the brown robes of the Flames and Candles, but they all stood as still as stone. The air hummed and shimmered with the waves of Current and shaping power. The distant burst hummed against his bones like the outer edges of ripples, waning and growing stronger in turns.

The other Lights felt it as well. As they stood still, their eyes shifted about, searching for the source of their confusion.

"What is that?" asked a boy half Rylin's age. He thought the young Flame might be from western Vodess.

"It's nothing we're permitted to know about," a short, dark-haired Candle girl answered. "It's council and Solas business."

Rylin already ran into hard times when the Solas kept secrets. He had no desire to see how much more pain their silence could cause.

"That may be enough for you; but not for me." Rylin walked a determined stride down the hallways. The younger

Lights followed him. Until now, they were ready to abandon hope of getting answers. Rylin's conviction changed that.

The council chamber of the Ard Solas was at the top of the five floors. It was a circular room that allowed different entries from various points. It was situated in the center of the level. The hallways that held various offices and studies all converged to the entries of the chamber. Most of the offices were empty. Each waited for a new Ard Solas to rise and be worthy of claiming it. With only three Ard Solas remaining, this floor was often filled only with a crushing silence.

Rylin brazenly shoved one council door open and entered, ignoring the customary Current Charged knock. The Solas of the new council stood together in a circle at the center of the round room. The room was filled with large rings of wooden chairs facing the round open center. The high ceiling chamber was illuminated by a large white Current Sphere, hovering high above the gathered council. The Solas were dressed in silver robes, while the silver robes of the Ard Solas were marked by color coordinated collars of their crafts.

`The lead Ard Solas, his collar brown in favor of Geomancy, was a towering man who turned to face Rylin. His name was Martenen Delak. He was the long-time leading Geomancer of Teril, overseeing the progress and harmony of all the farmlands. He held a reputation to be as slow-acting and cautious as the stone he was attuned to.

"Have you forgotten your manners in your solitary training, Light Rylin?" Martenen's deep voice asked, chastising. "You were not called for this gathering."

"I will trust that none of you were too locked away to sense those waves of Endless Current. Have you had enough time to debate and conclude that it was not so different from the battle of Katahn?" Rylin's snide questioning came out in a hostile spit.

"Know your place, Torch!" A yellow and silver dressed Ard Solas Aeromancer snapped. "You come here where you are not permitted, and you bare your anger at us with an obvious lack of decorum."

"The last time we felt such powers in use people died, our leadership died," Rylin reminded them with stern and level recrimination. "This time, it feels as though its northwest, someplace where our Order is not present. If people die, now, it is not our teachers and fellows giving their lives for those who cannot fight. Unarmed and helpless people may be dying. Allowing it once, we were caught off guard. Do you need me to speak aloud what it is to ignore our cause more than once?"

Martenen and the Aeromancer were about to assault Rylin with another reprimand when a younger Hydromancer intervened. "We are not ignoring this, Light Rylin. It is a matter of severe importance, and we will act upon it." His tone was calm and even.

"What do you plan to do about it?" Rylin failed to feign calm as he ground his teeth.

"That is a matter for the Solas, Light Rylin," The Hydromancer denied, sternly. "You must resign yourself with the trust that we will decide in a manner that is best for everyone."

Rylin nodded without a word and turned to leave the council chamber. The stares of the Candles and Flames tracked him before they followed. They thought the confrontation would be more severe. Maybe they even believed he lost his nerve, that he was so easy to placate.

But this matter was far from concluded. The council was given a chance to give him an honest and direct answer, and they failed.

The council would soon learn that if Rylin wanted to find the truth, not so much as Void Hands could stop him.

-7-

King Delkit Mayzeneth, ruler of Katahn'Sha, crouched low in a cutting thicket of thorny bushes. There were more than three hundred of his best archers hidden in the dense towering forests that bordered southeastern Perahl'Sen. They watched the rolling grasslands to the south under a gray overcast sky that promised rain. His thick, smooth hands retrieved a brass spyglass from beneath his forest green surcoat and held it up to his steel blue eyes. His bushy brown eyebrows furrowed. There were none of the usual signs that a Kasarin Warlord was ever present, and no sign of an approaching army.

Yet Tihl'Zen, the hub of three Stratian nations, was reduced to ash with no survivors. An army was out there, somewhere. He would make them answer for this second attack on his people.

It was not that he believed his allies in the Enlightened Sun were delusional, as Lycendrik assumed. There just wasn't enough evidence to connect Void Hands to the attack on the harbor city of Katahn. There was enough motive for the Kasarin Army to wipe out his smaller navy, destroy the harbor city, and raze Tihl'Zen. The only detail that was out of place was the time in between the harbor and Tihl'Zen: more than two years.

Lycendrik claimed that their confrontation with the Enlightened Sun must have left them wounded, forcing the Empire to recover. Delkit was not so certain of that. After a dozen battles with Kasarin Warlords and Pirates, Delkit understood his enemy a little. They were as proud as they were brutal. The Havoc Guilds in particular, embodied both traits. They spent years grinding down their fears and weakness until defeat would only come with death. If there were survivors from a Kasarin attack, they would press forward.

Delkit stroked his dark brown mustache in thought. He also knew all of this was known to his radiance; Fates favor his soul. Yelisian fought against the warlords six times. There were Havoc Guildsmen present during three of those encounters. Their reliance on evocation proved detrimental against the Grand Master Illumancer. His versatility was far superior to theirs. He had no trouble analyzing them and taking apart their defenses, as he always did.

So, the detail that nagged Delkit the most: why did Yelisian give up his body and spirit to an enemy he repelled with repeating ease?

Delkit shifted slightly in his concealment. He kept his painted chain mail quiet. He looked down at his long bow and quiver, reassured as much by his weapon as he was the archers behind him. If there really was a contingent of Kasarin Soldiers to the south, as Lycendrik told him, they should be within sight, soon.

Perahl'Sen's reports also didn't make much sense to Delkit. Tihl'Zen was many miles northwest of these woods. Why would the Empire make a broad circle that would lead them back this way? For that matter, why were so many garrisons and villages spared along the way?

It looked like Tihl'Zen was wiped out only by the Havoc Guilds. Everything about it bore their signature stamp of destruction. But the Magi of the Havoc Guilds tended to rely only on evocation, raw elemental fury. The Magi Delkit battled with never Current Read or Meld Walked as Yelisian called it. Why was this so different?

Horse hooves rustled the thick foliage behind him. Delkit stood up and readied an arrow in one smooth motion. More than fifty of his archers did the same; but Delkit gave a deep sigh of frustration.

"Fates, Lycendrik! You're supposed to be watching the coast for ships," Delkit breathed in irritation.

Lycendrik did not understand the concept behind an ambush. He wore a white surcoat over gleaming gold-plated bracers, greaves, and silver chain mail. He had the sense to tuck his long blonde hair into a gold-crowned skull cap; but with the shining raiment, he was riding around on his white horse. The stead creaked with the oiled leather saddle and gold fastenings.

Delkit was sure the Kasarin Emperor could find Lycendrik's location from the other side of the Maelstrom Sea.

"I arrived to make sure all is as well here as it is there," Lycendrik explained in his measured way, arching one eyebrow.

Delkit lowered his bow much later than his men eased their own weapons. The king of Katahn'Sha might be Lycendrik's ally. He might have agreed with the plans that brought them to this point. But while the young, silver-tongued king might have persuaded most of them, he had a tendency of blundering his plans like a Fates condemned fool. It was often enough to make Delkit want to put an arrow into Lycendrik's head.

In the last two years, Lycendrik increased the number of spies in the Kasarin Empire and pressed them closer to the Crimson Throne. He seemed more feverish to mark the Kasarin Empire for the attack on Katahn when the Order discovered the demon claw.

The result was inevitable. The spies were found, and the emperor declared war. Depending on how serious he was about his retribution would determine the size of the force he sent to Stratia.

"You are supposed to be several day's ride northeast of here, watching the coast," Delkit hissed in an annoyed whisper. "Their ships could make landfall. I want eyes on them and watching my backside."

"My cavalry is still there," Lycendrik shrugged. "The lancers will run down any crimson boots that touch our shores. We have got nothing to fear, there."

Delkit pinched the bridge of his nose after laying down his weapons. Lycendrik was possessed of the certainty that their enemies would stand still and allow a sword to run them through, without protest. If these were real Kasarin armies, they would prepare a successful landfall, first. Only their inexperienced warlords would allow drunken thugs to stagger blindly onto Stratian shores.

What Delkit would give to have Yelisian standing at his side to meet this threat? The Grand Illumination was one of the greatest reasons why the empire hesitated to invade. He incinerated ships that were still miles out at sea, using only the intensified light of the sun. He crushed entire fleets with giant conjured waves. On land, hundreds of pirates were pulled beneath the sand, up to their necks. Yelisian made it brutally clear that he would decide who would live and die in an attack against his homeland.

Now Delkit only had this idiot for an ally. The same idiot who instigated this war, to begin with.

Because of that, this new council of Solas claimed a stance of inaction. Delkit never believed, until now, that the Enlightened Sun would be anywhere but by his side to defend Stratia. Now the Kasarin Empire was sending a message that they could strike anywhere, anytime, and Delkit had no sorcery to stop them. This would be his most difficult defense, yet.

"You can task your men with courier errands," Delkit groaned. "It is beyond senseless for a king, in obvious regalia, to ride alone on the countryside. If I were them, an arrow would have already found your head."

Lycendrik looked like he was about to say something in his defense, but an agonized cry cut his protest short. One of Delkit's archers had fallen from attack. Fates! How did anything slip behind them in the forest?

Delkit kicked his bow up into his hands and readied an arrow. He pointed his weapon at the direction of the scream and lowered into a crouch.

"Down, you fool!" Delkit hissed at Lycendrik as he yanked at his gleaming surcoat.

All Delkit's archers stayed low, concealing themselves in the silence and the forest. Their eyes searched about for crimson and gold, waiting to unleash a lethal volley.

A gust of wind fell on Delkit and his men. It was the prelude of an archer falling from high above, as though dropped from the trees. His arms and legs were bent at backwards angles. Some of his clothing was burned black, and his armor was melted into his flesh. His eye sockets were black empty pits.

The panic was as chaotic as it was predictable. Some of his well-trained archers let their arrows slip, wildly. Others of his men were struck in the head and throat from the wild attack.

In the ensuing pandemonium, vines sprouted from the tree trunks. They gathered and entwined about the legs of the closest archers, tossing them high above the trees. Their screams filled the air.

Now, Delkit knew what they were up against. He knew why the other villages and garrisons were unharmed while Tihl'Zen was destroyed. He knew why he never saw them coming.

This unusual magic style was not the regular Havoc Guilds. These were the Elite Havoc Guilds, the Emperor's personal army of sorcerers.

Oh, Delkit finally knew how deep the emperor's wrath was, this time. The emperor was going to exterminate every Stratian man, woman, and child.

Delkit pushed Lycendrik forward to his horse, all but throwing him back on.

"We will hold them. Ride to the Zenith Citadel, as swiftly

as you can. Tell them Stratia is under imperial obliteration."

Lycendrik looked around, dumbly, eyes wide with terror. He started this war, but the young king clearly did not expect a retort of this magnitude.

Delkit grabbed onto Lycendrik's saddle and jumped up. He slapped his cheek, hard.

"Go Lycendrik, now! The Order of the Enlightened Sun must stand with us, or we will all die! Now go!" Delkit shouted before he slapped the horse's rump. The horse needed no other signal to gallop into a full sprint into the grasslands.

Delkit turned in time to witness a rain of firefly pellets of crimson flame fall from above the trees. The branches and foliage caught fire, instantly, filling the air with heat and thick clouds of choking smoke.

To his horror, he watched the pellets sear holes through armor and flesh with ease. It burned through muscles and bones, leaving opened black holes through the victims. His men died, thrashing as it burned through chain mail hoods and their skulls, straight into their brains. Dozens of his archers were dead in seconds.

Delkit tried to dodge the fire rain as nimbly as he could. Several times the rain glanced off his arms and legs, creating searing waves of pain. He ignored his wounds as best he could. Two thirds of his archers were dead. He needed to buy Lycendrik enough time to get away from their sight. He needed to be far enough away, and closer to the Zenith Citadel.

Fates, though! These imperial elites were not even in sight, and they already massacred most of his fighting force.

Delkit picked up the body of one of his archers and hoisted it over him; using the corpse as cover as he left the burning woods. The ambush was already reversed. It was time to see if he could draw the sorcerers out into the open. The fire rain fell from every downward angle, still glancing and searing his exposed arms and legs. The flames burned through the corpse, again and again, creating cauterized holes. The heat and smoke threatened to bring him down, robbing his air and his sense of direction. The roar of the forest inferno coupled with the screams of burning and panicked men.

Delkit staggered through the tree line, with clumsy lurching steps. His grip on his weapons and the dead archer were an overwhelming heavy press. The fire had already pushed into the grasslands, but the recent heavy rains and damp soil slowed its advance.

Delkit dropped the body and drew his bow, readying an arrow. His vision was blurred by tears and a struggle to breathe. He crouched low, and rotated his aim, scanning for hidden sorcerers.

A pair of black tattoo-covered arms, thick with muscle, appeared to his left and gripped the arrow. The arrow was broken as the hand squeezed. Delkit's eyes widened. Now he knew for certain that these were the Elite Havoc Guilds. The sudden Meld Walk was one confirmation.

But the giant arms, the black bracers covered in gold spikes, the wicked black tribal tattoos...these were all well known to Delkit. He felt any belief that he might survive this day, vanish to nothing.

This man was the supreme patriarch of the Havoc Guilds, the master sorcerer named 'the fist of the emperor'. His name was Zenen'Rol, and he was a scourge known to hundreds of islands now under imperial rule. The emperor sent this titanic man, rumored to be invulnerable, to any overly noticeable opposition, to end any defiance.

Delkit twisted out of the iron grip. He dropped his bow and drew a short cutlass and a dagger. Delkit measured Zenen'Rol and knew he was at a disadvantage. The bald dark man stood eight feet tall and covered with bulky tight muscles. His broad shoulders were draped with a burgundy vest coat that fell to his knees and was open at the front. He wore loose black pants. The scowl on his wide hard face spoke of endless rage and contempt. This was further conveyed by the three gruesome long scars that ran the length of the top of his head.

Immediately, two dozen more Havoc Guild Elite finished their Meld Walk in a wide circle around Delkit and the towering sorcerer. They stood in silence, their feet apart, and their hands clasped behind their backs.

Delkit ignored the ring of Magi. He knew they were here to impose a ring for a duel. The sounds of burning and dying archer's screams faded, one voice at a time.

"King Iron Wall, all alone. You brought so few men, and none of the Order," Zenen'Rol taunted, his voice low and deep, speaking with a nuanced Kasarin dialect.

Delkit grinned as he prepared to retort in perfect Kasarin. "We all agreed I could take you with a fraction of my fighting force."

It was a lie and a bluff. Delkit's bravado was a mask, and Zenen'Rol smiled, knowingly. Delkit wasn't fooling anyone.

Delkit rushed Zenen'Rol, howling. He held his dagger low, guarding in front of him, while his cutlass was pointed before him, from overhead.

The sorcerer only smiled, inviting him. He didn't change his casual stance and didn't move until Delkit struck. The sorcerer's arms began to shine with a metallic gloss. He slammed the dagger down and away, forcing the cutlass to change its trajectory to his abdomen. Delkit thought the sorcerer foolishly forced the weapon to his belly, but the towering man caught the weapon, painlessly, in his free hand. He twisted the point of the sword away, then smashed the blade with his other forearm, breaking it in two.

Zenen caught the broken sword tip and threw into Delkit's forehead in one swift motion.

King Delkit Mayzeneth, ruler of Katahn'Sha, the man who stood before a dozen warlord sieges, was dead before he fell. He had been named 'iron wall' because no pirate or warlord had ever attacked further than the shores of Katahn'Sha under his reign.

-8-

Kreshin hated being called on for large tasks. He didn't know what forced the council to recall him to the Zenith Citadel, but his instincts warned him of coming displeasure.

The line of Solas was long, stretching far into the hallway. There were not many of them left after the battle of Katahn, and not so many raised to their silver staff, but it seemed all of them were present. His fellow Lights talked in hushed and impatiently edged murmurs.

Kreshin was a Solas now, as well. He was raised a year after the Malkanor Inquiry. Now, he not only owned a red-oak staff, but he leaned against it often; reassured that he had something to support his weight.

So, now he leaned, appearing far more casual and disinterested than the other waiting Solas. He yawned with sleepy boredom, his hands and arms wrapped around his staff. There were supposed to be spells that Torches were tested on to be raised to the silver staff, but this formality was skipped with Kreshin. One of these was a spell to keep refreshed and alert even without the Endless Current.

There were other spells left out. He wasn't required to demonstrate adequate wielding of the elements, or Current Reading. He wasn't required to demonstrate fast Meld Walking. And he didn't have to demonstrate a moderate knowledge of history, alchemy or the intricacies of creating spell-shapes.

In the end, this was because Kreshin was relegated to the role of Lesser Solas. He was sent to travel between various provinces in western Vodess. His specialty was Domestic Polymancy. This frequently meant that he would transmute waste into materials that were needed; or revert it to its energy form in the Endless Current. Other than that, he would often find himself repairing damaged items.

It wasn't glamorous work for a sorcerer, but Kreshin didn't mind it. Larger roles in the Order often meant more dangerous work. He was content to be lazy, take his time, pace himself. So, he had to seek out reeking heaps of refuse to alter. It was better than risking his neck in fool battles between fool rulers.

Those sleepy days came to an end after the battle of Katahn. Every Solas and wandering Torch was summoned back to the Zenith Citadel. Not even Kreshin's lack of skill and power kept him from being recalled.

There were things that Kreshin couldn't understand about all of it. All Solas were here to train every initiate as swiftly as possible. While the more obvious point was that no Solas was really training anyone, there was also the matter of his lack of skill. He wasn't powerful or well-versed enough to guide the next generation of Solas. So, what was he still doing here?

"Do your thoughts ever stop whining?" Inquired a measured, male voice from behind Kreshin. "I can't think of a day you didn't try to hide and take a nap, Light Kreshin."

"If you don't like my thoughts, don't Current Read me, Light Merahl." Kreshin turned, feigned a scowl, then laughed as he gripped the tall Perahli's forearm in greeting.

Merahl smiled, his ivory complexion glowing in the expression. "I am surprised they were able to pull you away from your desk in the basement works."

"It's a very busy schedule they give me down there," Kreshin defended in mock offense.

Merahl laughed. "Oh, I'm sure. Watch dust until you fall asleep, then fetch a cup of peach tea. At least your transmutation isn't neglected."

"I would deplete Teril's orchards without it."

Merahl's blue eyes searched past the short Vodessian, scanning the line of Solas. "What do you suppose this is about?"

Kreshin shrugged. "Council matters?"

"Thank you for the educated observation, Light Kreshin. I can only imagine the faculties you deployed for it," Merahl drawled with dripping sarcasm.

"The Council does as the council wills. It isn't our place to comprehend them."

"That might have been true when we were Torches, but these are different times. That isn't the same council that tested us for our staffs. Do you realize how long most of us have been clustered in the Citadel?" Merahl relayed all of this in a cautious whisper.

Kreshin shrugged. He didn't really mind enough to keep track of time.

"It's been two years, Light Kreshin."

"The Order is still wounded and grieving. We have few Ard Solas and no Grand Illumination."

"That's not all we don't have. There are no trials to elevate the initiates. There have been none for more than a year. There are no talks of who will become Grand Illumination or who will be raised to the council of Ard Solas. There have been no mastery skill tests to see who can be raised to the level of Ard Solas. Fates, Light Kreshin! I am the Historian of the Order, and the Illumination's personal histories are still closed to me."

"Those histories were always closed to the Historians, Light Merahl," Kreshin reminded. "No one ever knew they were there until Light Yelisian died without a successor. No one thought to pay it any mind until the 'great discovery'."

"The demon claw is precisely why I must see those histories. We all suspect Light Rylin is correct to draw a connection between Katahn and his discovery. The Endless Current was used to battle something in the city that day."

Kreshin looked at Merahl, baffled. "I fail to see how that has anything to do with the closed histories."

"They marched to the harbor in battle regalia, Light Kreshin. Light Yelisian knew they would be battling something that day. I don't know who else knew; but Light Yelisian seemed certain of something that no one in the Citadel knew. I think he might have known the truth of history. I think the vaults of the Grand Illumination may contain so many hidden truths."

"And how does any of this have anything to do with the present state of the Order?" Kreshin pressed.

"Because we all have so much work to do, so much calling our attention, and we have done nothing for two years. Little solid training, no trials, and only a Torch has done anything to further our goals in the Order. His discovery has left libraries in turmoil all over Stratia, and we say and do nothing else. Katahn has left Stratia on the brink of economic collapse, and we do nothing."

"It's not like we can do anything for Katahn," Kreshin argued. "That barrier won't let anything through. Even if we could get through, Light Barahn reported that those burned remains will cause sickness to anything that attempts to reside there. He said it would remain that way for another century."

"Then we need to rebuild Katahn on new land," Merahl suggested. "We build a harbor. We take in requests from Katahn's destitute citizens, and we provide, as the Order has always done. We build it twice as large, to double the speed of the economic recovery. We have always done this. We forgot to do this for Nerinmor and look what happened for it. We cannot fail the people again, in that way."

Kreshin nodded. Even though he was lethargic and

unmotivated, he knew Merahl was right. Whenever the Order was called to violence, there was ruin in their wake. It was impossible to wield such catastrophic powers and not hold an obligation to the well-being of the people. The Order's ability to repair and improve was nothing short of miraculous. Now, the Order was failing in those duties.

Kreshin sighed with weary resignation. "I guess there is so much more a Lesser Polymancer can do."

Merahl patted Kreshin on the back. "You wouldn't be a lesser Polymancer if an Aeromancer is aiding your efforts."

Kreshin gave Merahl a sideways stare and was ready to say more; but the line of Solas began to file into the Ard Council Chamber.

The circle of seats filled quickly, leaving a few of the Solas standing close to the walls. Murmurs filled the room with incoherent chatter, adding to the sense of anticipation.

Ard Solas and head Geomancer, Martenen Delak, entered from a double door followed by a dozen of the new council of Solas. Their silver and colored robes were an ostentatious contrast to the humble trappings of the old Council. The bright light from the halls spilled in behind the council, casting long shadows in the room. The doors closed with a thunderous boom. The Council gathered a wave of Endless Current without warning. Before anyone could comment on the absence of manners, rods of white light, one foot in length, burst to life in front of every Solas in the room.

"All of you will grasp the rods and swear absolute loyalty to the will of this council of Ard Solas," Martenen ordered, his mountainous shape standing with expectation.

"Begging the pardon of the council," apologized Kera, "but this is forward beyond formality and decorum. What if we refuse?"

"Any Solas is free to reject the oath. If you do, we demand that you leave this chamber, abandon your robe and staff, and leave the Zenith Citadel, forever," Martenen answered.

A series of chagrined whispers resounded in the chamber. Nothing like this had ever been demanded in the history of the Order of the Enlightened Sun. Every Light was encouraged to possess their own mind on matters and follow their own will to do what was right. It was acknowledged that any ruling solitary figure would be flawed, never possessing perfect wisdom.

The short, round figure of the Pyromaster Barahn was the first to stand in defiance. "If I did only as the council wishes, I would never have found my true calling in the flames."

Kreshin was amazed, not at Barahn's rejection, but that he would say it so politely.

"That is, of course, your decision, Light Barahn," an older Aeromancer accepted.

"I would like to add that I already know what this is about, Martenen Delak; and it is shameful to say the least." Barahn abandoned the use of Order formality, insulting him by using his noble family name.

"It is nothing more than our Order moving forward through troubled times," Martenen defended, expressionless.

"You forget, Geomancer, I commune with the flames with the ease that I speak to you. Ashes and smoke are like whispered secrets for me."

At That, Martenen's expression shifted, paling.

"Worry not," Barahn waved a dismissive hand. "I won't influence the choices of my fellows. If they cannot follow their conscience on their own, then walking away is not the right choice for them. They should already feel how wrong all of this is."

"As I said, you are free to leave, if you wish," Martenen declared, but waited until Barahn turned his back before continuing. "Those students who remain without Sparks will be given instruction in whatever way the Council sees fit."

Barahn halted in his steps, clenching his fists. "Impossible, Martenen…"

"Address your fellows with respect," a leathery Hydromancer ordered.

"When it is earned, I will. Don't interrupt, Light Nikolt." Barahn shifted his anger back to Martenen. "It is impossible to train my student to be anything other than a Pyromancer. Light Teranen has walked too much of her chosen path, already."

"Then we shall have to start her anew, with a clean beginning," Martenen deflected, calmly.

Kreshin was baffled, but even more confused when Barahn's eyes widened with outrage.

"You can't do that, you mud roller!" Hissed Barahn, spit flying free. "Current Scouring is forbidden. It has been since three Radiances before your Spark, Kelteseus."

Kreshin leaned to Merahl, who was gaping with shock. "What is Current Scouring?"

Merahl blinked, dumbfounded, before leaning to whisper. "It is a method used to clear away any memories considered detrimental. Often, a person can lose so many years of experiences that it can break their minds and leave them crippled. That is why it is forbidden. It certainly shouldn't be used as flippantly as Light Martenen is implying. He wants to use it just to clear away the knowledge of a path a Light has chosen so that they can be placed on a path of the Council's choosing. It's tyrannical and barbaric."

"It's up to you, Light Barahn. Stay, obey, help us restore the Order in haste, or leave. In your failure, we will set Light Teranen on a course to avoid your blunders as the best Hydromancer she can be."

Barahn clenched his fists, flexing white knuckles. Kreshin felt the air become hot as a tiny ball of fire formed in the Pyromaster's hand. It flew across the room and struck Martenen on the right side of his face; impacting with the sound and force of an open-handed slap.

Barahn returned to the glowing white rod and gripped it with both hands. Most of Solas-all of whom had students like Barahn-did likewise.

Merahl stood up and turned to leave.

"What are you doing?" Kreshin whispered.

Merahl held no reservations about being heard. "I may not know what this is about, as Light Barahn seems to; but I do know this cowardice strong-arming is an act fit for the Mage Clans before their fall. It isn't a reflection of the Order I cherish that instructed me."

Merahl turned to face the Council and the Solas who gripped the rods. "I respect the honor of my fellow Solas, that they would do so much to protect the next generation of our Order. You are brave, and I will always think of you, fondly."

Merahl levelled a stern gaze of reprimand on the council before he continued. "All is known in the light. The light exiles the shadows."

With that, Kreshin watched as Merahl, knowledgeable historian and stronger former Solas, departed from the council chamber and the Order of the Enlightened Sun.

Kreshin was not as brave as Merahl. The Order granted him an easy life, to date. He didn't want to turn away from the comfort it afforded him. He gripped the rod of light in both hands.

Over two dozen other Solas held no obligations to students, and twenty-four of them departed the council chamber. Everyone else swore an oath of obedience to the council.

With no need to worry about further resistance, Martenen returned to his point.

"Your first directives from the council are as follows: You will not participate in unsanctioned conflict outside the Citadel walls."

Now, Kreshin understood what this was about. Even as unmotivated and lazy as he was, a queasy sense of guilt settled over him like a shroud.

Twice, there was the disturbingly aggressive bursts of Endless Current to the north and west. There were obvious signs of sorcery being used to commit violence. All Lights of the Order were present in the Citadel, so that ruled the Order out as either attacker or defender. The people of Stratia were under attack by magic, and with no Lights there to defend them, these one-sided events would be massacre.

So, the Order of the Enlightened Sun would sit in the Citadel and do nothing for the people of Stratia.

"Second, you will not pass any knowledge of these conflicts to our initiates in training." Martenen paused, looking over his oath sworn Solas. "You have all made the correct choice. The Order is in no state to rush into battle, especially when it is joined by kings who do not heed our wisdom."

So, that was what this was about. Martenen was allowing Stratian citizens to die because the kings wouldn't do what he told them to. All at once, Kreshin understood Barahn's anger and Merahl's dismay.

"Kasarin Havoc Guilds attack, and you are going to allow thousands of people to die as a child's way of telling Lycendrik 'I told you so'?" Barahn demanded, shouting.

"The Kasarins will kill, for a little while, to remind us to leave them alone, and then they will leave. The kings will never forget their wrath, or that their lust for battle cost them any assistance from us. They will listen to us, next time."

"There won't be a 'next time'!" Lorin, the youngest Aeromancer Solas shouted. "I helped three other Hydromancers tend to Lycendrik after he rode without food, water, or sleep for almost a week. He nearly died, riding so hard. We heard his delirious murmurs very clearly, Light Martenen."

Lorin paused, his gaze passing over all his fellow Solas. "Delkit Mayzeneth fell in battle. All of Stratia is under Imperial Obliteration."

-9-

General Metrias Fullen, commander of two thirds of Perahl'Sen's Lancer armies, and leader of the Pearl Griffin Squadron, watched the coastline to the east. He sat on a tall white mare. He watched from the top of a rolling, grassy bluff that tapered down to the shores and sandy beaches before the Maelstrom Sea. The day was wet and cold with drizzling rain. The wind whipped the white and gold standards of the Lancer armies.

It was a miserable day. It had been a lousy and uneventful week. Every day since his Majesty departed to report to the king of Katahn'Sha, the Lancer armies met on the same bluff, in disciplined ranks. There were five thousand lancers, and they all waited to engage an enemy landing that never arrived. It became nothing more than a pointless exercise that took up multiple hours of every day.

Worse still, the provisions were not supplied to last this long. His Majesty failed to establish any supply caravans to and from the capitol. Food and drinking water were running low.

Metrias sighed. Beyond that, his men were restless, and tired of pointlessly waiting. Several brawls were breaking out every night. Morale was dreadfully low.

There were few escapes from the tedious waiting. Both Metrias and his men would lose themselves, polishing their steel armor until it shone. They sharpened their lances and long swords and maintained the straps and surfaces of their shields.

War times were not something his men were accustomed to. While Perahl'Sen's army was large, and cavalry was effective, the white and gold equipment made them appear too flashy for militant action. They were more familiar with royal parades and honor guard work.

About half-way through the cold afternoon, a thick fog bank stalked in from the east. It rolled, undisturbed, over the crashing waves and grassy bluffs, swallowing everything in thick gray mist. It moved with such unnatural speed that the cavalry was lost in the gloom before they could turn away.

Metrias's horse pranced in place with nervous tension. Unable to see even a few feet away, he felt alone and exposed. The hairs on his arms stood up. While he could see nothing, he felt as though he was being closely watched. Murmurs from his men reached him, fearful and tense, but he couldn't make out their words.

Metrias couldn't lead a lancing charge in the fog. The lances would be as dangerous to his own people. He dropped his lance and unsheathed his long sword. The metallic ring of the blade leaving its scabbard was a welcome sound in the thickening silence. His men followed suit, creating a ringing song that filled the air.

Then Metrias heard crushing metal, bones breaking and ripping flesh. Somewhere, he heard a body fall from its horse, impacting against the grassy earth. Before he could process the meaning of the sounds, he heard the fall of another body to the earth. The deaths were so quick that the victims didn't have time to cry out.

One of the lancers trotted out of this mist, slumped to the side on his horse. Half the length of a lance was impaled through his sternum. The horse stopped and the rider fell to the ground.

Metrias' horse began to stamp with heightened fear, as he was lost in the fog, surrounded by the gut-wrenching sound of lancers impaled on their own weapons. He gripped his long sword with white knuckles. He did this for the reassurance of the weapon in his hand, and not in any certainty that he might be using it soon. The archers of Katahn'Sha had only ever included him in battle once, in his entire career. It was the only battle he ever fought. It was only against several ships of Kasarin pirates that proved both motley and unorganized. That battle was over in minutes.

This Kasarin sorcery was unlike anything the Lancer General ever heard of. It wasn't their common giant red fireballs or shards of ice they used to muscle through their enemies. This was calculated and creative. It was deadly in a new way. It seemed to adapt to the enemies they confronted.

Now, five thousand lancers were being butchered in seconds. Metrias would flee and report this catastrophe; but he couldn't see far enough to know where to run to.

Metrias felt the ground tremble. His horse cried out in fear, rearing up on its hind legs. Metrias was thrown to the ground on his back. Even with his armor, the hard impact knocked the breath out of him. Underneath him, the ground quaked. He tried to stand, but every time he propped himself up on his elbows, the tremors brought him back down.

When the quakes subsided the fog also began to fade. Metrias looked around in disbelief, shocked and sick with rising nausea.

A force of five thousand lancers were reduced to a few hundred. Many of them were impaled, their lances jammed into earth upon falling, their bodies bent forward and arched backwards in the air. Blood seeped out of their fresh wounds, trickling onto the grass in puddles. Some of their organs attempted to escape wider openings caused by the quakes. Soon, entrails would dangle free, and stomachs would fall to the ground.

Outside the carnage, a towering wall of stone and dirt circled around the butchered army, cutting them off from any hope of escape.

Metrias wasted no further moment. With himself and his men trapped, it would be simple for the Havoc Guilds to finish killing them all. He rolled to his feet and grabbed his long sword.

"To the walls!" Metrias shouted as he sprinted to the closest edge of the earth prison. "Use whatever you may, and break through."

Metrias found a patch in the wall that was more dirt than stone. He began to hack down with frantic determination, lunging his weapon through, trying to cut a hole for escape. He and his men would only have seconds in which to escape before the Havoc Guilds settled on a method to get rid of them. His mind flashed with images of the crimson fire rains they preferred. He forced himself not to think about being trapped and burned alive.

There was a loud grinding burst before one of his men screamed and died several hundred feet away. He didn't look, he could not afford to stop cutting through. It must have been some impaling spike of stone, or something just as cruel.

Several more screams filled the air. Metrias doubled his efforts, ignoring the growing ache in his arms. His lungs burned, as much from panic as the strains on his body. This wouldn't be how he would die: helpless, trapped, picked off one at a time. He would not wait for his turn. He would not let these Kasarin Sorcerers decide his end at their leisure. Metrias Fullen may not have experienced much battle, but he would break through. He would rush at least one of these sorcerers. He would claim at least one head before he died that day.

The clang of steel against stone was a continual deafening ring. The Perahli soldiers shouted and swore as they swung their weapons against the walls of the prison, again and again. Maybe enough of them would break through the walls and kill more of the Havoc Guild sorcerers. Metrias hoped so. He wanted to hurt their invasion, even if only a little.

A dozen more dying screams filled the air. Even without seeing the lancers, the sorcerers continued to kill them with each magic. Were they watching with bird's eyes from above? Could they somehow sense them some other way?

At last, a section of wall crumbled, revealing the grassy bluff beyond. Metrias crawled through the opening, gripping his sword with angry resolve. One head, he would claim at least one head.

Metrias was almost through the wall. His arms and head peaked through when something squeezed around his hips and ankles. He tried to pull his legs, only to fall on his belly. He looked back where several thick brownish red vines constricted and restrained him.

Several more vines sprung from the wall and grass, wrapping around his neck and wrists. He twisted his head, and the vines against his neck chafed and cut.

To the east, at the beaches and across the ocean horizon, bulky, tall-masted Kasarin Soldier ships dotted the view. There were more than a hundred, by an easy count. Each one would hold more than several hundred of the Crimson Empire's well-trained soldiers.

Metrias watched the coming invasion with despair. A small, calloused hand gripped the top of his white-blonde hair and yanked back, bearing his throat. He didn't try to struggle as another small feminine hand brought a long, serrated dagger below his chin and against his neck. She yanked the blade. Metrias felt hot pain on his neck while his life and blood departed him in seconds.

It didn't matter that he was about to die without seeing the eyes of his killer. All Stratians were about to die in the same miserable end as he did.

-10-

Amorlic Moarenroak leaned idly against the mossy bark of a broken willow. He flipped and caught a dagger in one hand as he waited, bored and a little impatient. His glossy black leather coat proved ample protection against the tree's rotting moisture and the cold mists of the swamp. His shoulder length yellow-blonde hair was tied behind the nape of his neck, adding to his roguish looks.

Amorlic had grown in the last two years, but like the world around him, he learned to control the flow and outcome of his growth. He was a foot taller now. While he had strong muscles to support him, they were of a size to allow swift precise movements.

That was the key to survival, of course: being swift and precise. Spiders leaped on their prey when they were too complacent. Serpents moved at blurring speed and had their prey in their mouth before they knew they were in any danger. There was no honor to any of it, just the quick and the dead.

This part of the swamp was colder, less inhabited by Nerinmor's native wildlife. It was two days north of his mother's swamp compound, a neutral location just south of the frozen Northern Wastes.

To Amorlic's right, on a moss and fungus covered knoll of boulders, a stack of wooden crates sat, guarded by two leather clad mercenaries. The two men were small and quick, trained at his mother's island stronghold far to the southwest of Vodess.

Amorlic was given the fighters by his mother, over a year ago, when he was the last survivor of a long and deadly contest between residents of the swamp compound.

The contest placed the future of the throne of Malkanor up for the taking. The game was between himself and the slaves she kept in the swamp compound. Her rules were veiled but clear: only one would survive to claim it, but all deaths were required to be untraceable.

Amorlic survived. His birthright belonged to him still. When he was offered a chance to return home, he declined, believing he still had more to learn from Nerinmor. His mother accepted but offered the token reward of two mercenaries as bodyguards.

So Amorlic chose these two: Rackten and Benaith. They were trained by a Kasarin Mercenary in every form of knife combat the master soldier could teach. So, alongside a belt full of perfectly balanced throwing knives, they also each had one more attached to a length of rope. In battle, the two brown-haired Vodessians were as quick as they were bloody. They also never spoke, and always followed orders to the letter. They stood still, their hands clasped behind their backs, and their feet slightly apart. They stood to either side of the crates.

The quiet of the cold northern bog made it easy for them to hear the approach of their clients long before they emerged from the mists. Amorlic stood up straight, sheathing his dagger in a smooth flourish as he turned to look at them.

There was more than a dozen of them. They were a motley rag-tag bunch covered in dirt. They wore patches of fur, leather, and bits of rusty metal plating. Only the leather of their boots was oiled to protect against the fetid swamp waters. There was no order or discipline in their approach. They swaggered in casual strides. Did these men have the skill to make use of the wares they came for? True, their massive swords and axes looked brutal, having the capacity to cleave through several men in a single swing, but there were signs of tell-tale rust and chipped metal. A real army might have a few hours of difficulty with them, but these men would not come away with victory.

The leader, a tall, broad shouldered man with long platinum hair and dark brown eyes, stepped forward.

"You are the one called Amorlic?" he boomed.

"I am. Did you bring fifty thousand Terilian gold pieces?" Amorlic demanded.

"May we examine the wares?" The leader demanded with a hard edge.

Amorlic shook his head. Just because this man was a larger fighter from the Northern Wastes didn't promise Amorlic's fear and obedience. "It is policy that we do not allow the clients to view the wares until we have confirmed the payment."

"How do we know you won't cheat us? That could be crates full of venomous serpents ready to spring on us."

Amorlic wouldn't budge on the matter. "Fifty thousand Terilian gold pieces." Amorlic spoke slow and condescending. "Do you have them?"

"It is difficult to trade Northern Rubies for Terilian coin..."

Amorlic gave a shrill whistle to his bodyguards, gesturing for them to gather the crates. No excuses would suffice. The man was either an idiot, or he took Amorlic for one. The Northern Rubies might be valuable, but the miners never gave them away or traded them with flippant disregard. The miners hoarded them until they were ready to cash them in for enough wealth to buy them grand estates. The mines and the glaciers often crushed and buried the miners before they could complete their caches. If anyone, other than a miner, attempted to trade with the gems, it was an alarming signal of murder and theft at best. It was obvious blood money that was impossible to launder. It would be traced back to Maesellen in a day.

"What are you doing?" The raider shouted as Rack picked

up one of the crates.

"Rubies are worthless to me. No coin, no trade."

"Wait, we have the coin," the leader shouted in haste, gesturing for a brown-haired axe wielder to come forward. He carried a large brown leather bag over one shoulder, which he dropped on the boulder.

Amorlic heard the clink of coin, but he paused to look at the bag, then at the axe wielder, then at the leader. Rack and Ben put down the crates. The two tensed defensively as Amorlic opened the bag and retrieved one of the golden coins for inspection.

"You could have begun with this," Amorlic observed in irritation. "Yet you tried to make excuses and offer trash."

The lead raider stepped forward, closing within a couple of feet of Amorlic, glaring. "I am tolerating much from you, little princeling. Why should I not just kill you and take what we wish?"

Amorlic didn't blink or flinch as he met the raider's gaze. "The price just went up. You will give us ten percent of all coin from future raids, and five slaves of our choosing."

"You tread dangerous ground," the raider growled.

The tiny needle prick got the raider's exposed forearm faster than anyone could register Amorlic's movement. The bigger man breathed through his nose with increasing rapidity but made no other move.

The seamstress needle was coated in a particular spider venom that found the brain and paralyzed the victim in an instant. The spiders were common in the southern Nerinmor swamps, so the supply was infinite to those who knew how to harvest it. The raider would live, though.

"Supposing I don't leave this swamp. Suppose her majesty is less than satisfied with the outcome of this trade," Amorlic grinned. "You and your men will have five days, at the most.

After that, you can be certain she will make you beg to be sent to hell. So, if you are done voicing stupid threats, agree to the terms, or get out of my sight."

Before any answer, there was a quick, wind-dashing sound. Two of the raiders at the rear stiffened before falling, face first, into the mud with a loud splash. Throwing daggers were lodged up to the hilt in the back of their necks.

Shouts filled the silence as twenty armored figures burst out of the mist. Their smooth swift sprint was alarming, considering the bulk of their crimson pleat armor edged with gold. They also wore golden helmets with tall crimson plumes. The men were tall, dark skinned fighters with hard brown eyes. They held long, curved, slender swords while small bucklers covered little more than their forearms.

The raiders only had an instant before the soldiers cut them down with wide, cleaving, horizontal cuts. The raiders were slaughtered before they could draw weapons.

Amorlic, Rack and Ben responded with greater speed. Rack and Ben dashed ahead, their dagger whips blurring around them in clouds that promised death.

Amorlic was quick to find an exposed inch in their armor, above the thigh. He hurled two throwing daggers forward, cutting into the thighs of two swordsmen. Had the daggers been normal, the prince would be dead in the next moment; but they were poison coated.

This toxin was one of Amorlic's favorites, and a marked difference from his mother's nightshade concoctions. He called it 'Orchard's Dream'. It held the favored spider venom as its base, but it was carefully combined with the powder of peach pits. The combination paralyzed the victim and killed within seconds.

Rack and Ben ignored Amorlic's first two targets, leaving them to die from the poison. Their daggers found the eyes and brains of two more soldiers.

Amorlic ran to another crimson soldier, his long daggers

in hand, and rolled around the shield, ducking low behind the fighter. He stabbed the back of the thigh without turning. He stood up to give another soldier a shaver's nick on the left cheek. Amorlic's daggers were coated in Orchard's Dream. He only needed to deliver scratches to his enemies. If his daggers ever ran dry, his sheaths held fast-applying vials ready to coat them anew. He could always make more at the end of any given day.

Rack and Ben whip cut the throats of three more before the remainder turned and fled into the mist. Amorlic gathered his daggers. Rack and Ben coiled their weapons. They were about to gather the crates when Amorlic whistled at them and shook his head.

"We know these are Kasarin Soldiers, and they are from the Crimson Throne. That was a trifle force. They believed us to be less than relevant, or the rest of our lives would be short. They may have sent a greater force to the compound. If I were my mother, I would hate to lose a stronghold much more than a few crates of merchandise. We leave the crates and travel fast and light."

Amorlic and his bodyguards left the clearing in the swamp at a full dash. They needed to cover the two days of ground as quick as they could manage. Amorlic would make quite a name for himself if he could mount an effective defense against the Kasarins. His mother would be generous for maintaining the secrecy of her rising empire.

-11-

Rylin's awareness floated in the emerald sky. He pulled against the cold blue moments of the past. He pulled against seconds and minutes, first, then days. His body sat in the center of the golden circle in his Temporal Study. He would have to travel weeks and miles. He trained himself well enough to withstand the effort with little strain on his will and body.

It would have been easier to project his awareness and eavesdrop on the council, just the other day; but Rylin would at least honor the formalities of council privacy.

If the bursts of Endless Current were the result of a one-sided conflict, as it was two years ago, then the victims deserved to have their final moments witnessed. They deserved to have someone identify their killers and seek justice against them. It was vital to learn as much about it as he could.

So Rylin projected to that first moment when he felt the violent ripples in the Endless Current.

Rylin slowed the progression of seconds and minutes and began resisting the cold and the pressure. His awareness moved away from the Temporal Study, through the thick walls of the Citadel and out into the hills and bluffs to the west. He rode on the still waves of raw energy, feeling himself draw closer towards those who spell-shaped it.

The direction changed to the north, close to the border

of Teril. The three-nation hub city of Tihl'Zen would be in that direction. He thought anything that would have happened to a favorite city to the Flames and Candles would be widespread knowledge in the Citadel, by now. The younger boys and girls loved the bakeries, shops, and the displays from the artisans of Perahl'Sen. If the younger Lights could spend a day idle, they would frequently choose Tihl'Zen.

Rylin stopped, his awareness floating above the fountains, walkways, and rooftops of the hub city. This was the source of the bursts in the Endless Current. He allowed time to resume to its natural flow.

There were hundreds of tall, crimson and gold clothed figures halting out of their Meld Walk. No sooner did they appear in the streets did they begin gathering waves of Endless Current and unleashing killing sorceries on the defenseless citizens. Disembodied as Rylin was, he could not be sickened by what he saw. While he thought he could prepare himself after the ocean carnage before the battle of Katahn, he realized nothing could prepare him for this.

Tihl'Zen only held a basic law enforcement for patrolling the streets and keeping the peace. They couldn't begin to defend the people, or themselves, against the raw fury of these magi. They cooked Perahli men and women with jagged lances of crimson lightning. Red fires reduced the city to ash in moments.

White-hot rage boiled in Rylin's awareness. Women and children who attempted to flee were decapitated by flying arcs of red energy. Blood sprayed free of their open necks. People hiding in basements and cellars screamed in agony as they were burned alive. The people of the three nations were helpless against the slaughtering invaders.

Caught in his growing fury, the Temporal Current shoved him back into his place in the present.

Rylin's body tensed, still lifted off the ground. A continual howl of rage sounded from his open mouth. His table, books, and chairs floated in the air, caught in the throes of his outpouring of anger. It was too destructive to contain in the Citadel walls. He Fold Stepped into the frigid mountains of the Northern Wastes to empty his rage. In his cries, the air shimmered and the snows swirled about him in a twisting maelstrom. For minutes, Rylin was the eye of his own rending storm.

Rylin traced the stupidity of it all back to its source. Two years ago, Maloric warned the other kings that any proven attempt to spy on the Kasarin Empire would be viewed as an assault on their sovereignty. When Rylin began to connect Void Hands with the battle of Katahn, Lycendrik's ego was bruised. The fool was so eager to be right about starting a war that he increased the number of spies in a desperate attempt to prove the Kasarin involvement with the loss of Katahn. They would have pressed a frantic search and found nothing before being discovered.

Now, for ego and territorial stupidity, the good people of Tihl'Zen were butchered to the last. None of them were involved in any of the decisions that led to the attack. Everything about their end was helpless. In each of the victims he saw the faces of his family and friends in the outskirts of Pahlinsor. These people were no different. They had no control over the events that decided their fate for them.

Facing and naming the anger that burned inside Rylin helped to cool it, if only a little. For now, he could reign it in and focus. This new Council of Solas would do nothing about these Kasarin attacks. Was this because they were keeping to the claim that the Order was too weak to fight? The more likely truth was that they wanted the teach the kings a foolish lesson for not heeding their counsel.

What good was a lesson to a dead student? If these Kasarin Magi were willing to commit to wholesale massacres, it was clear that no one was safe. Could the council not see that soon there would be no one left to advise?

Rylin projected his awareness to his Temporal Study and then Fold Stepped. He realized he shaped a vulnerable Fold Step to vent his anger, and inwardly berated himself for not following his self-imposed safety protocols. A Fold Step like that could have trapped him in the side of a mountain.

When Rylin returned to his circle, he projected a message to Ishell in the Endless Current. Even then, he began opening the Simulacrum locks on his crafting chamber and started rummaging for various items. The first item was the emerald.

In minutes Rylin heard the door to his meditation chamber open, and Ishell gaped, stopping to admire the crafting room for the first time.

"You made another room, but still you create no windows, Light Rylin," Ishell chastised as her eyes circled the surroundings.

"Bringing a pocket future into a distilled space is difficult enough, Light Ishell. Do you know how much of a task it would be to transport and distill a whole countryside just to give me sunlight and fresh air?"

"I am sure the answer is, once again, easier than you give it credit for. You need a lady's help again, so I will take some time to think about it for you."

Rylin didn't allow her to see his annoyance as he searched through a cabinet drawer. "I didn't call you to discuss the décor, Light Ishell. I called you because we all need to prepare."

"Leading with vague statements was your Spark's tendency. You should not make it your practice, as well."

Rylin spun on his heels and levelled his intensity on Ishell. "The Kasarin Empire has begun its attack!"

Ishell shrugged. "We all knew they would."

Rylin resisted the urge to grind his teeth. Her seeming disinterest was aggravating, but he pardoned her ignorance.

"They razed Tihl'Zen. There are no survivors. The Havoc Guilds Meld Walked in and slaughtered everyone. The bursts we have been feeling are them."

Ishell's eyes widened.

"Fates! I should have seen it sooner," Rylin swore. "I have been Fold Stepping in and out of the Empire. I saw their lack of military force in the streets. It should have been obvious."

"You idiot! You have been going to and from, with flippant disregard, when you know, better than anyone, what is happening?" Ishell shouted.

Rylin dismissed the tirade, shaking his head. "Calm yourself, Light Ishell. I project before I Step. I scout ahead to see if anyone is there, first."

"What of the people that can be questioned? Did you watch them, after? Don't you think any of them would think it odd that a Stratian sorcerer repeatedly appears and vanishes? It's possible you started this."

"You and I both know what started this, and we know it wasn't me."

"Maybe so," Ishell acquiesced, "but you can't ignore that you acted without full and proper discretion. We are Lights. We cannot charge about the world, recklessly."

Rylin nodded. "That is a fair point, Light Ishell, but I believe you digress from the actual matter at hand. Will you prepare with me? No one can win a war, alone."

Ishell's smile was slight. "That is the most sensible thing you have said, yet. Of course, I will; but there is much we don't know."

"Such as…?"

"The council already declared inaction before the attacks began. Nothing of this has been mentioned by any of our Sparks. Why?"

"To protect initiates in training," Rylin offered.

Ishell shook her head. "Kera would've said something. Fates! She would've already marched out there with Enriall Armor and a silver staff. Something is off kilter with the Solas,

Light Rylin. Solas Barahn should be popping his knuckles and cricking his neck."

"Do you think it has anything to do with Solas Merahl's resignation?"

"I am surprised you know about that. You could simply claim the truth, your way," Ishell suggested.

"No. We need to train and prepare."

"No, Light Rylin. Stop thinking like a muscle-headed boy. We need more allies. If not the Solas, and we must know why, then the strongest initiates in training. It is just as ludicrous to think of only two people winning a war."

Ishell walked over to stand beside Rylin, looking at the collection he placed on the table. "What is all this?"

Rylin picked up the emerald and tossed it in his grip. "To prepare, I may have to ignore some of the normal rules of training. I need to create any advantage that can be gained."

"You, yourself, have said that you create dangers when you ignore your training," Ishell critiqued with warning.

"I don't believe it matters when everyone is in danger."

Half a day later, Rylin sat on a stool before a tall weaving loom in his crafting chamber. He never imagined that the work of a tailor would be a part of preparations for war, but he would never find anyone in the modern era to complete this task.

It was true that he could have done this by transmuting the pieces of material or shaped the full coat. He could have gone anywhere in the world and paid a commission to have it made. This was no ordinary long coat. Rylin needed to craft this by hand. He needed to give it his full time and effort for it to better suit his purposes.

This would be a major breach in training, of course. An

enchanted object like this would be permitted only for a Solas. There would be two spell shapes saturated into this coat. Using it would be simple. Making it would be complicated.

Rylin continued to weave forest green threads together, melding them into the patches and lengths of material. It was a messy effort, but he never really attempted to make his own clothes before. He did have a few ideas to improve the quality, later.

On the table, beside the emerald, sat a green crystal flask. The concoction that would fill it was brewing now, bubbling and cooling in the bottles. Rylin lost himself in the tranquil cadence of the hissing steam and the crackling frost. The mix, by itself, was not magical in nature. Anyone with the knowledge, patience, and ingredients could make it. While the first two requirements were a simple matter, only Rylin's excursions to other lands allowed him to locate the highest quality of items.

Finding the herbs and flowers was easy. In some cases, buying them was difficult. Rylin couldn't just fabricate items right in front of stall and shop owners. These merchants went through great lengths to find rare flowers and herbs. He would only insult and belittle their efforts if he used Simulacrum to cheat their costs.

So, the difficulty was that Rylin could not spend Stratian currency in many of those eastern lands. He had to find trades and tasks in the more neutral lands to earn Kasarin platinum coins. If he muted his powers and dressed less like a Light of the Order and more like an eastern wanderer, the island natives accepted his aid. He was only a coin-earning hedge sorcerer, as they saw it.

As in the days when Yelisian trained him to find small ways to improve his will, Rylin didn't hesitate to use his powers to help farmsteads and fishing crews. It felt good to go out into the world, ask for little, but help a lot. He might be earning money, but he measured carefully. He paid attention for signs of what the people could afford, and he brought his fee into acceptable levels to match it.

Rylin also learned a lot about the Kasarin Empire. The emperor ruled over all of them. The Havoc Guilds, Warlords, and armies were an extension of his iron fist. Much of the population was the opposite of all of that. There were families and honest people just making a living, just as in Stratia.

Unlike Malkanor, the Empire did not over-tax its people, or wait for random citizens to abduct and torture. Knowing this, Rylin could not allow himself to let the invasion create an over-generalized view of all Kasarin people.

Rylin pulled a thread of forest green tight, with a surge of angry resolve.

He wouldn't allow the emperor or his armies to continue butchering the good people of Stratia, either.

-12-

Zenen'Rol stood as still as stone on the beach. His hands were clasped behind his back. His large angular face was expressionless. His eyes shifted among the soldiers of the armies, and he supervised with disinterest.

Tents and spike walls were erected. Cooking fires were started. Weapon and armor racks were built and placed. It was all done precisely and in minutes. It was their testament of imperial discipline.

Still, Zenen seethed with deep, angry impatience. Zenen'Rol was no soldier. He was a man feared by all in the Crimson Empire. As a magus, he was not only the leader of all the Elite Havoc Guilds; he was also the iron right fist of the emperor. He was at the front of every imperial conquest, and he executed every traitor to the throne on sight.

Zenen was a giant, even by the grand standards of the empire. He was taller, far more muscled, and his dark scowling countenance was enough to frighten men, women, and children into sudden obedience. His three scars on his head were created from hot iron brands, pressed to melt flesh and bone. They were a sign of devotion to his guilds and his emperor. The tribal black tattoos were symbolic of each of the lands he conquered in battle. He gained the unquestionable right to battle the strongest enemies in foreign lands, first. Their death was reserved as an honor for him to claim.

Zenen ground his teeth. Why were the greatest powers

of the empire needed here? All the magi were holed up like cowards, and they were not enough of a power to challenge him anyway. The Grand Illumination, the sorcerer that once held back warlords and lesser havoc guilds from ever setting foot in Stratia, was reported dead, along with the strongest magi of the Order.

That was the one reason why the empire did not invade straight away, two years ago. The destruction of dozens of ships and thousands of traders was alarming. There were some merchants that were only alive out of fear. They reported that the oceans became full of corpses and debris. When they first saw the strange black storms over the waters, they turned their ships back home and wouldn't sail again.

The emperor dispatched scout ships to verify these claims at a discreet distance.

All the claims were accurate and frightening enough that Zenen watched the emperor's hands tremble.

Unlike Stratia, the imperial military, the Magus Guilds, and all the imperial family knew the ancient truth. The common people of the empire didn't know, but that was only so that they could live and work, as they were meant to.

For two thousand years, the Crimson Empire watched Stratia with a wary and close gaze. There was little that could frighten Havoc Guild Magi. However, the empire kept an elite archive that held well preserved accounts of an era known as the Black Decade, a time when the empire was on its knees before an army of Void Hands. These accounts were required reading for everyone who was not a common citizen. These accounts often kept Zenen'Rol awake at night after reading these dark histories.

The dark wreckage in the Maelstrom Sea bore a horrifying resemblance. It almost began the war with Stratia right then. The emperor would not permit a second Black Decade. He would stamp it out before it could begin.

Except Stratia was much more wounded than the empire.

Their economy and coastal infrastructure was shattered. Stratia didn't seem to be in any shape for battle, much less conquest.

So, the emperor relented. He was wise and honorable enough to grant mercy to a crippled enemy.

That would have been the end of it, but then Stratians were spotted in the empire. These were not merchants, as the emperor hoped. These were moderately trained spies.

Then the number of these Stratian spies increased, much more so in the last year. Like an infestation, they began to appear closer to the throne each day, as bold as they were stupid. Zenen personally executed each spy (much to his delight) but that never brought them to a halt.

Then it was reasoned if Stratia could spare so many lives for espionage perhaps their wounds were a deception. Maybe Stratia was closer to covering the world in a second darkness than originally believed.

The empire would take no chances. They would not allow a return of such a nightmare. They would strike first and leave no chance for Stratia to strike back. Their people would die, and their lands would belong to the Crimson Empire.

Zenen's impatience grew by the moment. These beach camps were only the beginning. There were still twenty supply ships and three times the number of soldier transports. They waited at sea, taking turns to offload for the conquest. The whole thing might take days before the army was on land, with miles of camp and defenses established.

All the while, Zenen and the other Elite would have to watch and protect the armies as they landed.

From what? Zenen thought irritably. Only two days ago, Zenen and his magi wiped out thousands of strange looking horsemen. The white and gold riders never saw Zenen coming. They were butchered in under an hour. The bodies were piled up and burned before the first transport could make landfall.

The massacre took place about a mile to the west. There

were still mounds of dirt and stone that once towered over and trapped the horsemen. There were still the spots of black earth where the bodies were burned to ashes.

It was only partly because it was their custom and creed to burn them all. This time, Zenen understood why the emperor wanted no corpses in their wake. If the Void Hands were here, then every dead body was a weapon to them.

No chances would be taken.

Zenen held back his frustration and impatience. He knew the need to guard the soldiers. He was not some first year barely accepted magus with bleeding knees from the Trial of Glass. Discipline and patience did rule over his desire for battle and worthy enemies. On any other day, Zenen'Rol would stand placid on this beach, allowing the rush of Endless Current to bolster and empower him. He had been a sorcerer in battle long enough to understand the strength of a clear mind.

Yesterday, however, Zenen felt something unsettling.

There were colossal bursts in the Endless Current, first to the south, then again in the far north. The burst in the north was followed by titan waves of raw power that shoved against every present magus. After several minutes, the waves decreased and returned to the south.

The bursts in the south were far too great to ignore, but the 'waves' from the north were something else, all together. It was raw angry inner will, but that did not make any sense. A magus bursting with that much will was like a man lifting the largest mountain with his bare hands.

Zenen took a moment to calm himself, taking comfort in the sound of ocean waves and hungry gulls flying nearby for food. He listened to the officers shouting orders, and the soldiers who rushed to obey them. He felt the spray of the crashing waves and the cold winter wind on a dark gray mid-afternoon.

Zenen was calmed. He took further consolation in one fact. He knew the giant power was not a Void Hand. No magi had ever sensed the power of a Void Hand. They were all still safe in that regard.

But a power like that could have only come from one in Stratia's Order. The command to leave them be still chafed against Zenen's sensibilities. The power of Stratia's magi was comparable to the Havoc Guilds. Ignoring the Zenith Citadel felt like leaving a poisonous snake at his back, unchallenged.

The emperor reached some sort of tenuous agreement with the Order's new leader. It further aggravated Zenen that his loyalty to the empire didn't afford him access to the details of that agreement. Zenen was only permitted to know that the Havoc Guilds could not strike the Order unless the Order struck first.

Zenen hated waiting for his enemies to strike first, and he knew they would.

After all, as soon as the armies were fully camped and ready, Zenen and the other magi would begin Meld Walking entire legions all over Stratia. The Havoc Guilds prepared themselves with extensive training in Meld Walking hundreds to thousands of people at a time. The Ka'Rak, the sword soldiers of the empire, trained themselves to withstand the sickness from Meld Walking. All of them could attack upon arrival to any location.

This method was already tested a few days ago when a small squad of Ka'Rak was Meld Walked to the west. Zenen observed the success from the gaze of a transparent Scrying Sphere he projected into the skies above.

Zenen was disappointed to see three men kill a small squad of well-trained Ka'Rak, but the travel and observation still counted as a great success.

So, in several days Zenen would send his Scrying Sphere into the skies. He would find ideal targets to strike, analyzing their defenses for weaknesses. The cities and nations would fall in swift succession.

Zenen would deliver a vacant new continent to the empire. He would find and deliver the blackened giant blade of the Magus King to the emperor.

-13-

Creation's End was not a name he would choose for himself, but the fear it could generate might suit his purposes. The Ancient Ones promised he would have his true name one day, but he would have to earn that right.

Creation's End stood in the hard slag mounds and the deep, black, glossy trenches of the ruins of Katahn. Far to his right, the Book of Worms sat on a raised pedestal of black, melted stone. It was open, and the blood-soaked pages were revealed. Its scrawled words and diagrams of ancient Void Arts were only a fraction of its powers. Its pale blue glow illuminated the dark ruins on this cloudy midnight.

Several yards in front of Creation's End a tall, black, wraithlike figure floated. In its black hands, he held a transparent black staff. The Ancient Ones called this weapon the Scepter of Devouring, and it was favored by the Shadows Eternal. The black-cloaked man who held the weapon no longer retained much of his own identity. He gladly offered it when he sacrificed his body and soul to become a part of the Book of Worms. His human form could be returned at moments like this when the book required a human shape for its purposes. If the book had human souls enslaved, it could call on the spirits of the Void Disciples.

This Void Disciple once went by the name Makorin, and he was the Patriarch of the Order of the Void Triangle. The book summoned him because of his mastery in the shadow arts and his swift brutal fighting skills.

Creation's End held a similarity with his sparring master: he did not have a physical form of his own. He was a dark, transparent, human shape. It was difficult to acquire enough strength to take even this much of a form. He had help to do this. Where, once, he was in danger of disappearing forever, now he drew his power from the Essence of Stillness. This was a primordial infinite darkness that lay underneath everything. This essence was a part of the Great Mother, the venerated sentience of nothingness that came before all creation. That essence was also how he regained enough strength to sustain himself against the Endless Current.

Now, he was a phantom of two worlds, a discard in the world of the living, a growing power in the world of the dead.

The Book of Worms taught Creation's End how to survive and grow powerful. Creation's end satisfied justice in returning the favor. Creation's End pushed his new power into the eternal world of departed souls and found several hundred people the Book killed on its journey to Stratia. He pulled them out of eternity, smashed their will into perfect subservience, then returned them to the Book of Worms.

As a result, the Book could call on the spirit of any Void Disciple at will.

Creation's End let the cold hollowing Essence fill him. It scraped inside him like jagged shards of ice in his body before it stretched his will into hell.

A being like Makorin could only ever create his sorcery from Sol Fierest. If he were to try to use any more than that, the overwhelming magnitude of oblivion would scour his entire existence until nothing remained. It was true for every Void Disciple. It was why there were three sects of the Void Triangle. They compensated for everything that one could not do by drawing from the other two.

Makorin could only ever wield the Scepter of Devouring.

A Blood Gauntlet could only create the Rod of Torment, which would sicken and enslave with the blood of the condemned. A Hellfire Imbued could only create the Reach of the Inferno, a staff that burned any victim it struck.

But Creation's End was able to wield all three disciplines of the Void, separate or together. He could create a defense of the Devouring Maw, only to counterattack with the Annihilation Worms at the same time.

As he was able to use all three disciplines, he could also create a weapon that combined attributes of the three domains of hell. It was called the Staff of the Abyss. Until now, the weapon was reserved for the king of hell. In one strike, it could freeze and swallow souls, burn away undesired will, then sicken and enslave whatever was left.

Creation's End limited the raw ability of the staff. He would not take in the will of another person. He would not create hordes of undead slaves. If he was not strong enough to enforce justice, then he would hone his will and powers until he could.

Justice was his entire purpose. It was why he trained in these dark and forbidden disciplines.

Creation's End first approached the Book two years ago, with the intent to destroy it. He already felt the pain and poverty its devastation would inflict all over Stratia. The Book had already killed thousands, and a war was inevitable. The way for justice dictated a clear path, then. The Book must be destroyed to answer for the ruin it caused.

'*Hear us and decide carefully.*' The book spoke in his mind, urging him after he found it in the wreckage of a Kasarin Merchant ship.

'You wish to create justice, to end pain,' the book observed after he relented. '*Fear is a worthy motivator against the unjust. Fear of the punishment can end a transgression before it may ever begin.*'

He considered the truth behind the book's words. It was

enough to allow it to continue.

'We were the Order of the Void Triangle, the most feared gathering of magi, ever. What we did chills the bravest blood to this day.'

'Ask yourself this, enforcer: what would cause a murderer to stay his dagger with greater haste, a king's headsman, or one of our magi?'

The Book of Worms won that argument.

The energies of three hells swirled toward his waiting hands, gathering into the semi-solid black shape of the Staff of the Abyss. It was long, as tall as himself. As he held it, he felt the screams of billions of condemned souls reverberating inside him. He felt the hot relentless fury, and the cold cruelty of millions of years of demons coursing through him.

The weapons of the Void Triangle did not just allow the wielders to strike with the element of the hell they favored. They also created a fast bridge to the realms of hell, allowing for easier spell-shaping.

Makorin dash-floated at Creation's End. He raised the Scepter to strike at his head from above. Creation's End swung the Staff up and to the left, its high end left an arcing trail of violet hellfire in its wake.

Creation's End shifted the staff and swung most of the length in a low sweeping circle. The ground beneath the attack chilled with a layer of slippery hell frost.

Makorin's feet were in the air, so he tilted his head sideways at Creation's End. Makorin's faceless black gaze failed to notice the Sol Fierest cold snap freezing the air, hardening it to ice. The jagged hungry black ice reached up for the lower half of Makorin's body and held him still, up to the hips.

Creation's End gathered the sadistic malice of Blot K'Rark, the realm of blood breaking. A ball of red liquid filled with white chunks floated above his raised hand. Creation's End gestured forward, and the ball launched a wide drenching spray of blood and bone matter. There was hissing and rising steam vapors as the corrosive blood of the condemned ate through everything it touched.

Makorin was quick to respond with a man-sized swirling black vortex that began to pull everything with powerful winds. This was the classic Shadow Eternal spell called the Devouring Maw, a void that consumed and nullified the existence of everything swallowed into it. It was as powerful a defense and offense.

Creation's End answered the Devouring Maw with one of his own. The two powerful vortexes began to pull against each other to no avail. The clash of two forces pulling harder and harder against each other would have one certain effect: a massive explosion.

Makorin and Creation's End were blasted backwards, flying dozens of feet high in the air. The Book of Worms shielded itself with a spontaneous barrier of bone, remaining safely on the over-seeing pedestal.

'Well done. You shift between the disciplines freely. But never conjure a force with greater effect than you can withstand. You will create a moment of vulnerability for your enemies to seize upon.' The book pulsed with blue soul light with each word.

"The Devouring Maw creates vulnerability in its enemies," Creation's End argued, his voice a cold hollow rasp. "If I am made prone, I would do the same to my enemy, at least."

'You have been instructed in the way to sink into the shadows.' The book reminded him of a method that would allow him to move in and out of darkness at will. *'Do not always answer force with more force. If a force, before you, proves that powerful, move around it.'*

Creation's End nodded his understanding of the lesson.

'Learn swiftly. We must still increase your powers to an overwhelming level in battle. You have already learned and mastered the disciplines the Void Triangle knew in life, but your destiny is to do

what we never could.'

Creation's End did not respond to that. He did not enjoy his name and did not accept the future the Book offered him. Everything the Book desired was far beyond the scope of justice, stretching into total nihilism.

'*In time, you will fathom the injustice of life and death. On that day, you will seek to correct this transgression.'*

-14-

Ishell's hard-bottomed shoes echoed loud in the dusty halls of the dark sub-basement. A Current Sphere floated above her raised right palm, lighting the gloom of the long hallway ahead. It was narrow and cramped. Gossamer webs hung low from the ceiling, caressing the hood of her gray robe. She was not enough of a fool to leave her brown-blonde hair exposed to the filth and disuse.

The sub-basement was a forgotten level of the Citadel. The entry sat far away from the furnace room and frequented halls of the basement above. Several days after Rylin informed Ishell of the slaughter in Tihl'Zen, they ventured into an exploration of the Citadel. They would need a place to gather allies, measure abilities, and plan for a defense against the Kasarins.

Rylin believed everyone would need training, so he offered to create one of his distilled time spaces. Ishell noticed something Rylin didn't.

The Sparks might not speak about the Kasarins; but dueling and battle training had become a much greater focus. Kera pushed Ishell to spar with a staff and her strongest magic at an average of five times a day. Ishell couldn't predict when her Spark might start a duel. One instant, Ishell might be changing into a bed robe for the night, then Kera might Meld Walk into her tiny bed chamber and start a duel right then.

Ishell thought it was annoying to put her nerves on

constant edge, but she knew it was needed. A battle against their home could occur when no one expected it. No one anticipated Tihl'Zen's destruction. Why would the Kasarins do anything predictable now?

That was just what Ishell experienced from Kera; never mind the training every other initiate had to endure. Polymancers dueled with swords and shields in the hall, stopping only when one was too injured to continue. Those wounded were brought to Hydromancer healers. The Solas would step away for peach tea, leaving their students alone to heal broken bones and deep gashes.

These events led Ishell to reassure Rylin that distilling time and creating a training space was unnecessary. Without her guidance, his blind conclusions would be twice as catastrophic.

"It's so clandestine meeting in a dark basement like this," Borvis observed, finishing a Meld Walk to fall into step beside her.

Ishell gave a startled gasp before she slapped Borvis on the arm. "Fates! Light Borvis, you are going to make my heart leap."

"You do that to me every day, Light Ishell," Borvis flirted, his grin was wide as she glowered at him.

Ishell rolled her eyes. "It is neither secret nor 'clandestine' if they can feel you Meld Walk."

Borvis offered a dismissive shrug. "Our Sparks are all but shoving us into Enriall armor, and the council lounges on its laurels. I will give you a pouch from my father's treasury if they start taking an interest, now."

"The Baron of Len won't be happy if you wager away his coffers," Ishell warned. Len was a northern barony in Teril. Its farmsteads prospered to a moderate degree. It's Baron, like King Talik, never over-taxed.

Borvis's smile turned mischievous. "Who said I would have him know about it?"

Ishell slapped Borvis upwards against the back of his head, his brown hair ruffling. "Ouch!" Borvis whined, rubbing the back of his head. "What was that about?"

"That money is gained from the sweat and pains of the people," Ishell ridiculed.

"Speaks the Light who is going against the council's wishes."

"You know what this is about, Light Borvis. You would do well to remember this if we rush to defend your birth land."

Borvis stopped and turned to face Ishell with one of his rare thoughtful gazes. "That reminds me: why is it the Kasarins attack everything but the Zenith Citadel? They came to eradicate all natives of Stratia. So, why do they ignore us when we are all cloistered together, and the world presumes us weak?"

"Maybe we pose no threat in their view." It was a guess, but Ishell knew it was wrong even as she spoke it.

Borvis knew this too and he shook his head. "Our strength is irrelevant, and not a factor of their mission. They are no fools. Having proven that, they must know we will strike back, in due time."

"Our Order does not often succumb to vengeance, Light Borvis."

"Then they must know we will meet them to protect the people." Borvis sounded irritated with the correction. "My point is, they must know a confrontation is inevitable. Why do our Sparks train us for it, but no one goes out to begin the defense?"

They mulled it over, and their eyes met slowly as the realization dawned on them in unison.

"They can't!" They both exclaimed.

"And the Kasarins cannot attack us…"Borvis began.

"…because there is some sort of arrangement," Ishell finished.

"It must have been reached between the council and the

empire." Both were excited by the discovery as their breathing quickened.

"But the majority of the Solas don't agree with the decision," Ishell added.

Borvis's nod was emphatic. "It would explain Solas Merahl's resignation, and the others with him."

"It also explains why they are so determined to train us to fight," Ishell surmised, thinking about Kera's surprise duels. "They know we cannot sit idle while our birth homes and families burn. They knew we would discover the truth, and they knew we would do what they could not."

"Also, look how they prepare us," Borvis added.

Ishell paused to reflect on the duels and training. She thought she could follow most of Borvis's intelligent chains of thought, but he did leave her stumped from time to time. He was indicating a commonality, and she thought she could make it out, but it eluded her grasp and would not all come together for her.

"They are preparing us to fend for ourselves, Light Ishell," Borvis concluded. "And the way they prepare us, it's possible we may be warring with the Kasarins, alone."

It was a small jump of a conclusion, but Ishell recognized it was a realistic deduction.

That was overwhelming and frightening for Ishell. As soon as they moved to defend the people, they would be alone as they fought against the most battle-hardened armies in the world. The Solas would not be there to advise or offer their abilities if mistakes were made. The fate of all Stratia would rely on the magic and wit of students.

Ishell felt her brown eyes bulge as she leaned back against the cold dusty wall. Her breath became rapid as she shrank against the enormity before her.

"Fates!" Ishell gasped, almost to the point of tears, tears

that seldom fell from her eyes. She thought of all the families, all the hard-working men and women, and the children they cared for.

Ishell thought of her father, toiling away at his forge, the strong steady presence she relied on as a child.

If they failed to push back against this juggernaut force that came to lay siege, all these people would have no one left to defend them. They would all die. There would be no graves to honor the good they brought to the world. It would all be gone, wiped away by the Kasarin Empire.

And what was she that she thought she could stand in their way? Ishell was a sorceress and evoker with less than a decade to her skills. She was a girl, new to adulthood.

Ishell remembered her conversation with Rylin, in the Outskirts, before the Inquiry arrived. He all but accused her of dreaming lofty and chasing adventures. She defended herself by telling him that she wanted to be a part of a change.

Was Rylin more than a little right, back then? Did she give in to the impulses of a naïve thrill-seeker? Could all this be some bitter wisdom from fate?

Here she was, so confident that she could meet every challenge. And now? The lives of every human being, everyone she ever loved, were relying on her to stand alone between them and a force intent on massacre.

"It's so much…all alone?" Ishell whimpered and she hated how pathetic it sounded.

Borvis didn't seem to share her contempt. His eyes were genuine in their sympathy as he pulled her into his embrace and allowed her to weep against him.

"No one ever said you would do this all alone, Light Ishell," Borvis reassured her, his voice softening. "You and I found allies in the Citadel, strong skilled Lights who believe as we do."

Borvis raised her chin in a gentle hand to meet her gaze. "You know I will be with you. I have to."

Ishell was perplexed by his certainty to march into battle when she had to drag him out to train.

"Why is that?"

Borvis's face brightened. "I have to see their faces."

Ishell hated it when people made a point but never concluded it all at once. She did not bother to hide her irritation.

...Which only made Borvis grin wider. "I want to see the look on the faces of the Kasarins when they realize they angered the most powerful and violent evoker in all Stratian history."

Ishell laughed and watched Borvis's smile warm for it. She could never be sure which could be more infuriating: Rylin's intense bull-headed drive, or Borvis's jovial attempts at flirting.

This once, Ishell welcomed Borvis's attempt for what it was. He was trying to dispel her fears and bolster her confidence. This once, it reminded her more of what her father might do if he stood with her, now.

Ishell pulled herself free of Borvis's arms. "How many are with us?"

Borvis's shoulders slumped; his voice became meek. "Maybe a hundred at the most."

Ishell gaped. "We would do little better than Delkit or his archers, or the Perahli Lancers. The Havoc Guilds outnumber us by no less than ten times."

That last bit of information was not easy to acquire for non-Solas. Rylin was tracing the Kasarin movements in his Temporal Projection, so he knew everything they were doing, firsthand.

It wasn't easy for Rylin to watch the Kasarins butcher so many people. Rylin was angry after he emerged from his Temporal Study, after each Projection. He no longer let his will explode, as he needed to do after witnessing the events of

Tihl'Zen. While he did go far to the north to release his outburst, Ishell wondered if there was anyone in the world who didn't feel that explosion of will.

Ishell felt guilty for forcing Rylin to do all the spying alone. It was harder on him than asking him to go into battle with the invaders. It made her discussions with him tense, bordering angry, and she knew she did not hold the right to ask him to be any other way for it. Would she feel any differently if she were asked to gaze at such horrible events and do nothing? The answer made her respect the validity of his growing anger.

For now, the Kasarin Army halted its advance. The Havoc Guilds were overseeing the arrival of many thousands of soldiers. This meant Stratia had time to prepare; but it also meant the Kasarins would destroy so much more when they began to move again.

Ishell sighed, weary, then sneezed as she inhaled a breath full of dusty air.

In answer, a door opened several yards ahead into the gloom. Teranen emerged, outlined by the light of several Current Spheres from the room behind her.

The tall pyromancer looked at them with some impatience. "Are you two going to stand in this dusty hallway all day?"

Teranen was not the only adult in training to answer the call to defend Stratia, but she was the first and perhaps the most eager. It wasn't just her hot-headed demeanor as a pyromancer that brought her to the fight. Before she was recruited by the Order, she spent years protecting the outcast northern barony of Dunell. When she heard what happened to Tihl'Zen her anger caused her body to erupt with a burning aura of white fire. She would be happy to trade blows with the Kasarins for it.

"Are they all there?" Ishell asked.

"Light Erissa counted ninety-nine. If Rylin did not create this room as large as he did." Teranen paused to shudder. Ishell knew the pyromancer found time sorcery to be unnerving and confusing. "We would be hard pressed to meet like this."

Ninety-nine, about half of the Order of the Enlightened Sun. Even if the Order stood together, they would number only a fraction of the Havoc Guilds.

"They are waiting for you to speak to them," Teranen informed Ishell.

Ishell was surprised at that. "Do they not wish to hear from Light Rylin, more?"

Teranen shook her head. "He spends too much time in his study. They do not see enough of him. When they do see him, he is withdrawn and angry."

Ishell nodded while she walked into the light of the secret gathering room. There were many voices around her, but they all fell silent as she walked deeper among them. Adults and children alike turned to look at her. They were looking at her to lead them in this war. They were looking at a blacksmith's daughter to lead them to victory. She thought this, and her fears revived with greater fervor. They were placing their faith and survival in the hands of a girl raised as an outcast in a shoved aside village.

Ishell stopped to look at the faces around her. She was not surprised to see the Blood Scathe Twins. They wanted to use their grotesque magic on people, any way they could. Red-haired Light Erissa stood next to Teranen. She was half the pyromancer's age, but she was eager to help bolster the pyromancy with her own aeromancy. Ishell knew Erissa idolized Teranen. Though Erissa was a much more experienced Light, she admired Teranen's strength and endurance.

Ishell empathized with this admiration in her own way. She did not know as much about Teranen's personal history, but everyone knew Maesellen's cronies were all afraid of Dunell. The great Flame Witch never allowed the people in the cold village to come to harm. Squadrons of thugs were sent away with melted weapons and shattered armor. Wanderers lost in the forest would find their way following one of her floating orbs of fire. When these travelers came to Dunell, the villagers would offer them food and a place to rest the night, helping them on their journey.

Ishell looked down at an unusual pair of expectant brown eyes belonging to a white-haired boy. His name was Merice, and he was the only remaining Illumancer. He was only ten years old. How could anyone let him be here?

"Light Ishell, these are dark times," Merice reminded with a stern and wise patience that was beyond his years. "My magic needs to be here, to exile these shadows. Will you allow your elements to be idle as they are soaked in Stratian blood?"

Ishell could not decide in which way she felt more stricken. Current Reading was a skill for the Solas, and Merice did so with casual ease. Furthermore, his wisdom and articulation reminded her a great deal of Yelisian.

In seeing Teranen, the Blood Scathe Twins, and Merice, realization combined and stirred within Ishell. She felt her confidence return as she walked to the far end of the tall wide room. She gathered Endless Current into her voice to be heard by everyone. She also shaped a cushion of wind to lift her up to better be seen.

"I know that you all know as I do," Ishell began. "We know all the death and ruin caused by the Kasarin Empire. We know they pause, but not to grant us mercy. They gather more forces. When they move, they will begin to overwhelm all of Stratia."

Ishell let that sink in. "As so many times before, we, in the Order of the Enlightened Sun, won't allow this."

"What of the Solas? Will they join us?" asked a brown-haired middle-aged man.

"They have not been permitted to fight, yet. At this time, there is no reason to believe they can." Ishell's answer was blunt.

Murmurs filled the room, and some turned to leave.

"If you leave, you disappoint your Sparks, and you wound the spirit of our Order," Ishell warned.

"You want so few of us to fight against an army that has not been wounded on our soil? There are so few armies left between all of Stratia," informed a dark-haired geomancer, with irritation.

"Then you are too blind to see what I see." Ishell pointed at the Blood Scathe Twins. "Sanguimancers, and Illumancer, Polymancers and Elementalists of every kind, a legendary Pyromancer, and over a dozen well-trained evokers. We have skills, some of which are alien to the empire, others with great magnitude."

Ishell paused and her gaze narrowed with intensity as she looked to find her fellow neighbors. "This I speak to my people, gathered from Malkanor. Think of all that you once were, think of every day you starved or stumbled to find a single drop of water to drink. Think of the fears that once attempted to bury you for years. Think of the love of those you held dear, as you fought one more step, one more day, even as our betters tried to crush us. That same love brought us all here. We love those we left behind, so much that we strive, every day, to fathom the depths of our powers."

"And who are we now?" Ishell let her voice rise. "Are we the slaves and meager we once were?"

"No!" rang the voices of the Malkanor Lot.

"And we know this because we are far above all that tried to have us die in obscurity. The Kasarins seek to do the same. They wish us dead in unmarked graves. But we did not give this pleasure to the highborn of Malkanor, and we certainly won't give it to the Kasarin Empire, will we?"

"NO!"

Ishell's voice was a shout of fervor, by now. "Those we cherish, those who inspired us to find our greatest selves, they are desperate and vulnerable. Without us, they will be forced into this terrible fate. As we did, when we lived beside them, we will stand side by side and take our slim chance for survival and hope, where there would be none otherwise. There will be no dark obscure graves for them, and can you tell me why that is?"

"THE LIGHT EXILES THE SHADOWS!" Came the roaring intonation from the determination of one hundred Lights of the Order.

"When we fight, we honor the sacrifices of all our Sparks and Solas! Just as they did in Katahn, we draw the line in the sand before our people. We declare to these murderers 'We are the Enlightened Sun, and we cast aside your shadow'!"

As the Lights shouted with passion, it was clear that Ishell shared in their abandonment of doubt and fear. If this was Stratia's only defense, Ishell knew anyone would be hard-pressed to dismiss it.

Rylin was not in the room, and Ishell kept him out of her words. It was not because she thought he should stay out of the war. She wanted everyone gathered to rely and depend on themselves and each other. She did not want them to use him as a crutch for the days ahead.

'Still,' Ishell thought to herself. *'He would be one of the most powerful and unique Lights on the battlefield.'*

If the other Lights were going to draw strength from him, Rylin needed to be among them more.

-15-

Aemreen Tahkaer walked down the center lane of the Outer City, a place once called the Outskirts. To her mother's dismay, she walked alone. To the dismay of her handmaiden, Lady Arayse, she was dressed, from neck to ankles, in chain mail. She wore a short-sleeved leather jerkin, loose enough to allow ease of movement. She also wore black leather boots and bracers, with a long saber sheathed at her hip.

Aemreen's father was happy to see her don weapons and armor these days. He was, after all, the Lord General of Malkanor. While he supported all her life choices, she knew he held out hope that she would succeed him.

That was not why Aemreen felt the need to forsake her dresses, most days, and chose to equip herself this way. Contrary to belief of other nobles her age, it did not have as much to do with the Kasarin attacks, either.

Ever since the death and memorial of Yelisian, fates favor his soul, King Maloric and her father returned more determined to protect the farmers and workers from the cruelty of the aristocracy. It became a continual struggle against Maesellen, who was supported by her lackey barons and the thugs they recruited. While Maloric and her father could not prove anything against the Malkanor nobility, the armies of the nation warred with a seemingly infinite onslaught of thugs.

The conflict reflected on the people. They were not taxed heavier, and their homes were in good repair. They kept food to eat and coin to spend. But the hordes of thugs were spread all over Malkanor, kidnaping and assaulting outside the swift reach of Pahlinsor. They stalked and prowled villages and highways, waiting to rob travelers, or take them to be sold into slavery.

What was needed was connecting evidence, which they lacked. Aemreen was certain these thugs worked for the baronies, who, in turn, answered to her majesty, Maesellen Moarenroak.

Regardless, this meant the soldiers were spread thin, on patrols from border to border. There was no one left to protect the Outer City or its people. So, Aemreen took it upon herself to work with some of the residents to keep her father informed. She also settled conflicts and interrupted any crimes that occurred.

Aemreen didn't have much to worry about when it came to the farmers or the families. They were a warm, close-knit community. The exception was, of course, the miners who sometimes returned from the mines that bordered southern Nerinmor. They were a remnant of a history that no one in the Outer City welcomed. They were often drunk, frequently violent, and always angry. The miners were trapped in the times when their families had little to nothing. Their failure to provide created a desire to drink away their failures.

Change would never allow for people to stagnate on old ways and bad habits. The Outer City felt this truth. Aemreen was glad to be witness to this truth, as well.

Aemreen walked the cobbled streets under a warming late winter sun. It was noon. Children were playing in the streets. Mothers and fathers worked together to carry baskets and carts full of spring seed in preparation of the coming season. Aemreen carried her skull cap under her left arm, leaving her free to wave to familiar faces with her right hand. Her long brown braid swayed back and forth below the middle of her back, out of her way.

Aemreen looked about her and smiled. The Outer City was a good place. It always reminded her of the best of the nature of

Malkanor. It was enduring, patient, and caring. She felt happy to look after it and protect its people for her lover.

Aemreen paused, letting her emerald eyes wander in daydreams as she thought about Rylin. He was both the happiest and saddest thought in her mind. She thought a lot about his touch, shy and tentative as it was, and his bright blue eyes. She was happy to think about the time they did have together, and it hurt her to know that it was not time for them to have more.

Aemreen stopped her wistful thoughts and massaged an ache in her shoulder. The leather and chain mail were not tight or restrictive, but after a while the heavy weight pressed down on her. She had grown stronger in the last two years. As a young woman, she was not as dainty or frail as her noble peers. Her hands were more calloused since she took up more training with the sword. Her complexion was a little darker from adapted sun exposure. Though she wore armor for a man two sizes larger than her, it only served to conceal the fact that her curves were more defined. Alongside this, the muscles in her arms and legs were more pronounced, though not bulky. She was as strong as any soldier her father ever trained.

Patrolling the Outer City was not the only obligation Aemreen filled her time with. All her activities were distasteful to the Queen, of course, but the King and her father were full supporters of her choices. So, if she was not patrolling and training, she was reading apothecary journals, or helping Pahlinsor's healers in their work.

Further up the street, emerging from the flat plains beyond, came a boy a few years younger than Aemreen. He was dressed, from the neck down, in loose airy black. He waved his arm high, causing his shoulder length brown braid to bounce. Though he smiled, his dark brown eyes were intense and piercing. A faux ruby-pommeled long sword and a gold handled dagger were sheathed at his hip. He walked with a fluid, ready grace that came easy to him for all his training.

Joriken Beranahl, Aemreen's protégé and partner in

protection, closed the distance and clasped Aemreen's forearm in greeting.

"You're late. I expected you several hours ago," Aemreen criticized.

Joriken shrugged. "I just returned from one of the southern baronies."

Joriken was absent for more than a week. If not for the help of the blacksmith Errnik, Ishell's father, Aemreen would have patrolled the city alone.

"Some of your father's soldiers were ambushed," Joriken informed.

"Walk with me and tell me more." Aemreen led the way past the single-floor, dark, gray homes.

Aemreen gestured for Joriken to hasten his point.

"I stopped the thugs. Two dead, the rest won't walk. I broke a few knees and severed a few ankle tendons." Joriken raised a halting hand before Aemreen could speak. "They won't talk, but I observed something in their fighting. They are a little better than thugs, but their training leans heavy on a single thrust to the middle. I think they are accustomed to ending their fights with that method."

Aemreen nodded. The single thrust technique was a favorite among soldiers posted at the southern borders with Vodess. Their skirmishes were generally with bandits that had grown too greedy, hoping to loot the more remote homes and lesser estates. The skirmishes often took place in narrow canyons. The soldiers would lead the thugs into a bottle neck space where they could end the conflict with a thrust that would be difficult to deflect or evade.

"If they won't talk, did they have any evidence connecting them to Earl Mejin?" Aemreen asked, hopeful.

Joriken sighed with annoyance. "No. They had the appearance of Vodessians, brown hat, tan, casual movements.

They also donned what might be expected of thugs. Any other day I might stand back and wager a gold piece in favor of the soldiers. They were Phoenix Legion."

Aemreen didn't bother to hide her surprise at that last bit. While the Phoenix Legion made up the bulk of Malkanor's army, they were also her father's favorite and most well-trained soldiers. He drilled them, often, and was never disappointed with them.

They also did not tire so easy. Together, they numbered over three thousand, last she counted years ago. They never separated into patrols of less than twenty. They held the tendency of halting skirmishes in less than three minutes due to partial Kasarin methods taught by her father.

"How many were in the patrol?" Aemreen dreaded the answer she might hear to that.

"I counted eight."

That chilled Aemreen. "Do we know if they were attacked by Kasarins?"

Joriken shook his head. "I don't know. I did not ask." Joriken turned to draw her into his solemn gaze. "They looked like broken, empty men. They had a wagon between them, for the bodies I think."

Aemreen knew that if it wasn't the Kasarins, then the other truth was just as bad. Either one meant that her father's soldiers were being pushed back. The Phoenix Legion never lost men, before. Her father trained all Maloric's men too well to die against thugs.

There was a thought that chilled Aemreen more. What if the Kasarins attacked Malkanor while Maesellen and her lackeys continued their foolish struggle to reclaim servitude from the people. The Empire would tear both sides apart with little effort.

"Any word from Torch Rylin?" Joriken changed the subject with a sly gleam in his eyes.

Aemreen controlled the impulse to sigh. "No; but given how things are, what time would he have?"

Joriken laughed. "Only as much as a time sorcerer wishes."

Rylin made a habit of Fold Stepping to Aemreen once a month or so. While the Order insisted on inaction, and remained withdrawn from the world, Aemreen assumed Rylin remained busy. But she did not get a visit from him in the last few months.

Joriken seemed about to offer optimistic reassurance, but as he opened his mouth, a man's screams sounded from the fields to the north.

Aemreen and Joriken sprinted toward the source of the cries, unsheathing their weapons. Aemreen strapped the skull cap onto her head with a leather buckle under the chin. She insisted upon the adjustment when she discovered, even with her thick hair, her head was a little smaller than the previous owner of the helmet.

Two more cries sounded from the same man's voice. The cries drew closer with each sounding. Aemreen knew the victim was running to the Outer City. Several more men and women dashed into view, fleeing for the safety of the village. Aemreen and Joriken were forced to swerve around them.

Aemreen spotted a young farmer couple. The wife held her husband's hand, running in the lead. The dark-haired man's free arm hung limp, with a bone deep cut on the upper arm and shoulder. Blood spilled free to his fingers while he struggled to keep pace under the blood loss.

Behind them, five red and gold heavy armored soldiers chased with murderous intent. Their curved, long swords were held in both hands at hip level, ready to deliver a killing strike.

Joriken rolled low, rising into a kneeling position in front of the lead soldier. He brought his long sword up in time to halt a strike for his head. He flipped his dagger in his grip and jammed it through the soldier's left thigh. He jumped high and impaled the soldier's neck with his long sword. When he landed, he kicked the soldier free of his weapons.

Aemreen approached another soldier before he could close in on the wounded couple. The soldier attacked with a flourish that would have cut most Stratians to ribbons. Aemreen parried and deflected as swift as the blows came. She gave a silent internal thanks for all the time she spent training with Joriken. He insisted on learning everything she had ever learned from her father.

As the soldier's long sword began an upward cut at her middle, she blocked low, bracing the dull side of her saber with her free hand. Sensing the two-way opening, she delivered a quick, high, arcing kick to the side of his head. She lifted her sword and swung in a half circle, cutting his neck. As he fell, Aemreen heard another soldier charging over him. She struck with a jarring backwards kick before doing another half spin, running the point of her saber between his eyes in a powerful lunge. She lashed out with a sideways thrusting kick that sent the soldier off her weapon.

Joriken finished cutting down one more soldier, and Aemreen joined him in approaching the final swordsman. They moved slow and cautious, allowing a chance for him to flee, or drop his weapon and surrender. Instead, he hardened his stance and tightened his two-handed grip on his weapon while they circled him.

Aemreen moved in front of the red soldier. As Joriken circled to the rear, he dashed in. Joriken anticipated the backward stab and blocked down hard with his long sword. He spun and jumped high, twisting into a sideways thrusting kick to the back of his armored head.

The soldier stumbled forward, his face meeting with half of the blade of Aemreen's saber with a wet crunch. Aemreen relaxed her lunge, and yanked her weapon free of the soldier's head, letting him continue to fall, face first.

Aemreen sighed with weary exertion while she wiped her

blade on the fallen soldier. It was not her first life taken, thank the fates. Some years ago, there were thugs that tried to escape from her father and cut down unlucky farmers of the Outer City that were in their way. They forced her to discard her last naivety then. Even before that, she watched as some of the healers in Pahlinsor tried and failed to save lives. As a result, death and bloodshed were no strangers to her.

But killing was a little too easy for Joriken. He gave her a wry smile.

"Two lunging thrusts to the head."

Aemreen could not evade returning a slight smile. "What of it?"

"I remember someone telling me not to repeat the same maneuver..."

"Sage wisdom. I am glad you follow it," Aemreen attempted to stop him.

"I think it was that self-same maneuver," Joriken pressed.

"You have strange gratitude. We are still alive, against five Kasarin soldiers, no less."

As if to argue the point with Aemreen, screams sounded from the Outer City. Plumes of smoke burst to sudden and sporadic life, exuded from the homes.

Joriken and Aemreen dashed back to the Outer City at a full sprint. The running and fighting began to take its toll on Aemreen in the armor. She pushed against the heat, sweat, and ache that weighed down on her. She and Joriken were all the people had. It was her worst fear realized.

While her father and the Phoenix Legions were spread throughout Malkanor, the Kasarins began their assault, right in Pahlinsor.

-16-

Zenen'Rol sat cross-legged on a plush maroon rug in a dark, thick canvas tent. His eyes were open and unblinking as he stared into the depths of a cloud of red glowing mist. The faint light cast by the magic etched his angry face in stark and frightening detail. He ground his teeth as he watched several squads of Ka'Rak and three young Havoc Magi blunder the most simple task he could have assigned them.

This dark stone city in the west should have been easy to wipe away. Even with a city and a towering black palace within a few miles, its defenses were weak. There were no patrolling soldiers, all the members of the order remained holed up like cowards. There were no walls or defensive structures to hinder them. The landscape, itself, seemed an open invitation to attack. There were only flat plains and a growth of vegetation most Kasarin farmers would hesitate to call woods.

Some of the contingents were released from the Meld Walk in the farmlands where the servant caste worked, and it seemed like they would strike down any who thought to flee. But then a boy and a girl in armor arrived, and their fighting skills were unique among Stratians. If Zenen'Rol was not already burdened with the task of overseeing the beach arrival, he would have Meld Walked to challenge them, himself.

It grated on Zenen's combat sensibilities. Five Ka'Rak were cut down like first conquest soldiers, fresh from the Empire's training camps. They were dead inside of minutes. While it was true that there were clear Crimson Empire skills present in the two defenders, five Ka'Rak should have been able to fare much better than what he witnessed.

Hoping the assault was not an entire botch, Zenen shifted his attention to the middle of the paved city streets. Homes were burning, in places, and that was a good sign; but he met with further frustration as the transparent scrying sphere hovered over a blacksmith's forge. A burly, shirtless figure, only a little shorter than Zenen'Rol, stood outside. He was surrounded by ten Ka'Rak, and he held them back with a giant sledge and a double-edged war axe. Several Ka'Rak were cut down, bleeding and dying in the street around the balding, blonde smith. Their injuries were massive, lethal within seconds, as their internal organs fell onto the cobbled grounds.

The smith's strikes were wide, and powerful, forcing the Ka'Rak to maintain a wary distance from the crushing arcs.

Where were the Havoc Magi? Zenen's scrying sphere lifted higher, searching the streets for their presence. He was furious to find they were causing random explosions to various homes while the Ka'Rak were facing the defenses unaided. Were they so young and arrogant that they found addictive fascination in random and meaningless devastation? He needed to rein in their concentration.

As Zenen looked closer, he had little time. The boy and the girl were about to intercept the smith. If the three joined forces, and this contingent remained scattered, this offensive would be routed.

"What nonsense are you novices engaged in that you forfeit victory?" Zenen projected his angry shouts across the distance to the Magi. "There is a defense, near to success, in the center of the streets, not a quarter of a mile away from your games-playing. I will not tolerate another humiliation, like the swamps of Nerinmor. Concentrate and conquer."

With that, Zenen was satisfied to watch the three magi call to thirty Ka'Rak, gathering their forces to wipe away the defending efforts.

Zenen sighed, breathing in the calming smoke of incense. If he were less an expert of 'Fire Rivers', the method employed to gather Endless Current while obstructed with anger, he would not be able to maintain these vigils.

Zenen released the red-hued haze of the Scrying Sphere. the tent was illuminated only by the glow of a single red candle in a brass stand. With the concern of failure diminished, he could turn his efforts to expediting the landing.

Rylin sat in his Temporal Study, floating, his eyes closed. Watching the activities of the Kasarin army proved tedious for several days, now. They were only moving to land more soldiers. Their Havoc Guilds were as silent and still as statues.

But this tedium worried Rylin. For the first few weeks, the Havoc Guilds left a wide trail of blood and bodies everywhere. But this stillness left an uncomfortable tension, their anger was a thick force in the air, even in the numerical calm of the Temporal Current. They would move, again. Time was growing short. Their impatience would only be satisfied with greater levels of cruelty when they struck again.

That time came with little warning, catching Rylin off guard. Several squads of the famed Ka'Rak armies gathered, accompanied by three Havoc Magi. The Endless Current swirled around the entire gathering before they vanished from sight.

It happened with swift abruptness. The Meld Walk was a common skill to the Order, but shouldn't the aggressive Havoc Sorcerers require wording and gestures? To become part of that infinite vibration of energy, one needed to still their thoughts and emotions enough to be unclouded by them. That would have to be a second nature for a Meld Walk with no spell-shaping. This was something Rylin never witnessed from them. He collected his scattered thoughts from their stricken confusion.

It was not important that they knew how to do it. They needed to be followed and watched. Rylin's awareness rushed to catch up to the stream of ripples in the Endless Current left in their wake. Their union with energy made it difficult to do anything more than follow, tracing their ripples west across the land scape. Meanwhile, seconds were ticking into minutes. Time continued to move outside of the Projection. These Kasarins would certainly find their next target. They would strike with all their pent-up fury. Unsuspecting people would be left in bloody and burning heaps.

But something worse tickled Rylin's thoughts. They moved far and deep past the Terilian farmlands. They did not stop to lay waste to those villages. They remained westbound, ignoring the north and Nerinmor. They continued an unerring path straight into Malkanor. Rylin inwardly prayed he was wrong, that they held no interest in the Outer City, or Pahlinsor, or the baronies and villages that surrounded.

Five Ka'Rak departed the Endless Current just to the north of the Outer City, in potato farms and apple orchards. They wasted no moment and felt no Current sickness. They struck swift and without mercy.

Rylin knew every victim. Two men arched upwards, against the curved, long swords that skewered them from behind. A foot of slender steel burst through their sternums, before they were yanked upward to do more damage to their heart. Blood fell in thick streams from their gasping mouths. Beckray and Torit were ten years older than Rylin. When Rylin was smaller they would hoist him up in these apple orchards to allow him to pick more fruit for his mother.

A young couple, only a few years older than Rylin, tried to flee. The husband already received a deep gash on his arm for his efforts. His head would have been split open if he didn't move when he did. Rylin knew this man as Tarik, and he lived several huts to the south of Rylin's hovel. As a boy, Tarik skipped stones at a small pond in the woods. Now, his wife pulled with desperate yanks while he struggled to remain alert from the blood loss. His efforts were doubled as he screamed for someone to save his wife.

Rylin recognized the sight of Joriken at once. Taller, dressed in black, with a broader physique, he barred the way against five Ka'Rak. There was a heavily armored guard as well, but there was something strange about the soldier's posture and movement. Rylin looked closer and noticed the soldier was a woman. He gaped with alarm when he saw the face and knew Aemreen was standing in defense of the Outer City. His lover, Aemreen Tahkaer would meet the Kasarins in battle with only a boy to assist her. She would be split open and burned to ash, in the end.

That was the last of watching and doing nothing Rylin could tolerate. He opened his eyes and sprung up from his sitting position. He rushed about his study, gathering only three items. The coat, he whipped onto his arms and shoulder in a snapping flourish. He placed the emerald flask in his pocket. He hefted the smooth length of the long emerald staff in his hands. The golden runes-etched into the end- sparkled. The transparent emerald length sounded with a heavy '*whoosh, whoosh,*' as he gave the gleaming weapon an experimental spin.

Rylin locked the image of the north fields of the Outer City in his mind. He saw everything just as it was in projection when he closed his eyes. Then he Fold Stepped.

Errnik was outside his smithy. Aemreen and Joriken skidded to a halt to either side of the burly smith. He held back seven red plated soldiers with a double axe and his heavy forge hammer. Three red and gold figures were crumpled in heaps, mangled in pools of their own blood. They paid the price for underestimating the Outer City smith master.

"You must have made the Barons most cross, Errnik," Aemreen teased. Her eyes shifted among the remaining soldiers. "They hired Kasarins to rip down your forge."

Errnik grinned without turning. "It's my overwhelming charm."

One of the soldiers backstepped in time to avoid a braining strike from the smith's hammer. He stumbled over two other soldiers behind him.

Aemreen and Joriken leaped at the opening. Aemreen flicked a wide arc from her saber, causing a thick spray of blood from the soldier in front. Joriken wheeled around Aemreen and rammed his dagger into the forehead of the soldier on the right. He lashed out with a high sideways kick. The impact sounded a loud crunch of red metal and bone on the other soldier's head. Errnik greeted the dizzied and stunned soldier with a disemboweling cleave from his axe. Errnik yanked the blade free, trailing intestines and chunks of broken armor.

Victory was in sight. The other soldiers hesitated from the sight of the swift defense. Their eyes shifted from the bloody heaps of their fellows to the enemies who waited. The explosions and the quaking cobbles were still. Silence granted a moment to breathe. The screams of frightened villagers were no longer in evidence. Aemreen wanted to believe they bought the people time to flee to safety. There was no way to be certain, and no time to investigate.

Smoke and plumes of bright red fire still licked the skies. The acrid black clouds made a choking miasma filled with the reek of blood and death. Still, Aemreen dared a calming breath.

That was the only reprieve she would have. The soldiers back stepped cautiously. They melded into an approaching contingent of red plates and long swords from the south. Aemreen turned her head to the north. The sound of heavy boots in marching cadence preluded the sight of another contingent of Kasarin soldiers. A hasty count revealed no less than thirty soldiers. Their swords were drawn. When they closed the distance, they would cut them to ribbons in one unified strike. There would be no chance to deflect.

Aemreen turned her attention to the south in time to see another arrival. The soldier's feet hammered a unified halt as three figures appeared. They materialized from the air itself.

They were not heavily armed or armored, but this made them even more intimidating. They wore long, open, sleeveless red vest coats over black pants, and boots. They wore black leather bracers covered with brass studs. Their heads were shaved, even in the case of the two tall women. A series of scars and black tattoos decorated them like badges of honor.

Their grins were eager, and their eyes shone with a hunger for slaughter.

Their fingers were encircled by tiny strands of crackling red energy.

Fear settled with cold disregard in Aemreen's belly. These were Havoc Guild Magi. These were the people who bathed Stratia in blood and ashes. They lost none of their number in battle, yet. Aemreen, Joriken and Errnik were the only obstacle to Malkanor sharing in the fate of their victims.

Their chances of survival could not be found. Maybe, they could outmaneuver the Havoc Magi. They might be able to withstand a trial of attrition with the soldiers. That was only separate. The combined forces were more than sufficient to put them down.

Aemreen sighed, collecting her resolve. This was not the day for death she planned on. There was no help for it, and no escape from it. Her life would buy time for escape for the people.

While her regret was an obvious one, Aemreen would not yield to it. No tears would fall. She leveled the intensity of her emerald eyes on her enemies.

Aemreen brandished her saber in a flourish. Her saber sang a shrill metallic song of steel. "Which of you dies first?"

No one stepped forward.

The Havoc Magi continued to smile. Their grins did not change.

The Soldiers held their swords ready, but there was no sound of creaking plated armor, no boots grinding against cobbles. No one moved a hair's width.

Aemreen's lips curved into a smile of her own. This was no ordinary pause before conflict. This was no stop in a moment at the end of a person's life.

Joriken and Errnik relaxed, their faces creased with confusion. Who could blame then? Aemreen knew that this sort of event last occurred in battle seven millennia ago.

"Invaders, I wish to introduce you to someone." Aemreen relaxed her own stance. "This is Torch Rylin, of the Order of the Enlightened Sun. He would speak, but his words might come too quick for you to fathom."

Rylin stood between the circle of soldiers, and the three defenders of the Outer City. His Displacement Cloak was a reflex, cast upon arrival, quickening his every move. He closed his eyes, seeing only numbers and places fill the darkness of his thoughts. The Temporal Current moved with the steady rhythm of gears on a wheel, clicking inside him with mechanical precision.

Rylin stretched his awareness into each of these clicks. He felt their logical symmetry in his grasp. Each one moved into him with eldritch light. He felt the glow permeate his being, uniting him with time itself. His mind stretched outward. His fingers turned and opened each of these hidden bolts and locks.

Rylin cast far beyond the spheres and cloaks he was accustomed to. He shaped into the gathering around him. He projected a Stasis Field. With a *'boom'*, emerald energy burst outward in a wave. The Stasis Field trapped all the Kasarins in the Outer City.

Rylin projected the remaining Temporal energy into his emerald staff. It bucked in his hands, with rapid force. Dozens of shimmering balls of energy hurtled at the Ka'Rak. They soaked into the weapons and armor, absorbed into the metal and wood. A mix of ambient moisture and fast-moving time seeped into the equipment, hastening their decay. Tiny brown flakes fell, first. The weapons and armor crumbled into particles that piled on the cobbled road.

The soldiers were disarmed. Rylin altered the flow of time on the Havoc Magi. He swept his staff low, cracking against their shins. They fell in a motion that was lethargic. When they landed, Rylin calmed his thoughts. The Endless Current answered his inner stillness with a swift wave of vibrations and energy. After a shaping, restraints made of stone reached out of the cobbles. They clasped tight on the wrists and ankles of the Havoc Magi. Time slowed for Rylin, and he spoke then.

Rylin jammed the end of his staff against the throat of the Havoc Sorcerer, he spoke in fluid Kasarin. "Your attempt to invade this city has failed. I leave you two options of surrender. You Meld Walk back to the Crimson Empire, and never return, or you will Meld Walk back to your camp without the ability to Meld Walk again. Whichever way you choose, you will not harm Stratia again."

The woman on the left laughed with defiance. "You issue demands of us in a farmer's tongue? Your threats are swine and beets, boy."

"Only death will stop us from wiping all Stratians from the world." The Sorcerer spat against the staff.

Rylin sighed and rolled his eyes. "No, not 'only' death. You will regret your choice. Savor your next Meld Walk, you will not shape another."

Rylin braced himself and closed his eyes. He winced as he

began to shape his next Displacement Cloak. This would hurt him, as well.

The Temporal Energy hummed through his staff and spread outward from the choking point. It created a growing dome of emerald light that cocooned the magi. The light contracted, seeping into their skin. The effect was immediate.

The skin on their hands began to crease and wrinkle, sagging away from brittle bones. The skin on their heads shrank and drew tight, revealing crags and hollows. Pock marks and moles dotted their faces. Their bodies shriveled, and their clothes drooped from stick thin frames. Their eyes sank into the hollows of their sockets. Their lips thinned and pulled back from yellow teeth.

Rylin withdrew the aging cloak. He shuddered with distaste. It was a forbidden magic among Chronomancers against living victims. These three were a decade from their grave. The green glow vanished. He withdrew his staff and dismissed the bands of stone. He offered his staff to aid them in standing.

One of the Havoc Sorceress's slapped the offer away. She cried out as her bones protested with arthritic agony. She looked at her shaking hands with wide horrified eyes.

"One Meld Walk," Rylin reminded them. "Together, you might be able to take your disarmed Ka'Rak with you. This was your choice, it stands."

Rylin dispersed his various anomalies of time. Everything returned to normal flowing movement. Rylin braced himself for the inevitable price to pay. He needed to see the Kasarins leave. A visage of strength was needed to force them away.

Rylin turned to see Aemreen, Joriken, and Errnik. He looked them over for injuries. The blood that covered them was not their own. Rylin sighed with relief and wrapped his arms around Aemreen's waist.

Before Rylin could savor a kiss that waited months to

occur, a cold pressure began to squeeze deep into his brain. He fell to his knees, gripping his head. His skull was viced with tremendous unseen force. His arms and legs drooped with leaden weight. His palms scraped against the blood-stained cobbles. He opened his mouth to scream, but no sound escaped his throat.

Aemreen gathered Rylin in her chain-mail arms. His vision began to blur and darken.

Two thoughts escorted Rylin into unconsciousness. He was first grateful that the Kasarins were not here to witness this.

And would he always lose consciousness so close to home?

-17-

Martenen Delak strode confidently down the dark corridor toward the open light and cold air of the entry foyer. His heavy, silver-trimmed, brown robes of an Ard Solas billowed behind him in flowing waves. His thick, dark, oak staff sounded loudly against the marble floor with every other step of his right foot.

Martenen was a tall man, with broad shoulders and thick corded muscles. His hood was up, concealing the shining brown hair, tied in a short tail behind his neck. He had deep, dark brown eyes and rounded cheeks over a short-trimmed dark beard. He seldom smiled, leaving furrow lines of careful considerations. He wore soft, short, leather boots that lent well to his long, measured strides.

Martenen joined the Order only five years after Yelisian. He always thought the Illumancer to be little more than a thoughtless showboat. He wondered, often, what Kelteseus ever saw in him. He answered to battle far too much. He never studied all the lore at his fingertips. He took way too many risks with more lost than gained. He never followed up his decisions with proper after-study. All and all, Yelisian was a wound on the Order. His leadership ended in a way that was as just as it was predictable. Martenen would have laughed at the fulfillment of the inevitable, but Yelisian left the Order in shambles.

Now it was up to Martenen to clean up more than half a century of unchecked chaos. Of all the Lights Kelteseus could have chosen to lead the era, he chose the worst. Yes, Martenen believed himself to be the best choice, but he would have gladly accepted Matisia's leadership. And look what happened to her! Sent out to Malkanor where her mind and talents were wasted; another example of Yelisian's thoughtless blundering.

Now the Order stood on a potentially fatal precipice. Even before the fool, Lycendrik, started his efforts to prove the Empire's involvement with the loss of Katahn, Martenen knew that a war between rulers was coming. Martenen quickly chose emissaries to negotiate with the emperor. Meeting with him was difficult enough, arranging a non-violence pact was harder still. The emperor held a long grudge with Yelisian. It took a lot of bartering and compromise to get him to see that the Illumancer's era was over.

In the end, when the Order survived, they would have to serve the emperor in an unofficial capacity. Yes, they would be treated harshly-as inferiors-for quite some time; but the Order needed to rebuild, anyway. It was only right that they should truly begin all over, again.

It was also true that bartering meant the vaults of the Grand Illumination. While Martenen didn't know where the hidden libraries and reliquaries were, he agreed that the Order would help locate them, and give the Empire unrestricted access to the contents.

It was a steep price, but Martenen believed it created a balance for the Order to survive in a very new world. He could not save everyone, and now he believed it was wrong to try. Stratia was a land steeped in corruption and fools. Malkanor was a breeding ground for elitist slavers. Nerinmor was a ruthless bog where depravity reigned. Vodess was too slothful and weak to ever rise to any possibility. Katahn'Sha couldn't think without the Order present. Perahl'Sen was dainty, fragile and too playful. Only Teril seemed noteworthy, and they allowed everyone to feast off their labors so often that they would never discover their strength.

Of course, Martenen could not divulge any of this to his fellows in the Order. He could admit that he agreed to a holocaust, and that the Order would do nothing about it. So, if they were all going to survive, he needed to nip this uprising in the bud. Somehow, information had slipped to the non-Solas. Solas were training their students for war, everywhere, and they were even holding secret gatherings like rebellious adolescents.

At the head of it all-to Martenen's dismay, but not his surprise-was Yelisian's incorrigible student, Rylin. Martenen would not refer to him as Light Rylin; and after today, he would never need to, again. For the sake of patience, Martenen allowed his rogue solitary training and loud antics. As a Geomancer, he endured his lack of manners and respect.

Then, against obvious council rulings, Rylin gathered information about the Kasarin attacks. Martenen didn't know how he did it. It was like the whole Katahn incident that way. Martenen might have just taken his gray robe, demoting him to Candle, for it; but, in direct violation of every rule of the Order, Rylin engaged in battle against a Kasarin detachment in Malkanor.

Martenen didn't care about Rylin's reasons. He had already proven far more hot-headed and volatile than his mentor ever was, and twice as dangerous. Rylin was on a clear path of self-destruction. If he wasn't cast out, there would be no Stratia left. The Order needed to distance itself from Rylin's inevitable catastrophic explosion.

As Martenen came within view of the entry foyer, he saw the council already flanked an empty space and stood before the assembled Order. He stepped out into the overcast gloom of the late winter day and halted between his council fellows. A cold wind blew in from the hills to the west, clashing and mingling with the ocean sprays of the east. Martenen felt as though even the white of the Citadel lost its warmth.

That was to be expected, he thought. There were hard times ahead. They had to make cold decisions if any part of

Stratia was to survive.

Martenen gathered Endless Current through the stone, then projected it back out in the ground, creating an undetectable ripple that would carry the sound of his voice.

"Lights of the Order of the Enlightened Sun. I thank you for coming to listen." Martenen believed starting with a friendly note would garner their cooperation. "I know you are much more informed than I wish you were. I want you to know that I didn't create ignorance out of malice. I wished only to protect the members of my most cherished Order. Violence rages beyond these walls. Blood is shed, needlessly. I know you are all worried about your old friends, your families that cared for you, and your birth lands."

Martenen paused, allowing his words of sympathy to reach the gathering. "I held back this information because we must find any means of diplomacy first. That has been the way of our Order since it was founded. We never answer violence with more violence without considering the possibilities. I believe such chances are present here. We can come to a long-awaited agreement with the Kasarins. In doing so, we give a better future, not only to Stratia, but our entire world, as well. We must come to an understanding, not conflict."

Martenen's gaze scanned the Lights before him. The Solas, of course, remained silent as they stood against the wall closest to the entry door. He placed them there to prevent the Lights in training from doing anything unreasonable. He knew, as he watched their clenched fists and tight jaws, that the Solas wanted, very much, to make their disagreements plain.

Martenen scowled before making a stern declaration. "As you may all know, yesterday, one of our Order departed to meet the Kasarins in battle. For any Light in training, sorcery combat with those who do not possess this gift is strictly forbidden. War and battle are permitted only to the Solas of our Order."

"Furthermore, he was not instructed to leave, at all. These violations endanger the discipline of our Order and threaten the world we protect. As punishment Rylin is, henceforth, banished from the Order of the Enlightened Sun. When he returns, we will exile him to the Northern Wastes, where his power can harm none."

Shocked expressions, and several gasps were evident, even among the Solas. Banishment and exile were judgements that had never been passed before.

"Why would you do that?" A boy shouted back.

Martenen squinted, trying to locate the child who would challenge his wisdom. He didn't need to search long. A small, blonde-haired boy emerged from the front of his peers. He was less than twelve years old, wearing the brown robes of those who were not Torch level. Did this mouthy child discover his specialty yet? His brown eyes glared at Martenen with fearless, unhindered accusation.

"Because he would hurt everyone, Light…" for fate's sake! Martenen could not place a name to the boy. How could he be expected to know the name of every non-Solas?

"Merice," the boy finished, his voice hard, "and just as you don't know the name of every non-Solas 'upstart', you do not know the true heart of our Order. For safety, you toss aside the future of our Order like so much waste."

Martenen's gaze narrowed. How could a child sound so cold and filled with judging contempt?

"Light Yelisian refused to succumb to such cowardice. Perhaps that is what Light Kelteseus saw in him." Everyone with a rank higher than a Torch gasped at Merice's assessment.

Martenen's anger burned hot against the boy. Something about him reminded him of his long-time rival. The feelings stirred were as bitter as the bile climbing his throat. Was the anger causing him to feel sick?

And did this boy just Current Read Martenen? Martenen didn't sense any change in the Endless Current. There were no probing strands of magic.

More to the point: if Merice did Current Read him, how much did he now know? Only three other Lights on the council knew about his agreement with the emperor. If that knowledge were to spread before it came to fruition, the resulting insurgence would be disastrous.

Martenen realized that all eyes were on him. Merice called him out. There was an expectation that a leader could, at the very least, respond to a child.

"Rylin may have averted the loss of one city, temporarily. If we don't negotiate with these foreigners, if we don't talk, first, how can we avoid the loss of all Stratia?" Martenen delivered the challenge in patience.

"An interesting point, Light Martenen. So, why didn't we speak with the Kasarins before they devastated Tihl'Zen?"

That last came from Ishell, causing Martenen to grind his teeth. Of course, the fool girl best friend of Yelisian's destructive apprentice would challenge him. She was as rash as Rylin, and almost as full of destructive raw power.

"We didn't expect the attack any more than you did," Martenen defended. "There was nothing we could do about it."

Ishell snorted with cynicism. "Well, certainly, there was nothing you 'did' do about it. You did nothing about Katahn, including the pains of the people. You did nothing about the uproar in recorded history. There was nothing done about the slaughter of multiple Stratian armies. There has been a lot of 'nothing', Light Martenen."

"In our wounded state…" Martenen began a stammered excuse.

"We are not wounded. We are idle!" Ishell's shout drew equal parts nervous and approving stares from the Solas.

"Lower your tone, Light Ishell!" Martenen snapped back.

But Ishell would not be contained with such ease. "We are sitting idly by while our continent crumbles around us."

Martenen felt the gentle rush of Endless Current to Ishell. With nothing but a thought, she spell-shaped her voice to carry her words farther. Fates! These young Lights developed their skills much faster than anyone Martenen trained with.

"Light Rylin betrayed nothing of our beloved and sacred Order. He honored every lesson and wisdom ever passed to him. He left to protect our people. He honored the spirit of his Radiance, Yelisian, fates allow to revere his soul, forever." Ishell addressed every Light. She was answered with their rapt attention.

"If we are to honor all that is the heart of the Order of the Enlightened Sun, we must stop condemning his heroism and join him."

That last could not be tolerated. Martenen barely excused twenty-four Solas resigning. He only needed a reason to cast out Rylin, before, and the fool only gave it to him.

If that many Lights were to abandon the Order and march into battle against the Kasarins, Martenen's efforts would fail. The emperor would see it no differently than the Order breaking the agreement. At that point, the empire would turn its attention and wrath on the Citadel.

"No one leaves the Citadel." Martenen shouted. "I will not allow any more of you to endanger the Order, and any chance for peace. If any of you turn to walk, I will have all of you confined until either you see reason, or the conflict ends. I will not allow the Order to be tarnished by a mass exodus of renegades."

"You will have us confined, Light Martenen?" Layrienn's question was more of a playful challenge. "That would make the first real move we have seen from you since you tried to assume the post of his Radiance. Will you try to talk us into confinement, or will you show some mettle and force us?"

At this point, the situation was getting out of control. With each new voice, these renegades became more emboldened.

Under such fury, Martenen could not gather Endless Current as swiftly as he wished. His temper was at odds with his elemental affinity. He spell-shaped an earth spell.

The Solas gathered by the entry, scurried aside as a wall of thick gray bricks and mortar burst from the ground to seal the way out.

Heads turned to look at the impromptu imprisonment, then turned back to look at Martenen, He was gratified to see the shock and dismay on the Solas's expressions. That was short-lived as he saw the outrage and contempt on the faces of the rebellious students. How many of these Lights-in-training knew how to Meld Walk? His wall would be a moot point if there were that many. He would have given them another reason to depart. Rage did not make the best motivator for his well-thought plans.

"Those of us who will aid Stratia in her time of need, stand together for Meld Walk," Ishell shouted with rising defiance.

"Solas, seize all of them and confine them until they can each be Current Scoured," Martenen roared with fury.

The council around him turned, their eyes wide, their mouths gaping with shock.

"What? This Order needs a new beginning. This rebellion is an omen that it must be so." Martenen wondered why they could not understand something so simple.

The Solas did not move.

Martenen turned to them and howled. "Solas, capture them all!"

Still, no one moved.

"This is an order from the leader of the council. You are bound, by oath, to obey."

One of the Council Solas to Martenen's left, a Hydromancer, interjected with a murmur. "I believe the better question is how they can find the ability to disobey."

"They have to obey," Martenen growled in a tone that climbed to a renewed shout. "They are bound by Rods of Binding, they cannot disobey."

Now the Lights-in-training gaped with the same shock Martenen previously earned from the council.

"Light Martenen," Barahn stepped forward and shouted. "Let me explain a simple thing that has eluded you." The Pyromaster's smirk was smug and satisfied. "The Rods of Binding are not made with words, alone. They are also made with intentions. The collective intention of the council was that we would obey for the greater good of the Order. When you order us to imprison and maim our students, your command contradicts the intentions that bind us. This command also erodes the Rods, if only a little. Your bond with us is more tenuous now. Demand of us to harm our Order again, and the Rods will no longer restrain us."

Martenen's desperation grew as he watched the Lights-in-training cluster closer together. They were going to destroy the entire Order, and there was nothing he could do to stop them.

The Solas at the entry intoned in a unified shout. "All is known in the light..." It was an invitation. Their warm smiles beamed with pride for their students.

Martenen's anger climbed to a level that would not allow him to speak straight. He could only watch as the non-Solas turned and smiled back at their mentors.

"The light exiles the shadows!" came the combined intonation of the non-Solas.

The bubble of fury in Martenen's throat burst, allowing him to shout. "If you leave, all of you are hereby expelled from the Order of the Enlightened Sun. Your names will be stricken from the archives, and you will be labelled 'Renegades'."

Light Borvis (who Martenen only recognized because of his own extensive service to Teril) turned with a thoughtful grin. "'Renegade'...it has a certain charm to its sound." He mulled it over out loud. "I think the ladies will find it dashing."

The Solas answered Borvis's quip with a collective chuckle.

A moment later, a giant rush of Endless Current filled the foyer. Every able non-Solas who could shape a Meld Walk gathered close with their brothers and sisters who did not know how.

With that, the foyer was only a little better than empty.

-18-

Ishell tightened her belly and braced her bowels as the sudden stop jerked at her insides. The Meld Walk was not new to her. She shaped dozens of travels in the last two years. But blurring by at greater distance, as pure energy, could be taxing and disorienting. The body needed to be held together by force of will, lest every iota be dispersed throughout the universe.

Over a dozen Lights were not prepared for this. Ishell was assailed with a din of retching and dry heaves. Her bowels twisted with a resonating nausea. She closed her eyes and drank a deep inhalation of cool spring air.

The air was not fresh.

Ishell coughed as dust and old smoke scratched against her throat. She sniffed again, tentatively, using smell to take stock of the situation. There were other unpleasant odors, too vague and distant to identify. There was also the smell of coming rain, fresh and filled with cleansing promise.

Ishell opened her light hazel eyes to the dark gray clouds riding to the west of white overcast skies. She looked across the expanse of emerald fields to the south of the gray black homes of the Outer City. She walked in a dazed trance.

Several homes bore the burns and holes of tell-tale fires. A few were reduced to scattered mounds of rubble with scorch marks stretching into the stone streets. Those few homes were not burned by torch or blaze. The signs pointed to great explosions, sudden and devastating. Anyone in doors would have been killed in an instant.

Ishell neared the Outer City. Moans of the injured, coupled with the weeping of the grieving, broke through the blank wall of her trance. She staggered a step back, blasted by the energy of pain. Ishell was accustomed to different vibrations and energies. Ice formed when vibrations slowed to cold stagnation. Fire burst when vibrations were quick and excited.

Sorrow and agony, when amassed great enough, could strike with merciless force. Ishell braced her hands against her knees, gasping. The impulse to laugh, manic, warred with the crushing weight of sobs settling inside her. It was a madness that threatened to break her from within.

The reassuring presence of Borvis's hand on her shoulder was sudden and startling. The cry that escaped Ishell went skyward. It was greater than she intended, longer and louder. Her affinity was swallowed up in the throes of collective anguish, leaving her drowning and helpless. The scream was the air she needed.

After a silent moment, Borvis spoke in a gentle murmur. "If you wish, I can go and speak with the people."

Ishell wiped a rivulet of drool from her mouth before she stood straight.

"No. I am well. I can do this. It is my home. I need to do this."

Ishell walked. With each step she pushed down the part of her affinity that ran in tandem with the ambient pain. These steps, this discovery would be the least of the pains to bear. She needed strength and wit.

The soft rustling rasp of grass departed for the harsh crunch of broken stone.

There were more people than Ishell expected, with huddled clusters of unfamiliar faces. Their clothes were filthy with soot and sweat, marked with sheer cuts and wide tears. Mud and crusted brown blood caked in messy patches on their exposed skin. The strangers looked up at her with furtive eyes, tinted with traces of anger. Their downturned chapped lips hardened with scowls of recrimination and judgement.

No children played in the streets. Their fearful wails could be heard from within the dark confines of homes filled beyond capacity. The murmur of Outer City children accompanied these cries as they attempted to console their guests.

Ishell bore the piercing accusation that went unspoken against her. Their homes were gone. They nearly died. They lost loved ones in sprays of blood. Everything was inverted, dumping them into pain and loss. They were angry with her, but not specifically. She wore the gray robe of the Order, the same order that promised to protect them. Where were the Lights when they were needed most?

One man blocked her way forward. He glared, fuming with flared nostrils. He pulled on his blood-spattered tunic while several other people gathered closer.

"Some of this is my brother. But if you look, close," he yanked another part of his tunic, "you might find a part of my niece there, too."

The weight of the accusation pushed down against the top of her head. She refused to look away or speak. Some part of the Order needed to take this blow, and responsibility.

"The red ones came, the Kasarins; only the soldiers came, or I would not live to tell this to you." The villager paused to hold up his bloody sleeve. "They got my brother's wife first. They cut her so deep I could see her heart. My two nephews ran with us, but the oldest was cut through the eyes and brain. The other lost his legs below the knees."

"We ran, my brother with his little girl under one arm, and me. My brother couldn't see straight, on account of tears for his wife and sons. We were almost to the woods when they caught up to us. I turned just in time to see..."

The villager's lips trembled, and his chest shook with sobs. "They cut him in two, at the hips, in one swing. One swing!" He laughed with incredulity. "They must be stronger than woodsmen, or their swords are wicked sharp. My niece survived the first cut. My brother threw her ahead, before he died. She got up and ran. She learned to walk, only the week before, but she ran. Her screams..." He closed his eyes as he struggled with the memory. "You hear things, sometimes, that make you move faster, do more. My little niece screamed, she screamed so loud. I ran to her as fast as I could. I felt things in my legs snap. I had her tiny little hand in mine."

His eyes widened as he shouted at Ishell. "That's when they cut her head from her shoulders! I don't sleep now. Do you know why? Because she was quiet when they cut her head. Her screams stopped, and it was quiet, like night, like sleep."

He sighed. "I wish I died. I should be dead. But Phoenix Legionnaires arrived, standing between me and quick happy death. They were so tired, but they fought, anyway. Some fought to their last breath. They beat down the red ones. When it was over, there were only five legionnaires, and their swords were broken."

"And where was the Order?" he roared. "Where was their magic when they cut off the head of a babe?"

The crowd of refugees was a thick circle, now. There was no sympathy in their eyes. The mercy they were granted by the Kasarins was pointed at Ishell with their hard glares. Ishell stood as a symbolic representative of the Order, and the Order failed them all.

He glared, faint tears forming in his blood-shot eyes. Ishell didn't look away, and she didn't speak.

"So, what have you to say for the Order?" His voice lowered to a growl.

"You are right. We left you alone to die." The admission

tasted bitter on her tongue.

"What? No apologies? No excuses?"

"What would they give you that would ever make it well, again?"

There was a crunching pain to Ishell's cheek. Her vision darkened with spots of color from the survivor's round punch to her face. Ishell straightened as her vision cleared. She restrained her tears and looked at his clenched jaw. He opened his fist, and shook his hand, absently.

The Renegades arrived in the Outer City, but they could not pass through the tight-packed throng of people. The air was thick with collective sweat and body odor. The pungent reek of old urine on unwashed clothes was an overpowering cloud.

The Renegades observed and obeyed Ishell's visual unspoken cues. She didn't wrinkle her nose in disgust. Just as with the punch and the words, it was all a part of the Order's abandonment of Stratia.

"You can't give them to us. So why are you here? What difference does it make, now?"

Ishell lowered her head, then, but only as she lowered to one knee on the cold hard stone.

"We failed you all. Now, we are indebted to serve you, any way we can." Her eyes were lowered to the ground, and the ragged shoes that revealed his bloody feet. There were blisters and open sores in the grime of his feet. He would have run while his feet were cut and infected.

The silence was thick and tense. The air became heavy as Ishell felt the judgement of the people bearing down on her. These were her people. She once lived alongside them. She held an intimate knowledge of their toils and struggles. While they bled and died, she remained sheltered in pristine white walls. In this, she betrayed them. Her life was at their mercy, and she accepted that.

His feet turned and he walked away with no word. The small, calloused hand of a woman appeared in Ishell's vision.

"Get up. There have been enough slaves and pain among us. We need no more." Ishell was greeted by a shorter gray-haired woman. Her steely eyes shifted to indicate the gathered people. "But they would like to know why you are here."

Ishell looked around. The eyes fixed on her continued to press, as before, but with expectation. Women leaned with an impatient hand on their hips. Men stood with their heads tilted and their arms folded across their chest.

Ishell released a nervous cough before she raised her voice. "Our absence was wrong. We cannot make right the loss of your families. But if you allow, we will stay and help as best we can."

"Why would we need you? We live, still." The shout came from a man in the crowd. He was met with murmurs of agreement.

"Those homes look broken." Ishell looked at the crude lean-tos made from sticks and moth-eaten patches of clothes. "Some of you must be freezing at night." She looked at the feet of the refugees around her. Blood, pus, and filth were common sights. "Your wounds must be tended. I imagine there is little food to go around to so many."

At the mention of food, there was a chorus of rumbling bellies. Some of the people blushed as they gave their neighbors embarrassed looks of apology.

"Please, let us help you in your needs," Ishell pleaded.

A shout of defiance answered her. "We are not beggars in an alley. We worked and lived for decades. We don't need your coin or your bread. Take your pity elsewhere."

"And what of ours?" came the voice of a familiar man.

Kylor, Rylin's father, was unmistakable. He leaned against a wall with his arms folded, his dark bearded face patient. His coarse black hair was peppered with silver strands of age.

"You came. Your homes were burned. You were starving and bleeding. Did you not want our pity? Did you not want our aid?"

"That isn't the same. We were tired, desperate."

Kylor stepped away from the wall and spread his arms. "We all are. That is our burden in war. It is unfair and uncaring. We make up the difference. Do not be like the war that tries to break us. They come to help, take it. Bury your foolish pride." Kylor turned to Ishell. "Do what you came to do."

"Renegades, gather close to me." Ishell didn't turn, but the footsteps and the press of bodies were evident.

Ishell approached an old man with a beard like coarse wool over dark streaked cheeks.

"May I tend your feet?" Ishell asked, her voice soft, as the stooped old man slowly lowered to the cobbles. Ishell knelt before his outstretched legs.

"These people walked or ran because we were not there to escort them." Ishell spoke to the Renegades while she projected ghost strands of her will into the bloody feet before her. "They ran until their feet bled after their shoes split because we were not there. Now, we owe them their feet. Pay close attention. You will need to do the same for all these survivors."

There were slimy green places of infection that ran from the skin to the bone. Heat and enlarged swells pushed against the encroachment, preventing further spreading. Ishell's magic sought the filth and diseased tissue, pulling it free. The open sores and blisters oozed more dark green liquid as she did.

When that was done, Ishell shifted her magic. She cooled the swollen areas, forcing them to contract. Her magic pulled together torn skin and severed muscles. The wounds closed in minutes. It would have been faster, but Ishell's magic excelled in combat. Kera's healing talents revealed how far Ishell was from the title of Solas.

Ishell turned her attention to the soles and torn leather of the old man's shoes. She felt for the hum and vibration the shoes radiated, sensing their unique contribution to the Endless Current. It wasn't as raw or sheer as fire and ice. It was dull, and a little rigid in its pulse. That was how inanimate objects tended to be. The crafting and twisting could be a harsh transformation for any slow matter. Polymancers had so much more ease with it. They sought for the vibration of intention or the expression of crafting.

First, Ishell pulled and repaired as many fibers as were present. She thickened the vibrations around the soles, adding more to what was already present, sealing the holes.

The extended labor of unfamiliar sorcery pushed against her stamina. Ishell's mouth dried as her mouth murmured. Droplets of sweat tickled her forehead, threatening her concentration. Her fingers and forearms ached as they circled and twirled over the old man's legs.

But the work did end. Ishell blinked, certain that hours passed. The sky was overcast, but the dark gray of the storm clouds was little closer. The spell-shaping felt like long hours, but it was only minutes.

"Well then," Ishell exhaled. "Renegades do the same for everyone. Some of you will find some tasks easier. You may all have to improvise. This won't be our only labor before sundown, so work with haste."

Without a word, the other Renegades spread out. They sought the refugees and began the work, at once. It was strange to see boys without their first chin hair, tending to the feet of women old enough to be their mothers. But concentration and the flow of Endless Current was constant, even among the Candles.

Unfortunately, there were no Flames among the Renegades. It was a hard decision to make, but Flames were promoted to Candle after demonstrating some competence with the Endless Current. Without it, the battlefield would only exploit their vulnerability.

Borvis stepped close to Ishell. "I have yet to see Light Rylin."

Ishell nodded, absently, while she supervised the first attempts at mending and repairing. "We have only just arrived, Light Borvis. As our list of priorities go, he is beneath the needs of the people."

Borvis winced at the calloused assessment. Ishell ignored him as she knelt before a young woman swollen with pregnancy. She wasted no words. The woman's feet were a mosaic of dark bruises and deep gashes, spotted with blisters. A mid-wife would panic about blood-poison at the sight of them.

Borvis knelt beside her. "So, what then, after this?"

Ishell snapped with annoyance. "Look around. So many people, so little shelter. The coming winds will throw their rags into the horizon. The rain will pour through those burn holes. They will be ill with fever by dawn if we don't give them better."

"We are not Solas, Light Ishell. Even with more Current, the pulse of a home is complex. We can do little better than what they have."

"It is better than a torn shirt at the end of a stick. That is what matters. Now, will you act or sit on your laurels and hurl our limits in my face?"

It was an angry question, and Borvis blinked, leaning back as he squatted. "I'm more harm than help at mending wounds. I'll begin with the shelters."

Ishell nodded. Borvis stood up and walked away. It was the start of a long exhausting day.

-19-

Rylin opened his eyes to a squint. His eyelids were heavy and weak, pressing against his efforts with aches. The flickering dim, orange, light played with his skull-squeezing headache. In the mix of shadows, everything seemed like a faint glow dancing in water. It was late, and only candles broke the pervasive darkness of the night.

There was a deep silence, interspersed with the gentle sounds of quiet snoring. Strong winds rattled against panes of glass with random discretion.

The faint smell of roses clashed with a miasma of stale sweat, and thick body odor.

Rylin shifted where he lay, feeling the soft press of sheets and covers against his bare torso. His head rested against a thick down pillow. He pushed against the fatigue in his eyes, attempting to push them open, further.

The room was unfamiliar to him. How did Rylin get here? The last thing he remembered was the battle in the Outer City. Between then and now, everything was a fugue mix of kaleidoscope delirium. Everything was a garbled mix of voices and words that filled hazy attempts to wake. He could make little sense of it all. He knew there was the jostling of motion inside a velvet carriage. There were hands, so many hands. Some were large and hard; others were small and soft.

Rylin didn't recognize where he was, but he knew what

happened to him. His conscious memory clung to his mind with implacable tenacity. No amount of mad whirlwind events could strip him of the knowledge of what he did, and how he got this way. He read enough Golden Hourglass lore to understand the consequences of his choices.

Rylin turned his head both ways, trying to get his bearings. To one side, Ishell and Borvis sat in a deep, velvet loveseat, leaning against each other. Their gray robes were spotted with white stains of sweat and splattered with caked mud. They comprised the snoring chorus. Their dirty faces were cast in hard shadows from a candle on a table beside them.

Rylin turned his head the other way. Aemreen sat in a worn wooden chair. She wore a plain blue skirt and long-sleeved white blouse. Her long brown hair was braided into a circlet on her head, while the rest fell down her back and framed her face. Her chin rested against her chest. Her breathing sounded with quiet snores.

Rylin's blue shirt and forest-green long coat were neatly folded on top of an end table in a corner. His emerald staff gleamed in the candlelight, while the gold runes sparkled in the flickering glow.

There were so many questions that filled Rylin's mind. He sat up, and Aemreen's green eyes slowly opened.

"Where am I?" Rylin croaked, his voice parched with thirst.

"In one of the guest rooms in the west side of my estate." Aemreen stood up, going to a wide birch table where a pitcher of water and a glass waited beside a white cloth. "Which explains why you don't recognize it. You have been asleep and feverish since you fell in the Outer City. I had to bring you here, where a healer from Pahlinsor and I could tend to you. I feared for you when your fever would not break for more than two days."

Aemreen filled a glass of water and gave it to Rylin, he drank it in two swallows.

"Drink slower. You have been under for days. You will be weak."

The cool liquid washed away the dry scratchy feeling in his throat. Speaking came with more ease.

"I am sorry to have worried you and put you through this, my love," Rylin apologized.

Aemreen shrugged and smiled. "There are so many reasons you owe me no apology. I just wish I knew what ailed you."

Rylin shook his head. "Displaced Potential Reckoning. It is a consequence the Temporal Current metes out for meddling with the overall potential of another human being. I knew it would happen. I don't know how long it will last."

Aemreen sat on the bed beside Rylin. Her nearness filled his head with a giddy intoxication.

"If you knew this would happen, then why did you do it?"

"The Kasarin armies and nobility fight to the death with their enemies. For them, life is for the victors and death for the conquered."

"It is war, my love. That is how wars are always waged."

"I believed that if I introduced another outcome, one worse than dying in their eyes, it would cause them to pause and reconsider the entire invasion."

"Maybe if they were simple warlords, and scattered sorcerers, that might be true." Aemreen found Rylin's hand and clasped it. "But they are here by imperial edict."

Aemreen sighed. "The Phoenix Legions still battle the newly arrived Kasarin Soldiers. Though they are tired, and their swords break, they engage the invasion at every village and farmstead from Vodess to Teril."

"What is happening, Aemreen? Why are the Phoenix Legions so exhausted? The Kasarins do not yet send the Havoc Magi, or a more determined force. This cannot be their limits.

They were always prepared for much longer wars."

"They have been attempting to protect so many isolated homes and villages from well-trained brigands. The skirmishes have been happening for more than a year, just one feint after another. Only Joriken, Errnik and I have been able to maintain a watch over the Outer City. These slavers and thieves have been getting bolder by the week."

"So, someone is orchestrating these extended efforts to harry the Legions." Ishell added, as she raised her head. "Someone wants to sap the resolve and fighting power of the Legions. But their timing was poor. They disappeared when the Kasarins arrived. Now, we are trying to figure out where each one of these weary detachments of Malkanor's bravest are, so we can rally them together and refresh them."

Rylin nodded, mulling it over. "Unify our forces. It is a good idea. How many came from the Citadel?"

"One hundred of us were cast out, and we came straight away."

Rylin coughed with wide eyes. "Cast out?!"

"We are Renegades of the Order, Light Rylin. Martenen wanted us to disregard the death of thousands of people." Ishell winced against an unspoken memory. "No more. You may have acted early, and without warning, but this must be."

Aemreen raised her eyes to find Ishell and Borvis. "Their aid has been invaluable. They have been tirelessly seeing to the needs of the refugees. They have been trying to figure out how to find my father's wayward men, and their charges."

"Which brings me to another task: Light Rylin, we need you to begin your meditations tomorrow. You can find all of them in seconds."

Rylin lowered his eyes, ashamed. "I am not sure I will be able. I will try, of course. Displaced Potential Reckoning does include a temporary or permanent loss of abilities."

Rylin heard Ishell grind her teeth. He looked up to see her hands clenched tight. "Let me see if I am correct in this. You charge out here, you save our homes. You save my da', and for that I am grateful. But you thought to send a vague lesson to a ruthless enemy. A lesson so vague, it would have to be spoken to be understood. You knowingly risked losing all your powers, at best, in the thick of genocide against our people, at worst for the rest of your natural life. Light Porra and I can sense how the Endless Current seems to swerve around you, as though avoiding you."

Ishell leaped to her feet, shouting, with her fists rigid at her sides. "Did you stop for a moment to ponder what could happen if your fool plan to end the war in one metaphor failed? We need you, Light Rylin, and your brash arrogance has forced you to abandon us. We are only one hundred Torches and Candles, attempting to stand with thousands of broken and battered men. The Solas were forbidden to accompany us."

"We have been here two and a half days. Already we are blind and bone weary. Perhaps if you informed me of this, beforehand, I could have directed you to a more plausible solution."

Ishell stormed out of the room. Borvis woke and stopped at the door, looking back at Rylin, and then at the pile of his personal items.

"At some point, you are going to tell us what those are. They are radiating more power than half the relics of the Nerinmor Inquiry combined." Borvis shut the door quieter than Ishell would have.

Rylin looked to Aemreen as she closed her eyes in thought. "She is right to be angry with you."

"Do you share in her anger?"

Aemreen pursed her lips. "A little. I was there, my love. The battle was yours. You could have ended it any way you chose. With you here to help us, there is more than the war you could have assisted with."

Rylin thought about it a moment. He felt like a dullard as her meaning escaped him.

When the meaning did strike, it made him feel thrice the fool.

"I could have found the connections to put this mastermind in irons."

"We suspect it is her Majesty, trying to wear down the resistance that keeps her rule from being absolute. We have no evidence, no witnesses, nothing. His majesty won't simply take her head, or jail her on a king's edict, alone. He believes it would be the start of a tyrant's path. So, we support his decision. He is right."

Rylin nodded in absent agreement. Maloric was a good man. He was instructed in fair justice and king's ethics in the same study hall as Yelisian. He would never do anything that resulted in injustice.

Aemreen bent over Rylin, her rose scented hair spilling over his face as she kissed his lips deep.

She pulled away, her emerald-green eyes drinking in his face. "Rest, my love. I don't believe you will be unable to use your powers for too long. Gather your strength."

Aemreen blew out the candles on her way out of the room, leaving Rylin to lay awake in the dark. He already made costly mistakes, and left people in anger they held a right to.

Rylin's jaw clenched, and his hands gripped the sheets. Determination washed away his sense of embarrassment and self-berating. He bent his knee up, pleased to find his body could still obey his commands.

No matter how long he would be without his powers, he could still give his help in blood, sweat and pain. Rylin would only stop helping when he breathed his last breath.

-20-

The hot orange blaze of the fire burned several feet high, crackling and popping as it consumed wood. Teranen sat cross-legged within a couple of feet, drawing in more than the intense heat. She allowed her mind to mingle and entwine with the flames, becoming far more intimate than lovers. She felt its hunger, its raw demanding power, its desire to dance with defiant abandon, twisting and snapping against the dark and the cold. Her mind mixed with the brilliant hot yellow, and heaven-licking orange, breathing plumes of smoke into the night sky. Its dragon breath obscured the moon and stars.

Beyond the flames, several of the Renegades snored as they slept, using their robes for blankets and small heaps of long grass for pillows. Errisa slept, curled up a few feet from Teranen, while two Candle girls slept just a little further away from them. They all huddled close at the end of the cobblestone street at the south of the Outer City.

Teranen couldn't sleep tonight. Perhaps it was the strange environment of the well-kept homes, a few hundred yards away. Maybe it was the change in routine or being without a home. She was older than most of the Renegades, and she knew age demanded stability, a knowledge of things that would be familiar and reliable. This made the third time her entire world changed. Only her magic made her able to endure more, at least that was what she thought.

But Teranen knew, deep within, that it was more that she

knew she would have to fight. She had done so before. She forced Maesellen's thugs to withdraw many times.

The Kasarins would not withdraw. Thousands of men came to fight to the death. Teranen knew rage, knew how to harness the heat of anger; but she had never called on her fires to kill anyone. Now her fires would have to burn flesh, create screams, and end life.

Teranen hated it. She hated war, and she hated how she had to defile the purity of her flames. She looked down at her hands and arms, seeing the random web-work of scars. The ice and cold had given her those scars. Snow and rocks cut her as she tried to hold her son, as she tried to cling to her husband. They were both consumed in thick heaps of snow. She tried to dig, to reclaim them, to hold their lifeless bodies close for one more minute. The snows burned and cut her flesh, ravenously, for it.

Fire was Teranen's life. It was her redemption. It saved her and gave her a rebirth with purpose. She used the fire to guide lost travelers away from the ruthless hunger of the cold. She melted snows away from edible plants so that starving men and women could eat. She warmed freezing children and brought them light when they were afraid of the dark.

Yes, it had been Teranen's weapon at times; but she always found a choice in how to handle it. Fire gave her a world filled with love and hope, and she cherished it. While it was true that she was eager to fight the Kasarins after what they did to Tihl'Zen, and all its people, it was only recently that she acknowledged that it meant that she would have to kill.

Erissa stirred, and Teranen put a reassuring hand on her shoulder. It was a bit motherly of her, she supposed. She smiled as she watched the young Aeromancer snuggle against her palm. Dunell, the Order, all of them became her family. They never replaced the memory of her son and husband. They only added to it.

All of them taught Teranen beautiful lessons about fire and living. She knew, now, the renewing, caring side of the flames. To her, fire was passion and free expression, it was an extension of inner warmth, of inner light breaking the darkness. Yes, it also had fury and rage; but she would argue that to be true of all elements. All of them could destroy as much as they gave.

Teranen looked down to her side, at her neatly folded gray robe. Barahn insisted on embroidering, in gold, each rank on the inside of the lapel. So, she had a flame, a candle, and a torch sewn onto the inside of her robe. She was not as fast to reach that last as Rylin and Ishell, but Barahn said he met no one with greater determination than her.

Thinking of the short, rotund Pyromaster brought a sad, wan smile to Teranen. Even after only a couple of days she found herself missing the Order's only vulgar Solas. She viewed Erissa as a younger sister, but what did that make Barahn? He was no lover, certainly. That role was permanently vacated with the death of Borik. He held too much knowledge and wisdom to be a son, though she was a bit older than him.

Teranen chuckled under her breath. Maybe he was like an older brother, complete with excessive rough housing.

Before allowing her mind to drift further into it, Teranen cleared her thoughts of all but the fire in front of her. She focused her breathing, altering its speed and the movements it created in her body, attuning its rhythm to the fire. Her throbbing pulse sought the cadence of every pop and crackle. The rush of blood in her veins became one with the steady roar of the flames. She was the fire, and the fire was her.

After a while, Teranen felt the vibrations in the air, between her and the fire. She felt those vibrations permeate deep into her body. It was the soothing pulse of the Endless Current, and with it, she felt the world around her in a keen and sensitive way.

Teranen used the Endless Current to push into the flames, to allow her mind to become one with the intense heat. Then she stretched and pushed the boundaries of her awareness, reaching into the other fires burning in the night. She could see through campfires burning in the south and east. She saw through candles that lit the way forward through dark hallways.

Teranen was not just the fire that burned before her. She was every fire that broke the gloom all over Stratia. She could see whatever she wished. She first found her friend and teacher. He was sleeping, curled in a ball, on the Citadel furnace room. She was disgusted to see a pool of vomit under the side of his face. He came back to the Citadel after drinking, again.

Where did Barahn have left to find his hot rum? Katahn was gone. Tihl'Zen was gone. Every other city and village remained in constant fear of attack. Did he transmute his drink? It would make a first for him. He hated spells that didn't involve fire.

Teranen felt Barahn's heartache. It was why he lay in a drunken stupor so close to where they trained. The spell, Fire Scrying, was a method he taught her, recently, so that she could always watch over the people she cared for. The Pyromaster was a crude man, but he was also the best teacher she had ever known. She would not let him down, now.

Teranen reached through memories and fire, pulling the familiar hamlet of Dunell. The images caught in the smoke and tongues of flame blurred and then resolved. Teranen saw her once-charges asleep in their homes of wood and light gray bricks. While it was early spring, the mountain snows still covered the side streets and walkways. The tiny village was situated at a pointed border between Nerinmor and Vodess, just south of the Northern Wastes. It was never easy to farm in those lands. Mining and hunting were the major form of living there, with the mines providing meager amounts of ore. With it being at the center of three nations, and the boundary to the north, Teranen thought the village could become a vast hub-city.

But it wasn't what Dunell could be that drew Teranen's love for them. It was the people. There were maybe twenty families living in the huddled village, but they were hearty and enduring, as well as charitable and compassionate. Never once, did the people of Dunell view Teranen's magic with hostility. In fact, they always favored its practical nature in their unforgiving lands. To them, her presence was always a blessing.

The men and women were sad to see Teranen leave them to join the Order, but they also understood that she needed her talents to grow.

Teranen looked closer to the ends of the muddy streets of the village, and her brow furrowed. White, tall, wide tents were pitched. Blue and black armored soldiers stood at watchful attention, gazing beyond the edge of firelight.

Teranen seldom saw the Phoenix Legions, but they were instantly recognizable. But why were they so far north? The general talk was that the fighting was mostly in the south, before the Kasarins arrived. It was centered close to the borders of Vodess. The cold was a little too unpleasant for the thugs from the warmer nation.

That was not all that worried Teranen, though. There was a tired look to them. She saw gashes in their chain mail and brigandines, and deep dents in their bracers and greaves. Their deep blue tabards were torn and spotted with brown patches of dry blood. Their eyes were blood shot and furtive, shifting in constant fear. Their hair and beards were matted and untrimmed. Their swords weighed heavy against belts that hung loose at their hips.

These were Malkanor's best soldiers. They were known and respected throughout Stratia. They were one of the major reasons why Malkanor remained its own nation. So why were they so beaten?

Teranen looked deeper, making her own examination of the gloom. The village slept peacefully, but there was a painful tension in the silence. The soldiers seemed to anticipate something. The shadows and gloom felt like it circled and probed them.

Teranen took careful stock of the soldiers, remembering

everything Barahn taught her in the past couple of months. There were forty soldiers, twelve on watch and patrolling the tree line in shifts. Most of them appeared to be swordsmen with no shields. There were only a few polearms and spears in evidence, and only two long bows to be found. Their draws were loose and frayed, and their wood was splintered and weak.

Without shields, the swordsmen would have to rely on the pole weapons to make up the skill difference with the Kasarins. With so few, the Phoenix Legionnaires might last only a few minutes more against a Kasarin attack. The long bows were a negligible presence.

The entire assessment relied on a purely Kasarin Infantry assault. If the Havoc Guilds were present, Dunell would burn to the ground within an hour.

Judging by the shifting in the far away darkness, Teranen believed the Kasarins were close to making the same conclusions.

Teranen stood up. She put her gray robe on over her brown, thick, wool dress. She shaped a Meld Walk before anyone could wake.

-21-

Teranen's Meld Walk ended at a watch camp situated at the easternmost road of Dunell.

Startled and already at the edge of their nerves, three of the swordsmen drew their weapons at her initial appearance. They breathed a sigh of relief and sheathed their weapons after they saw her gray robe.

"Do not stay your weapons, yet. The Kasarins have been watching you for some time, now." Teranen spoke low, noticing that the tension was even greater here, in person.

"Why do they not attack?" asked a middle-aged soldier, waiting for her to introduce herself.

"I am Torch Teranen, formerly of the Order of the Enlightened Sun. I am part of a group of Renegades sworn to help defend Stratia. The only reason they do not attack outright, is the losses they have sustained against your comrades in the south. They are taking time to study you from the shadows. If they know as I do, they will attack tonight, likely within the hour."

That caused the three swordsmen to straighten. "Then we must rally our squads and meet them."

"What is your name and rank?" Teranen asked.

"Twentieth sergeant Ronkar Meraksis."

"Sergeant Meraksis, as I understand it, your first priority

is to get the people to safety," Teranen reminded.

"It is," Ronkar admitted, lowering his gaze. "But there are so few of us that we would be cut down in seconds for trying."

"Don't lose your honor, Sergeant. I will support whoever defends the evacuation."

In the next few minutes, any sleeping soldiers were roused and armed. They emerged from their tents looking weary and dejected, like men resigned to their last march, men that knew death was certain.

Their expression of fatigue and despair melted a little, giving way to a whisper of renewed conviction at the sight of Teranen in her gray robe. The Order didn't forsake them. They had a sorceress for an ally. They would live if they worked together. It did not matter that she did not carry the silver staff or wear the Enriall Armor of a Solas in battle. They were grateful and hopeful that any magi came to their aid.

Teranen saw increased movement in the shadows beyond the trees. Not all the families were awake and ready to escape. The Kasarins knew this. They knew the soldiers were at their most vulnerable, right now. This was the moment the Kasarins were likely to capitalize on.

Teranen closed her eyes and inhaled deep. The darkness of her mind filled with the image of her husband, Borik. Her fingers curled into the smooth locks of curly dark hair. Her forehead felt the press of his rugged jawline, chin, and lips. His hard dark features were common in Malkanor men. For the briefest instant, she felt his chiseled miner arms wrapped around her waist. She smelled the musky mix of earthen clay and thick woodsmoke.

"Borik, my first and only love," Teranen's thoughts were a prayer spoken in her mind. "I always knew such strength when I was with you, and when you held me close. The world was always well, again, when I looked into your brown eyes."

"Let me know your strength, again. Be with me so that I

can stand with these broken warriors. Be with me so that we can defend these good people."

A tear fell from the corner of Teranen's eye as her mind filled with the image of her dark-haired boy.

"Kaeden, my dear sweet boy. I have no right to ask anything from you, my wayward light of my heart. I failed you. If you ever passed from this world in peace (as I have hoped and prayed with every breath) then know that you have never left my thoughts. I am so sorry, and I hurt for you every day. If you ever believed in me, as your mother, believe in me, now. Believe in me so that I can do for these children what I failed to do for you."

Teranen's eyes were closed. The tears formed two hot streams down her cheeks. They were an offering in a prayer for her two most cherished spirits.

There was a low whisper, beneath the roar of a distant bonfire. *'You have never failed me. I feel my place in your heart, every day. Fight with all your spirit, ma!'*

Teranen cleared her mind of all but the sound of the crackling fires. She blocked out the sound of stomping soldier boots, clattering armor, and knocking doors. The panicked shouts were lost on her, as the Endless Current flowed from flames and into her, cutting through the cold mountain air.

'I am proud of you, my Teri,' the deep gentle voice of Borik filled the silence of her mind. *'The fates knew you were the best of us. That is why you lived on. We, both, love you. Now, set your heart free of us, my love, and give em' hell, Teri.'*

Strength and light-hearted will surged through Teranen. For the first time in her life, she could do anything. Far beyond the reach of her limits, she was a Torch of the Renegades, the Flame Witch of Dunell. She was a warrior magus.

Teranen felt the heat of three hundred men, pressing against the cold air from the darkness. These were the Kasarin Soldiers. Beyond them were ten Havoc Magi, poised in the supposed protection of the dense woods.

Teranen smiled. She raised her palms up, high. White hot flames sprang to life wrapping her hands in their embrace. These were her Heart Fires, a Pyromancer's purest flames of inner expression.

Teranen screamed, a sound filled with the fury of her conjuring inferno. In answer, a towering wall of ivory flames burst to life between her and the enclosing assault. It burned no trees or buildings, but any Kasarin foolish enough to dare crossing it would be burned to a blackened corpse. The wall spread in a half circle from the north to south, running the entire eastern edge of the village.

The road leading into Dunell from the southwest remained untouched for the fleeing villagers.

Teranen shouted with defiance into the night sky, while her forehead felt the twin heat of her eyes pouring candle flames of white. "If you want this village, Crimson Empire, come and get it!"

The Phoenix Legion halted their actions at the sight of the burning spectacle before them. As they watched her fiery act of defiance, they raised their swords high, and roared in a powerful cheer. Their spirits were filling with renewed determination. Their broken will to fight began to mend. They would fight as fiercely as she would.

In retaliation, geysers of water attempted to bubble underneath the bass of the wall of fire. The fires would not die so easily. With the added heat of Teranen's will, the water would require more time to douse it. As that time passed, twenty of the Legion Swordsmen ran in a clammer of metal, stopping in a defensive phalanx, twenty yards in front of her. They crouched low, poised and tense, their swords pointed at the geysers in front of them. The spear and polearms took up positions in front, ready to skewer anyone wearing red.

Sergeant Meraksis shouted out to his men as a central geyser began to wear down the fires. "Phoenix Legion! Defense formation 'v', cut anything that comes through. Protect Torch

Teranen at all costs. Tonight, we burn the Kasarins, for a change."

There was an answering rowdy laugh. Teranen smiled, finding herself in complete agreement with the Sergeant. Her hands swirled and arced, leaving artful trails of white fire in the air. She murmured a lyrical and incomprehensible language. The cold steel became a chilling press against her skin. The sharp edges of every blade caressed her senses.

All the metal blades burst to blinding life, wreathed in her white fires. The metal did not burn or melt, but their heat created beads of sweat on the arms of their wielders. It was a weapon imbuing spell she like to call the Dragon Tongue. The metal would not chip or break, and their edges would melt through steel and iron, burning the flesh of their enemies.

A pathway opened in the fire wall. It was a narrow path, only big enough for one or two men, and filled with clouds of hot steam. It was a bottleneck, and Teranen thought the Kasarins would not be fool enough to seize upon it.

But, in seconds, dozens of red and gold plate soldiers pressed into a dash through the steam. Their curved longswords were held low to make quick, powerful slashes.

They did not expect an eager Phoenix Legion with swords of white fire. The Kasarins found themselves charging into a massacre.

The Phoenix Legion cut down rank after rank of invaders. Their swords burned through polished Kasarin steel and armor with the ease of air. They made swift cuts through flesh and bone, severing appendages, and cleaving through heads and torsos.

The heaps of cauterized smoking carnage sickened Teranen. She had to lose herself in the continued flow of power to keep her focus. As a result, she felt the change in the air before the first razor arcs of crimson energy appeared. She moved swift, rushing to answer the Havoc Magi. She hurled head-sized spheres of white fire and gathered force at each arc. She shattered each one before it could reach the Legion Swordsmen. The air was filled a resounding cacophony of thundering, ground shaking explosions and flares of white light. Each crimson attack was broken.

Burgundy hued vines broke the ground around Teranen's feet, trying to ensnare her ankles. The dagger-length sharp thorns would shred her legs if they reached her.

Teranen screamed, lifting her head to the night sky. A surrounding pillar of white fire burst skyward around her. The flames incinerated the vines to wispy black ashes.

Teranen would not allow herself to be pushed back into a deeper defensive. The body heat of the Havoc Magi radiated against her, with acuity, in the night. Her eyes looked beyond her flames and found the red rush of heat in their veins. She saw them as plain as daylight. She could burn each of them with ease.

Teranen began spell-shaping, locking the presence of each magus into her awareness. Their heat and fury were like beacons in the night.

High above the trees the air shimmered into a massive globe. Seconds later the ground quaked, for miles, as the giant sphere burst in a blinding white booming explosion. Ten white comets, the size of a head, hurtled down in the aftermath.

Screams filled the air as the fires found their marks, slamming through the Havoc Magi. They were given no warning to flee or avoid their fate. They were blind and helpless as the flaming spheres burned through their torsos, leaving smoking black holes.

As Teranen killed the last of the Havoc Magi presence, a Legionnaire cleaved the last Kasarin swordsmen from shoulder to hip.

High above Dunell, the translucent, shimmering Scrying Sphere of Zenen'Rol vanished, taking his growing rage with him. He abandoned his decimated forces and the cheers of victory that howled into the night from the surviving village.

-22-

Zenen'Rol's boots stomped with anger, through the charred remains of the western coast town. His will of rage overflowed his body, creating tiny bursts of crimson lightning along his arms and legs. The failures who dared name themselves Ka'Rak gave him a wide berth.

The moonless sky was cold, its darkness further adding to the frightful expression on the giant sorcerer's face in the spontaneous flashes of red light.

They should all be afraid of him. Zenen demanded at least that much. That fear should drive them to unchallenged victory.

Yet, the lands to the east did not belong to the empire. The dark city of Pahlinsor should be ashes in the wind. He watched over his fellows and soldiers, and forcefully advised them to victory. Somehow, they failed. The dark city still stood, and the detachment was returned, enfeebled.

They returned accepting their fate of death in dishonor, of course. They knelt and offered their throats to be cut. It was not acceptable for any force of the emperor to withdraw from battle.

The three formerly young Havoc Magi, and the lost equipment troubled Zenen'Rol. The sorcery that was the culprit was unlike anything he ever encountered. Yet, the description stirred something in his mind. It was not a Void Hand's sorcery, but Zenen'Rol felt like he should be able to name and place it.

The Emperor's Fist put it out of his mind for now. Thinking about it, without answers at the ready, would accomplish nothing. He breathed deep, clearing his mind, taking in the faint sharp smell of fading smoke in the night air.

Zenen'Rol gave a perfunctory nod as his right- hand sorceress, Ken'Tekira, stepped out of concealment. She emerged from the gloom of a sparsely wooded field to fall into step beside him. She was a smaller woman, bordering on petite. Without her lean arms and legs, she would have been fitted for a child's size in combat raiment. The top of her head was shaved, clean, marked by a long deep scar that ran the length of the middle of the top of her head. Her dark brown eyes remained ever alert, scanning the shadows.

"You are brave to approach me, tonight," Zenen commented, his voice rumbling with warning.

Ken shrugged. "Fear, in the face of failure, is a cornerstone for weak cowards."

Zenen nodded, both in acquiescence and approval. Ken'Tekira was always Zenen's finest choice of student. After her Trial of Broken Glass, she had been assigned to a different master. Even as she stood up, her legs and palms dripping fresh blood, she beat her would-be master to death with a relentless barrage.

Such strength, determination and fury called for a greater teacher. Zenen'Rol was happy to oblige. Accepting her role as the student of the Emperor's Fist, he gave her the title of Dragon.

"You were not at the siege of the dark city." Zenen let his disdain become clear for her to see. "I was forced to send children to lead the assault. They might have succeeded if you were present."

"I am trying to locate the city of Gleaming Pearls."

"You stop for shining baubles, now?"

Ken scoffed. "Of course not. I am a conqueror and a war sorceress, first and always. But it was said to be close to the beach camp, and I have only seen ashes."

Zenen arched an eyebrow. "Then you already destroyed it."

Ken shook her head. "I never forget any village or city I burn down. I would have remembered something so grand. I studied my maps, at length. I know the capitol of Perahl'Sen is there. I sense deception, Master Fist."

Zenen nodded. "It is possible. The magi of the Order lean towards trickery and deceit. But it is an enemy alone and cut off. If they are there, they cannot move with us so close. I want you to leave that city be, for now."

Ken'Tekira stopped, turning to look with question at Zenen. "You wish me present to crush this defense Malkanor is presenting."

"Earlier this evening, I was forced to watch three hundred Ka'Rak and ten Havoc Elite getting decimated. They were wiped out by a lone fire sorceress and twenty battered men. Imagine my disgust as I watched our forces charge blind into a bottleneck. What Elite would have given such stupid orders?" As Zenen spoke, his fury sparks grew more frenzied, and Ken was forced to take a step back with wide eyes.

"Did we gain anything for it?" Ken'Tekira's voice sounded with a faint twinge of fearful hesitation which only made Zenen angrier.

"The village still stands, no Stratians were killed, and its people fled to safety. The reputation of our guilds will be severely questioned when word reaches the motherland."

Zenen'Rol was about to launch into a raging tirade when a Ka'Rak messenger arrived, panting as he halted from a full sprint.

"Lord Master Fist." The Ka'Rak knelt with his head lowered.

"Speak quick and careful, Ka'Rak Runner. My mood is

deadly," Zenen advised.

"I was instructed by Sub-General, Ma'Takal, to bring you to a farmstead, one mile north."

Zenen ground his teeth in anger. "Why is any farmstead still standing, here? Have you all become fools since we arrived in Stratia? Does the air create stupidity in all of you?"

The messenger kept his head lowered, seeming to understand that signs of weakness would end his life as he spoke. "The Sub-General understands the terms of engagement in Stratia, Lord Master Fist. He only conveyed that you are requested; and should see for yourself."

"You tread dangerous ground, Ka'Rak," Ken'Tekira warned. "Waste the Master Fist's time, and I will kill you, myself."

Zenen'Rol watched as the runner trembled ever so slightly. He knew it had nothing to do with Ken's threat. "If I may speak, boldly, I don't believe the Sub-General is wrong about this."

The crimson electricity that writhed around Zenen'Rol disappeared as his curiosity took over. "A mile north?"

"Yes, Lord."

Zenen'Rol did not waste his time with a night stroll. He cleared and calmed his mind, allowing an easy slip into a Meld Walk. The world blurred, for a brief instant, before he halted on a dusty rise of scrub and crab grass.

-23-

Zenen looked down the slope and realized calling the place a farmstead was generous. There were a few malnourished animals, grazing with abandon. They fed among crude squares filled with more patches of weeds than actual crops.

There were two adobe structures with worn and rotted redwood rooftops. One was an obvious choice for the animals to take shelter. Neither had shuttered or paned windows to keep out the wind and weather.

Zenen snorted with disgust at the sight of the negligence. He heard these Vodessians were more slothful than the normal Stratian. Not even drunken farmers in the mother land would have allowed this.

The Sub-General and a half squadron of Ka'Rak moved into place behind Zenen. The officer quickly read and identified Zenen's expression.

"Look closer before you claim my head, My Lord," the Sub-General urged.

Zenen sighed in frustration and narrowed his gaze for a better view.

What Zenen saw was almost enough to make him queasy. It certainly sent a chill through his skin.

Among the farming plots, he vaguely discerned the details of Ka'Rak armor and Havoc Guild Raiment. There were almost as many pieces of armor and clothing as there were torn and bloody appendages. Arms and legs lay in pools of blood. The pigs and sheep were so famished that they gorged themselves on human hearts and entrails, biting and crunching through the flesh and bone of torsos. Their mouths and snouts were smeared with blood, dripping chunks of human flesh.

Blood spots splattered the tan adobe walls. The front door hung at an odd angle on one bent hinge.

"Where is General Mez'Rahan?" Zenen demanded, shouting. "Why does a priority come from less than him?"

"He accompanied twenty Havoc Elite to the farmstead." Ma'Katal knelt and lowered his head. "There were screams from within the house, shortly after. No one returned."

"You know why we journeyed to Stratia, Sub-General. This is the sort of thing we burn to ashes, first. Yet, you call me as if there is some debate to it."

"Our torches fail us, and magic is swallowed up in dark holes in the air."

Zenen'Rol mulled the information over a moment. Everything about this was unnerving. He felt an urgent sense of warning. This farm was an icon of everything he had come to burn away, and yet it was different. It appeared to be the kind of slaughter and bloodshed he read about, regarding the Void Hands. But if it were them, they would not just enclose themselves.

His dark eyes narrowed. "Very well. I will see to this personally, and alone. If I discover that incompetence is at fault, here, I will claim each life that has failed me."

Zenen descended the slope as scrub brush crunched beneath his boots. The cicadas and night birds were absent, leaving only a weighted silence. There was no wind, and Zenen thought that was just as well. It would have only caused a downwind for the stench of animal dung and rotting human carnage.

Zenen drew closer to the farm stead. He saw the animals with better clarity as they raised their heads from the bloody grazing. There seemed to be hungry anticipation in their dark, glazed eyes. Did this diseased livestock look at him like he would be their next meal?

'Go on in,' Zenen read in their eyes. *'Challenge and be ripped apart. We hunger for fresh foolish meat.'*

Without a word, Zenen gathered the Endless Current and shaped the Blood Roses. The red tinted vines burst out of the ground, seeking, and coiling around the pigs and sheep. The vines tightened and twisted as they screeched and bleated into the night. The vines enlarged, tearing the animals apart in bursts of blood and bits.

Zenen saw the flickering glow of faint candlelight reaching out from the darkness of the crude house. He stepped to the front door and kicked it off its remaining hinge, in disgust. The door shattered into splinters against a wall in a small den. It was filled with broken furniture and ripped apart corpses from his army. Some were cut to pieces while others held deep gnawing and bite marks. Flies buzzed in the faint light of the den, frenzied by the stench of excrement, and rotting meat. The air was uncomfortable and muggy.

Zenen narrowed his eyes in the dim gloom. The adobe walls were vandalized with patterns and designs in blood, rather than the expected smears and splatters. There was something chilling about the pictographs and strange writing. It was unlike anything recorded in ancient lore, yet something about it filled him with dread and recognition.

The flickering orange candle glow spilled in from an adjacent room. From inside there came the sounds of clattering forks, and knives against plates. He filled every iota of his body with poised Endless Current.

At a small dining table, Zenen saw a child, a sandy blonde girl. Her stick thin shape was seated with her back to him. She held a knife and fork without regard for him.

The girl paused, placing the eating utensils on the table before putting her hands together.

"Great Mother, aid us, your children and flesh, that we may cleanse the filthy growth from your perfection." At this point in the prayer, the girl's voice began to change. It was far too deep and harsh to belong to any child or human. "Revel in their geysers of blood, in the screams of their crushed souls, as we seek to return all to blissful stillness."

When the girl picked up the knife and fork, Zenen noticed they were dripping with blood. Zenen circled the table in slow guarded steps, never turning his back to the little girl, as he stepped into the revealing glow of the candle flame. Now, he could see her face.

"Human flesh that has not yet been condemned is a rare delicacy, where I'm from," the girl informed around a mouthful, her voice cheerful.

Zenen'Rol looked at the plate before the little girl and felt his bowels twist in revulsion.

There was part of a burned rib cage, a blood-soaked human heart, and a tiny pile of eyeballs set to resemble grapes or vegetables. It was a macabre parody of a human supper. It was a profanity beyond anything Zenen ever encountered before.

The little girl's chin dripped with a thick stream of blood. Her fork stabbed another eyeball. She ate it, hungrily.

"Soul fruit is such a treat, a worthy delicious dessert," the girl admired in her human voice.

The girl looked up at Zenen'Rol. As he saw her eyes, he felt his inner chill deepen. The whites of the girl's eyes were washed over in blood red, surrounding fathomless black pupils. The skin of her face was mottled, cracked, and covered with boils and oozing sores.

The cases of demon infestation and possession were well known in the Crimson Empire. Zenen'Rol and the Purifier's Guild tended to deal with these instances with swift brutality. They would suffer no demonic presence, long, and offer no mercy.

But Stratia was different. They were ignorant of history, even as they birthed and raised the Void Hands. This demonic habitation persisted for far longer than Zenen ever would have allowed.

"But then, we wouldn't have this delightful conversation, Zenen'Rol, Master Fist." The demon girl read his thoughts and giggled with impish delight.

"Your time here is an afront," Zenen spat.

The girl's brow furrowed, and she wagged her bloody fork at him. "We tend to say the very same about you humans." She continued to chew and swallow the eye with a satisfied gulp. "Do you know when the child surrendered her soul to the Great Mother? It was an exquisite moment; something you humans would have called 'heart-breaking' or something."

The child paused, putting down her knife and fork while grinning with bloody teeth. "I took over her little body and she struggled and fought to take it back. You humans always do. But she was just a little child, and I have eons of experience in breaking souls. I made her watch as she ripped out her father's entrails. She watched while her hands pulled her mother's heart from her chest. She fell into the perfect nothingness of the Great Mother before I could finish cutting out her brother's brains with a rusted bread knife."

"Do all demons talk too much when they are in our world too long?"

"Your world?!" The demon child roared in a voice that shook the walls. She burst upward, floating well above the tabletop. Her eyes blazed with unholy red fire. "We are the Children of Nothing! Thou art but the fungus and feces that creation did hurl upon the flesh of perfection. She was first, always, and forever. And what art thou? A reeking blight, a stench that Great Mother can never be rid of. We are the will of the true beginning and the absolute end. We are an extension of she who is too perfect and beautiful to be stained by thee."

It was an act of will for Zenen'Rol to remain upright and unflinching. He felt tremors of fear settle deep into his chest and bowels. This cold fear was new and alien to him, but he would not disgrace himself by cowering before his enemy, now.

The little girl settled back into her chair, picking up her knife and fork to saw away at a bit of cooked muscle on the ribs.

Zenen felt this was his time to press forward for answers.

"You've been expecting me."

"What makes you believe that?" The girl reverted to her child speech and voice as she looked at her dinner.

"For one thing, I am still alive."

The girl shrugged. "Perhaps you are simply too strong for me to kill."

Zenen shook his head. "I do not think so. You have met my Havoc Elites magic with those infamous black holes your 'disciples' were so fond of."

The girl giggled. "The disciples are such a delight. They always elevate everything we teach them."

Zenen ignored the complement directed at history's most genocidal nightmares. "My magic met no resistance. Even now, I am filled with enough Endless Current to level a quarter of a city."

"Only a quarter? Tsk, tsk, tsk." The demon wagged her fork at him, again. "I'm afraid you're woefully lacking for your task, Master Fist."

Zenen pressed on. "I'm alive when so many of my Ka'Rak and Havoc Elite are not. You could have ripped me to shreds."

"Thou hath misunderstood mine meaning." The demon smiled as its old voice and speech returned. "Thine power is enough to contend with me, a while, mayhap to triumph. I hath come to grant thee a message. Thou wilt, inevitably, burn this place and prey to ashes when I am done. With mine words, thou wilt feel no victory gained, this eve."

"Thou hunt the Disciples of the Great Mother. They will certainly find thee, as certainly as thou wilt never find them. Know that thine powers, thine men, and thine 'secrets' shall not avail thee. Thou wilt come, face to face, with Crayaht'En. Thou wilt be among the first, and thou shall find thy powers far too weak."

"Why tell me this?" Zenen asked.

The child picked up the blood-soaked heart and bit deep, chewing thoughtfully. "This captain is completely damned. What did you allow him to do?" The child mocked a gasp. "Rapist..." she mulled over the flavor. "Oh, he did take his time about it. Some were courtesans of your emperor. You did not look in every home you burned, did you? He had plenty of time for the 'filthy Stratians'. And a thief and murderer?! How did you not see his growing wealth, or the missing bodies in the imperial court?" The girl shrugged. "You really should thank me. He spends a great deal of time in all three kingdoms, now. He burns, he is maimed, and he is hunted in Sol Fierest. It is rare to earn all three, but the heart never lies. I can taste his eternity, like dirt and ashes despoiling good meat."

"You have not answered my question, Child of Nothing." Zenen pushed with equal hesitation and impatience.

The girl's bloody red eyes widened. "See? Is it so difficult to use manners at this juncture? I expect no less from the Crimson Empire. You face your fears, never hiding from the truth, unlike Stratia."

The girl paused to giggle. "Entertainment, Master Fist. All the Children of Nothing desire to be as close as possible to what is to come. It may be the most wonderful play in the history of the stars. I could not help but come close enough to the stage to poke the King's Fool, no matter what may come of it."

Zenen's brow furrowed deeper. "But you know I will kill

you and burn this all to ash."

The girl shrieked with cackles of laughter. "Zenen'Rol, if I feared death, would I take hold of such a fragile vessel? You will burn this body, and I will return to hell to laugh about your fate with my brothers and sisters."

In an unnerving quick instant, the child's face became serious and bleak. "The part your histories never recorded is that Stratia never located the Order of the Void Triangle. They revealed themselves to the bickering Mage Clans, issuing a subtle ultimatum, months before they struck from the darkness. The point being, of course, that the disciples will never be found until they wish to be. By the Great Mother, you do not even know how they remained hidden for two thousand years, only to surface now."

"So, what of it, child?" Zenen spat. "Do you propose we pack up and go home? We just wait for the Void Hands to stroll up to the Crimson Throne?"

The girl's inhuman peals of laughter made Zenen's ears ring. "Great Mother, no fool! You wouldn't come back to an empire if you did? My brothers and sisters would be too disappointed. They would riot for it. This way, at least it stands a bit longer; as your reward, I say."

Zenen's look of confusion was plain, and the little girl answered before he could speak. "Send your Scrying Spheres to the motherland, Zenen'Rol. Some of my brothers and sisters revel early. The farms are discovering how much they love fire."

"Enough of this, demon!" Zenen'Rol clenched his fists. The walls trembled as coils of fury lightning licked his arms. "I'll play no more with your banter. You say I can kill and burn you, and I shall. You can tell your fellows that the Crimson Empire is here to burn away your influence from the living world."

Zenen'Rol reined in his disgust and revulsion, projecting a wave of force at the demon's neck. There was a loud, sickening crunch as every bone shattered from the base of her neck to the middle of her back. The girl's head slumped at an awkward angle before she fell sideways from her chair.

Zenen'Rol stormed out of the home and spell-shaped a huge sphere of imperial fire. It hovered in the sky, a moment, before it fell and slammed through the red roof top, incinerating the macabre scene. It was dirty work to kill a child. There was no honor, only shame to be found in it. But the little girl demonstrated the need for it in these foreign lands.

A demonic sickness spread throughout Stratia, and its infection could claim the entire world. It was better to amputate, and remove the disease, while there was still time.

Zenen inhaled the thick cloud of smoke and felt the heat of the fire on his back. A long shadow climbed the slope ahead of him, cast by the glow of the inferno behind him.

He thought about the demon's words. Much of it was the same, tired doomsday rhetoric every demon spouted before they were cast out. Some of it troubled him, though. Was he so focused on his mission that he failed to notice a change in his homeland?

And how did the demon know about 'the secret'? Zenen was one of few magi, in the entire Stratian conquest, to know about it. Many magi who were believed to be a risk of speaking about it already had their throats cut.

Zenen would have to send a Scrying Sphere into the east to verify the demon's claims.

Ken'Tekira caught up to Zenen'Rol as he ascended the summit of the rise.

"What comes next, Master Fist?"

"You will take as many Ka'Rak and Elite as you need, and you will crush down on Malkanor. Send a force to that stinking bog in Nerinmor, also. That fortress has stood for too long, already. They have no magi there, so send a small number of Elite to help make quick work of it. Finish it with haste."

"What will you do?"

Zenen was silent a moment as he reflected on the demon's words.

"I must return to the beach camp. I need to look in on something...troubling."

Zenen's irritation returned as his dark gaze snapped up to his Dragon. "When I am done, I will take a detachment to the Citadel. Leave me with three hundred Elite. Be mindful of who you allow to remain with me. The Order has, as I expected, broken with the agreement with our emperor. We are free to remove even their Stratian taint."

Zenen'Rol was about to leave his orders at that, but then he remembered the burning farm stead.

"Spread the word to our forces: the next time they see a place like this, they are not to approach. They are to send for twenty Elite, who are to destroy such a place from no less than three hundred yards."

"All is understood, and shall be done, Master Fist." Ken'Tekira bowed low before departing.

-24-

Martenen Delak stood at an east facing window in his wide bedchamber. It wasn't the quarters of the Grand Illumination, as he thought they should be, but they did afford a wondrous view of the Maelstrom and the bleak remains of Katahn. He Ignored the comfort of his bed, with its down mattress, and obsidian stone frame. He found no solace in the round smooth sand garden that occupied a portion of his room. He could not lose himself in the sparkling luster of the collection of quartz that decorated his shelves.

Martenen stared, restless and angry, out into the abyss of night, while they rest of the Order slept in peace.

In the past week many of the Solas challenged the limits of their new tenuous freedom from the Rods of Binding. Now any order he gave them was answered with a Contest of the Magus.

The barbaric custom resurfaced four years ago, as Rylin and Ishell fought over some trivial matter. Now, Martenen could not ask a Solas to so much as look left without being issued a formal challenge. Today alone, Martenen was fatigued by a Contest of Enduring Levitation, Haste Polymancy, and three occasions of Reflexive Elemental Defense.

What was worse? His two envoys to the emperor had not yet returned. It was only a day past due, but Martenen didn't know how many battles the Renegades rushed into during that time. Word of dozens of conflicts could have reached the emperor by now, and the hostilities could be fully renewed.

Martenen did not know these things for certain, and that vexed him to no end. If the empire was going to include the Order's destruction in the conquest, he could prepare for it if he only knew. He could act fast if there was still time to negotiate. Not knowing left him at a point of inaction that made him restless.

So, Martenen stood at his window in a flannel bed robe, allowing his bare feet to absorb the cold sensation of white marble against his skin. All the while his scowl found new limits.

Somewhere in the ruins of Katahn, Martenen was tricked by the sight of tiny blue flashes of light. He didn't know what to make of that. He never studied the barrier around Katahn and knew as much about the Spirit Arts as any Ard Solas. This was not the first time he saw the lantern flickers of light, though. They did vary in size and color, from time to time. Sometimes they reached a level of brilliance to fill his bed chamber.

Martenen shrugged. While he remembered little of his Spirit Sorcery training, he wagered the lights were a side effect of the barrier. The alternative was to admit to Light Barahn's disturbing delusions that sick fires destroyed Katahn, and that otherworldly forces were at work.

Martenen came so close to dismissing the drunken Pyromaster's claims, months ago. That was just as Rylin went and dug up the hillside in the middle of the night and found that strange claw. The stupid boy brought it to other Geomancers, and Martenen knew how that went awry. The boy offered a suggestion, and the fools latched on without proper study, investigation, and discussion.

There was no way the stone held a demon claw. It might be a leftover magical creation, or the last piece of an extinct species. But demons and Void Hands were nothing more than foolish stories told around the fires at night.

'Is that what you believe?' The voice that challenged

Martenen chilled his skin with its low, rasping whisper. The sudden intrusion was enough to catch his breath in his throat while he leaped up.

"Who is there?" Martenen whirled this way and that, his eyes dark and narrow as he scanned the bedchamber. He found no one.

'Do you know that light should not be able to escape a Spirit Barrier?' The voice sounded so close, within two feet. Martenen saw nothing, and only felt cold and watched.

Why did Martenen feel so cold? The breeze that came through the window was cool and scented with the promise of rain that would come by dawn. It was not that cold.

'All the wrong questions come to your mind. Still, you fail to answer any of mine. You ponder nothing of true importance, yet you believe the entire Order should fall over themselves to obey your every whim. Your entire world crumbles, and you barter away everything of meaning to preserve your own skin.'

"You are an intruder. Show yourself, now!" Martenen pushed anger into his voice, even as fear settled deep into his middle.

'Yelisian, Matisia, and so many skilled Ard Solas gave their lives to create the barrier. Many believe Void Hand Magic is imprisoned within, yet, like Lycendrik, you do not.' The voice observed as it read and scrutinized Martenen's thoughts and past actions with ease. 'So, if you believe Kasarins to be imprisoned within the barrier, why do you broker deals with the enemy of the Order?'

"Who says I believe it was the empire?" Martenen could not believe he was answering, allowing himself to be caught in a game that placed him on trial.

'There are no other culprits, Martenen. Even you cannot be so foolish as to believe they gave their lives and spirits for nothing.'

Martenen felt sweat bead with cold droplets on his forehead, as what he assumed to be an intrusion mutated into an interrogation. "So, what of it? I made a deal with those I believe may have destroyed Katahn. Where do you go with any of this?"

'I go to justice first, coward. You saw what happened to fellows of your Order, and in fear, you bartered away everything they held dear.' The cold accusations of the voice began to circle him, judging. *'They died with honor, and you disregard their sacrifice. You were never fit to lead the Order. Your Logic breeds self-preserving fear in you, causing you to abandon your principles at the first sign of distress. Kelteseus saw and read this weakness in you, and that is why you were never chosen.'*

Martenen felt naked and vulnerable under the press of judgment. He decided it was time to lash out with accusations of his own.

"And what of you, phantom intruder?" Martenen shouted with spittle spraying on his beard. "You enter my bedchamber with the stealth of a thief. You judge me, though I do not see the eyes of my accuser. You deem me to be a coward, but you speak from the safety of concealment."

Martenen was answered with a long silence. He hoped he was alone again, but he knew that hope did not exist. His skin crawled with cold and gooseflesh that made circling passes around his body. This was not over.

Lightning flashed in the black night sky. There was something about the storm and the intrusion that tickled and tugged at the Geomancer's mind with urgency.

The presence halted in front of Martenen. A dark, transparent, human shape materialized while still blending into the night shadows. Its broad male shoulders turned as it faced him. It stood only a little shorter than Martenen, and its dark shape drank the warmth of the air like a vortex. It radiated waves of forceful cold that permeated Martenen's bones and stung his skin.

A pair of fiery red eyes flared in its head. Martenen felt the weight of its hatred for him crushing down on him. He felt small and inconsequential under that hateful glare. His power seemed insignificant in its presence. The only reason it deigned to be near him, was to judge and sentence him. Martenen was too unimportant to hold a voice about it.

'All your actions were committed to avoid pain and death. You would have thrown every man, woman, and child in front of you to avoid that fate.' The eyes of the shadow flared with every word, but no mouth moved in the shadow. *'Your actions will destroy Stratia. All your brothers and sisters will be in chains, forever. In decades to come, the empire will bestow the title 'Order of Cringing Dogs and Swine'. All the honor will be gone. To avoid this fate, I must force upon you the fate you hide from.'*

There was no time to gather the Endless Current. Martenen quickly attuned himself to the stone of the walls and floor around him. Several man-sized spikes of stone pulled free from the surfaces. They floated in the air in front of him.

Before Martenen could launch the skewering volley, the shadow made a twisting gesture with its wrist. A pitch-black hole opened in the air between the Shadow and Martenen. The hole pulled debris, stones from his shelves, and his entire assault into its fathomless depths.

When Martenen's attack vanished, the Shadow flicked its wrist again and the vortex disappeared.

'I did not come to tarry in your childish games. At this moment, the invaders soon gather to attack the Citadel. If you live, the Lights in these walls will be gathered, forced on their knees, and executed. They will not resist, and they will not fight.' The foretelling was cold, and dispassionate. *'Before the Renegades departed, all of you would have been dishonored and enslaved. Another more favorable option can only occur if you die, now. Accept it. Perhaps end your own life, and you can spare yourself great pain.'*

"I choose to end you, instead!" Martenen growled as he clenched a fist in front of himself. In response, four walls of marble formed up around the shadow and slammed together to crush it. The thunderous explosion left Martenen's ears ringing.

The room was filled with settling dust clouds that made him cough. The floor and walls were gouged deep with the rending sorceries he employed.

Before Martenen could examine the aftermath at length, every inch of his body stiffened with sharp cramping aches. His arms and legs locked and seized up into rigid paralysis.

The Shadow stepped free of the dust cloud. Its glowing red eyes moved within inches of Martenen's face.

'That choice was never a part of the selection,' the raspy voice whispered.

Martenen wriggled and thrashed against the sorcery bind, but his muscles would not budge. He pushed his will into the stone around him, trying to break free or strike at the Shadow. His will dissolved into nothing as soon as he projected it. He panicked. The calm was beyond him. He could not gather the Endless Current while the aches and agony flooded his awareness. He was helpless.

The Shadow raised one hand, pointing at Martenen. Lightning and thunder became a fervent barrage in the night. The pain in his body doubled. Everything below his neck stretched with an intent bent on tearing itself apart.

Martenen looked down in horror at his right arm. His skin split, from shoulder to wrist, down to the bone. Blood spilled and seared against his exposed nerves. He attempted to scream, but his mouth and throat would not obey. As another split ripped open his left arm, Martenen realized his body did intend to rip itself to pieces. The deep gouges became more rapid and frequent, choosing random locations on his body. His arms and legs were bloody bones when the rips began to tear into his torso. His abdomen and chest split, spilling their contents free. His robe was a bloody mass of cloth. It slid down his shoulders, searing whatever nerve endings remained.

Martenen was horrified to find himself still alive. His head was intact, unmarked but smeared with blood.

Martenen listened, in revulsion and horror, as his organs fell to the waiting heap of shredded skin and muscles with wet splashes. He begged for the pain to claim his conscious mind as his wet bones gave out beneath him. His head landed in the pile of his bloody remains. Why would his mind not shut down and let him die in peace?

Martenen realized the truth of his predicament far too late. He was not among the living, anymore. He was not allowed to take his place among the dead, either. This was Void Hand Magic. It was dark and cruel, and forbidden by just decree.

The final truth was that Yelisian and the Council died trying to prevent this magic from moving beyond Katahn. They failed.

Martenen's head gurgled and his chin and jaw ground against the wet heap on the floor. The pain continued, relentless. He was useless within his own mutilated remains. His eyes shifted about. His throat sounded a high-pitched rasping parody of breathing. He felt hundreds of pains of a body that was no longer attached to his head. Madness began a slow insidious invasion on the remains of his mind.

'*I am Crayaht'En,*' The Shadow spoke as it turned and walked away. '*I have passed the sentence of the Prison of Flesh. Justice is satisfied.*'

-25-

If Ishell's right arm was not covered in thick glossy obsidian, she would have a deep gouge in her arm, and the tip of a long spear through her heart. The spear dancer was dressed in the Havoc Guild vest coat and pants. He was an older man, favoring an unusual blend of empowered speed and conjured weapons. It was a noticed contrast to the common volleys from the fireball throwers, and vine conjurers of his younger peers.

Ishell's opening came much later than she hoped. The Havoc Sorcerer lunged forward with a powerful thrust of a serrated long spear. Ishell shaped the Endless Current in little more than a breath, causing a strong gust of force to slam into the sorcerer's backside. He stumbled forward. Ishell parried the spear off her obsidian gauntlet. She mouthed another incantation and brought her left hand up to his face. A wide stream of fire burst from her palm and incinerated the spear dancer's head until only a black charred skull remained.

He fell dead before he could scream.

Killing was nothing new to Ishell, now. Her first victim was a younger sorceress she left entombed alive in a mountainside close to the border of Teril. With the memory of the villager still vivid and clear in her mind, she refused to allow her hands to remain clean in this war. The simple act of avoiding bloodshed was a filthy transgression against her own people. They did not escape unscathed. Why should she?

The ground continued to rumble in chaotic fits. Giant

boulders, and massive ballistae bolts slammed into the homes, reducing everything to rubble and craters. Mothers, fathers, and children screamed in terror, as they were led to safety. Their guides were children, themselves. Most of the Candles were no older than twelve. The villagers only followed when they noticed the brown robes and calm demeanor.

Torches and Legionnaires worked in groups to repel the Kasarin soldiers and hold back the siege rounds from striking the people. Powerful gales of wind halted the devastating arcs while walls and spikes of stone met the rounds in air, causing dusty explosions.

Two Kasarin swordsmen charged at Ishell. The warm afternoon sun reflected in a blinding glare from the steel of their long swords. Ishell mouthed two more incantations. The power that she wielded began to itch inside her chest and bowels. It was a warning sign that she had to ignore. Her hands shot forward, flinging a spray of water that hummed and sparked with electricity. The two swordsmen ran into the spray before they could think better of it. They halted in their steps as the electricity coursed through their swords and the metal of their armor. They thrashed and convulsed. Their mouths foamed with white. Their eyes rolled and steamed before they fell.

Ishell stopped to thought project into the Endless Current.

'Light Borvis, those siege rounds are getting frightfully close. Tell me the villagers are almost out, or that you are close to driving a counter-offensive right into the wood hinges of their ballistae.'

Borvis answering thoughts were tense and defensive, as well as sarcastic.

'Why would I do that when I can entertain the ladies with wondrous displays of flowers?'

Kaysienn interrupted with an annoyed snort.

'He won't get anywhere, anytime soon, if you keep

shouting your thoughts loud enough for every magus to hear. Let him be, Light Ishell,' There was a pause in Kaysienn's thoughts before she continued with a hint of admiration. 'Light Borvis is busy transmuting shrubbery out of the heads of the hot-headed witches.'

Ishell didn't bother to point out the irony of Kaysienn calling anyone hot-headed. The images that were conjured by Kaysienn's description did cause her to shudder.

A towering wide wave of crimson fire barreled down the dirt street heading toward Ishell. Timbers and foundations, that remained, were obliterated into ash. The juggernaut fire magic cremated everything in its path.

Once more, Ishell calmed herself, stilling her mind as the Endless Current howled into her, searing against the inside of her body. She screamed as she held up both hands in front of her. The raw power was shaped and converted into an equally massive wall of freezing water. The barrier bent against the clash of red fire, buckling like hammered metal. The water did not give. The collision halted with both forces dissipated. The streets filled with an obscuring cloud of steam and mist.

'You could have saved a lot of effort if you had done that sooner,' Borvis sent his complaint.

Ishell mentally shrugged. 'They waited so long to use any of their trademark flames.' Ishell turned her attention to another location in the battlefield, trying to obfuscate her thoughts from Havoc Magi. 'Light Porra, tell me you nearly have all the villagers out of here. We could really use some Aeromancer and Geomancer magic on their siege weapons.'

The heavyset Hydromancer responded with a hint of irritation. 'Rushing us will not hasten the Meld Walks, Light Ishell. I am already under strain with so many fractured legs. You need not inhibit my concentration further.'

The Hydromancer was silent a moment, but Ishell felt the scrutiny of her probing magic. 'Do something about that wound to your left arm, Light Ishell. If you move around much more your veins will break, and you will bleed and fall.'

A silence filled the streets as the Kasarins tried to gain their bearings in the artificial mist. Ishell took the moment it afforded her to look down at her arm. A deep gash split the muscle of her upper arm, nearly to the bone. A wide stream of hot red ran down her arms and elbow to pool on the ground. The spear dancer seemed the most likely to be the cause, but Ishell knew the Kasarin swords came close to cutting her open on several instances.

Ishell looked up and around at the thick clouds of white vapors. She could make out the shapes of several of the heavy armored Kasarins probing ahead with the point of their swords. They moved slow and cautious. Their plumed helmets shifted as they sought their next victims.

Ishell could remain still and undetected from the soldiers until the steam cleared. If she healed herself now, the Havoc Magi would find her in the same breath. It was a risk Ishell would have to take. Ishell placed her hand over the long gash. As soon as the Endless Current flowed toward her, she felt the same happen for the Havoc Magi. Ishell quickly calmed herself beyond the gathering of Endless Current. She felt the air, allowing herself to sense each warble and eddy around her. She felt the quickening of vibrations in the hands of the Havoc Magi, before they held spheres of crimson fire. Ishell was far more subtle. She was already prepared with dozens of anvil sized spheres of water. The water balls remained hidden in the air high above their heads. She allowed the waters to fall and douse the spheres of fire, and their shapers, just before they could wind their arms to throw.

The attack was not as lethal as she would have preferred, but it was enough to break their concentration. With a moment taken from both the soldiers and the magi, Ishell finished shaping a healing spell on her arm. She watched as the Mend Shape knit and sealed all the severed muscle and skin.

A moment later, the clouds of vapor faded. Five crimson

soldiers dashed at Ishell. Their sprint was fluid, and their hands were at the ready on their weapon hilts. Ishell stumbled over a clumsy shaping of a blast of air. The conjured wind caught her attackers as her face came within an inch of the gleaming tip of a curved sword. The soldiers were hurled backwards off their feet.

When the Kasarin soldiers landed on their backsides, they were pinned down with a lethal volley of arrows. Not one projectile missed its mark. Several Phoenix Legion Archers stood with long bows far down the street. Ishell wished she had a moment to wave a hand in thanks.

The Endless Current began to shift and divide outside of the village. The Havoc Magi were focusing on something else. The shift allowed the Renegades a moment to breathe, outside of the siege weapons and soldiers, but Ishell knew it was only for a moment. There was little time to act. She needed to move and think faster. Where was Rylin's Displacement Cloaks when she needed them?

A violent surging wave of Endless Current began to swell and rush into the village. Ishell's eyes widened with alarm when she realized it was heading toward the Candle Geomancers that were defending the evacuation. Ishell didn't know who it was, but so much at once could be dangerous for any one of them.

It was too late to react. White light flared in the heart of the devastation, dimming the radiance of the noon sun. Ishell shielded her eyes, only an instant, before a powerful gale began to tow debris towards the south of the village. What few buildings remained were yanked into the inexorable force. It would have been a moment of opportunity if anyone could stand straight.

Then there was an ear-ringing thunderous boom. A blast of concussive force slammed into the ruins of the village. Soldiers and unprepared Lights were hurled off their feet, northward.

Borvis's voice was a cracked echo in Ishell's silent mind. 'If we act fast enough, we can get the rest of the people out of here in a blink.'

But the broken way Borvis sounded told Ishell that something bad happened. Something that would not allow such an action to occur. She knew what that something might be.

'What happened?' Ishell knew they lost someone to that explosion.

'Light Aerina dissolved into the Endless Current. She shaped too many defensive stone spheres at once.'

The silence that continued was a blessing for Ishell. She thought about Aerina. She did not know the girl well, but she had already proven to be a promising Geomancer.

Aerina possessed a decent amount of skill for an eight-year-old girl.

Ishell's fists tightened into trembling white knuckles as she fought back against the tears that threatened to overwhelm her. Not yet, but soon, she promised herself. She directed her heartache and weariness into anger. She changed the anger into precise concentration. There would be time for tears, later. She would allow herself that time, soon enough.

Ishell's thoughts projected with a tone of grim resolve, this time for all her fellows to hear. 'Change of plans, Light Borvis. I want every Polymancer and Geomancer to shield every Stratian within five miles of the village center. Everyone else is to bolster the energies of those shaping.'

Borvis sounded wary and suspicious as he answered. 'What will you do?'

'I am ending this, right now.'

Ishell shaped the Grasping Winds and began to rise off the ground. Her ascent was slow, at first. But she quickly began to climb dozens of feet into the air, as winds whipped around her. The Kasarins were quick to notice the anomaly, and their siege weapons began to seek her out. The massive rounds could not find their mark in her, as the winds shifted her to the left and right with the ease of a leaf.

The Havoc Magi tracked her flight, soon after. But their attempts to take her out of the sky were only elemental, and Ishell felt them even as they formed. So high above the ground, they could only answer with more of their trademark balls of flame, and it was as redundant as it was useless against Ishell. She doused each fire before it could spring to life.

With so much spell-shaping, Ishell knew she should be in danger of meeting Aerina's fate. Her will felt doubled in her angry determination. Children were dying to protect the helpless. She could not tolerate any more, this day.

Now, Ishell was far above the reach of the Kasarins. Trees and people, even the ruins, all seemed so small and irrelevant from her vantage. She pressed the force of the Grasping Winds around her head to give her more air before she could feel light-headed.

Tiny bubbles of brown began to boil up on the ground, throughout the village, like a series of blisters. The Stratians were safe. It was time to spell-shape before the Kasarins could devise some way to stop Ishell.

Ishell maintained a pressure to the Grasping Winds that allowed her to move on the air as though walking a solid road. Her arms and legs began a slow rhythm while she sung in a low voice filled with exotic incomprehensible words. As she danced and sang, she began to quicken her movements, and her voice began to rise in pitch, creating snapping syllables. Her hands clawed and raked the air, her legs arced in smooth sweeping kicks. An observer would call it a soldier's hand combat drill, and an exotic dance.

A magus would feel the building Endless Current. They would feel the spray of energies, or the whirling like waterfalls and the movements of clouds. A magus would know an elaborate spell-shape was at hand.

Some of ancient Evoker history, kept in the Citadel

library, dated as far back as the Dragon Tooth Clan. They were a clan dedicated to battle, profit, and superiority. They were as proud as they were fierce in battle. Nearly all of them were Evokers of legendary skill and power. None of them had achieved the third tier in evocation, but it was a common belief that they were only centuries away from achieving it.

Only bits and pieces of their lore survived for two thousand years. Some of their advanced spell-shapes were too complex and powerful for the Enlightened Sun. So, many of the books collected dust in the back of the library.

Until Ishell found them. She read deep and with fervor, spending many hours of many days lost in their ancient pages.

There was a spell-shape that always drew Ishell's attention. It was the creation of a famous sorceress named Kaeshin. The spell-shape was lengthy, exhausting, and completely overwhelming to its victims.

Ishell added one variation to Kaeshin's spell. The original spell called storm clouds closer. As Ishell continued to move, the Endless Current began to materialize into the clouds she needed. As she spun and whirled, tufts of white dark and gray began to hurl out from her arms and legs. The mists began to spread further and further away, filling the sky around her.

Ishell glanced down to see what the Havoc Guilds planned for their final assault. Dozens of siege weapons and thousands of soldiers began to appear. Meld Walks were completed by scores, as a crushing number of reinforcements arrived. If Ishell was not prepared to act now, the Kasarins would have obliterated the village and killed its inhabitants in minutes.

But everything came to a halt, below, as the storm clouds spread and filled the sky. Ishell's movements were a blur. Her voice climbed to a piercing shriek that reverberated against the horizon.

The spell-shape was named the Song of the Thunder Gods. Only three sorceresses ever mastered the use of the shape.

It was a spell that was, thus far, exclusive to women. The first was its creator, Kaeshin, the second was her student, Daeshriel Moarenroak, first queen of Malkanor. Ishell would be the third.

Temperatures and frictions were created in the clouds. The results were sparks of white light in the misty masses. The energy flashed, more and more, licking the makeshift clouds with eager anticipation.

Then it was instant pandemonium. Between the clouds and the village, the air was filled with thousands of raging towers of jagged electricity. Every exposed target on the ground was struck by wrathful lightning. Peel after peel of thunder shook the earth, accompanied by dying screams and shouts of panic. Catapults and ballistae were reduced to blackened slivers. Everything not covered in domes of earth was obliterated by the furious onslaught.

The Song of the Thunder Gods raged for a time Ishell could not measure. The relentless savagery the Kasarins set loose upon the defenseless people of Stratia, the sacrificed lives of children, all were revisited on the invaders with a determined fury of instantaneous massacre. This storm was here to put an end to this force. It would not abate until every Kasarin within five miles floated as ashes in the wind.

All the while, Ishell pushed more and more of her will into the spell. Her desire to protect her people and her fellow Lights became an all-consuming drive, feeding her will.

Traces of the Kasarins became non-existent in the blackened earth. Ishell relaxed her will, releasing the Endless Current that powered it. The clouds began to fade and the Grasping Winds slowly lowered Ishell back to the ground. The earth was pock-marked with deep, black craters where the lightning rained down. Most of the bodies were obliterated by the massive bolts, overwhelmed by enough electricity to burst. Other bodies were cooked black, their armor and flesh were melted and fused together. Ishell's hair began to rise as she came close to the ground. There was a sharp smell in the air that mingled with the stench of burned bodies. There was an ever-present hissing and hum that sounded in the otherwise silence.

The domes of earth crumbled away, and the occupants raised their heads and looked about with wide eyes. The village was gone, but no complaint was made as the Kasarins were also absent.

Borvis was the first to approach Ishell. His narrow, bony face was dirty, but streaked with dried tears from only a moment ago. He wrapped his arms around her, pulling her close.

The Phoenix Legions and the Renegades continued a swift, uninterrupted evacuation. They would take the refugees to Pahlinsor.

Ishell was grateful for Borvis just then. She felt emotionally exhausted and raw. She felt cracks in her resolve, and a weakness in her knees. She leaned into his chest and finally allowed her tears to run free.

Aerina was not even the first child they lost in this war. Children were pouring energies beyond their limit to match the Kasarin brutality. They were not trying to be heroes. They were not seeking glory. They were trying to protect the people with every ounce of their being.

Aerina was the twenty-first child dissolved into the Endless Current in this war. Ishell promised herself she would not allow any of them to be forgotten.

-26-

Rylin and Aemreen were both exhausted from their labors in the Healer's Triage. They sat on a small patch of soft grass and violet wildflowers, on the bank of a calm, large pond. Towering pines and oaks circled in a protective thick ring, before the woods far south of the Outer City.

They were both dirty, covered in sticky, dry sweat, blood stains, and reeking of sharp medicine smells. But neither of them held the energy to care about that. Aemreen leaned her head against Rylin's shoulder and held his hand in her lap. Rylin lost himself, burying his nose in her long, soft, brown hair.

Aemreen wore a short-sleeved red blouse (which masked the blood stains better) and a long, black, loose skirt. It was a practical choice, and far better than Rylin having to find a river for his own single outfit, every night. The dirt and wear he acquired made him miss Current Cleansing.

"That was a well-placed wrap to the Corporal's chest," Aemreen complimented in the dim twilight.

Rylin listened to the nightbirds and kissed the top of her head. "Thank you, love. But he would have bled too fast without your salve. It looked combined, but local. Where did you learn to make it?"

Aemreen squeezed his hand. "The base is from the book of the Bren Sisterhood. But many of the herbs do not grow near enough. An herbalist from central Pahlinsor had to take a week of study with me to find the substitutes we needed."

Rylin kissed her head, once again, but paused as remembering struck him. He withdrew from her for a moment, patting down his long coat and clothes. He hoped he didn't lose it, praying to the fates that it did not fall.

Aemreen turned to look at him with bewildered green eyes and a raised eyebrow.

Rylin breathed loud with relief when his fingers brushed the smooth hard surface.

"I meant to give this to you, sooner. It's why I was gone for so much longer before the attacks." Rylin extracted the gleaming green flask as liquid sloshed inside it.

Aemreen gasped, her eyes wide, as she accepted the flask with two reverent hands. A tear glistened at the corner of her eye, but she laughed. "It's so beautiful; but what is it, my love?"

"It's Mithridate, made from ingredients from their purest locations."

Aemreen covered her mouth in an expression of shock. "Rylin, that is sixty-five ingredients, and from every land on the face of Pravahs. Not to mention the delicate distilling process. And what is the container made from?"

Rylin smiled. "It's shaped from the same emerald as my staff. If my powers are restored, the emerald is young and vibrant enough for a Chronomantic Enchantment. I can cause the flask to be full whenever it empties."

Aemreen's eyes were lost in thought a moment before she shook her head. "I can't allow such a short step in my own training. I would rob myself of the chance for understanding."

Aemreen ducked into Rylin's sight, closer, before kissing his lips, deeply.

"When it becomes empty, I want you to fill it with me."

Rylin smiled and pulled her closer in his arms.

Aemreen rested her head against his chest but held up the flask for her own scrutiny.

"Emerald flask and staff, green coat…." Aemreen mulled it over, out loud.

Rylin understood the rest of the question before she could finish.

"The Temporal Current, and its energies, are green. When I use a green focus, much like Porra's flask of water, the Temporal Current gathers, and shapes faster, and with greater ease."

"So, then color may be relevant," Aemreen voiced before she smiled with mirth. "I allowed myself to believe magic was more colorful just to make displays for the rest of us."

"Some are just for color. Light Ishell tints her lightning to violet. But there are times when she does it to add a challenge to her training. It requires greater concentration to change the color of every bolt. But Light Kera changes the color of her own lightning to green, because she dilutes it with earth energy for more power."

It was a lot of mechanical talk, and Rylin was surprised that her interest did not falter for it. Her desire to learn as much as she could was one of the many things he loved about her.

Aemreen's forehead creased. "What about the Kasarins and their red magic?"

Rylin paused. It was unavoidable that talk of the Havoc Guilds would surface, even here, between them. Images of women and children with their heads severed in orchards and fields came to his mind, unbidden. Images of men, unaware in the woods, screaming and dying as red fire rain burned completely through, came next. The brutality and death were a haunting procession in the depths of his mind. But, as a reward for his vigil, Rylin was permitted greater insight to his enemies.

"There is something in their training, I don't know what it is. The Endless Current usually is best when a Magus is unclouded by thoughts and emotions. But their rage is, somehow, so natural to them, that it comes in a breath. It changes their magic. Their red fire is hotter than furnace flames. The raw Current and anger causes electric bursts from their bodies. All of it seeps into their vines."

"It seems like that is the bulk of their spell-shapes," Aemreen observed.

"It is all that comes easy for most of them. They battle in such fury that they must do what comes naturally for such clouded minds. Our anger does not afford creativity in battle."

Aemreen breathed a weary sigh. "They have to have some sort of limit with their devastation."

"It is also taxing on them. Fighting so angry is very draining. But that means their methods for training are more brutal so that they do not succumb to pain and fatigue, so easily. Fates," Rylin snorted, "they force new magi to crawl on broken glass for hours before they battle a master, simply to be accepted into the guild."

"That's horrible! How did you learn of this cruel tradition, love?"

"From the same merchants who helped me find what I needed."

Aemreen fell silent, leaning her head against him. Twilight faded, and a large full moon crested the east, above the tall trees. Evening birds fell into silence, and cicadas filled the void of their absence.

Rylin held Aemreen in silence, randomly kissing the top of her head. He was content in the quiet, content to abandon talk of the Empire. The days were long and merciless, filled with good people that starved, bled, and died right before their eyes. Stratia's populous was never massive. So, every loss was a deep wound.

"There are days, but for a moment, that it is all so much," Aemreen spoke without turning her gaze from the moonlit reflection on the still pond. "All the death, the fear, the pain from all the people. I can't free them of all of it. Those times, I simply want to run to you, and tell you to take us away from all of it."

Rylin nodded but remained silent, kissing her hair. It was a tempting wish: the easy way. He didn't hold all of his powers, so he couldn't stand for his people. He could not honor the memory of his Spark, the way he wished.

But both reasons were why he could not flee from this war, either. He could not agree with this option, but he doubted Aemreen felt differently than he did. It was just her need to voice her weary and breaking heart. She only needed Rylin to listen.

"First Maesellen, then Katahn, then Martenen, then the Kasarins. Do our obstacles ever grow as weary as we do?"

To that, at least Rylin could offer reassurance.

"We tire, but not alone, as they are. Even tonight, Light Porra, Light Merice, the healers and herbalists excuse us…"

Aemreen held up her hand. "Forcefully."

Rylin laughed and nodded. "…Yes, forcefully. Allowing us to gather strength to stand, again."

It was just after they bandaged the corporal. Something of their tiredness must have revealed itself, because Merice and Porra insisted they rest. They began pushing them out of the triage.

"These dangers, the Fates favor us by giving us only one at a time. They do not unite."

"But they do seek to drive us apart, forever," Aemreen observed, pointedly.

"Perhaps," Rylin acquiesced. "All but a devoted philosopher would go mad, pondering why."

"Are you one such scholar?" Aemreen teased.

Rylin laughed. "Fates, no. Human Intricacies are best known by healers who tend to human wounds."

Aemreen looked at Rylin with feigned accusation. "Do you

dare to taunt me?"

Rylin only laughed harder. "And provoke the most feared sword in all of Malkanor? Never. I must possess a sliver of wisdom, at least."

Aemreen laughed with Rylin. For that moment, under the bright moon in the cool darkness of a spring night, they were allowed to laugh, to love, and to put aside the anguish of war. Until midnight, when they returned to the Outer City for sleep, it was enough to restore their broken spirits.

Aemreen kissed Rylin's lips deep, one more time, before she left to sleep in her father's field command tent.

-27-

Maesellen Moarenroak stood at a high balcony, tapping her red-lacquered fingernails against the stone rail. Her deep red lips were pursed in a scowl as she watched with boredom and waited with impatience. A stick thin blonde Vodessian girl fanned the heat away while Maesellen's mind wandered.

Maesellen hated idle thinking. It was little more than an escape for the addle-brained. She steered her thoughts into a determined progress. Her first focus was the city she looked down upon, as much literally as figuratively.

"What collection of fools would build such a city as this?" Maesellen thought out loud.

The dainty servant woman did little more than blink. She possessed the wisdom to prevent words from escaping her open mouth. A dead or missing servant might be impossible to ignore, but Maesellen could make the girl's life miserable, regardless. The Queen of Malkanor could be counted on for creativity and resourcefulness.

Which Maesellen would need when the day came to claim Malkanor and rebuild it.

"Our defenses face east, toward Teril. The city is designed that way. What threat do they imagine would come from there? Stray flocks of sheep? Yet, the west of the city is wide open. The palace wall faces grass. Were Vodess not a haven for brains in a stupor, their marauders could seize the capitol before their next meal."

As Maesellen expected, the girl only managed to look away, nervously. No tightened grip on the peacock-feathered fan, no sign of intelligence at all. She showed no hint of irritation that she, and her homeland, were insulted.

Maesellen turned her cold blue eyes back to the city. She watched the preparations at the edge of the merchant quarters. She squinted against the bright noon glare. She raised a shielding hand above her thin eyebrows, below the beginning of her long black hair. The pressure against her tightly woven braid shifted her diamond crown.

Tents were erected in the mile-long space between the edge of the merchant section and the start of the Outer City. These provided a triage for the wounded legionnaires. To Maesellen's disgust, refugees were treated in these shelters. The malnourished were fed, the injured were healed, the people were allocated temporary residence, and Malkanor's resources were wasted. As the only nation that gave the Kasarin's any lasting resistance, it would have been wiser to gather their strength and coordinate a precise counter-offensive.

A headache boiled in Maesellen's head as she watched resources squandered on rescuing one backwater peasant collective after another. If the people truly wished to survive, they would have pooled their newly gained finances into establishing their own defenses.

That was the problem with these benefactor bleeding-heart altruists. No new and noteworthy strengths were revealed, and would-be heroes were siphoned of their paragon attributes.

The truth and result of this was evident in the weighted difference between the Havoc Guilds and the Enlightened Sun. The Havoc Guilds would take their members, at will, from the people. They would cultivate what they could use and discard the rest. Their ideals were second only to imperial law. They could direct their ambitions and rise to lofty positions of prominence. They allowed other directives to be carried out by less combative guilds, like the Purifier's Guild, or the Enchanter's Guild. Maesellen respected them for their drive and sheer focus, even if she feared being ripped to shreds by them.

In contradiction to these refugee sections, Maesellen was pleased to see the long, rigid lines of patrolling Phoenix Legions. Mejin's thugs fought a grueling series of hit and run assaults that left the legions weary. They were careful not to allude to her involvement, but the toll it took on the people should have caused a mistrust from the masses. In time, Maesellen's hidden forces could have rushed to Malkanor's rescue, staged a fake war against the Vodessian marauders in her employ, and cast out Maloric, Marcelles, and any other fool in her way.

Now, the presence of the Legions was a boon. Maesellen could not deploy her own forces without exposing herself. Her senses of self-preservation and her ambitions were at conflict for it, but there was no help for that.

There was a small gathering of people outside the city. They would vanish and reappear in different locations. Her hands tightened to white knuckles against the black granite.

The Renegades, as they called themselves, continued to train in skills they thought would help against the Kasarins. The Renegades were the only reason the legions were renewed and refreshed enough to fight. The coordination between sorcery and soldier proved to be a great advantage. But these were the same magi who were her greatest obstacle, even without the approval of their superiors. If anything, the division in the Enlightened Sun could doom everyone in Stratia that much sooner. Maesellen certainly couldn't marshal her own forces while they remained. She would be judged and imprisoned before her next breath.

And who else could last longer than a blink against the Havoc Guilds? The Renegades were motley, mostly children, barely organized, and far too few; but the fates favored them with moments of blind luck, time and again. Only last week they returned from a concentrated attack against a village far to the southeast. Somehow, the combined efforts devastated the entire Crimson Detachment.

"Favor us with your contemplations," intruded a female voice. The cheerful invitation drew a startled cry from the Vodessian girl. She all but jumped out of her skin as two girls of the same age appeared from thin air, to either side.

Maesellen smiled, an uncommon expression, somewhat forced. She smoothed her thick, red, silk gown as she turned. She already waited an hour in the miserable heat of the late spring. She felt sweat trickle in the folds of her gown, despite the constant fanning. But this was a moment she awaited eagerly.

"Your majesty," greeted the taller dark-haired girl. The two curtsied in unison, inclining their heads in a low nod. "It is an honor to meet you. I have long waited for a chance to converse with you."

Maesellen's surprise was evident in her arched eyebrow.

"Leave us." Maesellen dismissed the serving girl. When the Vodessian was well outside of hearing she looked her guests over.

They wore the gray robes that were donned by no less than the intermediate magi of the Order. Their faces and figures reflected women of the same age. But that was where the similarities ended. Maesellen felt an automatic liking for the dark-haired girl. Her clothes were plain, and she didn't adorn herself in any way. But there was a sense of crisp focus and self-control. There was kinship and connection to be found in her hard blue-eyed stare. Everything about her spoke of a woman who would demolish anything between her and her goals.

Maesellen already liked her even before meeting her. She knew a great deal about these twins, likely more than they would find comfortable. Kaysienn might be hinting at the same advantage over Maesellen.

A chill seeped into Maesellen's spine as she looked

at Layrienn. Where her sister was an image of order and calculations, Layrienn's frayed appearance and wide, blood-shot eyes were a vision of madness and chaos. Kaysienn's clothes were clean and precisely creased. Layrienn's were wrinkled with rust-colored stains. Kaysienn's lean muscles spoke of great speed and strength. Layrienn was bone-thin, wispy, and delicate. Her white-blonde hair ended in tangled snarls just above her hips.

Kaysienn glanced in the direction of the departed servant. "A Vodessian hand maiden? In Malkanor Employ?"

Maesellen smiled, knowing what sort of people the twins were. Sharing a few secrets might be harmless.

"Her and her fiancé fled from marauders into the pass of Borkray, several years ago. My agents found them. They knew to give me the girl for inspection. She works to earn his freedom."

"What of her would-be husband?" Kaysienn's curiosity was piqued.

Maesellen shrugged. "I wager he gave an alligator a severe belly-ache with as many flesh-boiling toxins as I administered."

Layrienn drew within inches of Maesellen's face, her smile mad. "Do you not fear the attentions of the Order when you speak of such things?"

Maesellen did not blink or shy away as her own smile remained. "It is a wonder Yelisian never tended to either of you. Perhaps he felt smug even when you appeared after the Kenden Estate in eastern Nerinmor was painted with blood. It is a wonder you survived such a grisly massacre."

Kaysienn's eyes brightened with knowing, and her scowling lips quirked up into a smirk. "The same could be said after the bad wine that claimed Baron Movis and his court of seventy-five. He so nearly had enough support to take the Nerinmor throne. His majesty of Malkanor pays this no mind. Perhaps because the deadly fungus in the wine looked like the result of poor aging, to the unobservant. Did the bodies burn as well as a heap of dolls, I wonder?"

Maesellen flinched, but her liking for Kaysienn doubled. No one ever discovered the fungus to be an excretion of the combination toxin she developed. If the Baron had claimed the throne, it would not have been long before he discovered some of her secretive activities. At the time, Maesellen had yet to construct her Nerinmor strong hold, her first base of operations.

Few people knew about the night Maesellen abandoned her childhood. The dolls were a much more personal story from an older time in her life.

Maesellen allowed herself the first real laugh she had in a long time. "You must tell me how you evaded the Grand Illumination. His ability to read people was exceptional."

Kaysienn's smile sharpened into a wicked grin. "The Order knows of only one of my abilities. I can manipulate the iron content in the blood, true enough. My greatest talent lies in alchemy and poison. Do not confuse this for the work of some meager apothecary. Poison and mixtures speak to me. I can alter them. With my two abilities, I can change the blood mixture in a body in specific ways. I can alter the vibrations the body exudes into the Endless Current. His Radiance saw only what I wanted him to see."

Oh, Maesellen loved the girl more each moment. If she could have chosen her daughters, the twins would be her first choice.

Layrienn chose that moment to interject. "Do you suppose we could find more pretty servants and playthings while we are about in Borkray?" Kaysienn blinked at the sudden shift in the conversation. "They would make fine gifts for her majesty."

Maesellen fought down her hidden revulsion for the clearly insane twin. "What would place such delightful young ladies in such a filthy collection?"

Kaysienn sighed. "It is another liberation campaign. The Kasarins have surrounded the valley, from one side of the canyon to the other."

Borkray did hold a strategic advantage. It was nestled at the mouth of a miles-long canyon. The walls of the canyon were sheer drops, enclosing an open defile all the way to Vodess. Borkray was flanked by dense woods to the north and south. To the east was an expanse of plains that broke against the face of a tall, wide mesa.

To Maesellen's dismay, Borkray was surrounded only by a thick adobe wall and guarded only by a small garrison of poorly trained militia. It was a wonder the Kasarins did not already reduce it all to ashes. Then again...

"A hostage trap," Maesellen thought out loud. "They are trying to draw you out."

Kaysienn nodded. "Exactly so, your majesty. Their siege weapons are pointed at Borkray from all over the valley. A heavy command and assault force are at the ready, watching from the plateau. The garrison has already been crushed."

Maesellen paced a moment, her eyes lost in thought. She pursed her lips in consternation as she lent the brutish invaders a thought of respect. They were aware that the new coalition would come to the rescue, and the Kasarins would demolish the town just as quickly as the would-be heroes arrived. A force that heavy could level the canyon mouth.

The failure to protect the people would shatter the morale of the Renegades. The rest of the battle would be a foregone conclusion.

The Kasarins might not be the muscle-headed fools everyone thought they were. Their study and understanding of their enemies seemed thorough. This strategy, alone, held so few counter-methods. Only an equal study of the Kasarins would grant any chance, at all. The Kasarins would sense any attempt to scry or scout them.

The Renegades might be lost, but perhaps Maesellen could preserve the two precious treasures before her.

-28-

Amorlic's black leather long coat billowed behind him as he walked the inner perimeter of the compound. The muggy fetid night air was alive with swarms of buzzing mosquitoes and flies hungry for blood and corpses. The former could be found with ease, but Amorlic didn't want the bodies to create sickness in what few people they still had. The bodies were dumped in heaps outside the compound. Alligators would come for the meat, and they would harass any nearby Kasarins.

Frequently spaced torches and fire pits created greater heat and light. There would be no stealthy surprises in the night, but Amorlic felt an uncomfortable sheen of sweat all over his body. If his coat had not already proven ample protection against mosquitoes and lesser projectiles, he would have packed it away already.

There were carefully placed stacks of barrels and vats kept along the inner walls. Some of the contents were explosive and were kept well clear of open flames. There were barrels of caustic acids and nerve toxins that were kept in their own locations. They were brought up from the laboratories below because the chemists were eager to witness their efficacy in battle.

The forge smiths were also eager to see how their blade and snare designs fared. Amorlic was quick to oblige them. Entry ways and walls were rigged with trigger panels attached to lethal spring blades. The tightly coiled snares generated tremendous force. Coupled with the heavy blades, the traps could crush plated armor and rend flesh from bone with ease.

Amorlic would like to think these things would help him rest at night. He masked his fatigue well. His anger commanded a strict and deadly compound. But he could not predict when the next Kasarin siege would occur. The mist obscured their presence and movements. This permitted only hasty reactions, never prepared planning. In the past three days, the Kasarins attacked five times. Each assault was progressively larger and fierce.

Four days ago, marked the first intervention of the Havoc Magi. In blind conditions, they were more dangerous than normal.

It was a stroke of genius that every mercenary employed by Amorlic's mother was trained in the use of Kasarin blow darts. It was simple for Amorlic to take up the same training in the past week. Since then, he had all the tiny munitions coated with Orchard's Dream.

Now, while the sorcerers proved devastating in their first few minutes, the constant lethal rain of darts from the compound was just as deadly.

A black-haired, apron-clad smith emerged from a door leading to the underground keep. He wiped his sweaty forehead as a thick cloud of smoke billowed in his wake. He inhaled deep, and his blue eyes showed his relief at drinking in the cool spring air, however rancid.

Amorlic narrowed his blue eyes. "That better not be from a mistake to our latest design."

The smith blinked and stuttered. "No, Lord Keeper. It is only the tar and pitch used to hold the bolts. It has to be hot until we apply it to the joints."

The smith laughed nervously but Amorlic was not deterred or amused. "How is the coil force on the automatic function?"

The smith lowered his eyes. "Still slow. The metal in

the springs is weak. The firing force and reloading speed are limited."

Amorlic's impatience boiled as he gripped the cuffs of his leather sleeves. "We have incendiary chemists as well as the best metal smiths in Stratia. Yet you cannot forge a strong enough metal? I have already coated all the waiting munitions in Orchard's dream. The other smiths have already prepared suitable mass compartments and bolts durable enough to withstand the applied force."

"I am aware, Lord Keeper…"

"Do not think to patronize me, smith. We have snares made of steel strong enough to crush their armored soldiers. We have enough of these traps to cut down their ranks before they come within view of our walls. So, why is this task incomplete?"

"As you said, they are in the hundreds of snares hidden in the swamps. We have no supply chains, now-no incoming iron or steel. Perhaps if we had a magus…"

"Fates! Can none of you live beyond magic?" Amorlic howled. "No more excuses and limitations, smith. The difference between life and death, for all of us, is our ability to improvise. The Kasarins are clearly weak-willed and stupid because they lean too heavy on sorcery as their crutch. Now, be ingenious or be dead, smith."

Amorlic was about to turn away when the inner foyer became illuminated by a brilliant, blood-red glow.

"Cover the incendiaries, now!" Amorlic shouted, not pausing to look up at the signature ball of flame. "Smiths and spearmen, to the barrels. Darts, to the walls and find that fire flinger, quickly."

On the shouted orders, an organized pandemonium erupted. Armored and aproned men spilled out of foundries and barracks. Leather clad men with crossbows and blow guns filled the wooden catwalks of the walls.

The fireball crashed with thundering force, but otherwise

dissipated. The chemists had devised several flame-resistant concoctions. Amorlic ordered the walls and rooftops to be regularly slathered in it. It was done, every week, after his first encounter in the swamps, north. The arrival of the Havoc Guilds was a foregone conclusion by then, and they were ready for it.

The incendiary barrels were moved below ground within minutes, while the corrosive concoctions were rushed to the outer walls. These would be ready to dump onto any that passed through the snares.

Amorlic retrieved a crossbow and ascended a set of stairs to the outer wall. He mumbled his complaints at the mist as he scanned for any trace of incoming sorcery. He listened to a hushed silence, waiting for the sounds of screaming men, and snares crushing bodies.

As was common in the nights in Nerinmor, the bogs gave a ghostly green glow to the mist from rising gases. He hoped the ever-present light didn't mask the quick, tell-tale flashes he was looking for. It was fortunate that the swamp was too dead, filled with stagnant noxious water, to allow their stealthier rumored vines. There were some natural boundaries even sorcery could not break.

Every marksman on the wall knew to remain silent, and watchful. If anything stirred the mists, they would unleash their projectiles.

The mists stirred, violently, as shadows began to tear the darkness apart. Screams sounded from every direction, as well as the strange sound of singing metal, and squelching rips. Something intruded on the attempted Kasarin assault on the compound. It was fortunate that none of his men triggered their weapons, waiting for a truly clear sign of a threat. There were too many silhouettes, and too much obscurity to identify actual threats.

This might not have stopped them from assailing the mist with volleys before, but there was an undeniable sense of warning in the air that stayed everyone's hands.

Amorlic could not believe what his eyes were attempting to convey to him from the vague shadow play. Were bodies being hoisted on air from implacable sharp spikes that came from everywhere? Impromptu spears and twitching dying men looked like they were creating a thicket that shielded the compound. The Kasarins looked trapped in horrible death throes, like flies caught in snares.

"If the Havoc Guilds were there, you would be dead now," a woman whispered in Amorlic's ear, as she appeared directly beside him.

Though her voice was teasing and playful, Amorlic whirled about with his crossbow. His bolt was aimed between the eyebrows of a pale, aquiline face. Though she was attractive, Amorlic did not ignore the crazed gleam in her blue eyes. Her lips seemed poised to break into a toothy mad cackle. Her blonde hair was a few shades brighter than his own, falling straight down in her back to her hips.

Then Amorlic noticed the tell-tale closed gray robe. The girl was, at the least, a Torch of that accursed Order.

One of the few things Amorlic enjoyed about the compound in the swamp was the lack of interference from the self-righteous fools of the Order.

"If you have come for justice, or some such, I promise you won't live to report this place to the Citadel," Amorlic threatened, his fingers poised tightly on the trigger. The other marksmen hesitated, briefly, before a sorceress of the Order, but they knew not to defy the Keeper of the compound. All weapons were levelled on the girl.

The girl cooed as she approached to caress the crossbow with her fingertips, staring at the deadly point absently. "Your highness, if I wanted to do anything about you, I would already be playing with your entrails."

That last was not only a sign of madness, but Amorlic knew that no one in the Order would ever speak with glee about carnage. The baffled curiosity that struck him made him wonder who, exactly, he was speaking to.

"Who are you? Why are you here?" Amorlic took a defensive step back, the crossbow still aimed at her.

"A new partner to your mother." The girl managed an expression of innocence as she stepped within three inches of the lethally poisoned tip.

"If you get within one more inch, Layrienn, you will die!" Shouted the warning of another woman in the foyer. She had a harder edge to her voice. "That poison is everywhere, and it has a potentiation I have never seen before." There was a pause, but Amorlic did not turn his attention to the speaker. He would deal with the closest threat, first.

"That is alright, my dear sister. No one here will lift a finger to harm me." Layrienn sauntered over to a cross bowmen, caressing the draw and trigger of his weapon.

The unmoving soldier was rigid and tense, but a sheen of sweat soaked his forehead. His breathing struggled and hissed through his nostrils, and only his eyes followed the mad girl.

Amorlic readied his own bolt to find its home in the sorceress's forehead; but paid a moment more attention. All his men were tense, but their weapons were redirected, slowly, to Amorlic. One man began to clench his teeth as he turned the weapon slowly back to her.

The blonde girl looked at the crossbow handler with her lips pursed in pouting disapproval. "Oh, don't do that. You won't be alone if I want to play with you."

The soldier's face contorted with agony. He dropped his crossbow, as five other men around him fell to their knees. They dropped their weapons and clutched their chests.

The girl walked over to her first victim and knelt in front of him. Her words continued their mad playful coo. "You know the blood around your heart is almost as hard as a stone, yes? I can change that, but it just would not do if you pointed your sharp toys at me again. You would not do that to me again, would you?"

"**NO!**" The man was allowed to shout.

The girl turned her blood shot eyes back to Amorlic with a feigned plea. "But now we have to wonder if his highness cares enough for his brave men to ease his hand." Her face twisted into mad mirth. "Or will he stand by while I play and play to my heart's content."

Amorlic said nothing. Threats from a mad girl should not be given more than hostile regard. But this would be a wasteful blood bath in a short second. He could kill her, unless her magic found him, first. But she might force his men to release a volley better reserved for an army if he did.

And why wasn't she using her magic on him, as well? Perhaps it was better to hear them out, then decide from there. The tension on his finger eased ever so slightly. In answer, a collective exhale of relief passed through his men. The five endangered men stood up; but refused to pick up their weapons for the moment.

"You may take ease, your highness. We are here to help." The other woman attempted reassurance.

Amorlic spat from the corner of his mouth. "Then you may leave the way you came. We need none of your witchery, here."

Layrienn closed her eyes and drank a full inhalation of fetid swamp air. "Two hundred twenty- six," she exhaled.

The other woman objected. "I see maybe seventy-five."

"Not all are above ground, Kaysienn. I feel their blood pump so fierce. Such toil, they must be dripping with sweat." Layrienn opened her eyes and took a slow step around Amorlic's crossbow. She drew close enough to whisper in Amorlic's ear.

"Three minutes."

Amorlic side-stepped and refocused his weapon, while

confusion played on his face.

"That is how long this tomb and funeral pyre will last against a serious Kasarin assault." Kaysienn shouted the answer to his unspoken question.

"The dead bodies, out there, tell me everything," Layrienn giggled. "You have them so vexed. A bunch of lowly, ordinary Stratians," Layrienn feigned a whine before making a stern face and a mock deep voice, "against big strong magi, and thousands of swords."

"They would be sending Elite, already, if they had any to spare," Kaysienn added. "But Malkanor is drawing the majority of their forces."

"Fire and vines, fire and vines," Layrienn drawled in boredom. "It's different from those that came before, but that is all they ever do. They are not artists, like us."

"Or like you, I see," Kaysienn complimented. "You really must tell me about this venom. How are you able to make so much? And is that peach pit dust? That should take ten times what you used. What synergy did you use to activate it in such a way?"

Amorlic did not look to Kaysienn as he pondered how he should respond. Regardless of the mad sorceress's claims, Amorlic and his men could handle the Kasarin threat.

But if they were truly sent from his mother, then refusing or murdering them would greatly displease her.

Amorlic hated sorcery. He was cast into these swamps because of magic. A peasant overwhelmed him twice with magic. The same peasant won the affections of his betrothed with magic. History recorded the Order's abuse of power against the nation he now stood on, with magic. Magic was responsible for obscuring the lines between rulers and the ruled. There was order, a form of peaceful stability, that existed only when such boundaries remained unchallenged.

Furthermore, Amorlic berated a man, only moments ago,

for codependence on magic. Now, there were these two witches, and because they were sent by his mother, he could not be rid of them.

Amorlic lowered his weapon and eased his stance. "Lower your weapons, marksmen. They are emissaries of Maesellen Moarenroak. We can go about as we were. The threat was false."

"Oh, it was a real threat," Layrienn approached, whispering, running her fingers in a caress on Amorlic's leather coat. "There was time for us to play, and their screams were such sweet music. It was such a delightful game."

"The crimson ball of flame was their only attack before we took them by surprise and killed them all," Kaysienn simplified for Amorlic.

Amorlic sighed, disregarding Layrienn's insane seductions. Unfortunately, his mother would advise him not to waste offered talents. If they proved useless or inconvenient, he would kill them without a second thought. They were here, now, so he would have to use them to solve the compound's shortages and weaknesses.

"How are you with materializing?" Amorlic turned his inquiry to the sane one of the two.

Kaysienn was an opposite to Layrienn. Where Layrienn was a soft blonde with mad glee exuded in an intangible miasma, Kaysienn was dark-haired, with hard features, and a scowl as endless as his own. Nothing about her was soft or gentle. Everything from their clothes, their hair, their shape, and their walk was different from each other. One a reflection of order and control, the other's glimpse into madness, and self-abusive seduction.

"You mean Polymancy?" Kaysienn asked. "We are very adept with it, as long as we have our focus implement."

Amorlic wondered what could enable their craft in such a way, and if he would be better for knowing.

Layrienn would leave nothing to his imagination.

"As long as the blood flows, running in rivers, rivers." There was an ecstasy in Layrienn's voice that chilled Amorlic.

"Blood is the focus of my twin sister's magic. The toxins, poisons, and blood iron…" Kaysienn emphasized her point by producing a vial of green liquid from her belt, beneath her robe. "…are mine."

Amorlic did not expose the rest of what he wanted from them, yet. He would observe and evaluate their worth before deciding how many of his projects would include them.

-29-

Zenen'Rol stood in the white granite courtyard of the Zenith Citadel of the Order of the Enlightened Sun. He stood with his feet apart and his hands clasped behind his back. He glared with unveiled disgust; contempt etched into his dark countenance.

The sky was thick with dark gray clouds, and the cool air promised rain. Dozens of Ka'Rak herded gray and brown robed men, women, and children into the open courtyard. Though he stood at the forefront of two dozen Havoc Elite, and several hundred more magi in reserve outside the walls, it seemed all a waste. Even the seven hundred Ka'Rak would have been better placed anywhere else in Stratia. The Order offered no resistance.

The air was noticeably cooler here, in the early summer. With only a little humidity from the Maelstrom Sea, lightning began to flash to the west, beyond the strange white edges of the Citadel. A loud crackling followed distantly in the wake of the lightning. Perhaps some of this Order of fools might say that a storm was coming. Zenen would argue that the storm was already here for them.

If nothing else could be said of the weather, and the way the Order was so easily corralled, Zenen would concede that it was a good day for executions.

An officer of the Ka'Rak approached Zenen'Rol and knelt on one knee with his head bowed. "Lord Master Fist. We have located the members of the council. They are in chains and on their way."

Zenen nodded wordless agreement, and the officer hesitated a moment more. "There is one more matter, Lord Master Fist."

Zenen ground his teeth. Every time an officer had an extra 'matter' in this conquest, it tended to be an unpleasant surprise for him. "Out with it."

"We believe we located the quarters of the leader of the Order." The officer paused, and Zenen only had to give a warning glare before he pushed forward. "Only it could not have been, Master Fist. The chambers looked to be the sight of a great struggle, and there were the remains of one corpse. It looked like everything inside was ripped out into a pile with the bones placed on top. More disturbing still: the head was mostly intact and animated to a degree. It looked like…"

"Necromancy!" Zenen hissed in revulsion.

Struggle and challenge or not, Zenen had all the reason he needed to kill every Stratian in the Citadel. The demon child was wrong in one respect: he found the hidden Void Hand, and he was not too powerless to stop a black decade before it could begin.

If ever Zenen could feel invigorated by righteous exultation, it was now.

Over the span of another hour, every magus of the Order was brought before Zenen. The twelve, now leaderless, council members were in chains a few feet in front of him.

Zenen paced in front of the council, glaring, his hands clasped behind his back.

"Which, among you, is a Void Hand?" Zenen demanded, twisting his mouth around the slurring Stratian language.

The council looked at each other in confusion. Zenen would not allow them to continue with feigned ignorance and denial.

"An officer of the Crimson Throne reported a work that is, without a doubt, Necromancy. All of our warriors know to fear the fate of lying to me more than failure. They know I will know the truth, without fail. So, I repeat…" Zenen annunciated slow and deliberate. "who…here…is…a…Void Hand?"

Only silence answered Zenen'Rol. He continued to pace before the council, allowing his anger and impatience to be conveyed fully.

Zenen could not believe that this was the same Order of the Enlightened Sun that repelled warlord after warlord. Their magic was supposed to be the formidable descendant of the Five Mage Clans. Yet how easily were they gathered up, like sheep to the slaughter. Now they were like whimpering brats, too afraid of pain and punishment to confess and own their crimes.

Why wouldn't they struggle or confess? Why, in the Citadel, were they such cattle, while outside they were the greatest obstacle Zenen ever faced? Was this how the Order of the Enlightened Sun wished to meet its end: meek and on their knees?

Well, what did it matter, anyway? They were all going to die. The Void Hands would die with them, concealed though they were. Zenen gave it a mental shrug and levelled his focus on the task at hand.

In Zenen's experience, no organized resistance could survive without its leaders to guide them. Perhaps even the nonsense beyond the wall would come to a confused end without their leaders.

"Council of the Order of the Enlightened Sun," Zenen addressed them in a declaring shout. "For your treachery against the Crimson Throne itself, and evident complicity with demonic arts, you are sentenced to execution. Do you have anything to say for yourselves before you bleed and die?"

"We can still serve the emperor, as Martenen agreed," begged a middle-aged dark-haired man. "All our studies, findings, and artifacts can belong to the empire. This 'allying with Void Hands' or some such, it is superstition and stories. See reason, I beg you."

Zenen paused, but not to consider the plea before him. He watched the chagrin and outrage on all the faces behind the council. Zenen watched fists clenched with white-knuckled fury. All this bartering was new to them. They seemed to want to bash the councilmen's face almost as much as they wanted to defend themselves. Something was amiss with their ill-placed self-restraint, and it made him feel uneasy.

Zenen did not look at the trembling council sorcerer. His hand slashed a wide quick arc with a curved dagger concealed in his vest coat. The gurgling sorcerer clutched the gushing wound to his neck. Blood flowed down into his severed windpipe, filling his lungs, and drowning him. As he fell and continued to bleed to death, he pulled his fellow council back with his weight still chained to them. Zenen grabbed another man with long red hair by the throat. Emperor's Thunder coursed down his arms and into the councilman's spine. He could not collect himself under the blood-red electric onslaught and could not defend himself against his death by electrocution. Smoke poured out of his mouth, ears, and nose while his eyes began to boil and melt.

Satisfied that the council magus was dead, Zenen threw the smoking remains onto the hard white marble with a loud crunch. The remaining ten council members fell on their backsides.

"Take their heads and mount them on poles along the road to Katahn." Zenen ordered, as he turned his attention to the subordinate magi behind the council.

Zenen approached a tiny blonde sorceress who looked strangely unbroken by the continued deaths of her leaders. He stared down at her with undisguised disgust.

"Are you truly such pathetic cowards?" Zenen mocked. "We come to your lands, unchallenged. We butcher your old and young, alike, cleansing your filth from the land. Now, we walk into your citadel as though it is ours, and we dispose of your leaders like animals to the slaughter. Still, you do nothing, here. Will you not harass and slow us as you do in Malkanor?"

Something of Zenen's words came as a surprise to the small woman. She smiled, inclining her head to a round dirty man behind her.

"Do you hear that, Light Barahn? Our little Renegades are giving them grief.

The scruffy bearded man laughed. "I knew my Light Teranen would give them a bloody lip."

"I thought I felt Light Ishell shape a very unusual magic." The small woman's smile broadened into a mirthful grin. "You must have backed her into a corner and made her very angry."

Zenen paused. This was not the frightened whining of cowards. These magi seemed very eager for a fight, yet they didn't. They seemed as though they might have planned things without their leaders for a while now.

And what was this talk of Renegades? Zenen began to wonder if he should have killed many of the magi, first. Maybe he should have rained down fire and death and been done with it.

The last man and woman of the council begged for their lives. The Ka'rak mercilessly began to saw off their heads at the center of their throats. Whatever Zenen might regret of it, it was done. He could only go forward with the scouring of the Citadel.

"Your time is up, Order Witch. You will die next. Have you anything to say for yourself?"

The small woman approached within inches of Zenen'Rol. He was taken aback by her bold smile. Somehow, he thought maybe nothing was as it seemed, now.

"My name is Light Kera. I am a Solas Evoker of the Order of the Enlightened Sun. On behalf of all my brothers and sisters who hold dear the true spirit of our Order, I have only two words for you..."

All at once, the Endless Current filled the courtyard, rushing to the inviting call of every Stratian magus before Zenen. Its sudden fury and overwhelming force howled, creating an actual wind, stirring dust and debris in swirling funnels. The ground began to groan and tremble beneath his feet. Fires began to erupt around the fists and eyes of the magi without burning them.

"…Thank you." Kera coiled her right fist back. Zenen had no time to react. Her right arm was coated in thick black, iron and she punched him in the middle with a colossal uppercut.

The force of the blow knocked him off his feet. He landed hard on his back with the breath smashed out of him. His head hit the ground with jarring impact.

For the first time in decades, Zenen'Rol was struck and injured. He was too stunned to comprehend it.

-30-

Kera was satisfied. She felt refreshed and cleansed as her iron-clad fist bowled into the Kasarin's gut with a solid crunch. Like every remaining Solas, she felt the power of the Rod of Binding slip away, like puffballs in the wind. Every death of the council released them, more and more.

There was no need to call the other Solas into action. They all felt their chains of inaction break. Kera was not alone in feeling guilty that she should rejoice in the needless deaths of the council. She regretted that it was their only key to freedom.

But now, the Order was free to follow their ignored natural impulse. It was wrong to be safely hidden behind these walls when Stratians were dying everywhere. She was ashamed to have to discard her heritage just to survive beyond the extermination.

It made Kera ache that she couldn't stand with her most treasured student. She wanted to face this threat together. She wanted to witness all Ishell's studies come to fruition. She wanted to see her use all her strength and knowledge. She would gladly stand with Ishell, not as a mentor, then; but as a sister-in-arms.

Kera could imagine such a thing giving Matisia, her mentor, a smile filled with pride.

At least now, they could all honor their student's courage. It was time to make the Crimson Empire regret their invasion.

The roar of bonfire-sized flames reverberated across the courtyard. Kera felt the intense heat of Barahn's signature blue Heart Fires while he laughed, raucously. The light of his fires dimmed the overcast gray and filled the courtyard with an azure hue.

"Come, my boys! Let's have ourselves a rowdy time by the fire!" Barahn laughed harder as he dashed ahead, deftly juggling and throwing balls of blue fire with deadly accuracy.

The Havoc Elite that stood behind the giant leader conjured walls of steel to block the fiery assault.

The swordsmen charged around the walls to cut down the Solas before their next spell-shape. The Havoc Elite were quick to shape tendrils of crackling electricity that wrapped around the curved blades.

The Aeromancers stepped forward in determined strides. They conjured howling gales of wind and shoving force. The soldiers only needed to slice the air before them to negate the defense and calm the air.

Barahn sighed. "Better leave this to me. You're only breathing on them. Get the Flames and Candles out of here."

Barahn ran, with reckless abandon, into the thick of the soldiers. They tried to slash and cut him down. Their blades turned into red puddles of slag as they met his aura of fire. He laughed and began delivering hard wild punches to their faces and ribs. His fists burned through armor and helmets leaving smoking black burns with every impact. Men stopped to grip their burns and scream.

"Come on, boys! You have to bring more than your breadknives to me," Barahn taunted as he continued to dance and weave through the fray.

The Aeromancers gathered the children with urgent haste. They hurried them out of the courtyard into the safety of the halls of the Citadel. Everyone else remained to hold back the Kasarins and cover the withdrawal.

Kera dismissed the iron covering her arm, with a shake of the wrist. The metal casing fell in a cascade of dust. She settled into a deep calm. She opened her hands at both sides. With only a thought, she shaped two lengths of loose green electricity. They were nearly identical to Matisia's combat favorite, the Lightning Whip.

Kera joined Barahn, lashing and whirling like a crazed dervish. Her whips crackled, snapped, and hummed and hissed in the air. Each impact against a Kasarin caused them to fall into lethal convulsions. It might not have been the ideal battle partnership Kera could ask for; but she could admit that her lightning and his blue fires made a devastating compliment to each other. Their attacks were all over the courtyard, leaving no room for the Kasarins to press in.

The Havoc Elite began to gather more Endless Current, and Kera watched as the walls were ripped into thin, razor-sharp, spikes that floated in the air. The attack would do nothing to Barahn, his fiery aura would melt the projectiles. As the stone lances were hurtled forward in a crushing volley, Kera heightened the speed of her movements. Her whips twirled and spun in an emerald cloud that smashed the spears before they reached her.

One lance managed to split through the continual flourish. It cut a deep gash that ran the length of her right calf. The searing pain threatened to drop her to one knee. She resisted with an angry shove of her will.

The Geomancers quickly raised slabs of the marble floor in front of the Solas, halting the stone barrage. Kera's offered protection gave her a precious moment to dispel her whips and mend her wound.

The top of the marble slab burst thunderously. Where the wall stood, the giant Kasarin's fist punched through with a steel coating of his own. Kera rolled back, clumsy, and startled, only an inch out of the reach of the hand reaching for her neck. He kicked the lower half of the stone out of his way, irritably. His steel fists sparked with crimson lightning. His lips were peeled back in the most frightening snarl Kera ever witnessed on a human expression. The three scarred gashes on the top of his head pulsed with tense fury.

"I am Zenen'Rol, Fist of the Crimson Emperor; and I will be shamed by Stratia no more!" The juggernaut sorcerer howled, spitting with fury.

Kera back-pedaled, trying to keep out of the raging sorcerer's reach. One strike from him would cripple, stun, or kill her.

Barahn spun about with an acrobat's flourish. In the building momentum, he conjured two balls of blue fire, as big as himself. He hurled them with the ease of apples. They slammed into Zenen's back. The giant man stumbled forward but was otherwise unaffected. The fires did not even burn his red vest coat.

But it did buy Kera an instant to act. She conjured a single, much thicker, whip of emerald lightning. She lashed down low, at his ankles. To her shock, he did not thrash in the throes of electrocution. As it wrapped around his legs, Kera gripped the whip in both hands, and yanked as hard as her body would allow. To her credit, the giant fell on his back.

The swordsmen charged ahead to substitute their fallen leader. The Polymancers walked forward to meet them. They altered the weight of the soldier's boots and swords. The weapons and armor became so heavy that the soldiers fell, face first. The Geomancers were quick to seize the moment. They softened the marble grounds beneath the over-burdened soldiers. The crimson swordsmen sank from sight, their screams fading to sudden silence.

The blue of Barahn's Heart Fire was eclipsed by a sudden blood-red glow from high above. Kera looked up and saw hundreds of balls of red fire casting aside the gloom of the clouds.

In the time she looked, Zenen was back on his feet.

"Hydromancers and Evokers, watch the skies!" Kera shouted, knowing she could not take her attention away from the sorcerer in front of her.

Barahn rushed at Zenen's back. The Kasarin spun to him at a speed that belied his size. He delivered a whipping thrust kick that sent the Pyromaster flying backwards.

It gave Kera an instant to shape her signature Four Element Crush. The marble floor rippled with chest high waves from behind Zenen. Two dozen lances of sharpened ice formed in the air to his right side. Thirty fist-sized balls of orange fire hovered to his left. When the fire and ice volley dashed to converge on him, she levelled her fingertips in his direction. Ten crackling lengths of emerald lightning blasted from her fingertips to join the barrage.

Kera used the magic once before against Rylin. She believed no one could duplicate his evasion without Chronomancy. She was certain no one would survive it if she didn't want them to.

Zenen steadied his balance against the waves of stone, riding with them. He projected a wave of crimson flames from his right hand, melting the ice. His left hand made a lifting gesture. A thick slab of iron burst up from the ground to halt the flames. The slab turned red with heated impact but achieved his defense.

Zenen puffed his chest against the electric assault. He eagerly absorbed the lightning. He was unaffected.

Kera began to feel desperation creep over her. This titan seemed impervious. He rose swiftly from anything that caused him to fall. If she didn't find a way to stop him, he would close the distance and break her. Her panic and calculations were not helping her, either. The calm she utilized at the beginning of the battle, was gone. She felt the hiccups of the Endless Current, burning and chafing inside her. Her thoughts and emotions were a resisting force to the Endless Current.

Yet, Zenen's apparent rage caused no such conflict with the flow of his powers. How could any magus manage so much in such white-hot anger? She was starting to persist only with raw will, and that was starting to take a heavy toll on her.

Barahn could not offer as much help, now. His Heart Fire waned, turning orange. Swords were only becoming red hot as they passed through the fire. He was receiving dozens of cuts that ran deep along his arms and legs. He still burned and struck down dozens of the soldiers, but many more continued to pour through the entrance.

Every other Elementalist and Evoker remained preoccupied with the descending volley of red fire. The creativity of the Polymancers was pushed to the limit against the press of Havoc Elite magic.

Vines began to break through the walls and floor, splitting marble and granite. Their dagger-long thorns ground against stone, promising much easier tears in flesh. The Geomancers turned their attention, trying to crush and shred the vines with stone blocks.

"We can't hold the courtyard much longer," Barahn's voice projected into Kera's mind. "They have the numbers and stamina to wear us down, here."

"If we withdraw, they will tear us apart as we flee," Kera projected back.

"Backstep to the corridors, and I'll hold them in a bottleneck at the arch. Take five evokers with you."

Kera blinked with confusion. "Why shouldn't I help fight them? Why break into another group?"

"Because, wherever the children have been taken, it won't be safe enough. They need to be protected better."

"What do you have in mind, Light Barahn?" intruded another Solas from deeper in the Citadel.

"Get them to Light Rylin's study. As soon as they are safe inside, destroy the door."

Having been one of the few Solas to read and study the Chronomancer's tomes, Kera knew she held an observer's knowledge of time sorcery. She was surprised that Barahn took the time to learn, as well.

"They could be trapped in there forever, Light Barahn," Kera warned. "Or, without the door to tether the errant future to our time, it could dissolve and kill them."

"Those are risks, yes," Barahn admitted as he began erecting successive walls of fire while he and his fellow Lights withdrew. "But you know the third possibility."

"They could all be safe and well until Light Rylin repairs the door and connects the time, anew. Only a Chronomancer could do it." Kera reluctantly supplied the answer.

"If I am wrong, Light Kera, then it would be no different than their fate, here. It's a chance we have to take."

"Why not have all of us go into the study?" Kreshin asked as they all gathered into the entry to the hall. A thick wall of fire stood between them and the Kasarins.

Kera answered out loud. "For one thing, the door can only be destroyed from the outside."

"More importantly: some of us need to stay and rough up our guests a little." Barahn turned his head and gave a toothy grin. "It would be awfully lazy of us to leave all the work for our wonderful Renegades."

"What do you think he meant about the Void Hands?" asked a blonde geomancer with a deep gouge slashed into his cheek. The cut oozed blood and left his right eye swollen shut. He spoke with a ragged wheeze.

Kera wanted to tell him it wasn't a good time to talk about it; but she wasn't sure they would get another chance.

Kera shook her head, slow and solemn. "I don't know. I

think the details were between that giant man and the officer, but they were speaking in Kasarin. With Martenen being dead, sometime before the council, I think that has something to do with it."

No one needed to ask how Kera could be certain Martenen was dead. They were free of the Binding, which could only be true if all the spell-shaping leaders were dead.

"More of their work surfaces, and we won't even be able to solve their mystery," Barahn grumbled. "Every time something is discovered about them, death follows the answers."

The time they discussed this was a generous standstill, but Kera knew they would all have to move, soon, if they were going to save the Flames and Candles. She didn't know why the Havoc Guilds didn't already make their move. In a fight of fire against fire, Barahn's orange flames were inferior to the Kasarin crimson fires. He was much too cut and exhausted to call on his blue Heart Fire.

"If you know all that, then get moving Light Kera!" Barahn shouted after Heat Reading her.

Kera directed five evokers and Kreshin to follow her. Several geomancers were left behind to defend against the vines and bring down the arch when Barahn dropped his wall of fire.

Kera let her senses drift into the Endless Current, searching ahead, above, and below. Invisible tendrils of magic snaked through the stone, passing through as incorporeal as a ghost.

Kreshin caught onto her efforts. Together, their magic searched for the hidden Aeromancers and the younger initiates. It didn't take long to locate them. They were in the first basement level, several rooms away from the furnace chamber. They began to race down the halls, enhancing their running speed with Endless Current.

Urgency restored normalcy to Kera's efforts. Her breathing became labored, and her legs began to feel leaden.

As if fate chose to exacerbate matters, several Havoc Sorceresses finished a Meld Walk several yards in front of Kera. They brought five soldiers with them. Their blades sparked and hissed with the same red lightning that sliced through wind magic in the courtyard.

The soldiers rushed with their blades pointed ahead in two-handed grips. The evokers stepped forward to meet them. Bursts of will and mumbled words called daggers of fire into their hands.

The sorceresses were just as quick. They sent five metallic lengths coiling out of their palms. The metal was covered in sharp, deadly barbs.

Kera moved to meet the attack with a pillar of stone. Kreshin's Polymancy was slightly faster. She felt him strain with the Endless Current as he transmuted the cutting metal into green vines covered in ripe red grapes.

Kera turned a quizzical expression to Kreshin. He shrugged his shoulders. "I make practical materials out of refuse, all day. What would you have of me?" Kreshin's thoughts projected, defensively.

The odd transmutation caught the sorceresses off guard. Kera seized the chance. As quick as her wrists twisted back, she held a pair of conjured silver daggers with a rare Polymancy of her own. She hurled the blades with deadly precision. One lodged between the eyes of the sorceress on the right, while the left woman took the blade, to the hilt, in the center of her sternum.

Kera turned to find a younger evoker woman barely holding off a flurry of one of the soldiers. She stepped back, in defense, trying to lock his curved, long sword with her two flame daggers. His attacks were swift and relentless, pushing her further and further.

Kera rushed to strike the soldiers exposed back. Another soldier reversed his sword point, from behind the evoker woman, and drove a low reverse thrust with both hands, while the blade moved along his hip. Half his blade lodged low into her spine, crunching through bone. The evoker arched back and stiffened. Her eyes went wide, and her daggers vanished. Her first opponent slashed across her throat, while her unexpected attacker yanked his blade free. He swung his blade in an upward arc on an older dark-haired evoker in front of him.

They were losses too sudden to follow or believe. Even without their red lightnings, or the assistance of the sorceresses, their weapons still dealt death as quick as any magic. The confines of the hallway were more familiar to the Order, but they were also advantageous to the Kasarin fighters. It was a miscalculation even on Kera's part.

Kreshin, Kera, and the three evokers pulled back from the swordsmen, warily. Kreshin had a cut from his upper arm to his chest. Blood soaked his gray robe. He was breathing heavy, and his eyes drooped, either from exhaustion or blood loss. Kera knew he wasn't very strong to begin with. It was a credit against his usual nature that he would even fight at all. She regretted every condescending thought she ever had of him. She hated that it was too late to take it back.

"We both know the Aeromancers are already moving the Flames and Candles," Kreshin projected to Kera, closing his eyes for concentration. "The Kasarins are likely Meld Walking wherever they can sense us. I'm not going to be able to run far without Current Enhancing, so you need to run ahead as soon as we have an opening."

Kera looked to Kreshin, openly bewildered. "Why now?" She sent back.

"Because I watched Light Merahl do the right thing. We watched all our most promising students do the right thing. Our teachers died doing the right thing. It was never the easy thing, Light Kera, only the right thing. I've done the easy thing, every time, Light Kera. I just watched the council and Martenen die doing the easy thing. They begged, they bartered away their souls. They were so helpless as they whined."

Kreshin opened his eyes, advancing on the soldiers. Kera felt his resolve gather much more Endless Current than anyone ever believed possible from him.

"If I seek the easy way now, they will only chase me, find me. Then I will have to beg. I will have to discard my dignity, forever. I have to pay for my cowardice and indulgence, now, or I will die both indebted and dishonored."

As Kreshin finished projecting his thoughts, Kera watched the air shimmer around him. There was a watery ripple that passed through his clothes. In the wake of the ripple, his clothes were changed to white robes and gleaming, crystalline, Enriall armor. He held out his hand to the side, and his red oak staff passed through the ceiling. When it obeyed his summons and found his hand, it changed into a staff of silver. She could only guess how he managed to imitate the enchantments placed on the Solas battle gear.

"I am Solas Polymancer Kreshin, of the Order of the Enlightened Sun." Kreshin's voice thundered down the length of hallway. "I advise you all to leave before I turn you into small lizards."

-31-

Kreshin moved, empowered by the Endless Current, but he never expected he could do so much. His silver staff blocked a sword cut for his head and changed the weapon into a brittle twig that broke afterwards. He struck another soldier's right ribs and changed his armor into a tattered brown farmer's shirt.

At the same time, Kreshin's Enriall Tunic allowed a healing wave of energy to pass through his skin and into his bones. It did not mend or pull, as the elements did. Kreshin only imagined each injury as whole, unbroken, and it completed his image.

As Kreshin continued to fight, he felt like the purest expression of Polymancy. He could change anything around him to whatever he wished. He could alter the reality of anything. There was no place for wounds, and the weapons that made them, because he didn't wish for it.

Kreshin had always been lazy and unmotivated, taking his place in an ignored setting so that it would be easy for him. Only now, as Kreshin stood and took his first determined steps, did he realize he had chosen a path as a master of change. It didn't have to be a world of ease and simple pleasures only for himself. He could give that world to everyone.

Kreshin's insightful ponderings cost him. One of the soldiers moved more skillfully than he expected. He moved in a series of uncommitted feints and cuts, careful not to connect with the silver staff.

The soldier managed to create complacency just long enough to pierce low, stabbing into his right knee. Kreshin screamed as hot pain brought him down. The soldier yanked his blade free.

Kreshin never trained himself to hold his concentration under pain like this. It overwhelmed his perception and shoved away his reach of the Endless Current. He fell to his back and rolled to his belly to find Kera.

"Run! Find them!" Kreshin roared against the pain.

A new pain blasted into his back. The bones of his spine broke. He struggled for breath as liquid created hot streams at the corners of his mouth. Everything in his torso was ripped apart. It was worse when the soldier shoved and twisted the weapon inside him.

As Kera watched Kreshin die at the feet of the Kasarin soldier, she understood the hard fate they all faced. Maybe, as Barahn was cut in the courtyard, and Zenen'Rol proved too much for any of them, the Pyromaster knew it as well.

This was the end of much of Stratia, in the way they had known it. Survival was no longer a certainty, for now. It would only be a destination for those fortunate and skilled enough to make the entire journey. Whatever would become of the nations after that would only be witnessed by those who lived to see it.

The Order of the Enlightened Sun would not be so fortunate. They had come to a point of facing a united empire with a divided Order. They would be found too lacking to live through this day. Maybe this was inevitable since the loss of Yelisian, Matisia, and all their great leaders. Maybe, in that way, the Void Hands had won; and no one could see it that day.

But Barahn was right. All that was left for them was to

save the children. The division in the Order, and its destruction, was not a price they would be forced to pay. They were blameless in all this. The last breath in the Zenith Citadel would be paid so that they would remain, justly, alive.

So, Kera ignored her tears. She called on her Steel Titan Gauntlets, again. She delivered two crushing punches that opened the way ahead. Heedless of the Havoc Magi who would sense her, Kera let the Endless Current flow through her without stopping. She let the raw waves of creation fill her, burning inside her almost to the fatal point of dissolution. The white stone and fading Current Spheres blurred around her in a mad kaleidoscope. She could feel the Aeromancers and the children, far ahead, climbing the steps from the basement.

Just a little more time, Kera begged of fate. Let Barahn hold them back, just a little longer.

Dust and rock fell in loose cloudy showers in the archway where Barahn knelt. His breath burned with each heaving exhalation. The entire right side of his face felt raw, as though the skin and muscle had been peeled away. His gray robe hung from his bloody round body in wet dusty tatters. Thick smoke and hot fires filled the hallway. Much of it was Kasarins he had burned until they were black and brittle. The sharp reek of burned meat saturated the oily clouds of smoke.

Barahn was the last Stratian in this hallway. His fellow Lights lay in broken heaps, wet in pools of their own blood. Barahn was only allowed a moment to gather himself because the Kasarins could not see through the smoke. They didn't know that there was only one remaining: a weak and bleeding Pyromaster.

Only Barahn's resolve kept the Endless Current flowing through him. He drank the heat of the fires, feeling their soothing embrace against the press of encroaching pain. When that failed, he knew the agony of his wounds would shove aside the presence of the Current. He would be left with only his will.

Then there was the big Kasarin to contend with, Zenen'Rol. The giant sorcerer had not joined in the fighting in the arch. What was he doing? He could not be on the ground, still. The man shrugged off the elements with ease. He was too large, fast, and powerful to exchange blows with.

But this was never going to be a battle to drive the invaders out of Stratia. Barahn felt the body heat of well over a thousand Kasarins, even as he and his fellow Lights were gathered up. He knew, even then, they couldn't win. If the council had released them from their oaths, rather than beg for their lives, their combined might would have been more damaging.

That was retrospect suited for another person. Barahn knew that was more pointless than hindsight and regret. Any time now, the Kasarins would advance on the crumbled hallway. Barahn held no delusions about the outcome. It was time to decide how he wanted the end of his life to be.

Barahn thought about his fiery-tempered student. Teranen began her training, sullen, reserved, and full of determination. That last trait drew him to mentor her. Her early stoic demeanor was a small fire, all its own. He never got to tell her, but she had already surpassed him. He had begun teaching her skills that he had only theorized about for years. If he had another week or two with her, he would have demanded she be tested for the level of Solas. Her passion for self-expression had become unrestrained, while her concentration and forethought remained extraordinary.

Barahn was so proud of her that thinking about her caused a steaming tear to fall down his cheek. In the end, she did as he hoped she would: she chose to stand for her virtues as well as those of the Order.

Barahn placed a palm on the ground and pushed fire through his skin. His hand melted a red-hot imprint into the stone. The burn did not darken or cool. He believed Teranen would walk in this hallway, again. She would find his handprint. She would read his final moments, and his last thoughts for her.

"Nothing has brought me more joy than instructing you, Light Teranen," Barahn conveyed into the burn mark. "You have become the great fire I knew you would be, the first day I laid eyes on you. When you see this, know that I love you, my white phoenix. I gladly give my life so that you may triumph, as I know you will. What comes next for the Order is in the hands of you brave Renegades."

Barahn stood up, slowly, ignoring the pains that seared over half his body. He heard heavy boots crunching against loose stone and burned bodies.

Through a cloud of smoke, the massive shape of Zenen'Rol lead several dozen soldiers and ten Havoc Magi.

Barahn smiled, a wide, broad, toothy grin that stung his face. "Come on in, Kasarin guests."

Zenen'Rol's grin was filled with knowing and certainty. Barahn could tell the giant thought he would kill Barahn as easily as his other victims.

Let him think it, Barahn thought to himself with a smugness of his own. *It will make this so much sweeter for me.*

Barahn flung his arms open wide. Fire and Endless Current answered him, eagerly. The flames that filled the hallway abandoned their feasts and rushed across the air. His skin absorbed the fire and Endless Current with equal thirst. Even as his insides seared in protest at so much power flooding through him, the presence of the fire soothed and bolstered him. He drank in more and more each second.

"Come on in," Barahn shouted, laughing boisterously. "I'll cook a grand feast for you."

Zenen'Rol's eyes widened with horrified realization. He began shouting orders in Kasarin, gesturing for his army to withdraw from the hall.

Barahn closed his eyes for a moment. It was a moment that possessed a generous amount more time than he thought he had.

Several familiar shapes formed in the silence of Barahn's mind. Foremost, he saw the tall, wiry shape of Yelisian. He saw his dark, narrow, hard face. The Grand Illumination smiled at him, warmly. With him stood Matisia and Dera, the two Ard Solas Barahn respected and revered the most.

"Do You see, now? I told you his true path called to him," Matisia told Yelisian.

Barahn remembered the day they spoke of. It brought a smile to him as he remembered Matisia arguing to the council. She defended a boy's decision to study the flames exclusively, even as the council pushed for more Domestic Polymancers.

"You were right, as always, old friend," Yelisian admitted. "I may study my enemies, but you always seem to know our families and allies far better than I do, most times."

Barahn felt another hot tear fall from his eyes as he listened to the acknowledgement of the few people who had always understood him the most.

"Look at him," Dera marveled, smiling. "He would defend the light of our Order with the radiance of his brilliant flames. We were right to call him one of our own."

"Go ahead, Light Barahn," Matisia urged him on, knowingly. "Say it, then join us in our work."

Barahn opened his eyes, and they burst with blue fire. The blue fire poured from his fingertips, out through the pores of his arms and legs. His fire reached out, expressing the heart and spirit of his being.

"All is known in the light," Barahn shouted, defiantly. He smiled as flames began to erupt through every orifice in his body. "The light exiles the shadows; and today, it's going to roast your Kasarin backsides like pigs on a spit!"

Barahn's body and will could take in no more of the fire and Endless Current. His nerves and skin began to burst, one cell at a time. A high-pitched keening screamed in the hallway and out into the courtyard. Hot wind and blue fire began to howl and roar outward from Barahn. It cremated the remains of the bodies. It melted and broke white stone, casting it away.

A moment later, as his nerve endings seared with all-encompassing pain, Barahn's body dissolved into the Endless Current. The resulting explosion of blue fire made a fused crater that ran into the basement. Five floors collapsed in a radius of several hundred yards. Hundreds of Kasarins were burned or crushed, the flames catching some who fled beyond the walls of the Zenith Citadel.

The Kasarins did not look to the city of Katahn. Had they done so, they would have noticed the dome of spirit energy as it shimmered with azure light.

Kera stumbled and fell hard on her side as the Citadel shook to its foundation. Her ears rang and bled from the snapping boom that followed. She felt the hot gale of the Endless Current blast through the halls in a massive wave. Kera felt the intense heat and knew, without a doubt, that Barahn was dead. He must have created a tremendous explosion with the last of his life, just to give her enough time.

Kera struggled against her aching and battered arms and legs. The fall ripped away the Endless Current from her; but she was only a hallway and a half from the basement stairwell. The Aeromancers were almost to the top. She could meet them at the hallway T-junction. From there, they only had to backtrack four hundred feet to the south, to find Rylin's Temporal Study.

There were several small ripples in the Endless Current. The Kasarins were Meld Walking to scour the halls.

Kera gritted her teeth. She pushed her arms and legs to run at a sprint. Her legs felt a need to stagger and fall again. She would not allow it. She could no longer afford to bolster her running ability. The Havoc Magi would intercept her with ease if she did.

Doors passed in the corners of Kera's vision. The Current Spheres were beginning to die down. Only daylight from around the doors lit the way forward, now. Kera realized that soon the Citadel would be empty of life, silent and hollow. The great sunburst white bastion, which stood for knowledge, wisdom, and unity, would be a broken empty ruin. Two thousand years of the most powerful and wise men and women were part of the Citadel's intrepid history. All of them lived, studied, and died to serve and guide the world.

Kera understood Barahn's final choice, and the final choice of her mentor's and idols. They were confronted with an inevitable outcome. In the face of that, all they could do was decide what they held most dear and were willing to die for.

"Light Kera!" Exclaimed a dark-haired young Aeromancer man. "Fates! Am I relieved!"

Kera rounded the corner, almost sliding sideways to the ground. "Follow me, and hurry! They Meld Walk to us, right now." She did not stop and look for their compliance. They ran the length of the west wall. She was glad just to hear their footsteps behind her.

Kera swore as she felt a Meld Walk end just a dozen yards behind them. The Aeromancer men and women whirled to face the Kasarins, shoving the children further down the hall.

"Fire and lightning will destroy a door quicker," shouted a petite Aeromancer in a tone that cancelled argument.

Kera did not have time to turn and help, in any case. She continued to lead thirty boys and girls to the Temporal Study. She felt intense heat across her back as the hallway was filled with a bright blood-red glow. Screams of burning and dying men and women sounded, even over the roar of the crimson inferno.

Still, Kera and the children ran. Kera admired the bravery the children demonstrated. They did not weep or speak, only ran. They were as disciplined now, as they were always trained to be. If the Renegades defeated the Kasarins, there was no doubt that such children would rise to the challenge of rebuilding Stratia and the Order. That thought filled Kera with hope.

And Kera knew, that if anyone could drive away the invasion, Ishell could. She believed her student would be a strong needed component to the future of the world.

At last, Kera reached the knob of the dark wooden door and opened it quickly.

"Hurry, get in!" Kera shouted, even as she gently pushed them into the separate space and time.

As she ushered in the last little red-haired girl, she turned to face Kera.

'Will we die in here?"

It was hard to answer a question like that, truthfully, to a child. Kera fought back her tears and lowered to one knee, placing her hands on the girl's tiny shoulders.

"I don't know," Kera softly voiced the truth. "But if you are out here, then you will die."

"Will you?"

Kera looked down and away. She reminded herself that she was speaking to a young Light of the Order, not just another child. It was wrong to lie to her fellow Lights. They were her family. They were everything to her. Every wrong she ever committed against them was a wound inflicted on herself.

"Yes, I will," Kera answered, gravely, before meeting the girl's now tearing eyes. "If all goes well, the Renegades will come home. Light Rylin will get you all out of here when the war is over."

Kera heard heavy footsteps and she sprang up to her feet.

She slammed the door shut.

Kera turned to see the giant Zenen'Rol. He barreled down the hall at a full sprint with a curved dagger in each hand. He covered yards with each stride. He would have the first move. He slammed his full enormous weight into her, shoving one dagger deep into her abdomen.

Zenen hissed. "You have played quite the game with me, little witch." Spit flew free from his growling lips. The intrusion of the dagger ripped inside her. He lifted her up with the weapon. His raging dark face filled her vision.

Kera's eyelids grew heavy while her mouth gaped open. She could not escape what was about to happen. The tip of his dagger angled up, scraping against the inside of her ribs. Her lungs were cut and filling with blood. She struggled to breathe. Her feet were off the ground.

Kera's eyes found the door to the Temporal Study. She steeled herself against the pain. She smiled and a hot trickle of blood formed at the corners of her mouth.

"I have… one more… game… Kasarin." Kera paused, coughing blood into Zenen's face. She struggled against her heavy left arm and pointed at the door. She mumbled a few words and poured her will into her hands. A ball of orange flame, as big as her head, dashed from her hand and slammed into the door. The force of the blast sent ember-edged pieces flying every which way.

Beyond where the door once stood, there was only the white marble of the wall. The children were either dead or alive, but they were out of Kasarin reach.

Kera smiled, knowingly. "Keep away…I win."

Zenen angrily twisted the blade against Kera's heart before slamming her to the ground with a loud crunch. There were dozens of broken bones. She lay face down as blood continued to pool underneath her.

As Kera died, she hoped Ishell would find the letter that

was tucked away in the walls of her study den.

-32-

Rylin sat, cross-legged, on the cold stone floor of a dungeon cell. The cell door was open to the dark hall. He was here, of his own volition, to study in complete silence. A single candle cast its glow from several feet in front of him. Its solitary light heightened his concentration for many of the tasks at hand.

Some of his powers were returned to him. Rylin could shape simple fire and mend spells, and that restored some of his sense of self-worth. But he needed to do so much more. The Renegades needed more from him, now more than ever.

On a straw pallet beside Rylin, sat a tall stack of books. These were all filled with the most advanced mathematical methods and theories. He would need their knowledge, above all else. He only recently began to understand that numbers and patterns were not just a way to shape Chronomancy spells. They were used to commune with the Temporal Current.

These last four years, Rylin cast hundreds of Displacement Cloaks. Only now did he know that a square represented an area. A triangle in a hexagon was a symbol of self. Numbers could be the size of an area, how many people, a difference in speed or potential. By themselves, they meant nothing. If they were infused with Endless Current, a conversation with the Temporal Current might occur. If they were infused with Temporal Energy, an exchange and partnership was created.

Rylin's partnership was temporarily severed. He could not have all his powers restored, yet. But perhaps he was left with a basic connection to the Endless Current for a reason.

For that, Rylin thanked the Fates that Garic, Malkanor's high-born tutor, held one of the largest personal libraries in Stratia. All his personal tomes were a collection of highest academics. His math shelves, alone, were an entire wall that predated the fall of the Mage Clans.

Several weeks ago, Garic found Rylin sitting alone at his old seat in the royal study hall. Garic was delighted to see him. He gushed at how Rylin was his fastest learner. Rylin smiled.

That was not all Rylin remembered of his first days in the study. The tutor held nothing but contempt for him when they first met. After a threat from Aemreen to invoke an opinion from Maloric, Garic was quick to change his approach.

Later that same day, threats were no longer needed. Between the copied mind of Yaekrim, and Rylin's own will, Garic poured through book after book with him.

When Garic found Rylin sitting alone, studying, he looked at the book in front of Rylin and scoffed.

"Geometry, and its practical applications? Fah!" The short, velvet-clad, bald man shut the book. "This is a dunce counting stones compared to our intellect, Torch Rylin. I'll have you waste no more time on such dull-minded basics. His Majesty gives me personal quarters in the north wing of the palace. Arrive there in an hour, and we will go to my collection. I'll introduce you to the ponderings and calculations of pure genius."

Rylin complied, and Garic was true to his word on all accounts. Where the Citadel library boasted the largest collection of magic, history, and alchemy, Garic's was as grand in a different direction. Rylin was amazed to see such a high-walled collection of every non-magical study he could imagine.

Rylin found a small step ladder beside the math shelves, and he climbed to get a better view.

"May I borrow some of these, Master Garic?" Rylin meekly requested while his eyes never strayed from math variants he could only dream of.

"I expect utmost care, and swift return to their precise location." Garic grinned as he acquiesced.

Now, along with the stack of books, he kept a small, leather journal and ink bottle with a long-feather quill beside him. Over the past week, Rylin attempted conversations with the Temporal Current, again and again. He recorded all his failed math formulae, ruling out one theory after another.

"Today will be different," Rylin vowed in the dark, damp confines.

It had to be different. Rylin needed it desperately. He tried to help the Renegades ever since their arrival. He would help Teranen ignite city watch fires and streetlamps. He would help Porra and Merice in the healer's triage. (Though, he could only help with moderate cuts and abrasions.)

But even as he helped them, Rylin saw the scorn in their eyes. Ishell only managed several words at a time for him. He did not fault their recriminations. His actions held a heavy price, and he was not alone in paying it.

Rylin needed to repay the Renegades for his selfish failure. Today would be the day he honored his debt. The town of Borkray needed to be a place of great victory for the Renegades.

Rylin retrieved a small rock from his long coat, raising to one knee. He traced a triangle within a circle on the ground. Then he surrounded the circle with a double layer of numbers. If all went well, he would need the circle.

Rylin stood up and closed his eyes. He was grateful to have found an unused part of the palace dungeon, where the silence was absolute. Had the fighting with Vodessian Marauders continued a few weeks more, even this sub-floor would have occupants and distractions.

Rylin let his thoughts fall away, one by one. Little by

little, his mind slipped into the soothing oblivion of silence. It wrapped around him and absorbed him, like the comfort of a warm bath.

As he drifted, he became open. The constant thrum and pulse in the air was not as strong as it used to be. Much of his inner being was sealed away, even as his will demanded so much more. It was a thirst that needed much to slake, but he was only allowed tiny drops.

So, it took Rylin much longer to hold enough Endless Current to properly infuse his hands.

First, Rylin traced the geometry of self in the air, leaving behind pale green lines of Endless Current. He traced equations for distance, populations and potential events reduced to zero. For each of these equations he traced a question mark around the symbol of self.

In a shocking flash of action, Rylin's tracings vanished. His body tensed in a grip of unseen implacable force. His eyes rolled into his forehead. His head rolled back against his shoulders. His awareness was yanked into an all-encompassing emerald limbo.

Different equations began to take shape in the air in front of Rylin, filling his perception to the point of a migraine. He realized he was in front of the sentience of the Temporal Current. It was speaking to him.

Rylin followed each equation, ignoring the throbbing ache in his skull. It was a repeating series. In moments, Rylin began to understand the numbers until they became words. Then it was a voice in his mind.

The same words were spoken in accusation, over and over.

What the three might have done will never be accounted.

Rylin responded, tracing golden lines in the air before him. His own accusation was plain.

"In their place, you have permitted the end of many potentials."

The response was dismissive.

Total conclusion is the outcome of all potential. I do not permit imbalance by taking from total conclusion.

Rylin needed a moment to understand the response. As best as he could discern, total conclusion meant death. Time needed to keep a balance by yielding to death.

Rylin was frustrated and confused. How was death viewed as a natural event, but quick aging was a transgression?

The Temporal Current read his confusion.

Total conclusion permits the summary and counting of all actions, and their contribution into other potential. A hastened potential allows the continuation but not the contribution. The equation continues, but the events are garbled.

It was difficult to follow the Current's precise and linear logic, but Rylin thought he at least saw a glimmer of hope. There was an unaccounted flaw.

"Would death have been a preferred outcome for the three?"

The answer seemed an annoyed but wary repetition.

Total conclusion permits a final counting.

"What contribution do the three make now?"

The three have been concluded, their contributions counted.

Rylin suspected as much. The Kasarin Combat Forces did not allow failure. They did not flee, and every battle was to the death. The three Havoc Magi would have been killed to give back their dignity.

Rylin smirked. His hands traced an event where he killed the Havoc Magi. He drew a comparison to the actual event that took place. Each equation held the same outcome: death for the three.

The answer was a begrudging reluctant silence.

Rylin pressed his advantage. He traced a frantic series of numbers and squares.

"There are many total conclusions, now. Many should be disputed. My ability to dispute these conclusions is diminished because of the three that met total conclusion, regardless of my actions."

The silence that followed seemed thoughtful. Rylin waited, patiently.

The Temporal Current mimicked his earlier equation of self, surrounded by question marks. One question mark vanished. In its place, a line stretched outward before it was cut in half.

Before Rylin could respond his thanks, his awareness snapped back into the dimly lit dungeon. A series of glowing green lines filled the air, fading slowly. Some were his own, others were the formulaic responses of the Temporal Current.

Beyond that Teranen stood, eyes wide.

"Fates, Light Rylin! That was quite the trance."

Rylin blinked, as much in confusion as to moisten his eyes. "I thought you and Ishell were helping Errnik repair legion gear."

"I glimpsed you through his forge. I had to see what this was about."

Rylin nodded. Teranen would have seen him through his candle flame. She would have used her Fire Scrying to solve the dilemma with Borkray, but the Havoc Guilds would have sensed her presence in the Endless Current.

Before Rylin could say more, he felt a tingling along his arms and legs, causing his hairs to rise. Looking at Teranen, he knew she felt the same thing. An instant later brought a roaring wave of Endless Current, smashing through their being. It came from far into the east. They both gasped.

"What is it?" Teranen asked.

The waves of Current waned and surged. Each one was an outburst from a different spell-shape.

Rylin knew what such magnitude and frequency meant. With a sense of urgency, he sat down in the triangle. It was difficult to calm his mind. There was a battle of sorcery. There were few in Stratia that could rise to that challenge. But this was a two-sided conflict. All the Renegades were in Pahlinsor. So, who was it? The questions flooded his mind, drowning away his needed clarity.

"Light Rylin, stop!" Teranen snapped in a brisk shout. She sat down on the other side of the candle.

"You will accomplish nothing that way." Teranen reached down to the candle. With one hand, she scooped under the flame. It floated above her palm and moved to her index fingertip. She lifted the flame until it was eye level with Rylin. It was close enough to warm his face.

"See the flame and think of nothing else. Breathe."

Teranen's voice was soft, and it lulled him into compliance. He saw the orange halo around the yellow center. Its brilliance drew his gaze. All his thoughts were lost in the light. They dissolved, melted in the heat of the fire. His breathing slowed. His lungs took longer to fill with air. His body relaxed and the tension left him, one inch at a time.

"Well done," Teranen congratulated, quietly. "Now, try again, Light Rylin."

Rylin closed his eyes and the Endless Current answered him. It was not as little as before, but it still wasn't the filling waves he was accustomed to. Inside the embrace of the Endless Current, he pressed for the sharp ticking pulse of the Temporal Current.

The energies did not inflict crippling agony on his head, this time. Those energies did not respond right away, either. When they did fill Rylin's perception he felt the weight of an omnipresent scrutiny. He might still feel intense pain if he asked for the wrong thing.

Rylin pressed his mind into the ticking pulse all around him. He was surrounded by the emerald hue of the still present moment. He saw the massive rolling shimmer in the air from the battle in the east. Rylin began to float up and out into the east. He moved swiftly, passing through stone walls and earth with incorporeal ease.

Temporal Projection was restored to Rylin. As he crossed half-way through Teril, everything began to blur. At first, it was a dulling of hard edges. Then, definition of clouds and farms began to overlap and bleed into each other. When he flew over Katahn'Sha, everything was lost in a blurry haze, as though he was viewing from underwater.

It was not the cold or pressure the Temporal Current usually imposed for projections that went too far; but he understood what happened. The removed question mark represented his restored ability of Temporal Projection. The line that was broken in half signified his ability would be decreased.

Rylin would not be able to discover the truth of the conflict. He could only speculate with everyone else.

So, Rylin's awareness snapped into the skies above Pahlinsor. He began to float west.

If Rylin could not discover what conflict transpired in the east, he could at least offer a solution to the conflict in the west.

-33-

Ishell crouched low in the lush, wild grasses. The green stalks were as thick as her arm, and almost as tall as herself. The heat of the summer sun beat down, filling her lungs with a hard pressure to breathe. She remained silent, taking slow and smooth movements that reminded her of the crabs walking on the beaches of Katahn. She listened for the heavy footfalls of the Kasarin soldiers.

Ishell paused, easing the tension in her legs for a moment as she inhaled slow, quiet, and deep. She could smell rich soft dirt and the musky pungency of the fields. She carefully brought up her arm and wiped a thick layer of sweat off her forehead with the sleeve of her gray robe. She wanted to Current Project to Rylin, to ask how much further, but it was too great a risk.

It was a boon that at least one of his Chronomancy abilities were restored, and with it a greater ability with the Endless Current. It was not enough for active participation in battle, but he filled the critical role of viewing the Kasarin activities and deployment. His inability to view the eastern coast still chafed in a way Ishell could see and sympathize with. But it was a step in the right direction, and she would take it without question.

Several days ago, Rylin conveyed the Kasarin placement of ballistae and catapults in the miles around Borkray. Rylin gave them exact deployment of their forces from the mesa to each siege weapon. Without his Temporal Projection, that information could only have been gained at the cost of all the people trapped in the town.

More than a week ago, The Havoc Magi had Meld Walked all over Borkray and killed every patrolling town guard they had. By morning the next day, the militia heads were impaled on bloody stakes in a wide semi-circle all around the eastern gate. It was a warning to anyone that tried to leave.

Now, the Kasarins had over three hundred people trapped as hostages. Any move to free them would have alerted the Kasarins, and the siege weapons and Havoc Guilds would have scoured the entire town to ashes and bodies.

Rylin's attention was on the forces overseeing from the top of the mesa. Ishell, and a group of Torches, were preparing a sneak attack on the siege weapons. Teranen and a handful of evokers were leading their own ambush against the Havoc Magi. If all went correctly, all the forces would be in place at the same time. Then they would simultaneously dismantle the entire Borkray assault and evacuate the townspeople to Pahlinsor.

They all had difficulties in their tasks. Ishell and the Renegades needed to move in silence through treacherously loud fields. Teranen was at the head of five hundred Phoenix legion soldiers. They abandoned their breastplates and cuirasses in favor of black, matte chain mail. But this did not completely dull their armor to silence.

Then there were the waiting dozen Meld Walking Candles. The boys and girls were far better trained now. In the past week, if they were not dueling and practicing with the Torches, they held other training.

When Marcelles Tahkaer noticed the Flames and Candles were dying in battle, he was quick to offer help. He knew, as Ishell did. They were dissolving in the Endless Current when the pressure of combat pushed them far beyond their limits; causing them to act in haste. The Phoenix Legions would ambush the students in intense struggles that simulated the battlefield. They managed to convince the students that they were in real danger from all sides.

Ishell thanked the Lord General, often. The boys and girls were no longer dissolving in the Endless Current.

The pepper-color haired veteran general only smiled. "Your Renegades save so many of my men, Torch Ishell. Why would I do less for my miraculous benefactors?"

Ishell pushed quietly to the edge of a clearing in the grass before she withdrew into concealment. The grasses were flattened in a wide circle meant to give enough room for the towering catapult and give the men a clear view of anything moving too close. This catapult was as large as her da's smithy. There was a pile of man-sized boulders covered in a sticky layer of black pitch. Beside the giant pile stood a muscle-corded Havoc Sorcerer. His studded bracer hands were clasped behind his crimson, knee length coat. He appeared bored and disinterested. Several soldiers stood at the ready around the levers and draw ropes, while ten more milled about in a lax patrol. They had no reason to believe anyone would attack this location.

Ishell waited, staying silent in the concealing fields. No move could be made until Rylin signaled that everyone was in place. Ishell took stock of the scene before her, analyzing it to determine how she would take it apart. She needed to disarm the catapult and dispatch the sorcerer in the same quick move. Even if the munitions were not ignited, the spheres could still crush anything in their path.

Ishell wasn't too worried about thirteen soldiers. She only needed to make sure they could not retreat and regroup. She was already very accustomed to their first strikes. The curved blades were ideal for slashing, and with both their hands ready at the hip, they preferred a wide cut, anywhere from neck to thighs. Occasionally, they would gather and strike in unison, but these soldiers were glory seekers. They wanted to claim the pride of single-handed kills.

The Kasarins held a lack of creativity that bordered on predictability. This was evident in both their swords and sorcery.

But they would always make up for it in overwhelming force. Ishell also knew not to get too complacent with their signatures, or they would try something different and catch their enemies off-guard.

Ishell looked up through the pointed green stalks. The sun was two hours past noon. Well, there was no rushing a precise effort like this. She looked down at her grass-stained knees. She felt the dampness soak through and mingle with her sweat. She promised herself a long hot bath that night.

Ishell cleared her mind. She tensed deeper into her low crouch. As soon as the signal came, she would lash out in an instant.

Ishell ached with stiffness when the signal came, an hour later.

"Now!" Rylin's voice snapped into the Current Projection.

Ishell sprang out of the grass, her arms coated in obsidian. In one punch, she reduced the munition basket to splinters. In another loud crunch, she struck the sorcerer's back, crushing the center of his spine.

She added a length of sharpened stone to the knuckles of her gauntlet. She punched and pierced the fallen sorcerer's skull. The crunch of bone and the wet splash of brains reverberated to her hands. She moved too fast for the soldiers to stop the assault. They were stunned and confused at the sudden attack.

From far away sounded thunderous explosions. Ishell felt the earth tremble beneath her. The soldier's tedium was upended into total pandemonium. Bursts of mushroom fire and clouds of thick black smoke erupted across the distance.

Ishell moved with speed augmented by the Endless Current. Her stone bladed gauntlets struck down six of the soldiers before the rest could draw their weapons.

As Ishell expected, her knowledge of their methods allowed her to fight them with ease. Knowing she already held the advantage, they pressed at her in unison. As they cut at her, she parried their strikes and caused three of them to stumble. Their missed steps staggered the others and allowed Ishell to evade the remaining attacks with ease.

After a failed concentrated effort, the soldiers fanned out, circling her. They feinted with probing stabs seeking for openings, hoping to delay her until reinforcements arrived.

Ishell refused to give them either chance. She gathered a heavy burst of Endless Current. She shouted, and a thick wall of towering fire erupted in a wide circle around her. She projected a wave of outward air into the fire. The bent fire wall instantly embraced and devoured the soldiers and the remains of the catapult.

After screaming and burning, the soldiers fell in charred heaps, lifeless. Ishell created dozens of spheres of water and doused any chance of a wildfire.

Ishell paused in the aftermath, feeling for the ripples in the Endless Current. Borvis had his objective under control. There was a steady sense of contained power from the other Renegades as well. The siege weapons fell quickly.

But the high ground in the northeast gave Ishell another impression. Teranen's spell-shaping hiccuped with uncontrolled bursts as she struggled to keep the attention of the Havoc Guilders. The evokers also projected chaotic waves. Their situation was not under control.

Ishell closed her eyes and slipped into a Meld Walk. She Followed the ripples without her eyes, and with certain ease.

When the Meld Walk ceased, Ishell was forced to steady her balance against the violently shaking ground. Explosions, and the shouts of men and women, filled her ears until they rang. Heat seared against one side of her body before she realized she stood directly beside Teranen. Her white Heart Fire blazed around her body, blending into the light of the mid-afternoon. Ishell felt her robe and dress start to warm while her arm blistered. She took a step away from the roaring inferno, projecting a barrier of cool humidity against further burning.

Teranen stood in a braced stance, one leg locked behind her. Both her palms were raised in front of her. Her hands blasted with a double stream of white fire that clashed with five streams of crimson fire. Five Havoc Magi were on the other end of the clash of fire against fire.

Teranen's lips were pulled back in a snarling rictus. Her eyes blazed with both the white fire and furious concentration.

"Are you going to stand there or help, Light Ishell?" Teranen did not look away from her struggle. "We all have our hands full helping the Legions cut down these Guilders. Doing two things at the same time is quite the chore."

Ishell glanced around in a hurried assessment of the battle. She noticed the shimmering white fire that surrounded the spear and sword points. Teranen's Dragon Tongue allowed them to slice through the spells and weapons in single strikes. But this also meant that Teranen's awareness was spread throughout the top of the mesa. Ishell knew that her own insides would burn with pain from prolonging two such spell shapes. She didn't know how the Pyromancer could keep it up.

Ishell saw an easy opportunity to end this battle. With so much heat filling the air, all she had to do was create well placed pockets of cold air to cause friction clashes.

Ishell moved swiftly. She spoke in a rising mumble as the Current flowed into her fingers. The movements of her hands slowed and cooled the vibrations in the air. She allowed her affinity to probe into the summer and the fiery heat, seeking the best placements for the bursts of cold. She shoved them into conflicting pressure. The resulting disharmony crackled and popped with flashes of white energy.

Now that the tiny lightnings filled the air, Ishell needed to direct it. She pushed the pockets of conflicting air, moving them where she wanted.

The Havoc Guilds were too slow to realize a subtle spell

shape was upon them. Tiny sparks of electricity seized into their arms and legs, numbing them. The lightning jabs left tiny singes wherever they landed. In seconds, the Havoc Guilds began to convulse and fall into the electric paralysis. They were not instantly dead, but the Phoenix Legion would put them to a swift end.

Ishell stopped spell-shaping and the cold air pockets succumbed to the heat. The tiny lightnings vanished.

Teranen released the Dragon Tongue and relaxed. Her Heart Fire waned before she turned to look at Ishell with a raised eyebrow.

"If you keep strutting those shapes, I may have to use other elements."

Ishell sighed wearily and chuckled.

Smoke and electric ozone filled the air with a sharp stinging odor.

Ishell was surrounded by a quarter squad of Legionnaires. They took up positions around her the instant she began to perform her lengthy spell-shape. Now that it was done, they added their efforts into the bloody work of killing the paralyzed Kasarins. There was no sparing the 'Guilders' as the Legionnaires called them. If the Soldiers showed unyielding drive to battle to the death, it was much more pronounced in the Guilders. As distasteful as Ishell found it, there was no choice but to deal death to them whenever the chance presented itself.

And Ishell hated every moment of it. Ordinarily, this spell shape would have permitted her to save lives. This time, she only made it so much easier to slaughter them.

And did they show such reservations to the villagers when they cut down children? Ishell challenged herself, inwardly.

Ishell was startled when Teranen placed a hand on her shoulder. The woman was beside her without warning.

"It is war, Light Ishell. It is how we protect all that is close to our hearts."

Ishell sighed. "I know. But this? Burying people alive? It feels so wrong to use these methods."

"It is life or death for all of Stratia, Light Ishell. We do only what we must."

Ishell admired Teranen's simplicity and implacable resolve. Ishell knew the Pyromancer held a similar view to this bloodshed as she did. It was self-evident in the color of her Heart Fire: white, the purest of fire expressions. But at what point was Teranen able to put aside her revulsion and set herself, without hesitation, on doing what was required of her? Why could Ishell never truly find such a point for herself?

No, this wasn't the only truth to the Flame Witch of Dunell. The instant certainty came from a much deeper source. As Ishell only just observed, children were being butchered. To a mother who would give anything to hold her son, again, there was no thought that she showed too little mercy.

Ishell admitted she envied the Pyromancer that unwavering clarity.

"I know, Light Teranen. I only worry that I may cross the same line these conquerors did, and find the same beast prowling within myself."

Teranen gripped Ishell's shoulders and turned her to face her directly. Ishell was forced to meet the absolute sincerity of her hazel gaze.

"We Renegades stand with each other, Light Ishell. We face all our enemies, together, be they Kasarin or the cold that creeps within us." Teranen drew Ishell close in an embrace. "Maybe we don't emerge, unscarred, but I would never let you lose yourself. Continue to guide us, and we will stand with you, Evoker."

Ishell gathered a steadying breath and withdrew from Teranen's arms. She looked to the emerald fields below the sheer bluff and into the west. She saw dozens of clouds of smoke that surrounded Borkray in a perfect half circle. She felt the Meld Walks of Candles as they escorted the people out of the town and into the safety of Pahlinsor.

Many of the Torches arrived. They began Meld Walking detachments of Phoenix Legions back to Pahlinsor.

Ishell allowed a moment to take it all in. Borkray was expected to be a bitter struggle. The Kasarins were ready to break and kill the Renegades, here. There was an unexpected irony to that. The Kasarins expected a total rout for this town. They were right. One side was wiped out, while the other sustained no casualties. Most importantly, the people of Borkray were safe.

Borvis approached, standing beside Ishell. He was covered with dirt, sweat, and blood. He whistled a cheery tune as he spun a small metal sphere on his fingertip.

Teranen raised an eyebrow before she left Ishell with a knowing smile and a wink.

Ishell laughed. "Do you have any idea how ridiculous you look?"

Borvis whistled a sharp high note as he popped the ball into the air. He caught it behind his back with one hand. He stepped close, sliding his feet, before he dipped her back in one arm. He reeked heavily, of sweat and bloodshed, but she ignored it. She would make him cleanse himself, later.

"You are intoxicating when you dance such a flawless General's ball."

Ishell felt her cheeks flush. She looked around, self-consciously and inverted, to make sure they were alone.

"I did no such thing, you buffoon." Ishell laughed while she quickly kissed his lips.

"We lost no one, my jewel. All the townspeople were rescued." Borvis kissed her back.

"Then will you not kiss Light Rylin to thank him, as well?" Ishell teased while she stood up. "His Temporal Projection and coordination were impeccable."

Borvis flushed nervously. "Ah, I would…but Lady Tahkaer would be most cross. Have you seen her with a saber? After that, she might be my healer. That would be thrice as painful."

Ishell laughed and punched him in the arm. "Come on, you dolt. There is no romance to be found in this bloody aftermath."

When Borvis and Ishell arrived at the eastern end of the street, at the edge of Pahlinsor, she was not prepared for the greeting she received.

Hundreds of blue and black armored Phoenix Legions surrounded the entirety of the Renegades. They were a thick, impassable throng that formed a surrounding perimeter in silence.

One soldier, his face covered in blood and ashes, raised his broadsword high into the air.

"Re…ne…gades." He shouted, "Re…ne…gades." He repeated before another soldier joined him, unsheathing his broadsword.

One by one, other soldiers joined in. They continued to repeat the chant, unsheathing their broadswords, pumping them in the air and chanting in a roaring shout. Their declared adulation climbed to a din that shook the ground and sounded into the skies.

"Renegades, Renegades!" The chant filled the late afternoon summer sunlight.

-34-

Ken'Tekira strolled the edge of the mesa that overlooked the valley to the west. In the breezy late sunset, she tried to make sense of the aftermath spread before her in the golden light.

In the silence, she made no sense of any of it.

Earlier in the afternoon, Ken'Tekira saw two dozen giant ruined patches in the tall grasses. Though she could not seem them, now, the broken and charred placements were well etched into her mind. There were an equal number of heavy ballistae and incendiary catapults poised to devastate the canyon town. Any sign of an enemy-and compromised placement-would result in an all-out siege from every remaining force.

Ken'Tekira looked at the town at the mouth of the canyon, nestled in dense woods. With its meager walls to defend it, she should be looking at a giant heap of rubble. There should be Stratian corpses burning.

Ken'Tekira kicked a golden Ka'Rak helmet in irritation. Its red plumes spun, end over end, as it rolled off the precipice. The only dead, here, were from the Crimson Empire.

How was such a monumental failure even possible?

Ken'Tekira also explored the town, earlier in the afternoon. The gates were closed, but it was completely abandoned. There were no fires, no ruins, only belongings and homes left behind.

The winds whispered across the darkening plains. A Ka'Tarth-one of the few scouts and trackers employed in conquest-peeled away from the lengthening shadows and knelt between two dead Ka'Rak.

Ken'Tekira did not turn to acknowledge his presence. She waited for him to report.

"They are all dead at the camp in the east, at the base of the rise, Dragon."

Ken'Tekira ground her teeth. She already viewed the relief and watch camp. Every Ka'Rak and Magi was dead. That wasn't the most perplexing part of it, though. They looked like they were killed without alarm or struggle.

"This I already know, Ka'Tarth. What else?"

"I followed two narrow trails from the north and south. They appear to have moved small, unnoticeable forces into position at the camp."

Ken'Tekira's eyebrows tensed. There was still not enough explanation for how the entire crimson force was wiped out without one Stratian death to show for it. Battles would always be two-sided conflicts. Death occurred on both sides, and in high numbers. The emperor sent more than enough of a force to withstand those losses.

When battles only held death for one side, it wasn't a battle anymore. It was a slaughter. Ken'Tekira inflicted enough of her own massacres to recognize that truth. Slaughters were the result of an inferior force being overwhelmed by something far greater.

But, by the eternity of the empire, no force of the emperor was inferior. Ken'Tekira could not accept such a clear demotion of their superiority. She could accept the defeat resulting from the strange sorcery storm. There were losses on both sides, then. Dunell was the result of a stupid choice made by the Elites, that night.

But this was baffling.

"Ka'Tarth, answer in truth. How do you think this could have happened?"

Ken'Tekira faced the tracker, his weathered eyes shifted as he licked his lips.

"I believe that this level of coordination is impossible without a very deep knowledge of enemy placements and behavior patterns, Dragon. Most of the camp was cut down by sword, while everything else was destroyed by sorcery."

"More to the point," intruded a leathery Elite woman as she climbed a steep rise, "the Endless Current at each placement feels as though it was an exact bane to each over-seeing magus."

"They knew precisely how and when to strike, all at once," Ken mumbled.

"If I might boldly add, Dragon, this precise an operation is impossible," the tracker added. "Even for a trained magus, gathering this much information takes months of scouting and detailing. All while avoiding detection. This force has been stationed here for more than a week, possibly three at the most."

Ken's eyes narrowed. "Do we have a traitor?"

The Elite veteran shook her head. "Inquisitors and the Enchanter Guilds vetted every Ka'Rak, at length, long before departing the motherland."

Ken whirled at them with fists clenched. "Then how was our force taken to task by children and battered soldiers?" She shouted as fury lightning licked her knuckles.

"Dragon, if I may," the veteran sorceress offered, earning an impatient gesture from Ken, "this is not only watch and observation. The precise timing suggests an understanding of assigned posts and times allocated to each placement. Those would only be known in conversations between Elites, officers, and subordinates."

Ken nodded. "Those conversations would only be spoken in Kasarin."

"Barring treachery-and regardless of the magic-whoever acquired this detailed information is fluent in the dialect of the motherland."

Ken nodded again. Her dark eyes were blank in thought. Delkit Mayzeneth, King Iron Wall, was the last encounter who spoke Kasarin. But this culprit was a magus. It was the only explanation for the level of espionage without detection. So, this was a skilled magus that could speak Kasarin.

She wondered at the report of the three young Havoc Magi who were disgraced. Could it have been the same mystery sorcerer? But if it was him, why was he not seen since the disgrace in Pahlinsor?

Regardless, Ken'Tekira knew the plan to break the Stratians, here, was a failure. She held the rare chance to learn from her failure in battle, and triumph next time. The Crimson Empire seldom awarded such opportunities. She closed her eyes, listening to the rustling grasses and feeling the warm evening wind brush against her. She calmed the fury of her mind to review what she knew.

The Stratians were given time to observe everything and exploit that knowledge to the fullest. It may not seem enough time to anyone else, but it was clearly generous and ample for this smaller force. So, an attack force could not encamp itself close to a siege for that much time.

The second was a point driven home for weeks. Though the Havoc Guilds tried new spell-shapes from time to time, the versatility of Stratia was superior, even among their children. While this was insulting, Ken could not deny it.

So, what the Havoc Guilds lacked in creativity, they would always make up for with numbers and raw fury. Stratia was utilizing strengths and weaknesses. Ken'Tekira needed to do the same.

Ken smirked with cunning. This knowledge was the start of a truly ruthless strategy.

Solas Merahl stood up, his legs stiff and aching. He blinked, allowing his eyes to adjust to the morning light. Solas Nerilisse, a short, heavy-set aeromancer, five years his senior in the Order, sat down. In her cross-legged position, she assumed her shift. The transition needed to be seamless, undetectable, and subtle.

That was the only way twenty-four Solas could protect the people of Perahl'Glae.

The group of former Solas gathered in the shining city only days before the Kasarins began to claim the beach. That was only one hundred miles to the east. The Solas were only present to distract themselves with the artistic beauty of the capitol city. It turned out to be a coincidence that saved hundreds of lives.

Merahl, and several other Solas, established the illusion that the city was nothing more than another decimated heap of cinders. Elements were weaved together in an intricate sequence that needed to be maintained at the four cardinal edges of the city. The Current flowing into the ritual illusion needed to be constant from each direction.

Merahl, and seven other Solas worked in exhausting shifts to maintain the illusion. All the other Solas were dedicated to tending to the city's needs.

In the first week, the white-garbed citizens seemed to understand the need to stay inside the city limits. If any of them were to leave the protective illusion, the Kasarins might see an unscathed Perahli leaving a charred ruin. It would not be long after that the truth would be known to the invaders.

Over a month after that, the citizens grew restless. They began to gather at the edge of the city, demanding to pass beyond the borders.

Perahli were never known for violence, so the city guards

only needed to bolster their numbers and increase the patrols. It was the first time, in centuries, that their prisons held more than one hundred offenders.

With sixteen Solas seeing to the city's needs, the food and water were unlimited, and the streets remained clean. Often, this meant they achieved the former by seeing to the latter. Transmuting mundane materials was, after all, a simple ordeal for a Solas.

Merahl walked the streets of ivory. The stones shone with a rainbow brilliance that gave the city is namesake: Pearl Gleam. The streets were lined with smooth, pleasantly rounded buildings that allowed the sun and moonlight to reflect everywhere.

There were islands of raised ivory stone spread throughout the middle of the streets. These were filled with rich Terilian soil that nurtured a myriad of both common and exotic flowers. There were also small fruit trees planted in the center of each of these islands. They provided a comfortable shade and a delicious treat at the same time.

In the silence of the morning, Merahl heard the bubble of water fountains. Some cascaded along crystal, tiered platforms, while others sprayed, artfully, from openings in ivory sculptures.

Merahl walked through several gardens and plazas, underneath balconies from open-air bed chambers and art galleries.

Merahl drew in a long breath of cool morning air and marveled at the city. True, he was born and raised in Perahl'Sen, but he was from a much smaller town, and its level of beauty and expression was only a portion of the wonder, here.

Despite the grandeur, the people believed it was a prison, now. The Perahli national spirit was free-natured and inquisitive. The people wanted to explore, to know and experience new things. All of them were artists and scholars.

Merahl looked ahead and saw a small blonde woman storming toward him. He ground his teeth in restrained frustration. Sometimes the people could be insufferable and impatient, complaining at the slightest discomfort.

"Solas Merahl," the white silk robed Perahli noble woman began, "I come with a written permit from Queen Behrain granting me departure."

Merahl sighed and glanced in the direction of the white, cloud-caressing spires of the palace. Of course, with Lycendrik sealed away in his chambers, the people went to their secondary ruler. The problem was that her majesty never held a mind for ruling. Everything about her presence was purely symbolic. Lycendrik wouldn't have been much better, but the Order could at least reason with him.

"Lady Daginae, her majesty is under unusually high stress, these days. If not, I am certain she would remember that no one can enter or leave, no matter the reason. It is for everyone's protection." Merahl tried to keep the bored annoyance hidden as he spoke.

Daginae came closer, thinking to intimidate Merahl with her angry blue-eyed glare.

"I am duchess to the largest estate in all Perahl'Sen. I am confidant to her majesty, herself. Last night, I had the humiliation of falling ill. Can you surmise the cause?"

Merahl knew where this was leading, and he held no patience for it. One of the easiest and cleanest ways to provide an infinite supply of food was to revert any material to its purest energy form in the Endless Current before changing its vibration and giving it another form.

Nobles such as Daginae believed they were eating waste.

"Can you tell one iota of air from another, Duchess?" Merahl asked with renewed patience.

She stammered. "Well, no…but that is not important."

"It is for this tiresome debate. What we work with is even smaller than an iota of air. It's everywhere, all throughout creation, travelling so fast that we cannot perceive it. The tiniest of tiny, moving from the farthest star into the blood in my veins, faster than I can blink."

Merahl gave her a stern scowl. "So, there are two certainties here: there is as much a chance you ingested divine light from a faraway world as a chance you ate last week's refuse. Second, you likely fell ill from inebriation. I suggest a decanter or two less, next time."

With that, Merahl shoved his way past the Perahli duchess. He ignored the indignant gasp that followed him.

Merahl did not feel like finding an inn. His night was long, exhausting, and he knew he could sleep anywhere. He saw a long bench. It was several yards from a bronze statue of a fully plated soldier, his sword raised high. The point of the blade gushed water down to a bubbling pool beneath it.

Merahl pulled off his brown travel cloak and wrapped it around himself as he lay down on the ivory bench. The location fronted a basin of roses and orchids, giving Merahl a soothing aroma to drift into rest.

The aeromancer sighed, thinking. He wanted to leave the city, too. His bones felt the urgency to depart. He felt the violent shockwaves in the Endless Current. A war was being fought (no longer a one-sided massacre). He felt the restless need to rush into the fray to end this madness or die trying.

Merahl also felt the clash in the south. When it stilled, he knew the Zenith Citadel had fallen. His home for decades was gone, and there was no way of knowing who was left to tell of it. There was no way they would have all survived, but he hoped that many had fled.

-35-

Rylin shuffled his feet in ragged weary steps, dragging his low boots against the dark gray cobblestones. He was physically and mentally exhausted. It was two days since the victory of Borkray. He spent days in Temporal Projection, studying the Kasarin layout and tendencies, stopping only to relay the details both in writing and speaking with Ishell and Teranen. Just as they toiled and trained hours of their day, preparing to ambush and dismantle the siege, he rarely stopped to rest or eat during those days. He would return to those exact moments around the mesa, over and over, heavily scrutinizing everything he saw.

Now, Rylin also had a deep-seated headache that continued to throb with force all over his head. His earlobes ached. His sense of reality was a little distorted from forcing himself to play through a continuous déjà vu. The world shifted in a surreal way, hazy, and dream-like. He pushed himself through each task even as fever threatened to claim him.

But how deep a price did every Renegade pay to rescue each Stratian? How much strain and agony did each child Candle endure? There was pain and death paid at every turn while he remained in Pahlinsor. If his friends had to pay such a staggering price, he would make himself pay as close to the same toll as he could.

But Rylin would not allow that victory to become the end of his efforts. He did not celebrate, and he did not stop to rest. In the past couple of days, he pushed himself to help the malnourished and injured refugees of Borkray. His Mend shape was in almost constant use. He had greater strength with the Endless Current after pushing himself with Temporal Projection like he did. His Mend could restore broken bones, repair hemorrhaged and battered organs, and he could improve blood circulation or slow it. He spent the last two days at Aemreen's side, in the healer's triage. Merice and Porra were also a steady presence.

If not for the boy Illumancer and the Hydromancer, he would have pressed on, even after Aemreen departed several hours ago.

In the first half of the day, Rylin sat in Temporal Projection again. He had to excuse himself, several times, to regain his strength, but his efforts did not reveal anything of great importance. After the total victory of Borkray, the Kasarins held a silent and unmoving position just east of the Terilian border. So far, none of the Terilian farmlands were damaged, and the people were unharmed.

The Kasarin focus was squarely on Malkanor. Rylin saw it in the placement and reinforcement of their armies. Malkanor defied annihilation, stood against them and survived. It confounded everyone because Malkanor was not the greatest military power in Stratia, even as they held the potential for it. The Phoenix Legions were only known in western Stratia, and only as enforcers and peacekeepers. On their own, the Kasarins would have done away with them as swiftly as they dispatched King Delkit and his men.

The Renegades were the component that changed that. As Light Teranen demonstrated first: when magic and swordsmanship were united, it was a greatly enhanced force. This was something the Kasarins would need to consider carefully before provoking.

After Rylin left the tall, wide, white tent, he attempted to Fold Step, once again. He was met by a wave of exhaustion that made his knees buckle. He sat down on the dark cobbles to recover for a few minutes. The Temporal Current allowed him to have some of his Projection restored, but it was not yet time for anything more. But there was much to suggest his penance was almost complete. A feeling of tightness in the Current, that made him think of anticipation.

Not wanting to strain any welcome with the Tahkaers, and not wanting to exhaust the resources of the inns where the Renegades slept, Rylin walked into the Outer City, towards his mother and father's home. He could help them, at night, while he was there. Each little chore he did for them, with or without the Endless Current, was another way to push his will.

Tonight, as his feet stumbled with heavy fatigue, he was late. The streets of the Outer City were empty and quiet. A sliver of the moon slowly made its rise over the dense woods and sprawling fields in the east. Tall black iron torch posts cast their bright orange glow as they lined the walkways. The windows to the single floor homes were dark. The people already found their beds for the night.

Rylin arrived at his mother and father's squat dark gray home. A single candle flame cast its tiny glow from a window ledge. It was left by his mother to welcome him, allowing him to find his way to a meal and a place to sleep. They would be sleeping now, but they would try to greet him in the morning.

Rylin entered and found a bowl of stew filled with bits of meat and vegetables, as well as a thick slice of bread. He projected a small wave of heat into the bowl to warm it. He sat down before the glow of the single candle and ate with a fervor that surprised him. He really should tend to the needs of his body with more consistency.

As Rylin ate, he thought more about the Displaced Potential Reckoning, and its place in the history of the Golden Hourglass Clan. It was obvious they had encountered it as well, or it would not have been recorded. Thinking about it was preferable. It stopped him from senselessly dwelling over his regrets.

The histories stated the Chronomancers meddled with time in reckless ways. If they were disbanded, as a result, why was their lore so well preserved?

It was not the first time Rylin wondered about this, but this felt like the right time for answers.

What if they took similar calculated risks that Rylin did? How close was he to repeating history? How many Chronomancers were crippled by Displaced Potential Reckoning? Did they ever fully recover? Were there worse punishments?

Rylin finished his meal. He lay down on a small mattress in a corner room. He covered himself with his forest green coat for a blanket. He opened the book of the Histories of the Golden Hourglass Clan. He read until his eyes drooped heavy with the pull of sleep.

Nothing came from his examinations. Rylin projected a tiny burst of air at the candle flame before he drifted to sleep in the darkness.

The halls were unlike anything Rylin could have imagined or dreamed of. So, this was a vision. They were wide, and cavernously spacious. There was a layer of perfectly smooth crystal over the floor. Beneath it was a series of gold and silver cogs of varying sizes, everywhere. Their purpose was indecipherable; but the Temporal Current manifested and channeled through them. The walls were made of silver, inlaid with emeralds cut into geometric shapes and equations.

The Temporal Current hummed everywhere, eager to aid, guide, and supervise. Its potency was so tangible that Rylin could almost reach out and touch it. He walked, his shoes echoing loud. There were doors made of lustrous gold. Each had observation windows made of emerald, smoothed to perfect green panes.

The rooms were all empty of people. Rylin peeked into some of the chambers. There were gold table and silver chairs set with green silk cushions. There were golden bookcases filled with tall thick tomes, covered in fresh leather.

There were several familiar meditation circles, far more elaborate than Rylin's. The floors and golden stands held emeralds containing pulsing Temporal Energy within. Their placement seemed perfectly aligned for advanced spells and rituals beyond anything Rylin had ever learned. There were also empowered emeralds dangling from the ceiling, at varying heights, from hair-fine threads.

As Rylin looked closer, he noticed the emeralds were not placed only for advanced spells, alone. They were perfectly placed for every mathematical gesture Rylin had ever learned. The results would be awe-inspiring, no matter the level of chronomancy performed.

Rylin was in a vision to answer his questions about the Golden Hourglass Clan. He was so excited he began a sprint to search for people. If he could find one fellow Chronomancer he could learn so much. It was a chance he thought gone with the death of Yelisian. He felt giddy as blood rushed to his head. He could have giggled like a child. He wanted to sleep and remain in this dream for years. This was a chance to learn as much as he could from this vision.

It occurred to Rylin that he could go into any of the chambers. He could look at the shelves, locate study journals and spell books in minutes. But books survived the coming seven thousand years. Rylin was alone with that knowledge in his own time.

Every Light of the Order could share and relate their knowledge and experiences, but he was alone. No evoker or elementalist would truly feel empathy for the growth and trials of chronomancy.

Now, Rylin could find out why. The Temporal Sanctum, as he knew it was called, was empty so far. He ran at a full reckless sprint, listening for steps and voices. He did not think he could talk to them, and be heard, but he could learn the truth that evaded him for so long.

Rylin heard the distant murmur of conversing voices over his own running feet. He wondered if these visions involved any true use of Chronomancy at all. He knew if there was any chance of that, a Chronomancer would detect his presence. But that seemed less important to Rylin, now. All that mattered was that he was in the infinite interior of the Temporal Sanctum. This excited Rylin because, in a way, he was home.

What must it have been like in the apex of its time? How did they distinguish between novices and masters? How did new initiates spend their days? Did they run for miles through sand dunes to increase their will? When did they use Temporal Projection to rise and tower over their previous limitations? How many people walked these halls during their golden age? What did they look like?

As many questions as there were, Rylin had so many more. His thrilling sense of wonder was boyish in a way he never allowed himself to feel before.

Rylin skidded to a halt at a respectable distance from two men.

One was a tall, dark-haired man wearing plain white robes and carrying an ivory pearl staff. Rylin knew he was from the Supreme Radiance Clan, Yaekrim's clan. Judging by his confident posture and commanding presence, Rylin felt certain this must be the Supreme Magus of this era. Yaekrim's memory confirmed it as well.

The other was a shorter, stout-muscled man with long platinum hair. He wore ornate, silver, silk robes. He held a gold staff that housed emerald gears and turning cogs at its ends.

Rylin was fascinated to see the deference the Supreme

Magus bodily conveyed to the Chronomaster. As he watched the two conversing, he realized this master must be the Temporal Arbiter. It was a title bestowed upon the leader of the Golden Hourglass Clan. He was not familiar with the name of this Arbiter, and there were no portraits of him in any historical tomes.

"Please, don't do this, old friend," the Supreme Magus pleaded. "Recruit, teach, start anew. Don't discard it all. The other four clans need you. They need the Golden Hourglass. All of Stratia will always need you."

The Temporal Arbiter laid a reassuring hand on the Supreme Magus's shoulder wearing a sad wan smile. "No, Stratia doesn't. I believe in the abilities of the remaining four clans. I believe in their united strength, knowledge, and wisdom. They will be enough to guide our world."

"We need you to lead us, to show us our strength, as you always have." The Supreme Magus countered. "Do you not see the lives you saved? Do you not see the lands you caused to flourish? Kings, who once gathered their arms in complete hatred, determined to shed blood, and the Golden Hourglass stopped them until they were ready to part as brothers."

The Arbiter nodded and closed his eyes. "I know this. The good we do-so many well-placed intentions- and we think to do more, beyond our abilities. It has caused a lack of respect for the forces we ally with."

"To what harm? What persons were injured or lost? We found no trace of anything you claim."

"That is the only reason I am sane and lucid enough to soundly pass this judgment." The Arbiter spoke calm and patient, even as the Supreme Magus was desperate.

"...because you set straight the mistakes of your brothers and sisters."

"You must understand, even with all our accumulated wisdom, even with all the good and powerful people in our clan, we all broke the rules of time."

"Your clan should have led all five clans, you know." The Supreme Magus slumped his shoulders as he mumbled sadly and lowered his eyes.

"No, we should not." The Arbiter ducked into the Supreme Magus's sight. "All the greatest of humankind's achievements will always be under the light, old friend. If we were to lead, we would cheat the fates. We would be little more than jaded immortals, feigning a level of understanding far beyond our reach."

The Temporal Arbiter straightened and stepped back.

"Have you done as I asked?"

The Supreme Magus nodded. "Aye. I selected your secondary option."

The Arbiter shook his head in dismay. "This is the only chance we will ever have to destroy the lore. The Temporal Current will only dull the protective enchantments on the books for a few more days. Once I return the Temporal Sanctum to the Endless Current and the bygone futures, the enchantments will renew the defense of the books."

"That is what I am hoping for. You may have never found an ideal keeper for the craft, but I must hope where you despair. Maybe one will come who is equipped to withstand the knowledge and wisdom in a way you dare not hope for."

The Arbiter bowed at the hips. "It is your decision, of course. I will hold you no ill-will as long as you do as I wish with the final tome."

The Supreme Magus nodded before turning away. "The lore that you decreed condemned was already reduced to ashes and dust."

The two masters walked in separate directions. The Supreme Magus left through the open, towering double doors. Rylin followed the Arbiter deeper into the Sanctum. He listened to the mesmeric grinding and hum of the golden staff in the silence of the halls.

"So, what did you do?" The Arbiter asked without turning.

Rylin stumbled over his own feet baffled and startled. Did the Temporal Arbiter speak to him?

"I am speaking to one in future penance, am I not? Displaced Potential Reckoning? Tell me what you did without revealing anything that will disturb coming events." The Arbiter turned and looked directly at Rylin.

"How can you see me? How do you know I did something?" Rylin asked with suspicion, but he felt dizzy with disbelief.

"The Temporal Current allows a look into history as a way for a Chronomancer, under penance, to gain required wisdom before they regain their powers. I confess, this conversation is an oddity. Pondering how this came to be is enough to drive either of us insane. Normally, I would not speak to one in your predicament. The Temporal Current does not usually permit it. But I am alone here, and I am the last. What we discuss can be allowed, so long as I take it to the grave in silence."

Rylin nodded, mulling over the words. He needed to speak carefully. He understood the Arbiter's wary misgivings. Time was linear, but the future was an ever-changing nebula. It held many branches that off to events that constantly ceased existing, because there were choices that always changed it. For the Arbiter, talking to a student so far in the future should not even be possible. It hinted that there were some things in the future that were immutable. That, alone, was enough to cause a person to shutter.

"You did not know I could see you. You are from far away. Our clan is gone, where you come from. That is why you know so little. Yet, I sense what is locked away from you. There is great ability in you, though it is crudely used. Your skills make me think of an Adept, yet you have more than enough power for a

Master. It is only refinement of your skills, and infusion of other crafts, that keep you from truly deserving the title of Expert. I do respect the balance you strike in body and will. Most of our masters impose increases in will through the body, alone."

Rylin's head spun for a few moments more before he pushed his mind back into order.

"Why? Why is there no one to teach and show me? Why do I only have books? Why is all of it gone?" Rylin raised his eyes and narrowed them as he pressed his questions.

The Arbiter sighed as he leaned against a wall. "You are not the only one who must choose his words with care. What is not known in the future is to stay mostly unknown. Answer me first."

"I accelerated age on three people. I risked it as a means of sending a message, trying to disperse a volatile situation."

The Arbiter nodded, appreciatively. "Tactfully phrased. Did it work? Was your message heeded?"

Rylin shook his head. "It was a waste of time and my powers."

"It would have been worse for you if it wasn't. Do you know the two things we are least allowed to affect?"

Rylin nodded again, reciting. "Potential and event."

The Arbiter smiled, and clapped Rylin on the shoulder. "You answered your question as well as mine. Perhaps he is not wrong to hope, after all."

Rylin woke up, his eyes opening to discover bright sunlight spilling through the den windows. He flung aside his covers when he realized it was only an hour or two away from noon. He dressed and straightened his hair, quickly. He needed to find Ishell and resume his watch over the Kasarin forces.

That was when he felt it. There was no need to watch the Kasarin forces. A massive wave of Endless Current shoved through him, an echo of intense sorcery. It was followed by another, and then a series of bursts. Each one was large, pushing against his lungs, but they varied as well. There were hints of moisture, cool water on his tongue. There was heat warming his skin, before it was cooled by a gentle breeze. There were other sensations warring for recognition in his awareness.

That was the point of it though. It was war, it was battle. It was in the east. Judging by the intensity and the ease that he could identify it, Rylin knew it was as close as Teril.

While he slept so deep in the vision, the Kasarins must have struck against the nearby village of Thriwald. It was only three recently constructed farmsteads close to the Terilian and Malkanor Border. It was hoped the three families that resided there would one day cause it to flourish into a town. That hoped seemed dashed.

The Kasarins must have struck before dawn, forcing a defensive response from the united Stratian force. It would have been in haste, with no preparation and little strategy.

Rylin ignored the breakfast left for him at the table. He slipped into Temporal Projection with a thought. Rylin sent his awareness over the vast plains and rugged woods to the east. He allowed time to move in its normal green hue, only seeking the defensive force in Teril. The journey did not tax his will in the slightest, even without a drawn circle and a sitting position.

Rylin located Thriwald in seconds. There were sprawling flats of crops growing in neat order at the base of a hill, climbing high to the east. Each of the modest farmsteads were little more than several brick and wood homes, as tall as several flights.

Rylin felt a hard jarring sensation jolting against his awareness. He forgot that it was nearing midday meal, a new respite Maloric imposed to keep the laborers of Malkanor in good health. Rylin's mother and father would have returned home only to find him standing in a trance.

Rylin pushed through the intrusion to observe the battlefield. There were catapults and crimson spheres of fire hurled about to the east of the farmsteads. Fields were ablaze with flash fires, filling the skies with a thick oily smoke that started to dim the sunlight. Craters of crushed and detonated earth marked both east and west, as the gray and brown robed Renegades tried to deflect the devastating siege munitions. Hundreds of Phoenix Legion corpses were maimed and left in the fields where they would burn, soon.

The Renegades were rallied together in a tight defense, but their backs were pressed to each other. There were hundreds of Guilders maintaining their assault at a safe distance while the Ka'Rak numbered in a crushing wave of thousands. This force was at least four times greater than the entire combined force of Renegades and Legions. Imperial Fire and blood red vines assailed the Renegades from every direction.

The Kasarins were surrounding and isolating the Renegades, creating a perimeter that was too thick for the unifying force of magic and swords.

Rylin saw something that sent a surge of panic flooding through him. Marcelles Tahkaer, and five Legionnaires, stood battered and cut off, surrounded by three dozen Ka'Rak. Their chain mail was already broken, in places, revealing deep bloody cuts beneath. There broadswords were marked with deep chips that would soon crack and break.

Rylin searched a moment to find a clear patch of undisturbed farmland, about a mile west of Thriwald. In a couple of Fold Steps, he could aide Marcelles.

Rylin opened his eyes, his teeth rattling as his mother and father shook his shoulders.

Rylin blinked several times. "I'm alright, Ma'." Rylin reassured, chuckling as he gripped her slim shoulders. "I was Temporal Projecting, trying to find out what has transpired since I slept so late."

Leain's light blue eyes were filled with relief. "I'll never grow accustomed to this."

Rylin wanted to give his mother and father more reassurance, but there was not enough time.

"I have to go, now. Ishell, Aemreen's father, they are in mortal danger."

"Don't do anything foolish," Kylor cautioned, his dark brown eyes stern.

Rylin snapped his fingers, summoning his coat to wrap his shoulders, and his staff into his hand. Both answered the call of his restored will and power. The Temporal and Endless Current flowed through him with a hunger for crafted purpose.

Rylin winked and grinned before he shaped his Fold Step in a thought.

-36-

Rylin's second Fold Step placed him at Marcelles's side. He was close enough to wrap him in his own Displacement Cloak of increased speed. Rylin stood in a wide stance with his emerald staff ready in both hands.

Rylin kicked up a cloud of dust at his feet. Before the dirt settled, a Dust Mimic stepped free of the debris.

The Dust Mimic cast a displacement Cloak of its own. It stepped forward and rapidly deflected dozens of sword-strikes every second. The Mimic was a blur of motion, moving everywhere at once. At first it stood just before Marcelles, then it blurred, the staff already halting a strike at a Legionnaire's throat, twenty feet away.

Rylin chuckled. "You know, my lord, I never realized I appear that way."

Marcelles stammered with sounds that conveyed uncomprehending disbelief.

"It is requested that we return alive. I'll not allow your daughter's heart to break, this day." Rylin cast a separate variation of the Displacement Cloak over Marcelles and his five Legionnaires. They would move three times faster, now; and the variation would help them adjust to the increased speed.

"I must see to the Renegades and the villagers. My mimic will remain with you. You will not fall today." Rylin investigated the distance where Kasarin soldiers massed in a concentrated force. Raw, rippling waves of the Endless Current surged from inside the mass of bodies. Roaring groans sounded outward from the center.

Rylin stopped a curved sword aimed at his hips with a projection of Temporal Current into his coat. A Stasis Cloak caught the weapon and broke it into shards before dispersing. He Meld Walked through the soldiers to stand with his fellow Lights.

Rylin stood between Ishell, Teranen and Borvis. Ishell did a double take in her glance at him.

Rylin wasted no words. He channeled Temporal Current into his staff as a dozen Stasis Spheres launched into the sky to seek out the catapult rounds. They crumbled into dust as they collided with the halted time.

"Did you rest well, Light Rylin?" Ishell managed to jibe. She whirled to deliver a round crushing punch to a soldier in front of her. Her arms were coated with a thick layer of jagged obsidian stone.

"Well enough to count, Light Ishell. Did you know there would be so many, or did you desire the thrill of being vastly outnumbered?" Rylin spoke even as he let his staff float beside him, and he began to shape a moderate Stasis Field. His hands blurred with emerald trails of energy before a fifty-foot radius, directly ahead, ceased all its movement. Everything in that space was halted in time.

It was a temporary solution, but it did close away one direction. This would hinder the Kasarin press a little.

Rylin crouched low and scooped a handful of dirt. He needed to shape a little, this time. When he blew the dust free of his palm, four more Dust Mimics emerged.

Rylin limited their functions to defending against the Kasarin Soldiers. It was a conserving endeavor. Even so, he was surprised to find his will and his stamina were not taxed in the slightest. Several months ago, his insides would be raw with so much sorcery at once. Coming back from his penance allowed him to return stronger than he was before.

But Rylin learned a terrible lesson from his battle in the Outer City. He learned that his powers would not grant him the luxury of going through war with clean hands. He naively believed a demonstration would settle things without blood and death. His arrogance created only so much more pain for the innocent.

That was a moment in the past. If the Kasarins would only permit life to be a spoil for the victors, then Rylin would harden his resolve. He would deal death as swiftly as they would.

Rylin felt the gathering Current long before he saw a large ball of trailing red fires arcing high overhead. It was going to fall on the Renegades.

Rylin held his hand up to the coming attack. He poured the Endless Current into his coat.

"Ionsu!" Rylin shouted as the imperial flames converged on him. It was a word spoken in the ancient language of the Fabricators. It meant 'absorb'.

The golden runes along the lapels of his coat began to glow. The ball of flame decreased in size. Several feet away from his hand, it was a little more than the size of his fingertip. Then it vanished.

Rylin calmed his mind to a soothing clarity. A massive wave of Endless Current howled through his being. The runes of his coat blazed with greater intensity, becoming golden fire. The Torch Renegades around him turned to look at him with wide eyes and gaping mouths.

"Dubailt!" Rylin roared at the top of his lungs. This word translated as 'duplicate'.

A volley of dozens of spheres of Imperial Fire hurled outward into the ranks of Kasarin soldiers. Each ball was as large as the one Rylin stopped. In every direction, blossoms of red fire burst into the sky with thunderous explosions. The ground trembled and quaked. Burning, screaming Kasarin bodies were cast high into the air.

Rylin walked forward through the thickening haze of smoke. The cries of dying men were lost on his singular clarity. He reached into the rigid linear energies of the Temporal Current, focusing it into the end of his staff.

Surviving soldiers rushed to cut him down. Rylin met them with a barrage of head-sized Stasis Spheres. The soldiers were struck in the head, chest, and extremities. The result was a gory mess as running soldiers left their heads and hearts behind them. Sword arms ripped free. Soldiers fell screaming, clutching the bleeding stump where their leg once was. Blood soaked the ground while body parts floated in the air.

Rylin Fold Stepped in front of a Legionnaire on his back. Rylin's staff was over-head, catching a downward strike. He let it slip free to grind against his coat's Stasis Cloak. Bits of glittering metal showered the ground.

Rylin projected another Stasis Sphere into the Kasarin's chest. He gasped and fell dead as his heart seized.

Rylin was devoid of mercy, now, and filled with a deep focus that drove him from one soldier to the next. The Legionnaires gradually regrouped with the Renegades. The battle began to slowly change. Where, before, the Kasarins divided and trapped the Stratians, there were now great swaths of Kasarins being struck down.

Among it all, Rylin Fold Stepped and dealt swift cruel death at every turn.

Rylin's strange mirror images held off the press of the decreasing Kasarin soldiers.

That gave Ishell a moment to stare with undisguised bewilderment at the ceaseless onslaught. Her shoulders sagged.

Her childhood friend, the meek and selfless boy she had always known, moved with unbelievable speed, and struck with an otherworldly precision. The waves of Current at Rylin's call shoved against the Renegades with force.

This was not the gentle boy who always helped Kylor and Leain in the fields. Rylin was a titan, here, a being possessed of one unavoidable objective: to kill every Kasarin unfortunate enough to fall into his sight. He showed no fatigue that would prevent him from reaching that goal.

"Fates, Light Ishell!" Borvis gasped. "But he is a terrifying one."

Ishell could not think of anything to say against that. She was stunned, herself, but she could neither agree nor disagree. This was a side of Rylin she never expected. His aggression was cold and methodical. He would appear at any point where the death of a single Legionnaire would begin a new isolation for the Stratians. It appeared he felt the possible shifts in battle.

Not much could be called common knowledge about the Chronomancers. Ishell read many books from the Dragon Tooth Clan, and where there were mentions of the Golden Hourglass Clan, there was one common agreement: the battle-hardened warrior evokers would never stand in battle against even an Adept Chronomancer.

Only now, as Ishell watched Rylin pierce deep into the Kasarin offensive, did she understand the proud clan's reluctance. It was a sight no Stratian Magus had witnessed in over seven thousand years.

"He is giving us an opening. Find Duke Tahkaer and let us rally against them," Ishell shouted as she spell-shaped more obsidian to armor her body as she charged west.

Jagged shards of sharp metal flew in a wide spray from behind Ishell. Borvis over-extended his energies to cut down anything approaching from either side. Ishell leaned forward into a shoulder first dash. The weight and hardness of her obsidian armor crushed anything directly in front of her. Curved swords shattered to pieces, followed by obliterated armor. Crunching Kasarin bones reverberated through the stone.

Explosions boomed in the east. Teranen gathered her Heart Fire and shaped giant blooms of sun white fire and melting heat.

Marcelles and several of his Legionnaires flurried into a speed-augmented counter-offensive. Though their armor and weapons were only a little more than useless, their movements blurred. Their broadswords flicked out to the smallest inch of exposure in the pleats of the Kasarin armor. Marcelles and his men held ample time to locate and strike at any opening, no matter how small.

One of Rylin's strange copies was present. It blocked any strikes the Soldiers could not deflect or parry themselves. It created more openings for the counterattack. The copy was possessed of the intention of defense, allowing everyone to push back.

Ishell ended her dash by vaulting herself forward. She slammed through the Kasarin mass before spinning and skidded to a halt beside Marcelles. She shaped a wind vacuum that pulled the air out of the Kasarin's lungs. They fell gasping for a breath that would not come.

"It has been an ill morning, my lord," Ishell commented, drily. Her voice was a muffled echo in her armor.

Marcelles smiled. "Aye, but it seems our fortunes are changing, Torch Ishell."

'If you would follow me, I think Light Borvis might be able to spare a moment for your present condition." Ishell looked over his broken chain mail and cracked sword.

Marcelles shook his head. "There is no time for that. Torch Rylin has given us a chance to drive the Kasarins out of Teril. It would be a waste to sit on our laurels as a reward to my son-in-law's generosity."

Ishell nodded in agreement then blinked in realization to the Lord General's words. Did she hear him, correctly?

Marcelles chuckled low under his breath as he ran ahead to regroup with his soldiers. His few accompanying men dispatched the last of the Kasarins around them before blurring to catch up.

Ishell shook away the moment of confusion. She spent half a year training for strength and endurance. That helped with the bulky obsidian armor. But she also had to mentally maintain several Current augmentations for decreasing the strain of weight against her, while increasing the mobility of surrounding her body in stone. Confusion and distraction were dangerous threats that would slow her down.

There was no time to waste. The Obsidian Juggernaut shape was seldom attempted for a reason. The prolonged channeling of Endless Current, in three different ways, had dissolved many magi in battle for centuries. It was a testament of her own strength that she could add her other evocations to the demands, but the inside of her ribs chafed with warning.

Marcelles covered half the distance to several squads that were surrounded by a thick perimeter of crimson armor. Ishell began a full, ground-shaking sprint towards the thick of the mass. She burst into the outer edge of the crimson force, swinging her stone clad arms left and right. Red and gold armored bodies were cast up into the air like leaves in the wind. At a safe distance to either side, Marcelles and his men cut through column after column of Kasarin soldiers. The steel of their swords created shining blurs, leaving sprays of blood everywhere.

The effort was visible to the embattled Phoenix Squads. There were the sounds of renewed fury as the Kasarins surged backwards against the sudden ferocity. Caught between Ishell, Marcelles, and two different sides of the Legions, they were cut down within minutes.

With the two forces reunited, they quickly lashed out at

the immediate Kasarin force, to devastating effect.

In the ensuing silence around Ishell, she allowed a moment to release the Obsidian Juggernaut, and the Endless Current. The black stone crumbled, fell into piles around her feet, and then sifted back into the earth. She braced her palms against her knees, laboring to catch her breath. She was covered in a sticky thick layer of sweat. There was no time to mend any but the most serious sword cuts. She was battered with the promise of many bruises to come. She was exhausted for maintaining the Endless Current for so many hours.

She looked further into the east, close to the rising incline. All of this was a trap, of course. They attacked the villages with a smaller force to draw the Legions and the Renegades out. It was still a force twice as large as anything they faced, before, but she believed ingenuity would prevail, again.

When they arrived, the Kasarins revealed a force twice as large as she expected. It was four times greater than anything they ever battled before. Such a force was overwhelming enough, but they began dividing the Legions from the Renegades in short order. Over a dozen Lights and hundreds of Legionnaires were cut down in the first hour.

Ishell and Marcelles managed to rally a stubborn defense on either side of the battle after that. It was a stalling effort. The Kasarins held more than enough reserves to wipe out the last of the Stratian resistance in a day.

Ishell hated to admit it, but Rylin's timing could not have been better. Her own sense of self-reliance and pride was wounded for it, but she would shelf it as a small price to pay.

Ishell watched the Kasarin ranks, close. Each foremost column burst into fonts of red liquid. Where the Kasarins were foolish enough to rush at Rylin, only swaths of sickening carnage remained.

The Kasarins could not pin him down to any one place, either. His Fold Steps saw him at any given location he chose, moving hundreds of yards in an instant.

The Kasarins were pouring down the slope of a miles-wide incline. Rylin's Fold Steps were carrying him further and further uphill. He was only as alone as he wished, creating any number of copies of himself.

No one ever discovered how much Endless and Temporal Current he could endure, and for how long. While Ishell's training made her a powerful sorceress, Rylin's unorthodox methods in chronomancy gave him an unfathomable wellspring to tap into. Even now, he showed no signs of slowing. She doubted his insides felt any searing at all.

A cool breeze blew in from the south. Ishell straightened and inhaled the invigorating wind, deeply. She had enough time to rest. It was time to rejoin this chaos.

Ken'Tekira watched with dismay and disbelief. Her strategy was flawless, even if it was obvious once her trap was sprung. It was a simple, unavoidable conclusion. For several hours, she divided the Stratian resistance and set about a trial of attrition. With such force in her favor, victory was a slow brewing certainty.

For hours, the catapults were positioned around the entrenched targets. With the press of swords, heavy siege weapons, and Kasarin magic, Ken'Tekira was only minutes away from the final crushing blows against the Stratians.

Now, her fists clenched white with impatient anger. Her eyes widened at the visibly plain disturbance in the field. The catapults launched their heavy rounds, only to do nothing more. She watched over a dozen blossoms of Imperial Fire explode among hundreds of Ka'rak.

From there, the battle inexplicably shifted against her in minutes. Ken'Tekira felt the enormous waves of Endless Current that rushed to a single point. There was a strange tint to that Current, a power with a variety she was unfamiliar with.

It was the same power from a short time after Tihl'Zen. This had to be the mysterious sorcerer at the battle in Pahlinsor. It was the same sorcerer she believed responsible for the massacre at the canyon town. It was terrifying and massive. It was an easy equal to her mentor's power, maybe greater.

And this sorcerer was climbing the hill in fast strides. He left bloody death wherever he passed. The hillside became slippery, soaked in fresh blood. He was coming straight at her.

For the first time in Ken'Tekira's service to the emperor, she debated fleeing. She could order a full retreat of her remaining forces. It was a rare order for a leader in conquest, subject to disgrace.

But running at the appearance of this sorcerer was inexcusable. Ken'Tekira would be even more disgraced if she fled before meeting this challenge. Her name would be stricken from the archives and written in the tome of cowards.

All the same, she knew it would be prudent to face him with an escape plan in mind.

"Ka'Rak, Gauntlet Formation, to me!" Ken'Tekira shouted. Crimson soldiers ran to create a wide double line facing each other. They were poised into their severing stances, one foot far back, posture low, with the hands above the grip of their swords.

Ken'Tekira could not help but smirk in anticipation, despite herself. How long had it been since she met such a challenger in single combat? She faced enemies possessed of greater power than her own, before. She prevailed, then. Perhaps she would, now.

Rylin approached the summit of the rise in dozens of Fold Steps. The soldiers behind him slipped onto their backsides as they attempted to traverse bloody grasses. He saw the double file of poised soldiers forming an obvious walkway to the top.

Did they believe he used too much power in his climb to be able to defend himself, now? Did they think his insides burned with the Endless Current? Did they believe he was anywhere close to his limits?

This all felt so dream-like to Rylin. In a dream, a person can run forever without getting tired. A person can touch the sun with wings of candle wax. It felt that way, now. It felt as though his body and spirit defied reason and logic, existing only to realize his imaginings.

With a negligent wave of Rylin's hand, shadowed by a trail of green light, the swords of the Kasarins around him were encased in Displacement Spheres of aging. The swords browned with rust before crumbling into flakes in their scabbards.

The soldiers looked at their disintegrated weapons with gasps of disbelief.

Rylin looked to the top of the summit. A small woman with corded, whip-like muscles stood with her hands clasped behind her back. She was dark-skinned, with a menacing scowl on her hard features. A long deep scar-a sign of loyalty to the emperor-ran along the middle of the top of her shaved head. She wore the long red vest coat and signature loose black tunic and pants of a Havoc Sorceress. Her arms were covered in black tattoos and black leather bracers.

Rylin knew this woman, both from description from Kasarin Laborers and his numerous Temporal Projections. He already had a thousand reasons to end her life.

"I am Torch Chronomancer Rylin of the Order of the Enlightened Sun." Rylin formally introduced himself, speaking the Kasarin dialect smoothly. His months of study and interaction were clear.

Ken'Tekira arched an eyebrow before raising her head to laugh.

"Fool! Your order is no more. My master, Zenen'Rol, already crushed them."

Rylin wanted to deny the claim, but he knew what he felt far into the east, over a week ago. The trail did end in Katahn'Sha.

Rylin also knew the terrifying whispers that surrounded the use of the name Zenen'Rol. If he was present in the assault on the Zenith Citadel, with as divided as it was, there was a good chance that everyone there was dead.

Ken'Tekira meant to break Rylin's fighting resolve with this claim. He would not humor her. No matter what she might claim, she was very wrong.

"Your claim is as unimpressively incomplete as your efforts to destroy Stratia," Rylin retorted, his voice cold, quiet, and even. "In both instances, Ken'Tekira, Dragon of Zenen'Rol, the Master Fist of the Crimson Throne, we…are…still…here!"

Ken'Tekira stopped laughing and glared at Rylin with a gaze that would have frightened anyone else.

"I will correct this error. You are children, novices, and battered soldiers. The least you could have done is gather finer disciples."

Rylin answered with a chilling smirk before Fold Stepping to her right. "Do you suggest a revered village witch? The best Pyromancer in the world?"

Ken'Tekira lashed out with a dagger hidden at her belt. Rylin was safe out of her reach with a Fold Step to her other side.

"Or perhaps you would prefer my best friend, heir to the greatest mysteries of evocation. She is a prodigy of Stratia's lineage of most powerful sorceresses."

Ken'Tekira attempted a backward kick to Rylin's middle, finding only air. He Fold Stepped back to her left side.

"I could find the student of the hallowed Grand Illumination, Yelisian, if you like," Ken'Tekira gathered a gravelly wave of hindered Endless Current. It was enough to create a length of crimson lightning. She swung the length in a wide circle, hoping to catch him in his next Fold Step.

"Ionsu!" Rylin shouted, and the lightning whip vanished, gathered into the runes of his coat. Ken'Tekira's eyes widened. She was familiar with the primordial dialect for Simulacrum.

"He would probably be an Adept Fabricator." Rylin tapped his chin with his finger, feigning thoughtfulness. He toyed with Ken's growing anger.

Rylin projected a burst of Temporal Current into his staff. The end of his weapon blasted Ken'Tekira with a Stasis Cloak. Rylin created a sufficient opening for her to understand him.

"But you might not enjoy that as much as you think. You see, he inherited the long-forgotten secrets of the Golden Hourglass Clan. His is the magic of time and space."

Rylin released the Stasis Cloak before projecting Endless Current into his coat.

"Dubailt!" Rylin shouted, whipping his free hand. His own length of crimson lightning struck the Kasarin sorceress. The electric shock knocked her off her feet. She flew back yards, skidding and tumbling head over heels.

Rylin dismissed the whip. "Also, that would be me."

-37-

Rylin kept a measured pace a long side the Renegades, though he wanted to hurry out of the commotion. His hood was up, shadowing his face, while his coat billowed behind him. His gleaming emerald staff tapped an even cadence against the cobbled road.

The inner turmoil was a sharp contrast to Rylin's outward facade. The battering heat of the sun lent a heavy weight to his thoughts. The worn and beaten Legionnaires appeared beside him from time to time. Though their armor was broken, and they were riddled with cuts and abrasions, they still laughed raucously and clapped him on the back and shoulder. They openly attributed their survival to him, and they offered to buy his next meal or a tankard of ale.

Rylin smiled in answer. They would not see the troubles that clouded his mind. He saved many of these men, just as they were about to be cut down. It would be an insult to them by denying their cheerful gratitude.

Marcelles Tahkaer maintained an even distance from Rylin. The Lord General's gaze bore down on him. Along with the heat and anxiety, the duke's heavy scrutiny made him feel a bit like an insect under a reading glass.

Rylin looked back and met the duke's gaze. His face was covered in bruises, his head was covered by his broken and bloody chain mail cowl. His sincere brown eyes met Rylin with warmth, as he greeted him with a broad smile. Rylin returned the expression while wondering at Marcelles's sudden and unwavering interest.

"There he is!" shouted a young corporal with a thick and rowdy accent. He was surrounded by several worn looking comrades. "The hero of the day, he is. I was almost cut down by three score of the red ones, and there he is! None moves an inch, and their swords crumble as though they had never been cared for in a hundred battles."

"He was about to cut them all down, anyway," Rylin deflected, remembering something similar being said by Errnik some years ago. A series of laughs answered him.

"You let us buy you a round of the finest and coldest," the corporal invited in a way that rebuked refusal.

"After dusk," Rylin begrudgingly acquiesced.

Rylin searched hastily for Aemreen. She would be here, waiting for her father and himself. He wanted to hold her close, to press her tight against him and feel her arms around the back of his neck. He wanted to bury his face in her hair and smell the sweet fragrance of roses.

Rylin also knew that Marcelles forced a choice on her. He wanted her to choose between donning the weapon and armor, marching into battle, or tending to the sick and injured. Marcelles made it clear that there was no wrong choice, but she needed to give only one all her effort and attention.

Aemreen's choice was clear even before she spoke it. She was a healer. She studied for years to heal people. Her conscience would weigh her down with guilt if she chose the path of taking lives over saving them. She remained in the healer tents, this time.

Rylin was so wrapped up in the looming shadow of his thoughts. He barely took notice of the growing distance between himself and his fellow Lights. But the wary and furtive glances they directed at him were as sharp as knives. They looked at him as though seeing a stranger. Had he really become such a pariah to them? This was their demeanor since the conclusion to the battle of Thriwald. What could have caused them to behave this way? Did he do something different or taboo in some way?

Such paranoia was a luxury Rylin could not grant himself. The Dragon's words followed him, taunting him. He gave them no room in the duel. Zenen'Rol's right hand sorceress would use that to off-balance him. She had to create a disparity that favored her, since her own strength and abilities were lacking.

But with the chaos of battle settled, Rylin examined it closely. Even as the Phoenix Legions returned, grateful to be alive, heartened by their survival against tremendous odds, there was no such mirth for him. He felt horrible for it. He didn't want to be the brooding one, or the gloom cast over everything. Pretense was the only other option.

But how could he celebrate when he knew that the home of the Order of the Enlightened Sun might have been destroyed? He needed to learn the truth and the specifics as soon as possible. But, if recent history taught him anything, he could not harbor the weight of this knowledge alone.

Ishell found Errnik waiting for her, some distance along the Merchant Way. She rushed at him, allowing him to wrap his tree-trunk arms around her and lift her high in a bear hug. He didn't pay much heed to her torn gray robes or her ragged blacksmith dress. He ignored the blood stains that had long since dried, turned brown, and caked. She was dirty and sticky with sweat, but the smith was just as happy to have his daughter safe at home.

Borvis joined them at a discreet distance. Errnik would have none of it. He eyed him up and down, his face stern and grim, before he allowed a new thunderous peal of laughter. He wrapped one arm around the wiry Polymancer's shoulder while keeping the other on Ishell's shoulder.

Ishell paused to give Rylin a glance over her shoulder. Rylin projected a thought back to her in the Endless Current.

Meet me by the fishing place, after sunset.

Ishell glanced back, again, and nodded.

It was still a long wait for Rylin's impatient need to know. The sun still burned high in a late afternoon. The refugees of Thriwald were already ushered to the triage. Talik would have taken them in, but Maloric and Talik reached a war time agreement. While Malkanor was able, Pahlinsor would be a temporary haven for all refugees until the Kasarin threat abated. It was a strain on Malkanor, and Talik hesitated to impose it, but Maloric's insistence won out.

"Rylin!" His grim thoughts were broken by the cry of his mother and father running toward him. Aemreen was with them. All three of them wrapped him in an embrace that threatened to squeeze the air out of him.

When they gave him room to breathe, Rylin looked at Aemreen. Her white blouse and sapphire cotton pants were stained with blood and sweat from her labors in the triage. He wondered how much he could do to help her, now. Yelisian once told him that the Chronomancers could halt time on the body and allow healers the time they needed to save lives. He was eager at the prospect of helping her in these new ways.

But his deeper thoughts must have peeked through to Aemreen. She looked at him with concern. "Something troubles you. What is it?"

Aemreen's emerald eyes searched his. She wanted to say so much more, but her gaze shifted to her father.

Rylin hesitated. "I don't know for certain, yet. It may be nothing. If it is a matter of import, it is also delicate."

Aemreen pursed her lips, her eyes suspicious before she nodded. "Promise me you will not bear this alone."

Rylin smiled. "I was just thinking that keeping such secrets would be foolhardy. I promise."

Aemreen's gaze shifted to her father, and she gave a

quizzical gaze of disapproval. "I will join you, shortly. My father looks a little worse for wear." Aemreen pushed passed the battered soldiers that stood in her way.

Kylor and Leain paused to measure Rylin with unique expressions. Rylin's cheeks heated before his mother and father looked at each other and laughed.

"I did not wish for you to remain silent during my words with her."

"We know, Rylin. We know," Kylor accepted, knowingly.

"But some words are best spoken without intrusion, dear," Leain added.

Rylin was led home by his mother and father. He listened, patiently, as they admonished him for rushing into such an obviously dangerous battle. He would not disagree or argue. They were only grateful that he was alive and well, and just wanted him to stay that way.

The sun was dim and broken by the tree boughs overhead. Rylin sat on the familiar boulder by the stream. The waters bubbled and sloughed over the rocks and forest debris. The fresh smell of the woods filled his senses and refreshed him. The cool air seeped into the sleeves of his coat, softly caressing the hairs of his arms.

Being here was a nostalgic step back to Rylin. This was the place of many days of childhood for himself and Ishell. He held up the mental gems of the past and present versions of who they were then, and who they had become. It was a pleasant diversion, even if it was a little melancholy.

The song of birds, and the skittering of squirrels in the trees gradually succumbed to the rhythm of cicadas. The heat of summer faded to the cool breezes of night. These lulling whispers held the hands of the weary, guiding them to sleep.

Rylin absently picked at a blanket growth of moss on the boulder. He looked over to a hollowed-out tree trunk. Inside, a rickety wooden crate sat, its contents wearing down to the passage of time. The earth would claim the crate and the contents.

Rylin smiled, wanly. No one would see or wonder what happened here, but the earth would always hold the memory. It was always as his mother said to him in the fields when he was a child.

The Endless Current whispered gently in the air, signaling the presence he was waiting for.

"Light Rylin." She appeared directly beside him, sitting close to him on the boulder.

Ishell looked down at the stream, absently.

"How does such a brook persist through so many years?" Ishell wondered out loud.

Rylin shrugged. "I don't know how such a thing can act with such defiance. It is a small stream. By rights, the bed itself should not be visible."

Ishell laughed, it sounded weak, but Rylin detected something genuine to it.

"It is not the knowledge of a Chronomancer I would ask this of." Ishell turned to force Rylin's eyes to her. "I am asking one stubborn being about the nature of stubborn things."

Rylin laughed.

The laughter on Ishell's face disappeared, then. "Light Rylin, I also need to speak with you. And I believe I must speak first."

Rylin tamped down his impatient need to know the truth and waited; allowing Ishell to speak her mind.

"You don't seem to understand why the Renegades looked at you the way they did."

Rylin nodded, remembering the tentative glances.

Ishell sighed, the weight of her coming words pressed her shoulders down.

"How strong do you believe you are, Light Rylin?"

Rylin shook his head. He never thought it mattered. Perhaps many magi pondered such things, but such thoughts paved the way for meaningless conflicts. Such vanity was dangerous for the pursuit of knowledge. If a magus already believed they were at the summit of their abilities, it would never matter how much more growth they could experience, they would never become more. It was better to place the peak of their abilities forever out of reach.

"Today, when we went to Teril, they sprung their trap. We could not break free. We lost more than a dozen Renegades, Light Rylin. The rest of us believed this was the day we would die. I was certain of it, myself. Their force was four times greater than ours. We came ready to hold our own against a force only double our own. Only forty Renegades fought today, Light Rylin. There was no question about it, with so few of us left. We were going to die."

Rylin watched as Ishell's hands trembled. She rubbed them together, trying to calm them.

"Before this began, you asked for my help. You asked for as much help as you could get. You said, 'no Light can fight a war, alone'. Today, you nearly did. What you did, it should not be possible, even in sorcery."

Ishell paused. Rylin watched the conflict of emotions play across her face. "It was more horrible that you didn't know or understand. I am certain no one has ever told you about your strength. You probably thought it was no different than any other Light."

Ishell waited. Rylin searched his mind and found he always did think of it that way. He would never allow himself to consider who was stronger.

"Why do you think no Solas would train you after his Radiance died? They were afraid of you, Rylin; and that was before, fates," Ishell chuckled, "...before you found ways to leap into more power. You did not do it because you were hungry for power. You only wished to match the demands everyone placed on you. For that reason alone, you could never see how far behind you left all of us."

"Today, I did not see Kylor and Leain's endlessly diligent son. I did not see the boy who used to come to this spot to go fishing with me. I saw a being that defied all reason and ripped apart an army with swift and cold precision. I was frightened by it. You never grew weary from it. What if we were on the opposing side of that? But you know what is more horrible than that? All these years, I have defended you. I thanked you when you pushed against the limits of an Ard Solas and saved my life. Only when I witnessed your power in battle did I waver and fear. I hate myself for it, Light Rylin. I am frightened of you, and I hate it." At that point, Ishell buried her face in her hands and began to shake with sobs.

Rylin was at a loss for words to assuage her fears. The only thing he could think to do was cautiously wrap one arm around her.

"You speak of my strength, but would it grant you comfort to know that your strength and knowledge is greater still?"

Ishell looked at Rylin, her cheeks wet with tears, her hazel eyes curious.

"I could not lead as you do," Rylin began. "I rushed off to battle, but I never stopped to consider those who might follow me. I never spoke with them or galvanized their fighting spirit. I never coordinated with the weary battered soldiers of our homeland. I only charged, without a second thought or a strategy."

"Even now, as my friend, you face your own fear to give me the truth. You have always been honest and straight forward with me. I have come to rely on that to see the path I must follow."

Ishell's tears subsided, and cicadas sang to them in the evening silence. Rylin allowed Ishell to feel the sincerity of his words, even as he contemplated what must come next.

There was no easy way for it. Ken'Tekira's words were a heavy pall, a crushing weight. As much as he hated to do it, he needed to share this revelation with Ishell. Even as she recovered from the turmoil of sharing one hard truth, he accepted he must impose one more on her. It was not a selfish inclination. He wanted to take this pain from her and investigate the truth on his own; freeing her of the consequences that knowing might bring.

But if Rylin could not acknowledge her strength and let her take the part of this burden that belonged to her, then all his words were hollow and pointless.

"There is a reason I called you here," Rylin gently urged. "This will not be easy for either of us, especially if my concerns are not simple delusions."

Ishell looked at him, baffled for a moment, before her irritation became plain. "Out with it, Light Rylin. Whatever it is, it will do more harm in its delay."

"When I faced the leader of the Kasarin detachment at Thriwald, Ken'Tekira, she said the Citadel has fallen."

There was a play of bitter emotions on Ishell's face before she settled into a hard-edged disbelief. "She was lying. All their forces were at Thriwald. There is no chance they held enough reserves for such an undertaking."

"Perhaps. But she added that Zenen'Rol was there. I know of him, Light Ishell," Rylin dropped his voice, as if speaking of the terror of the Crimson Empire might summon him. "The Fist of the Emperor is more of a monster than a man. Over the last fifty years, the empire has propelled its boundaries farther out than they have in centuries. They did this with him at the front of almost every charge. When the Kasarins speak of him, they speak in fear and whispers."

Ishell fought openly with irritation and uncertainty. "What do you propose, then? How will you discover the truth?"

Rylin sighed. "Not alone. You will discover the truth with me."

Ishell's laugh was incredulous. "What? You wish to Fold Step or Meld Walk so far east? They will send all their forces."

"Temporal Projection is the only way to know all that has transpired. Mind Slip is the only way for you to know it with me."

It was a reach, of course. The Mind Slip was an advanced version of Current Reading. It was more difficult as it required the Shaper, a Solas seeking to pass to Ard Solas, to experience the world through the perception and mind of another. It forced a Light to project their mind outward and surrender its individuality, becoming absorbed into the mind of another.

"You presume much, Light Rylin." Ishell warned. "That is an Ard Solas skill. Why would I know that?"

"I am talking to the same Evoker who changed the shape of the Song of the Thunder Gods," Rylin told her, flatly.

Ishell's eyes were unblinking, but unreadable. "I know the shape for the Mind Slip. But we will speak later about what your Temporal Projection should allow you to view."

Ishell said nothing more, allowing Rylin to say nothing as she turned to face him on the boulder. She began pulling the Endless Current into her. As her hands weaved, and her mouth mumbled words with her eyes closed, Rylin turned to his own task.

Temporal Projection was easy for him. His power was restored. He could reach deep into past events with little effort. When Ishell grasped onto his awareness, the weight against his mind was noticeable. Ishell was astonished at the skies and the emerald hue of the world in the Temporal Current. Her mind shuddered as they slipped into the cold forceful weight of moments come and gone.

In time, they discovered the truth. They were quick to locate the broken rubble of the once gleaming Zenith Citadel. The entire east face was a heap of molten stone, and black debris. Rylin did not descend into their home as they moved backwards in time. The destruction was plain, even from so high above. If he took them down into the halls as the attacks were occurring, it would become personal and injuring. Neither of them could withstand such a thing. Being so close to the deaths of their friends and teachers would break them.

The rain of bright red fires came; and with it, the cacophony of sorcery in attempts to save and destroy the citadel. Bright flashes of color filled the courtyard, flames devoured everything. Booming explosions filled the air and shook the ground below.

One figure moved away from the wreckage at a swift stroll. It was a figure that was much larger than the others. Rylin needed to see him up close. He swooped down into the cold blue, towards a sheer precipice that overlooked the Maelstrom. The large figure moved towards that bluff, alone.

The figure matched the numerous descriptions from Rylin's travels in the Kasarin Empire. Ishell gasped at the sight of him.

Rylin never encountered a man so massive and intimidating. Everything, from his black swirling tattoos to his thrice scarred head, radiated an aura of unyielding fury. He wore most of the same vestments as the other Havoc Guild Sorcerers, though much larger and thicker. His black leather bracers were covered with rows of brass spikes, and Rylin saw two curved daggers tucked into his vest coat. The weapons radiated the energy of an unusual enchantment.

It was enough. The Temporal Current shoved them back into their time and place. Ishell opened her eyes wide, before she narrowed them on Rylin.

"It doesn't mean she is right. We have to go back," Ishell snapped.

"Light Ishell, we know what we saw. Anything more will strip us down and leave us vulnerable."

"There could be survivors. They could be alive and hidden. They can't all be..." Ishell trailed off as her eyes began to water.

Rylin knew what his friend could not say out loud. He knew what she was desperate to discover. It was true that the specifics needed to be learned, to see if anyone lived. But they could not afford to discover that much while Stratia relied on the Renegades to fight for survival.

"For now, it is enough to know that she was not lying," Rylin finalized, grimly.

Rylin etched the sight of Zenen'Rol into his mind, playing it through over and over. With each replay, the dread that Zenen imposed dulled.

Rylin needed the colossal figure to be nothing more than another Kasarin enemy. That would make it much easier for him to face him down and kill him.

Ken'Tekira woke under the light of a full moon and a glittering sky of star light. Her dark eyes opened. She raised her hand to massage her head against an ache that hammered to her ears. Her arms and legs were twisted at odd and uncomfortable angles. A stream of drool fell from the corner of her mouth, seeping into the soil beneath her. Her clothes were torn and singed. Blades of grass tickled her nose.

The Dragon of Zenen'Rol was a mess, looking like a large animal chewed on her, then spit her on the earth to rot. But she was alive, and that was more than she thought she would be. The boy sorcerer was intent on killing her. Maybe he thought he did.

Of all the forms of death in battle she was ready for, this instance made her feel lucky to be alive.

Ken'Tekira never felt as helpless as she did in the face of that strange sorcery. There was nothing, in all her training in the Havoc Guilds, that could have prepared anyone for it.

Ken'Tekira untwisted her limbs. New aches and pains became known throughout her body. She stood up, slow and gingerly, taking stock of her situation.

It was difficult to discern the details in the dark of night. There were deep black craters, and large swaths of field burned to ashes. She saw the dark, mangled shapes of the dead. Their bodies were twisted, looking like bits of driftwood in a flat still sea. There were a small number of crows in evidence. They feasted on through the night, even as most of their murders withdrew long ago. The air remained thick with the acrid smell of smoke and the rancid stench of rotting flesh.

Some of the dead were Stratians, of course. A few were the Lights of the Order.

It was a gaping wound delivered to Stratia. As much as Ken'Tekira committed to her strategy, this should have ended the conquest. But as many Stratians were dead on this field, there were thousands more Ka'Rak and hundreds more Havoc Guild Magi, including Elite.

Ken'Tekira might have struck a blow to the Stratian resistance, but it was a greater disgrace to the forces of the Crimson Empire.

Ken'Tekira sighed with resignation. There was no help for it. She would have to report this to the Master Fist. She would not have to cut her throat. After all, she did face Rylin in battle, and did not flee. It was only uncertain how her mentor might react to this turn of events.

But Ken'Tekira was no meek novice. She was not a nervous little girl. Fearing consequences was for the weak.

Ken'Tekira calmed her thoughts, ignored her pains. She

gathered the Endless Current. She shaped the Meld Walk that would take her to the ruins of the Zenith Citadel.

When the blurring of the dark night came to a stop, Ken'Tekira was in the early dawn, far east of the field. She stood on a towering bluff that looked over the foaming waves of the Maelstrom. The precipice was only a few yards away. The waves crested over the shallows and crashed against the cliff face. To the north sat the black remains of Katahn, far beneath her current elevation.

Zenen'Rol stood with his back turned to her, his arms clasped behind his back. He was alone. His vest coat billowed and whipped below his knees in the ocean wind.

The morning air was cool. It was far more pleasant than the stifling warm air of the fields in Teril. The ocean fresh smell was a welcome difference. Down the cliff and to the west, on a low rolling rise, the Zenith Citadel stood ruined and empty.

Zenen relayed all that transpired here only weeks ago. The Order of the Enlightened Sun offered some resistance, but their sorcery was weak in comparison to Zenen'Rol's constant magic, the Flesh of the Immortals. He was the last practitioner of the sacred imperial sorcery. It was once common, before the Black Decade.

Zenen's unique training allowed him to shrug off every elemental attack hurled against him. This made him the emperor's perfect weapon against defiant magi.

"I anticipated your report hours ago, my Dragon. Did you tarry with your prey, awhile?" Zenen asked in sarcasm.

Ken'Tekira knelt in supplication, her eyes just below his knees. "I was struck by a Prefect's Lash, and I could not rise until a few moments ago."

Zenen'Rol spun about to face Ken with a cold raised

eyebrow.

"One of our own has turned on us?"

Ken'Tekira lowered her head in a bow. "No, Master Fist. An enemy sorcerer absorbed and copied my Prefect's Lash…"

For the next hour, Ken'Tekira remained kneeling as she relayed a full account of her defeat in Teril. She leaned heavy on how close she was to total victory before the young man, Rylin, appeared and turned it against her in minutes. She detailed everything about the strange sorceries that so soundly bested her.

Zenen'Rol paused, his eyes wide with surprise. "Are you certain he said he was a Chronomancer?"

Ken'Tekira looked up at Zenen's towering frame and nodded. Why was there such alarm on his face at that revelation? What was the difference between one Stratian elementalist and another?

Zenen read the confusion in her eyes. "Have you read deep into the archives?"

"I confess my reading was limited to renowned strategies and the required reading of the Black Decade."

Zenen'Rol disregarded her ignorance as his expression burst into an unusual grin. "At last! I believed this would only be a purge. I thought my only challenge would be found in a hidden Void Hand. Finally, a truly legendary opponent presents himself. Ha!" Zenen laughed loud into the night. "This conquest was not a waste of my skills, after all. Imagine it, Ken. Our ancestral guilds were never a close match to the Golden Hourglass Clan. When they disappeared, so did our chance to surpass them. This is the worthy challenge I never imagined I would find."

Zenen'Rol howled with laughter a little while longer. Then he looked down on Ken'Tekira as he beamed with glee. "Rise, Dragon. You are not disgraced. Had you prevailed, I would have been obliged and honored to surrender my position and privilege to you. Imagine it: Yelisian's disciple, a Fabricator and a

Chronomancer! I must duel with him!"

"Begging your pardon, Master Fist, but as you have said, this is a purge. We are to rid the world of all Stratians and any chance of a second Black Decade. Is such a frivolous side pursuit wise? What if you are also defeated?" Ken'Tekira asked, but she dreaded that Zenen already devised a plan for all of this.

Zenen'Rol's grin was almost boyish, if dark and twisted. "I have something for you to do, my Dragon…"

Ken'Tekira listened close. The first half of his plan was agreeable. Her stomach knotted with revulsion as he elaborated on his fail-safe plan. Unlike any strategy in the history of the Crimson Empire, this had a distasteful lack of honor.

She was also one of very few to know about the secret weapon developed by the Enchanter's Guild. The Enchanters who created this weapon were dead, which only allowed the creation of one such device. Ken thought one was too many.

Zenen'Rol acted in haste with the discovery that much of the Crimson Empire was bathed in purifying flames. Entire estates were reduced to ashes and buried in salt. It was a custom for lands lost to demons.

But did such circumstances truly warrant the use of the Seal of Stagnation?

-38-

Rylin slumped against the shaded side of a well in the center of the street. His hood was pulled far over his face while a cool damp cloth was folded over his forehead and eyes. The morning light was pale and blue. The sun was not yet risen above the plains and woods. The air was fresh and brisk in the early dawn.

But Rylin's head ached and throbbed. The desire to curl in on himself and moan it away was implacable. The morning birdsong hammered blows to the sides of his head.

The aftertaste of vomit and ale haunted every corner of his mouth, threatening renewed waves of nausea. Any more heaving would tear him inside out.

The first golden rays of sunlight climbed through the woods and spilled onto the roof tops and walls. Heavy footfalls approached Rylin. He peeled back a tiny opening of cloth. The lower half of the burly shape of Errnik greeted him.

"How is Ishell?" Rylin groaned, pitifully.

"Same state as you: dark quiet room, head over a bucket."

Errnik's cheerful booming voice was enough to force Rylin's brains out through his nose and ears.

"I...never knew you were so loud, Errnik." Rylin winced against a fresh wave of throbs in his head.

Errnik restrained an obvious booming laugh, reducing it

to a low chuckle. "How many did you have?"

Rylin knew better than to ask how Errnik knew what happened. "One too many."

"I don't think the Order ever let you drink, before. Must have been your first." Errnik sat down on the cool stone beside him.

At first, Rylin wanted to avoid any drinking or celebrating after discovering the aftermath of the Citadel. His mood was darker, gloomier. If the Kasarins were to appear before him, then, he would visit a far greater wrath upon them.

But as he and Ishell walked into the city proper, needing to clear their heads, they were greeted by a loud stumbling group of Legionnaires. As soon as the soldiers laid eyes on them, they would let nothing prevent them from buying Rylin and Ishell rounds of stiff ale to celebrate their unexpected return home. Before long, the ale replaced his anger and grief.

"It was the first and only. I do not understand how the miners ever believed it to be a suitable escape. Every pain I ever had, and a few I have yet to endure, came to me all at once." Rylin chose not to tell the smith that the heat of his proximity was squeezing his brains.

"Yet you choose this well for sleep, rather than troubling Kylor and Leain," Errnik observed with a commending hint.

Rylin lowered his head. His absence must have caused his mother and father to worry. "This is too great a disgrace. I could not look at them, this way."

"You could do one of those things the Order tends to do at times like this."

A familiar voice of a young boy spoke for Rylin. "In truth, he can't. He is in too much anguish to gather the Endless Current."

Rylin peeled back the cloth and leaned forward, peering around Errnik's massive body. The motion threatened to bring his bowels up through his throat.

Aemreen and Merice approached, side by side. Merice's brown farmer's tunic and pants were stained and wrinkled. His brown robe was crusted with dark blood stains. His blue eyes were red with pronounced veins of fatigue. His face was hardened with stern determination that belied his child years. His white-blonde hair was tangled and unkempt. The young Illumancer had foregone much of his vastly needed sleep, focusing all his energies into healing every individual that came into the triage. He was one of the most exhausted Lights among the Renegades. He often allowed Light Porra to sleep as he maintained a watch.

It was far more alarming to see the self-neglecting child retained a lucid mind through it all. Rylin could not have functioned so well for so long. The boy was worthy of far more recognition and applause than he ever received or asked for. In a war that threatened to directly crush children in its path, Merice stood as a valiant and defiant bulwark.

Aemreen's expression was not as forgiving as Merice. Her red lips were pursed into a disapproving scowl. Rylin was not accustomed to the hard edge in her eyes. Her arms were folded, and this caused him to notice she wore a modest long-sleeved blue silk dress embroidered with floral patterns. It was not a common choice of clothing for her.

"I want you to know my ire is centered more on my father's men than you. Regardless..." Aemreen approached and knelt close to Rylin. Errnik cautiously stood up and backed away, leaving Rylin to her scolding. At that moment, her rose scent, usually so pleasant and intoxicating, was too much for Rylin's sensitive bowels. "...these revelries are best reserved for the end of the war, not the heart of it, Torch Rylin."

Rylin might have managed an argument in his defense, but he recognized what an impulse like that truly was. It was childish and poorly directed, an attempt to mask his disgust with himself for letting himself be found this way. He would not allow his momentary self-loathing and embarrassment to inflict a wound on the love of his life.

"You are right, love. This was the wrong time for this."

Aemreen was visibly stunned by Rylin's total agreement. She must have believed this would become a shouting match.

Rylin forced himself to chuckle. "Wrong is wrong, my love. If the Kasarins were to strike, now, Ishell and I would be a liability. With honesty, I do not wish to do this again."

Rylin fought down his nausea and throbbing migraine to look into Aemreen's eyes as she measured him. He read her while she compared his resolve to other men, those who spoke making the same promises born of regret.

Aemreen looked to Merice and nodded.

Without a word, the Illumancer Candle approached Rylin. He placed a hand on Rylin's forehead, while he knelt and placed his other hand on Rylin's abdomen.

Rylin gasped with shock. He was struck with a sensation of being hurled into a deep cold lake. An invigorating wave of cool cleansing energy washed through his entire body. It sought out and rinsed away every intoxicated particle in his blood, leaving refreshed clarity in its wake. The pain, lethargy and nausea were wiped away in minutes.

When it was over, Merice fell back, landing on his rump. He did not bear the exhausted expression of a weary healer. His fair complexion was pale and wide-eyed with fright.

"You are not complete, Light Rylin!" Merice hissed in a whisper. "I have never seen this in anyone, but something is missing. Whatever this is, it has left a hole in your will."

Rylin knew what Merice was referring to. He thought the Rite of Separation would only leave behind a spiritual scar, too faded to detect. He did not often require a healer, so he knew the discovery should come as no surprise. He wondered if a Light discovered the same when they were trying to understand the

Displaced Potential Reckoning.

The only surprise in this revelation was that his will and innate abilities were not fully recovered from losing the Aspect of Vengeance.

Before Rylin could give the matter more thought, he sprang to his feet. The sudden move startled everyone but Merice. The boy's eyes went wide. The Candle felt it, as well.

"Find Light Ishell and do for her what you just did for me. Be quick about it. Go!" Rylin kicked up his emerald staff into his hand.

There was a play of confusion and worry on Aemreen and Errnik's faces.

"The Havoc Magi are in the Merchant Plaza." Rylin helped Aemreen to her feet and shaped an unplanned Fold Step.

Aemreen never grew accustomed to the disorienting sensation of being in two places at the same time. The gut-wrenching lurch that followed came as a relief. Rylin needed to warn her before he pulled her into one of his Fold Steps.

The complaint was irrelevant as they appeared at the far edge of the Merchant Plaza. Forty Guilders stood in rigid columns in the center of the square, oblivious to the giant gold block in their midst. There was a dozen of Pahlinsor's residents, and their eyes were furtive and fearful as they pressed tightly to the walls at their backs.

The Guilders stood with their feet apart, even with their shoulders, while their arms were clasped behind their backs. Their dark eyes glared ahead, as their vest coats billowed and snapped in the breeze. If the Lights of the Enlightened Sun were disciplined, the Havoc Guilds were rigid, seething with deep fury.

At the head of the imposing mass was the most intimidating small woman Aemreen ever laid eyes on. There was a long, deep scar running from the top and center of her forehead to the back of her neck. She was shorter than Aemreen, but her corded muscles seemed as hard as stone. Her face was comprised of hard angles, chiseled into submission by the scowl on her thin lips.

"Ken'Tekira." Rylin bowed low at his hips. The gesture seemed forced as his face barely restrained his contempt and anger at the sight of the Kasarin woman.

Aemreen wanted to know more, but the Guilder began speaking to Rylin in the Kasarin dialect. She wished she had taken time to learn the language from her father.

Aemreen understood little by the gestures and body language. But the offered white cloth that covered a rolled-up parchment letter held clear meaning. The Guilder offered her wrists for irons.

Aemreen gaped and her jaw went slack. Was this an official surrender? All night, the Phoenix Legions were loud and raucous about the sound victory in Thriwald. Aemreen found some of it hard to believe. But there was truth lent to the extreme tales when she saw the hesitation the Renegades displayed for Rylin. Did Rylin reap such a grand victory that the Kasarins were now willing to surrender? This accomplishment was unheard of in history. It was a better fit for fairy tales and legends.

Aemreen did not miss the slight smirk at the Sorceress's lips when she placed her hands out. Without such a deep scowl before, Aemreen might have missed it.

Aemreen did not wait a moment longer. She grabbed a fistful of Rylin's sleeve, yanking him away to a secluded distance.

Aemreen's voice was a hushed growl. "I don't know what this is, my love, but something is off-kilter. Her surrender is not absolute."

Rylin's answering smile was eager. "I know. It is

conditional. It may be temporary."

Aemreen planted her hands on her hips. "What are their terms?"

"I am to face Zenen'Rol, Master Fist of the Crimson Empire, in a duel. If I die, they will release themselves and continue their destruction of Stratia."

Aemreen groaned, resisting the impulse to pinch the bridge of her nose. "If you win?"

"All Kasarin forces will withdraw from Stratia, never to attack our lands again."

"Rylin, no. This is a trap."

Rylin shook his head. "I cannot ignore this opportunity, no matter the danger. This is my chance to end this war."

"This is exactly as it was before, Rylin. You try to take it all on, alone. You attempt to finish it in one stroke. You tried, and what did it do to you? You were stripped of your powers. Had you accepted that you were only one component needed for Stratia's survival, the war could have ended by now."

"You do not see what I see. This is a page of ancient history that he is trying to resurrect." The accusation of historical ignorance was like a slap to Aemreen's face. She would not allow her wounded emotions to obscure the need to reason with Stratia's best hope for survival. She loved him, dearly, but she could not fathom why he chose this critical moment to become a blind fool. "Eight millennia ago, the Kasarins struck at Stratia, just as they do now. The Golden Hourglass waited, hoping their powers would not be needed. In the end, they held no choice. When they were forced into battle, the fate of Stratia dangled in the balance of a duel between the Temporal Arbiter and the Master Fist. Arbiter Derakat Zorish prevailed with ease, and the Kasarins departed. Treaties were signed to forbid further aggressions."

Rylin's voice was excited and fervent. "Don't you see? Zenen'Rol's sense of pride and history dictate his need for this.

He wants the chance that no Master Fist has had in eight thousand years. He will put down all his stakes for this."

Aemreen held her ground in the face of his ecstatic optimism. "Rylin, there have been Kasarin warlords and pirates that have tried to raid Stratia's eastern shores for centuries."

Rylin looked at her with momentary confusion. She had to mask her relief at the opening. "When you combine that with this horrific invasion, it is self-evident that the Crimson Empire never obeyed the terms placed on them by the Golden Hourglass Clan. Maybe they waited several thousand years before they struck again. My point is they did. That is a refusal to comply with their terms of surrender."

Rylin's expression turned dubious and thoughtful. "You believe that if they did not honor their agreement before, why would they keep their word, now."

"Yes!" Aemreen breathed.

"But there is this point to consider. I have already overwhelmed them once. What kind of machination or deception can they hold in the face of that?"

Aemreen had to resist one impulse to grind her teeth, and another to wrap her hands around his throat. Why was he being such a fool, now? Where was this coming from?

Aemreen levelled her voice in a monumental effort of self-restraint. "Torch Rylin. Do you ever wonder why his radiance never spoke of your strength?"

Once more, Rylin's expression was dumbfounded. Aemreen knew that this was the point where he might be most receptive.

Aemreen pressed her advantage. "The most legendary of history's defeats were against opponents who could not accept the possibility that it might occur. Yelisian trained you without ever revealing your strength so that your arrogance would not rise and consume you. Please, my love, honor his memory and wishes. Heed my warning."

Rylin considered in silence before he sighed. "What would you have me do? If it is as Zenen'Rol proclaims, then I can end this without risking any more Stratian lives."

Aemreen wanted to laugh with relief. At least the humble modest man she loved was speaking, now. She could always reason with that.

"I just wish for us to prepare in case this is not what it seems. Either they came because they are certain that you are no equal to Zenen'Rol, or they came because they believe they have a way around your strength."

Aemreen allowed Rylin to have a moment to absorb that possibility. "We do not lower our guard to these 'prisoners' in the slightest. We have squadrons of Phoenix Legions bolstered by the Renegades, all over Pahlinsor. We establish check points. We watch for anything out of the ordinary. We have Torch Teranen help with guarding the prisoners. We know that her Heart Fire is hotter than their Imperial Fire. We can have these precautions in place within a few hours."

Rylin chuckled. "You are ever a general, my love. It is as though I am speaking with Light Ishell."

Aemreen laughed. "She is not here to say these things. As I say…"

"…you ladies band together when the cause is right," Rylin supplied.

As if summoned by thought, Ishell and Merice ended their Meld Walk a few feet away from them. Aemreen and Rylin spent another fifteen minutes informing Ishell of the situation and their solution.

Ishell raised an approving eyebrow at Aemreen's calculations. "I could not have measured it any better, Aemreen. Those are sound counter measures. Light Merice," Ishell turned to the boy Illumancer. "I would feel better if Aemreen was aided by a Renegade. She needs to move in haste. Can you help her?"

Aemreen did not relish the thought of the Order's fast

travel methods. Her stomach already began preemptive twisting in revolt. But speed was required. Zenen'Rol's challenge might only last so long.

Merice inclined his head in a bow. "Certainly, Light Ishell."

Aemreen and Merice departed to appraise her father of the situation. Rylin gathered a patrol to incarcerate the Guilders, while Ishell left to organize and assign the remaining Renegades.

All celebrations were put far aside. Aemreen Tahkaer felt a tension in the air that was unlike anything she ever experienced before.

A certainty seemed poised, for good or ill. The war would end today. Stratia's fate would be etched in stone. She found herself inwardly praying to the fates that the day would see Rylin back in her arms at the start of a time of peace.

-39-

Zenen'Rol stood in the lethal, freezing winds at the far north of the world. Even as gigantic as he was, the year-round snows wrapped his knees. Blinding snow flurries swirled around him, obscuring his vision, and forcing him to squint. He could not see far but he knew this plateau ran for several hundred yards before ending at a precipice that dropped a mile into the icy killing waters below.

Zenen'Rol allowed the Endless Current to create a searing wave of rage against his insides, causing him to become a beacon. The Chronomancer would be able to find it. He would be here, soon.

The Flesh of the Immortals was a constant armor against the deadly cold. It was an augmented endurance training that was unique among the Havoc Elite. Few could survive the years of grueling self-exposure. A sorcerer exposed their body to a constant element or weapon. They tolerated it for days and weeks without end. After months, a sorcerer was allowed a slight infusion of the Endless Current to expand their limits beyond the previous level of the weapon or element.

In the beginning, Zenen'Rol only sat yards away from roaring flames. When he finished training for heat, he would sit in the center of an Imperial Bonfire for days.

The same method was applied to swords, cold, lightning and wind. His lungs could stall breathing for hours.

On top of all that, Zenen mastered the mental training of Fire Rivers. This was a mindset where he could be filled with fury, yet the focus of his purpose provided a state like tranquility. This did cause the Endless Current to burn as it passed through him, but the pain increased his fury and will, escalating his power.

All this training brought Zenen'Rol to this moment. His armies laid siege to Stratia. He was on a mission to find a Void Hand. The Crimson Empire was consumed with hundreds of purifying fires to drive out the hordes of encroaching demons. It was as though the world was livid with apocalyptic fury, and the coming duel sat in the eye of the storm. Here, a revenge duel would occur, a moment of history repeating after eight thousand years. His blood rushed with heated anticipation.

Then Zenen'Rol felt it. There was the rush of an enormous wave of Endless Current tinted with a strange sensation. The snow and wind whipped into a great frenzy, repulsed by a maelstrom of power.

As quickly as it came, Zenen'Rol was left with dismay at what he saw. His worthy opponent was two feet shorter than himself, and barely a man. His shoulders were not massive. What few muscles he had were a fit for a dock hand or farmer. His dark hair and skin, as well as his hard angled features marked him as a Malkanor man. The only difference were his blue eyes, so bright against the dark backdrop that they seemed to glow. He wore a farmer's tunic, pants, and boots, but he also wore a forest green, long coat, embroidered with golden sigils of the ancient language. He also carried a long staff made of emerald with geometric shapes and numbers etched in gold at the ends.

Zenen never saw such a duality that baffled him as this boy did. He was not exactly frail looking, but Zenen did not find his appearance imposing, either. In fact, aside from his eyes and dark countenance, he was rather plain. But the power he radiated was an entire other story. Never did Zenen'Rol stand in the presence of something so massive that he had to conceal his trembling hands. It made him feel like a warrior in an old fable, standing in the gaze of a dragon.

"I am Torch Chronomancer Rylin, of the Order of the Enlightened Sun." The boy's voice was measured and collected, betraying no emotion.

Zenen smiled. How long had it been since he last issued the customary introduction before a duel? "I am Havoc Grandmaster, Zenen'Rol, Master Fist of the Crimson Emperor. Are you ready to join your beloved Order in the grave?"

"So be it," Rylin accepted with ambiguity. He flourished his staff and began to circle Zenen'Rol's left side.

Zenen allowed Rylin to take several paces before he struck as fast as a coiled snake. He whipped his hand out with a quick Prefect's Lash, while he created several Emperor's Roses to rip through the snow and bind his legs.

Rylin stepped out of the way of the burgundy hued vines with casual ease. He held his hand up to intercept the red lightning of the lash.

"Ionsu!" Rylin shouted. A sigil on his coat blazed with golden fire. The Lash was swallowed into a devouring unseen force.

Zenen'Rol recognized the rune and command word at once. He respected his enemy's ingenuity. Both the word and rune formed the word for 'absorb'. Rylin's coat was enchanted with powerful energy-eating magic.

Rylin spun away in a rapid flourish. "Dubailt!" A Prefect's Lash burst from Rylin's palm and struck Zenen from shoulder to abdomen. Zenen's body did not acknowledge the copied magic.

Zenen was already impressed and intrigued by Rylin's demonstration of the ancient art of Simulacrum. He realized that every sigil in the coat created a short-cut to the Fabricator's obscure path.

Zenen'Rol grinned as he unsheathed his two serrated, curved daggers from underneath his vest coat. He spun them in a blurring, open-palm flourish. If Rylin wanted to wield enchanted weapons and armor, Zenen'Rol could be an equal on that ground, as well. He rarely found cause to unsheathe both with the intent to call on their magic, but they would slice through most spell-shapes. There was no certainty they would cut through Chronomancy, but they would limit Rylin's versatility.

Rylin stood in a low crouch, tightening his grip on his staff. Zenen knew Rylin would try to stay low and use his smaller size for speed. It was time to show the Chronomancer that battles in the Crimson Empire were not so predictable.

Rylin waited, coiled, with a lesser Displacement Cloak already wrapped around him. He would move double his normal speed, now. Derakat Zorish ended his duel with the Master Fist in a humiliating swift manner. Their shame might have created lasting hostilities. If Rylin tried to keep an even pace, humor the giant's pride, perhaps there would never be another war with the Kasarin Empire.

Rylin directed some of his flow of the Endless Current at heating his body to survive. Then he subtly redirected his magic through the thick-skinned sorcerer. He never mastered Current Reading, he was adequate, at best, but Zenen'Rol was a desensitized target. Rylin could read basic information about him. Combined with what he knew from Temporal Projections, he thought he might be able to assess Zenen with some accuracy.

Zenen swept down low with a series of arcing cuts aimed at Rylin's thighs. If there were no Displacement Cloak, Zenen's attacks would have been too swift to defend against. As it was, both ends of Rylin's staff swept low, one end after another. Sparks flashed bright in the air from each clash, peppering the white snow. He stopped the cuts with strikes at the giant's bracers in rapid succession. His hands scraped against the crunching arctic snow.

Zenen spun with a thrusting kick for Rylin's sternum. Rylin did not have the exotic fighting training to counter it with his hands. He shaped a Fold Step, just before impact and reappeared at the giant's exposed backside. Rylin projected a tiny Stasis Sphere at Zenen's right shoulder, hoping to tear away a piece of muscle. Zenen moved with a speed far greater than Rylin expected. He whirled about, slicing the shimmering sphere in half with a cut from his dagger. Zenen halted the spin and lunged forward in a deadly stab aimed at Rylin's abdomen. Rylin barely managed to parry the attack with his staff. He did force Zenen to over-extend and stumble forward.

Rylin whirled about and brought the other end of his staff down on the back of the giants thrice-scarred head. In return, Rylin felt a searing pain across his lower back. Zenen'Rol fell, face first, into the powdery drifts. Rylin backpedaled as soon as he realized the Master Fist made him pay for his attack with a long deep cut.

Disgust overcame Rylin after a quick Current Read. Zenen felt nothing but an intense thrill in all this. The Kasarins were here to prevent further devastation by the Void Hands, whatever might be left of them. If Lycendrik did not act so brashly, if Light Martenen sought answers over self-preservation, the two continents might have come to an agreement and hunted the evil together. Rylin only began to unearth the dark chapters of ancient history when the attacks began. The knowledge could have been shared, and all of this could have been avoided.

The Master Fist was another matter, though. While he hunted anything of the demon magics down with fear and zeal, he also reveled in the bloodshed and death he caused. He was addicted and intoxicated by intense battle. He held only contempt for those who could not withstand him. To Zenen, common, good people of any nation were to be crushed under foot and cast aside.

Rylin harbored only one reason to humor him at all. If his ego and strong-armed pride were satisfied, perhaps this could all come to an end. It was a desperate hope. Aemreen was right to say Rylin had come ready to make the same mistake twice.

Zenen'Rol rolled away and sprang to his feet. He was oblivious to the layer of snow that coated the front of his body. His lips were pulled back in a tight half-grin, half-snarl.

"Quit trying to read me, boy. This is battle. It is no place for mind games."

Rylin was surprised. He thought the Master Fist could not sense his efforts. "For one so well-versed in history, I am alarmed you would say something so brutishly false."

Zenen howled and charged at Rylin. Moving only twice as fast was dangerous and slow. The towering sorcerer was not some lumbering behemoth. He was incredibly swift, with a versatile array of techniques.

Rylin mouthed mathematic equations and began to alter his Displacement Cloak. He moved four times faster. Each tightening of Zenen's muscles were visible long before he lunged and spun with a cut aimed at his throat. It was a lethargic effort to step back from the stab and duck under the slash. Rylin rammed his staff up into the exposed armpit and ribs.

Outside of the Displacement Cloak, Rylin's blurring speed added powerful momentum to the attack. The blow crushed bones and deadened nerves. Zenen dropped a dagger. It was instantly buried in the white tundra. His giant arm trembled with a pain Rylin knew the Master Fist was unaccustomed to.

Zenen'Rol staggered back, his teeth clenched as his lips foamed. "I'll kill you."

Rylin's retort was plain spoken. "No…you won't."

Zenen'Rol howled with fury. The Endless Current flooded toward the giant. How could he be so angry and still draw so much Current?

The snow on the ground bounced in excitement. The ground trembled. Zenen'Rol lifted into the air, held by a Grasping Wind. He stood far above Rylin's head. At the same time, something strange slithered in the snow against his legs. His pants were torn through as the lengths passed.

Rylin Fold Stepped far away from the precipice. A towering wall of burgundy vines burst out of the snow and ripped away the high bluff. The mass of vines and ice plummeted into the freezing waters below. The chunk of broken land shattered the thick ice with a cracking explosion.

Zenen'Rol was willing to tear apart the world for his pride and fear. This giant man was no different from Amorlic. Like Amorlic, he was a product of an elite cast that believed in breaking everything to achieve their petty goals. Zenen'Rol might not admit it, but this conquest had less to do with hunting down Void Hands and more to do with his glory-seeking.

Zenen'Rol floated in the air, his dark eyes alight with insane mirth. This was the kind of cruelty and malice that drew Rylin to seek instruction from the Order. Rylin vowed to put an end to this wanton malevolence, years ago. For the dead and the innocent lives lost from Stratia, it was time for Rylin to fulfill that vow.

For each of the unsuspecting lives cut down in Tihl'Zen, for the Citadel that Rylin called home, for the children who died fighting beyond their limit to protect the people, Rylin would have to kill this man.

Rylin felt more of the ground rumbling beneath his feet. Rylin concentrated and calmed his mind, allowing the Endless Current to flow through him. He shaped and spoke. The ground fell away just as Rylin pressurized the air beneath his feet. It held enough force to hold him up, but he would have to focus on every step, moving the air as he went.

But as Rylin stepped upward, the divided concentration weakened his Displacement Cloak. His familiarity with elemental magic was better than it was several years ago. But the combined efforts drained his potency. As he came closer to Zenen'Rol, the difference was noticeable. Zenen launched into a renewed flurry of cuts and kicks that strained Rylin's defenses. Rylin parried and deflected with his staff. He evaded the colossal blows while he maintained a continual awareness of where to quicken the wind. The rapid pace was grueling and mentally taxing. His will was bolstered only as he saw the sheen of sweat that beaded on the giant's skin. The Grasping Winds might demand less of someone more familiar with elemental magic, but Zenen'Rol's style of fighting was furious and offensive. He relied on his aggression to end his enemies in swift order. The anger in his Endless Current, the repeated strike after relentless strike, maintaining the Grasping Winds, and ripping the land apart were a clear strain. Rylin's movements were rushed, in the beginning, but repetition eased his coordination. Now, he could wear Zenen'Rol down over time.

That complacency proved dangerous for Rylin. A deep searing cut sliced the back of his thigh. Zenen'Rol's wayward dagger flew into his waiting hand.

The pain of the deep cut broke Rylin's concentration. The air cobble he stood on was sliced by the dagger's passing. He fell and sank deep into the snow. Rylin scrambled to his feet. He was only inches from a mile-long drop into the cold waters of the Stone Sea.

The daggers were an anomaly to Rylin. It should be impossible for anything to cut through a Stasis Sphere. How could any modern enchantment account for crossing paths with Chronomancy?

"The truth is that I was not certain they would." Zenen's voice bellowed from far above. He surprised Rylin with a Current Read he could not detect. "But I was promised they would cut through any living sorcery."

That was when Rylin knew he judged his enemy incorrectly. Perhaps Zenen'Rol diluted the Read with something easy to see and believe. He allowed Rylin to think he was just an unthinking brute, a dull-minded ravager. Zenen was not as exhausted as he let on. He waited for Rylin to fall into a trap of smug complacency, and it worked. Now the snow was turning red with the cuts in his back and leg. He was losing blood fast. Any attempt to mend would be a deadly opportunity for Zenen'Rol.

Rylin berated himself. Aemreen warned exactly against this conceited frame of mind. She might not have factored in the exact trap that waited for him; but fighting from a place of inflated ego was a costly mistake. That is why the ancient Chronomancers brought their full power to bare right away. When they entered, they already experienced the death toll of withholding their powers from the battlefield. It was far less costly to finish it quick and be done with it.

The ground began to rumble anew as massive waves of Endless Current surged toward Zenen'Rol. The air began to warm. A sharp tang of thick ozone filled Rylin's nostrils. The Master Fist seemed to agree that it was time to end this duel.

There was a spell-shape from the master tome of Chronomancy that Rylin found few opportunities to practice. It was a dangerous spell. It was nearly deemed forbidden and destroyed along with many other secrets. Unlike times before, Rylin studied the risks of this shape, and its demands. This was beyond any peril Rylin ever faced in Chronomancy. The benefit was that if he performed this correctly, and maintained it, he would overwhelm Zenen'Rol and end this duel.

Rylin poured all his concentration into his Displacement Cloak, hastening time as fast as he could manage. The trembling earth slowed to rolling hiccups. The air warmed at a much slower rate.

Then Rylin redirected his focus. He slipped deep into the linear patterns of the Temporal Current. Rylin recited mathematical equations in several different languages. His hands moved, trailing vivid bright streams of emerald light. The images were hard-edged shapes that united to form complex three-dimensional patterns. His emerald staff floated in the air beside him, glowing with bright green light. His hands moved and created glowing faceted cubes and dodecahedrons of temporal energy all around him. He spoke in languages unknown to the world.

The spell required half an hour to perform, but Zenen'Rol would see only slight twitches and green mist. He might have been able to feel the Endless Current roaring toward Rylin; and felt the strangeness of the Temporal Current. Little more than that would be fathomable to the Master Fist.

Then came the most challenging element of the spell-shape. As with the Fold Step, Rylin's awareness was in more than one place. Unlike the Fold Step, he would not choose one place to be in a moment. He would be in hundreds of places at the same time.

Rylin's concentration bucked and threatened to give way to dizzying vertigo. His stomach revolted with churning discontent and rising bile in his throat. The spell was about to give away and fail to his inexperienced efforts. Rylin mastered many spells with reckless abandon, but what was he? Was he a suitable successor to the Golden Hourglass Clan? Did he not prove, time and again, he was little more than a lucky boy, dabbling with powers better grasped by the most gifted and disciplined minds?

But this was not an effort to win an argument with his best friend. This was not showboating for the love of his life. Rylin looked at Zenen'Rol, and he saw the parade of thousands of faces. Rylin's first encounter of Zenen'Rol was the massacre of the people of Tihl'Zen. His bloodlust was unleashed upon them without warning or compromise. Ever since that day, their screams filled Rylin's mind. Each of their voices clamored over each other in his nightmares. They all cried out for one thing: justice.

Now, their voices returned to his mind, their cries of pain and fear changed into demands made in justified anger.

Rylin was not allowed to falter, now. Each shout added a piece of determination to his own. Their fury added to his resolute calm. Whatever he might have done before now, he was their instrument. He was an extension of their desire not to be forgotten.

Rylin did not just stand in a random number of locations as he gained control of the shape. He perceived his enemy from as many vantage points as there were victims of the slaughter of Tihl'Zen. He stood in the air, two feet in front of Zenen'Rol. He was in the bloodied snow. He was on a white tundra void, several miles to the south. He was on a broken piece of earth and ice, floating on choppy waters a mile below. He was in these places and thousands more.

Unlike the mimics of Simulacrum these were not copies of himself. These were all Rylin. They held knowledge, experiences, and the full will of him. It was a mad kaleidoscope of possibilities, converged into this one reality. Had he failed to control the mental demands, it would have created a personal paradox that would drive him insane.

With so many of Rylin drawing so much of the two Currents, the effect was violent. The winds and snows whipped in a frenzy. The air shimmered with a heavy magical pressure. The storm clouds above the arctic parted, allowing sunlight to pour down.

Rylin breathed relief. "I did not think I would ever have to shape Multi-Fold Displacement, but this needs to end."

There was another danger to the Multi-Fold Displacement. Rylin could not allow any of his thousands of selves to die. He could disperse the spell, but any death would be catastrophic on a personal and universal level. He, and the governing energies of creation, would acknowledge he was dead, while also recognizing he was alive. The result from the Temporal Current would be his complete erasure of existence.

The Multi-Fold Displacement was at fault for the loss of over half of the Golden Hourglass Clan.

Every Rylin swiftly shaped fingertip-sized Stasis Spheres. They launched a concerted barrage at Zenen'Rol. The giant's movements were too slow. He was engaged in an action that was half an hour old. He shaped the three imperial elements into massive destruction, unaware that Rylin had long since shaped a counter magic.

Zenen'Rol was oblivious to the danger. He could not cut through hundreds of Stasis Spheres shaped faster than he could perceive. All the spheres struck home all over his eight-foot body. With each inch he moved, his skin ripped away. His body oozed blood, while the halted bits of time retained his flesh and torn clothing.

Rylin released his Displacement Cloak. He listened to Zenen'Rol howl in agony. He watched the Master Fist of the Crimson Emperor fall to the snow as his Grasping Winds failed him. The Stasis Spheres faded, and the feared titan of the east was covered in a rain of bloody bits of himself. The snow changed deep red all around his body.

Rylin thought Zenen'Rol was dead or unconscious from blood loss. Then the torn, thrice-scarred head raised and looked up and around.

Zenen'Rol had trouble raising his head from the snow. His entire body was raw and flayed. He was covered in deep pock-tears that bled freely. Where did they all come from?

How did he lose such control over this duel? Rylin was far more than average, but he also fell into multiple traps. Zenen'Rol was about to finish him with the rarely performed Imperial Execution Shape. Now, Zenen was torn apart. He looked up and around and could not believe he was anything other than delirious. Rylin was everywhere!

Zenen did not know how this was possible, but he was barely alive.

This revealed two truths to Zenen'Rol. The first was that Rylin was taking him seriously now, where before he did not. That revealed a depth of power far beyond Zenen'Rol's ability to survive.

But survive Zenen did, in pain that was far beyond anything he had ever endured. Because he survived, he could mend his wounds. That was pointless if Rylin could overpower him again.

Which led to the second truth: Zenen did still have one way to win. The demon child said that it would not be enough against the Void Hand, but the demon did not account for other possible threats. He could use it, and there would not be a living Stratian left in five days.

Zenen'Rol strained against searing, bleeding muscles. He reached underneath his chest, and into the pocket of his vest coat. He found the smooth, cool, metal disc and pulled it free. He held it before his face a moment. He admired the chromium shine and flawless etchings. It seemed just a tiny irrelevant object. Only one had ever been created, yet it was such a devastating tool.

It was fortunate that there were no Current Readers as gifted as Yelisian, or Zenen would never have this chance.

Zenen'Rol gripped the disc in both hands. He pushed his will into his arms and into the Seal of Stagnation. Then he snapped the disc in half.

Zenen broke the tiny object. Rylin's spread perception snapped back into the single perception in the snow. The others vanished in the same instant. The winds died, and the clouds began to flood in on the clear blue they had been exiled from.

The cold and the pain of the two cuts flooded in on Rylin. He fell to his knees, shivering and crying out.

Zenen stood up, slowly. The bleeding craters on his body filled and mended in seconds. His clothes rethreaded together. His smile was cold and malicious as he walked toward Rylin.

Zenen'Rol knelt in the snow and gripped Rylin's head, forcing his gaze. Rylin struggled to remain alert against the encroaching cold.

Zenen's low voice broke the silence, with the Kasarin language. "You were never going to win, boy. We had plans within plans of our own, you see. We wanted to see how powerful you all were before we stripped you of your power. Now, this Imperial Decree of Obliteration can finally conclude."

Zenen'Rol let go of Rylin's head, allowing his gaze to sag. He stood up and walked away.

"Take this consolation to your grave, worthy enemy: you were far more of a challenge than I was ready for."

With that, Zenen'Rol vanished. Rylin could not feel the Master Fist wield the Endless Current for the Meld Walk.

Rylin was alone. He was stranded in the arctic, slowly freezing and bleeding to death. He did not have the power to do anything about it.

-40-

A great explosion rocked the city of Pahlinsor. The thunderous cacophony shook the ground. Every wall trembled. Shelves spilled their contents. Cobblestones cracked, and the dark gray buildings swayed, threatening instant collapse…close to the palace.

From the center of the palace, deep within the outer walls, thick black smoke climbed high into the air. Their source was giant tongues of blood red fire.

The patrolling Phoenix Legions were swept up among throngs of panicked residents and refugees. People screamed and ran every which way, gripped with confusion and terror. If the palace could be struck down so quickly, nowhere was safe. The soldiers tried to regroup and band together. They tried to restore order, attempting to direct the people. It was a useless gesture in the total bedlam.

In the middle of it all, Aemreen was struck with the full danger of the situation. It became evident in the triage tents.

Porra and the boy, Merice, looked at each other with wide-eyed horror.

Aemreen refreshed a splint on a soldier's fractured shin, ignoring his wince and quiet grunt. She looked over to the two healer Renegades. A grand boom reverberated to her. A deep cold dread settled in her middle.

"What is it?" Aemreen managed.

Porra answered with quivering lips. "It is the Endless Current. We cannot take it in."

Merice nodded his agreement. "Our will does nothing."

Aemreen only needed a moment to ponder the explosion and the inability of the two Renegades. An inkling began to creep into her mind, but she dearly hoped she was wrong.

Aemreen was on her feet. "Any soldier able to stand and lift a sword, do so now!" Aemreen's voice was a commanding shout in the tent. She moved behind an area partitioned by a canvas wall. She opened a wooden trunk and began to dress in a chain mail tunic and pants, casting aside her dress for leather pants and a thick wool shirt. The Legionnaires stood from their beds, silent and uncomplaining. Aemreen and the Phoenix Legions strapped on their steel bracers, boots, and skull caps. They strapped on their short broadswords and polled on their black leather gloves.

Aemreen finished arming herself and circled around the canvas partition. "Any change in your magic?"

Porra's answer came with tears at the corner of her eyes. "No. We cannot feel the Current at all."

Two more explosions shook the city, sounding from outside the tent, in the center of Pahlinsor. The screams of panicked people grew louder, sounding closer.

"Form up, Phoenix Legion!" Aemreen shouted. Every able and armed soldier snapped to attention at the foot of the double row of beds. They stood rigid, disciplined, and ready.

Aemreen continued in a brisk shout. "Our capital is under attack. We must get the people to safety, and we must drive the Kasarin threat from Pahlinsor. There is reason to believe the Legions must defend, alone. The Havoc Guilds are attacking, so we take every possible advantage. We fight under-handed, if need be, and we cut them down. First squad," Aemreen gestured to the soldiers to her right. "Group with the Renegades and guide the people to safe locations. Second squad," Aemreen shifted her attention to the soldiers on her left. "You are with me. We rally our scattered forces, and we cut down anything dressed in red, gold, and black."

Aemreen softened her tone, slightly. "I know you are all wounded, and you have already paid with pain in battle. I regret to demand this of any of you. Our homes and our people need us to lift our swords one more time."

Aemreen turned her expression and voice hard, again. "Let's hurry and get the people out of harm's way so we can keep this conflict direct. Now go!"

Aemreen reined in her own fear as she turned and led the soldiers out of the tent. She looked to the west, up the inclining street to the palace. The mid-afternoon sun became hazy from smoke. Three red infernos licked, with hungry intent, at the palace walls. In the streets, the deadly thorned vines ripped free from stone, seeking the people, tearing them apart in bursts of blood and flesh.

Aemreen turned her fear into hardened resolve as she unsheathed her saber. She led the charge into the city. Vines came at her legs and arms. She cut them down before they found purchase. The Guilders were not yet in sight.

Seeing a squad of the organized Phoenix Legion, the people began to settle down and accept directions for evacuation.

Aemreen saw a tall wiry Guilder reach for an elderly Stratian woman's throat. His hands and arms crackled with crimson electricity. Aemreen dashed while his attention was diverted. She skewered the sides of his skull with a charging lunge. She kicked him away and yanked her blade free from his head with a sickening crunch.

Aemreen's fears were confirmed in the city. The Renegades were stripped of their powers while the Havoc Guilds retained full use of their sorcery. She wondered if this anomaly was limited to Pahlinsor, or if it was a condition for all Stratia.

Was all Pravahs afflicted with this?

This must have been the full scope of the trap laid for Rylin by Zenen'Rol. The Kasarins could not defeat Rylin in a direct confrontation. They were certain to be wiped out with the full potency of the Renegades and the Legions combined. They needed to deviate around all Stratian sorcery.

Aemreen cursed it all, inwardly. She believed the trap would be an ambush for Rylin, or an attack from within Pahlinsor. She fully expected the dungeon break. Teranen could handle such an attempt with little assistance.

This tactic was beyond Aemreen's imagining. In the history of Pravahs, nothing like this occurred. She could not have anticipated this.

Ishell, Borvis Len, and several other Renegades stepped within Aemreen's view. The two young women nodded in wordless agreement before Ishell turned to help the Legions guide the evacuation. Ishell was powerless to fight, but Aemreen admired her quick rush to the task left open to her.

Aemreen found five Legionnaires guiding ten frightened residents. Ten, red-armored Kasarins appeared in the street, blocking their way.

"Watch your middle, and strike for the legs and head." Aemreen spoke as she located the Havoc Sorceress responsible for this offensive intrusion.

Aemreen ran to the sorceress. The dark woman saw her at the last instant and whipped at Aemreen with a dagger. Aemreen deflected the blow off her steel bracers before she delivered a disemboweling slash. As the sorceress gripped her exposed entrails, Aemreen impaled her through her chin in an upward stab.

The massive shape of Errnik bowled into the fray with a wide sweep of his hammer. Two red soldiers were flung high and far with the colossal strike. Joriken darted in from the other end of the struggle. He looked like a black wind, cleaving with abandon, leaving streams and sprays of blood in his wake.

"Errnik, take three Legionnaires and gather patrols to the north. Joriken, take four and go south." This would leave only seven injured men to follow Aemreen, but they needed to locate the legions with greatest haste.

Joriken opened his mouth to protest. Aemreen shot him a warning glare that forced him to sprint away in silent obedience.

Aemreen turned to the west, again. Her instincts and reflexes were only just enough to spare her life. She dived low, underneath a hot ball of red fire. She felt the heat sear her back through the thick shirt and chain mail.

Two of her seven men were not so fortunate. Two more balls of fire struck them in the face. Their eyes melted to jellied ooze. Their flesh was blackened to the bone in less than a blink. Their screams were brief before they fell back dead.

"Move like a Ka'Sorik gladiator all you want, little girl," taunted the familiar voice of the woman Rylin called Ken'Tekira. "I will burn you with the rest of this city."

Aemreen levelled her determined gaze on the small, menacing woman while she masked her sense of dread. She hoped to catch the Havoc Elite Sorceress by surprise. She would have cut her down without warning.

But the element of surprise was not on Aemreen's side. She was the only child of the Tahkaer bloodline, ancient allies to the throne of Malkanor and the Moarenroak family. She stood straight and readied her saber. She steeled herself against a fight she knew she was not likely to survive. She would account herself as the daughter of a warrior family.

She wished she could hold Rylin one more time. She wanted to tell him how much she loved him, and that she would cast aside everything to be with him, forever.

In Perahl'Glae panic created a murmur of hundreds of furtively hurrying people.

There were four Solas at work, in the four cardinal directions of the city. But their eyes went wide, and their faces paled. This was the first sign to the people that had grown accustomed to the unwavering presence of the former Lights. The people relied on the constant vigil they maintained over the gleaming city.

Nerilisse spoke first, her voice tiny with fear. "I do not understand. I cannot feel it, Light Merahl. I cannot feel the Endless Current."

Merahl's voice was grim and low as his eyes locked into the east. "There is every reason to believe our sorcery is gone, and with it our illusion."

Nerilisse visibly fought with her despair, seeking her resolve. "We must inform the city patrols."

Merahl nodded without looking away. "And whatever remains of the Perahli forces. They are all we have left to defend this city. We must aid them in whatever way we can."

Merahl's stomach went cold with dread as his fears materialized on the rolling hilltops to the east.

Hundreds of red and gold gleaming ranks of soldiers began to crest each rise.

With the illusion gone, the Kasarins knew that Perahl'Glae still stood. They were coming to destroy the capitol of Perahl'Sen, finishing the destruction of the Pearl Shine.

Lycendrik Derin, once the proud and clever king of Perahl'sen, looked east from his tower window over his shining city. Tens of thousands of Kasarins marched in perfect formation. They were ready to raze his kingdom.

Lycendrik looked at himself in a full-length, gold-rimmed mirror. He attempted to straighten the wrinkled lapels of his once white silk robes. They were stained, below the hips, with wide spots of unchecked urine. The robe was also spotted with splatters of faint brown and red, above his belly, from weeks of wine and ale spills. His face was covered with an unkempt brown beard. It was filthy from lying face down in a stupor on the floor. His once long, flowing, platinum hair was matted, oily, and tangled with dozens of thick snarls.

He wore nothing but his robe, anymore. He was naked underneath, and barefoot. He tried to stand up straight, in a semblance of regal dignity. He looked at himself in the mirror and cackled madly.

Lycenrik's blue eyes were glazed and cracked with a webwork of red veins. He did not sleep, anymore. The last time he tried, he was punished without mercy.

He saw the face of the brave king Delkit. He demanded to know why a coward of a king should be allowed to live when thousands died. After asking this, the Katahni King's face split and poured thick streams of blood.

That was only the most recent dream. There were dozens more that were just as bad, if not worse. He dreamed of mothers and children dragged, kicking, and screaming, before they were hurled on top of massive bonfires. He dreamed of miles of standing poles where his lancers were impaled through their backs and left to rot.

Lycendrik shuddered with cold revulsion. "Nightmares, so many nightmares," he whispered.

Then a tear formed at the corner of his eye when he thought of the words of King Delkit in his dream. He was right. Why should he still be alive? He looked out at the coming assault, marching against the late afternoon sun. It was an attack he personally provoked.

He punched himself several times across the cheeks, coloring his vision with spots. He was nothing more than a conceited fool! He believed righteous heroes always prevailed against villains in war. He believed that some sort of governing fate mandated that to be true.

War did not recognize the absolutes of good and evil. It did not shield the innocent. It did not grant self-proclaimed heroes some sort of invincibility. It was only blood and death. It was agony for everyone. Lycendrik was guilty of petitioning for its presence across Stratia.

If Lycendrik wanted to find a villain in all this, he need look no further than his own reflection. If he wanted to see evil brought to justice for the sake of the innocent, he only needed to bring it to himself for all his people to see.

Lycendrik turned away from his mirror and approached his open window. He climbed onto the ledge and stood up. He looked at the clear blue skies, the bright green hills, and his beautiful Perahl'Glae. His eyes streamed tears down his filthy cheeks. He never wanted to doom his kingdom, let alone all Stratia. He thought himself so clever and righteous as he maneuvered everyone into this war. He was a fool!

He looked at the shining pearl city and kingdom that was his. Perahl'Glae: Pearl's Gleam as it translated. It was such a fair jewel of a city. It was filled with expressive and brilliant people, and he failed them all. He condemned the good and the innocent to a death sentence. Well, for once, the king of Perahl'Sen would not force something on his people that he would not claim, himself.

"You're right, Delkit," Lycendrik murmured to deaf winds. "Why should a coward live on, when good people die?"

Lycendrik closed his eyes and walked off the ledge of his window, over a hundred feet above the ground. He walked to the death he unjustly fled, time and again. Before the people he once ruled, the nation that stood defenseless before the Kasarin armies, he passed his own death sentence.

Lycendrik hit the pearl white ground in a red splatter. His bones crunched loud, and his skull split. His eyes popped loose from their sockets as his brains tried to force themselves out through new openings. Blood began to pool underneath him, adding to the initial spread around him.

The Imperial Obliteration claimed the life of a second King.

Amorlic was not on top of the walls. The Kasarins assaulted with a fervor he had not witnessed before. Without the magic of the Blood Scathe Twins, (now huddled and whimpering in the corner of the barracks) this was the moment he had been waiting for.

The splitter traps and the poison stingers had already proven effective, cutting down hundreds of red-armored soldiers. The invaders came in the thousands, their sheer numbers crushed down on the compound, eventually passing the traps.

It was time for his ingenuity to reveal itself to everyone. The two women held no magic now. The Havoc Guilds rained down crimson fire and lightning. The bog willow trees were struck down and burning. The waters began a slow boil as the tall weeds began to ignite. Mist gave way to acrid smoke.

But Amorlic's repeating arbalests were proving invaluable to their survival. There were six, in all. Each was surrounded by a contingent of spearmen and archers. The arbalests spit an endless stream of poisonous bolts into the crimson waves, bringing down dozens of Kasarins in seconds. It seemed, for a time, that Amorlic would lead the compound to survive even this furious siege.

But the vines began to find their marks in the mercenary spearmen. The Kasarins discovered some way for their vines to persist, even in the fetid swamp nation, and they were quick to utilize the discovery. They reached up from the waters to pull them off the walls and boil them alive in the swamp. The bolt cases were beginning to run low. Runners attempted to cart freshly filled cases of munitions. The Havoc Sorcerer's claimed the lives of the runners, as well.

In the commotion, Amorlic stood in the foyer. He shouted orders and tried to maintain the defensive. He waited on the chance that an offensive opening would present itself.

It became painfully clear that the size and ferocity of this siege might be enough to sink the compound into the bogs of Nerinmor.

-41-

A strangely familiar voice sounded in the silence with sharp command.
"Wake up, Rylin."

Rylin did not want to obey. Pain and unbearable cold waited for him beyond the dark void of sleep. He knelt for a long time after Zenen'Rol left him to die in the arctic. It was pointless to do more. His back and his thigh protested with searing pain in his nerve endings. It was not content to remain so close to the open wounds. A dull ache spread throughout every fiber of his body.

Then there was the bitter cold, at first only biting at the ends of his toes and fingers. After a time, the needle-pricks of ice spread all over his body. He could only endure so much before he fell into the snow and into sleep.

"Wake up, Rylin," the voice ordered with greater insistence.

Rylin moaned in protest; but the sound of his own voice was enough to open his eyes. Beyond the darkness of his drenched hood, everything was white. His head was completely submerged in the snow.

"Do you not find it peculiar that your recollection is so clear?" the voice was somewhat muffled by the layer of snow. "You have lost a great deal of blood. Your wounds may be infected. Between that and the cold, you should be under the grip of a fever that will not allow you to remember your own name."

Rylin listened closer, trying to place the familiar sound of the voice. Under the circumstances, his mind was unusually clear, but his thoughts were still a little hazy.

Rylin's voice was a weak croak. "How...are you Current Reading me?"

"Ah, so you grasp a little of the predicament," the voice condescended. "I am, however, offended that you do not remember me. You do not remember that I have no need to Current Read you."

There was something to the voice: a cold, quiet contempt...yes, that is what it was. This was something that tickled at Rylin's memories.

"I have no time to jar the feverish recollections of a dullard. Suffice it to say, 'I have watched as you failed to wield the will to do what must be done'."

Those words snapped Rylin's eyes open. He strained to lift his head above the snow.

"You cannot be!" Rylin gasped.

The one who looked down on Rylin with unveiled disgust was an exact reflection of himself. He wore the robe, the tunic, the pants. Only the wounds were absent.

This was the part of Rylin that Yelisian severed in the Rite of Separation. This was Rylin's Aspect of Vengeance, a part of Rylin that sought justice in a way that was extreme, often cruel. It held a piece of his magical potential. It also claimed to hold the ability to determine the fated actions of people based on their present choices. Twice, its pursuits nearly branded Rylin as a murderer.

But Yelisian cast the Aspect into the erosion of the Endless Current. It was more than three years since Rylin's last encounter with it. He thought its dissolution was complete.

"Oh, I have been with you all along, Rylin." The Aspect

read his thoughts. "I guided you to discover the demon claw, and to discover the truth of the battle of Katahn. I nudged my will into your own so that you might recover from the Reckoning, sooner. I thought you would bring the Crimson Conquerors to justice. I never imagined you would fail due to pride and foolish ideologies."

"So…" Rylin began before he was interrupted.

"…why now? You are only alive because I wish it, Rylin. I gripped onto your life as you neared the brink of death. If I depart you will die. I am here to give you information, and then grant you a choice." The Aspect waited and Rylin nodded. What else could he do?

"At present, all Lights of the Order of the Enlightened Sun are powerless. Their magic is severed for the time being. They will remain this way for five days. This was the result of a secret weapon developed by the Kasarin Empire they called the Seal of Stagnation. It locks away the potential of every unwarded magus. The potency of their will, the Endless Current, these are out of their reach during this time. A search on the Havoc Magi would reveal a fresh tattoo. Most of them believe it to be decorative. This is the mark of the ward that protects them from the Seal."

The Aspect leaned closer to Rylin, narrowing its gaze. "It will take no more than five days for the Kasarins to kill every Stratian and burn away any trace they ever lived."

"You…lie." Rylin coughed.

The Aspect shook its head. "I have not lied in the past. I will not do so now. At this very moment, Aemreen is locked in battle with Ken'Tekira. Aemreen will die. Malkanor will be ashes by tomorrow's end."

Rylin's insides became cold and hollow, even as he fought with disbelief. Did he really hold her for the last time? Was she already no more than a fading wisp of vapor in his arms? Did he already lose everything she ever was?

But Rylin knew the Aspect would not share this information without an ulterior motive. He would begin with compounding his feelings of hopelessness.

Rylin looked up into the cold gaze of the Aspect. "Why tell me this if I am too late to save her?"

The Aspect's smile was more chilling than its blank malice. "It does not need to be too late. We can turn the tides against this entire invasion. They can end Stratia in five days. We can end them by nightfall. By day's end, there won't be a single Kasarin in all Stratia."

There was a forbidden overwhelming appeal to the offer. But Rylin remembered the last time he acquiesced to the Aspect's terms. It was the first time he ever used a concentrated Stasis Sphere on a human target.

The Aspect hardened its voice with anger. "Allow me to explain. You had the power, multiple moments, to end all this. You could have saved thousands of Stratian lives. Now, the rest of Stratia hangs in the balance. Their salvation depends on whether you will accept my aid; or allow genocide so that you may continue to cling to your self-righteousness and woeful hesitation. If you choose to fail Stratia, then I will abandon you to your fate. As I have stated from the beginning, 'I despise the lack of will to do what must be done'."

Rylin lowered his head, attempting to conceal his despair. He knew he held little choice. Whatever the Aspect planned, it was the only chance Stratia had for survival. Unlike years ago, when Yelisian still lived, this was not a matter of alternatives. There were none. Death was the only other option for everyone, and it was his choice to make.

"What would you have of me?" Rylin managed.

"I require control of us. I will save Aemreen, your mother, father, everyone."

Rylin nodded. "Do what you must."

Deep in a dense towering city of the Kasarin Empire, several red-robed men stood watch over an inferno that consumed a tall estate. The noble home was surrounded by a circle of salt before-hand. This prevented the escape of any demons or people under dark influence. The darkness of hell was a disease, and it would not be allowed to spread.

The entire manor, once the home of a lord, cast the night in the blood-red glow of imperial fire. Shadows flickered and danced in the darkness of the eerie red light. The intensity of the fire mixed with the summer heat. The air was thick with the reek of sulfur and smoke, forcing the Purifier's to wear red cloth masks.

Most of their work was done. All they needed to do was wait for the last timber to fall, and the last ember to fade. That was hours away, yet; but patience was required for the Purifier's Guild.

Then something strange happened. They saw movement from within the entry, deep beyond the bloody fires. It was a shambling figure. It was human in shape, but its remaining flesh and organs dripped away in melted ooze. Its spine and ribs were revealed, and the arms and legs were charred bones, held together by unseen force. It walked, lumbering one awkward step after another. A strange repetitious sound rasped from its throat.

The sorcerers watched in horror as it crossed over the salt-covered threshold. Such a thing should not be possible. It had never been witnessed in the last two millennia. One of two things had to be true for a demon to cross a line of salt. Either the demon was a lord of hell, or the world was about to undergo a major infernal event.

The Purifier's could only stand with slack jaws as the sound became a clear chant from lungs long since burned away.

"Crayaht'En...Crayaht'En...Crayaht'En..."

The chant filled the air over the roar of the imperial flames. This possessed corpse was not alone in its macabre observance. Other shrieking and growling voices united in their terrible zeal. It was the sound of demons caught in the throes of dark reverence.

Aemreen's arms were leaden, and her chain mail was covered in streams of blood. She knelt on one knee against the cobblestones, unable to lift her sword. Ken'Tekira would finish her soon. The sorceress was unscathed, breathing unlabored. She smiled down at her.

People ran screaming from the Kasarin Soldiers. Few Stratians made it far as their heads were severed by arcs of flat red energy. Blood sprayed the dark stones of the city, running into puddles and rivulets. Many more met their agonized end as they were cleaved and skewered at the end of the long, curved swords. Mothers and fathers protected the children with their bodies. No one was spared.

Aemreen gritted her teeth against her pains and in anger. "What are you waiting for, red witch?"

Ken'Tekira's smiled broadened. "I wanted to allow you to watch this city fall. I wanted you to know this was the only end for all of you."

Aemreen spat blood on Ken'Tekira's feet. "Stupid games for stupid people."

Ken'Tekira kicked off the blood spit and nodded in agreement. She yanked off Aemreen's skull cap and pulled her head back in a fistful of hair.

"Quite right. Why should I expect such filthy creatures to understand this irony?"

Aemreen looked up while her head was tilted back. She was forced to look at the sun, halfway in the western sky. Ken'Tekira's dagger was poised at Aemreen's throat, ready to slice the blood free. She stopped when she noticed the sunlight was beginning to dim.

Aemreen watched in fascination as the dark shadow of the moon began to overtake the sun.

It was the start of a solar eclipse. No one predicted it, not scholars or the Order. Had it been anticipated she would have heard people discussing it before now. Aemreen's belly filled with a cold dread. This was a rogue event, impossible even for sorcery.

While the sky darkened to an early night, a sound filled the air, repeating in cadence and rhythm. It was unintelligible, at first. There were so many shouts and screams, so much chaos of battle drowning out the sound. But the battle began to quiet in the face of this ominous phenomena. Neither Kasarin nor Stratian could help but stare into the deepening gloom, falling silent in the wake of that strange sound.

While the streets froze in mute terror, the sound began to clarify itself. They were voices, but unlike any voice from a human mouth. It was a combined screaming, gravelly chant. It was a repeating sequence of confusing words.

"Crayaht'En…Crayaht'En…Crayaht'En…"

Deep in the festering abandoned bogs of Nerinmor, there were hidden mausoleums and catacombs. The entrances were sealed away from sight by centuries of swamp muck. In one ancient era, these labyrinths were burial chambers for ancient rulers and their loyal servants. In a more recent era, though still ancient, these tombs were the meeting places of the Order of the Void Triangle. Here they would train, receive instruction from their demonic masters, and plan the various stages of their conquest.

The narrow halls and wide chambers were draped with thick gossamer cobwebs. The spiders abandoned these dank domains, recognizing that nothing living would ever belong here. Dust created a layer on the cracked stone floor, several inches thick.

It was no surprise when the stale, moldy air stirred, and shadows began to gather with intent and sentience. They began to slither and walk upright, called to the surface for the first time in centuries.

These shadows were not alone as they emerged into the swamp mists. Across the world, from within haunted estates and neglected graveyards, the shadows began to gather into the prevalent darkness, blacker than the early night itself. Their glowing blood red and fiery green eyes blazed with dark delight. Their harsh voices were united in a chant that echoed to every corner of Pravahs.

"Crayaht'En…Crayaht'En…Crayaht'En…"the sound continued.

The power was indescribable and massive, alien in every way. It changed him. He was no longer the young man, Rylin. He was filled with the Aspect's strengths and experiences as well.

During the time that Rylin trained in the Order of the Enlightened Sun, he learned to harness the two tandem forms of energy. While Rylin did this, the Aspect began to acquire the knowledge and skills of a different form of magic and energy.

This energy was not like the Endless Current, so it existed on a primordial level that was beyond the influence of the Seal of Stagnation. This energy was filled with raw cold, unlike the Endless Current. It was a ravenous force that desired to consume everything. It was hollow, and yet filled with fury. It required no clarity or tranquility from those who brought it forward. It scoured away obstacles such as unwanted emotions, or matters that might, otherwise, obscure the shaper's focus.

The Aspect shared this knowledge, and he knew this energy held very concentrated methods of crafting its actual shape. The effects of this energy, and its magic, created distinct changes in the human appearance over time. It adapted its wielders to better suit its needs. These changes were beginning to reveal themselves much faster with him. If it had a body, the Aspect would have experienced these alterations at a pace that mirrored the training.

Life and warmth were deemed an obstacle to the perfection of the dark stillness. Death was the closest facsimile to this non-existence. Color and bodily warmth in the skin were the first to disappear. What was left was a cold, clammy pallor of a drowned corpse. The lips also turned a cold blue tint.

The color of the human eyes was stripped away, as they were extensions of emotions and the soul within. In the absence of the vibrant colors, only two black pupils were left in orbs of milky white.

He no longer felt the cold of the arctic as he climbed to one knee. In the absence of the registered chill, the falling snow hardened to pellets, and the thick layers around him crackled with increased cold.

He also watched as the fibers of his clothes changed. One by one, every thread from head to toe was soaked in blackness.

The tormented wailing of a man cried out from inside his mind, as he stood up. His dagger injuries were transferred to the soul of a condemned murderer, deep in the bowels of Blot'K'Rark, the bloody realm of sadistic agony.

Filled beyond his limits with a new dark power, the black energy began to shove outward, lifting him off the snow with its inexorable force. The overwhelming darkness began to spill out of his body in the form of tiny, cold, black fires licking out of his pores.

In this new form, with so much knowledge, will, and experience; he was not simply a hybrid of Rylin and the Aspect. He was a vastly more powerful being.

In this new shape, he was Crayaht'En, he was Naejestrisis. Translating the demonic name to Stratian, it meant 'Spreading Negation'.

Naejestrisis probed into Stratia with ephemeral strands of dark energy, seeking the Kasarins. He felt them right away. Their emotions and purpose were heated and loud, even so far away. He felt the righteous fervor that brought them across the Maelstrom to burn everything in their wake. They were so convinced they were putting an end to any resurgence of the Order of the Void Triangle. The fools did not yet realize their actions only solidified its presence.

Naejestrisis did not identify with every ideology of the Void Triangle; but he also held no delusions about what he was now. He was the Void Disciple the Kasarins were hunting. What the crimson fools did not know was that Naejestrisis was the most powerful Void Disciple, ever. He held the singular ability to wield a full range of powers and shapes that his predecessors never could. Every attempt to do so, in the ancient era, was met with a complete erasure of existence.

Naejestrisis felt the fear that froze every Kasarin in the middle of their actions. They feared the sudden eclipse that darkened Stratia. They feared the global unified chant of the Children of Nothing.

Their paralysis made locating them so much easier. It

was time for Naejestrisis to seek out the Kasarins in Stratia and eradicate them all.

Naejestrisis opened his palms. The bitter, cold, dark of Sol Fierest bowed to his will. The searing ash of the raging infernos of Et Flaios burned eager to meet him. The corrosive blood that ran in lakes and oceans in Blot'K'Rark screamed and laughed in mad delight to play in his hands. Combined, the three realms shaped the long, semi-transparent length in his hands. It was a weapon and magical focus called the Staff of the Abyss. It held the destructive capacity and dark essence of the three domains of hell.

Beneath Naejestrisis, just above the snow, an inky black dot spread, becoming a wide pool. He sank into the darkness, feeling the terror and the icy predatory hunger that filled the realm of Sol Fierest as he passed through. He would travel with haste by crossing in and out of the dark world of madness and fear. He would emerge miles above a newly darkened Pahlinsor where he would return the furious extermination to the Kasarins.

-42-

The Kasarins were plain in the view of Naejestrisis. Everything was cast in a dim, colorless haze of gray, black, and white; but shapes and edges were well-defined.

The fear and hesitation below, poured from the souls of hundreds of human beings, mingled in the air. Their heartbeats hammered with hurried rhythm, creating thick pulsing vibrations. Their tense sweat left a saltiness that wafted upwards, lighting on his tongue.

There was a difference between the Stratian and Kasarin fear. Something ethereal and intangible defined their fears in the darkness, eager to be named. The Stratians felt the fear of believing that everything they ever knew was about to be swept aside. The Kasarins felt the dread that they found the beast they were hunting for, only to come to the suspicion that it might be too much for them.

The fears Naejestrisis felt from the Kasarins were not just from those present in Pahlinsor. He felt their blades still, their breath halted in their throats all the way to the edge of Perahl'Sen. In the darkness, caught in the sound of thousands of demons, they were paralyzed in terror.

Naejestrisis's cold blue lips curled into a tiny smirk. Anything he could sense, he could reach. He held the power to end this invasion in a few hours.

These 'Ka'Rak' and Havoc Elite would see the foe they sought. Naejestrisis began a slow descent that placed him in the center of the Merchant square.

Twenty feet from letting his feet touch the ground, Naejestrisis pulled deep from the infernos of Et Flaios. Purple, green, and red fires burst through the cobbles, roaring and entwining as they sought to break the darkness above. The air filled with the thick stench of sulfur and charred flesh. Screams poured upward through the opening of the first domain of hell, a bleak symphony of burning agony. Waves of smoke undulated in dark oily clouds from out of the hot base of the flames.

Naejestrisis spoke in Kasarin as he floated over a foot off the ground. His voice was cold, bleak, and quiet, like a storm on the horizon. It still reached every intended listener over the screams of perdition and the roar of the flames.

"Come for your prey, Ka'Rak. Come and claim your reward."

The pillar of hell fire was only ten feet wide, burning behind Naejestrisis's back. Its myriad glow illuminated the Crayaht'En for the Kasarins to see well enough. They abandoned their attention to the residents of Malkanor as they looked at him. Their fear warred with their sense of imperial duty, playing a conflict in their dark eyes. He waited, patient and unmoving, to see which among them would have the foolish bravery to strike first.

Twenty of the red armored soldiers crushed down their fears and approached from the edges of the square. They moved slow and fluid, their long swords aimed at an uncharacteristic stabbing angle. The flashing colors of hell fire created dancing shadows on the walls of Pahlinsor, casting Naejestrisis's grim expression into horrifying light. His palms were at his sides in open invitation.

Naejestrisis dared the Ka'Rak to come closer, and they did not disappoint. When they were close enough to run him through, Naejestrisis's hands thrust skyward. The hell fire pillar roared with greater intensity, even as it refused to burn the champion who summoned it.

The Ka'Rak blades came close, their blades inches from his clothes and flesh, but the swordsmen failed to account for the intensity of the hell fire or their proximity to it. The flames melted the incoming weapons into dripping red liquid before they completed their thrusts. Their armor began to heat to a brighter shade of red, but even as they screamed, he had much more in store for them.

Tendrils of purple fire, as thick as an arm, diverged from the pillar. They found their homes as they burned and cremated their way straight through the armored chests of the soldiers. Open holes smoked from cauterized gaping wounds.

The Havoc Elite were next to move, certain they could prevail where their subordinates died trying. Fifty of their famed Emperor's Roses split through cobbles and walls, seeking to rip Naejestrisis to bloody shreds. He clapped his hands, once, surrounding himself with a Devouring Maw. The vines were swallowed up along with the helpless remains of the fallen Kasarins.

Naejestrisis snapped his fingers and the ring-shaped vortex divided, gliding through the air, seeking the casters of the thorny vines. His expression was blank and stoic, as the Havoc Elite attempted to flee from pursuing darkness. None of the Elite managed more than ten yards before the vortex winds pulled and tore pieces of their flesh away. They screamed in agony as their bodies were ripped apart and swallowed into nothingness.

The Staff of the Abyss continued to float, dutifully, at Naejestrisis's side. He grasped his black weapon even as his senses pushed deep into the darkness of the eclipse. It was only a moment until he found what he was looking for.

Ken'Tekira's mix of fear and rage burned like a beacon in the concealing shadows. Her dagger was pressed against Aemreen's throat, frozen in the instant before spilling her blood. She was too afraid to finish killing her. Caught in the terrible black pandemonium around her, the Dragon believed she failed to prevent the advent of a second Black Decade.

Naejestrisis called upon the cold darkness of Sol Fierest, funneling it through his being. His mind projected out through cold strands of unseen magic. His magic circumvented the tenacity of her will, slipping around it with the ease of a serpent, and pierced into her soul.

Naejestrisis voice filled Ken'Tekira's head with the force of a debilitating migraine, dropping her to her knees. She screamed as she clutched her head.

"Dragon of Zenen'Rol, come forward and let us end what was begun."

The strands of Sol Fierest pulled Ken'Tekira, dragging her toward him. She tried to resist with the force of her will, but it only lessened her steps to a clumsy shamble. Her feet scraped along the cobbles, and her shoulders jerked and spasmed with each step. Her fellow Havoc Elite and remaining Ka'Rak watched her in the glow cast by Et Flaios. The Kasarin fear proved greater than their killing resolve as they watched their second most powerful magus pulled like a marionette.

The Dragon entered the illuminating view of the hell fire light. Her face took a moment of confusion as she processed what she saw. That melted to recognition, disgust, and fear.

Ken'Tekira gasped. "You!"

"That is irrelevant, Dragon." Naejestrisis reached for her, strands of Sol Fierest snaking forward in the darkness, invading her essence. He would satisfy a matter of justice with her, now.

The strands did not cause Ken'Tekira pain. She remained oblivious as she flinched from his raised hands. Naejestrisis found what he was looking for.

"Gather and shape as many of your strongest Prefect's Lashes as you can. Then you may strike me as hard as you are able."

Naejestrisis felt a twinge of discomfort as the Endless Current rushed toward Ken'Tekira. Its nuance and vibration were keener to his senses than before. She strained it through all the anger she could summon against him. She grappled with the Endless Current, unlike the Lights who allowed it to move through their will. How could she become so strong this way? It only served to exhaust them, quicker, and limit their creativity. It was no small wonder they could not invade until the Order was so weak and divided.

Two lengths of crackling, red lightning sprang to life in the Dragon's hands. Naejestrisis released her from his dark grip, allowing her time for flourishes and spins to build her momentum.

When the Dragon struck, Naejestrisis did not need to alter his speed as he did before. He met each strike with an easy deflection and parry from the Staff of the Abyss. After glimpsing into her soul, so completely, her strikes and techniques were well known to him. Each movement gathered more and more hell frost until he swung low and struck her left leg.

Ken'Tekira did not realize the danger of her situation until it was too late. She stumbled into a lunging step before her left leg snapped in two above the knee. Her thigh bled as she fell forward and screamed. Her abandoned foot remained standing and frozen in place.

Naejestrisis extended his left hand in the Dragon's direction. A mass of shadowy tendrils seeped out of his palm and wrapped around her. She thrashed in the throes of anguish as she was lifted off the ground. She remained in the air before him. Her leg bled a large pool below her, and her agonized screams filled the square.

Naejestrisis began speaking the primordial language of the Children of Nothing, shaping the essence of oblivion. The cold forces of the void scoured through him, delivering the collective energies of hell into his being. He focused on the realm of eternal fire. This was made easier by the opening in the merchant square.

"Et Flaios!" The voice that thundered those words sounded to the furthest edge of Pahlinsor. From Naejestrisis, the words sounded inhuman, harsh, and low.

In response, towering pillars of emerald hell fire erupted everywhere. In the city alone, hundreds of the emerald pillars pierced the sky. The outline of Naejestrisis was wraith-like in the eerie omnipresent glow. Each of these Pillars of Annihilation incinerated the body and soul of the Kasarins caught in the center of the flames.

Naejestrisis shifted the summoning energies, seeking out the realm of Blot'K'Rark. He pulled its presence up, yanking it through the earth until the corrosive blood of the condemned began to ooze through. The bloody rifts formed under the feet of thousands of Ka'Rak and Guilders all over Stratia. The tormented dead trapped within wasted no time grabbing the legs of the fresh victims. The Kasarins thrashed and screamed as they were pulled down into bloody perdition. Their flesh split and dissolved as they were pulled into the corrosive blood.

Content the Stratians were left untouched through the condemning sentence, Naejestrisis turned his attention to the last Kasarin in Malkanor.

Naejestrisis's voice returned to normal as he spoke in a low tone for the Dragon.

"So will it be with all of you."

With a yanking gesture from his left hand, Ken'Tekira's two lowest ribs snapped free and ripped out of her torso in a bloody spray. It should have been the end of her life, but Naejestrisis would not allow it. The strands of Sol Fierest held her spirit tight within her body. She continued to scream, unable to move. Her two ribs floated and spun quick in the air, polishing themselves white. Their ends sharpened to wicked points. Naejestrisis pointed at her, and the two sharpened ribs plunged deep into her eyes and skewered her brain.

With a flick of his wrist, Ken'Tekira's unliving remains were hurled into the open pit of Et Flaios, and the burning damnation within. He closed the fiery rift, and the city was plunged back into the darkness of the eclipse.

Pahlinsor was safe, but Naejestrisis left some of Stratia's invaders alive. He would sentence them, personally.

Naejestrisis floated in the abyss of the cold, infinite hunting grounds of Sol Fierest. The inhuman shrieks and growls of the Children of Nothing filled the blackness. His new name howled into the dark by the methodically cruel lords of hell. Many of them lowered to one knee or bowed their horned heads.

Naejestrisis knew more about the denizens of hell than any mortal was ever permitted. He knew their hierarchy and rulers. He knew which souls were sent to what domain, and what lords and functionaries would govern over them.

He knew that the King of Hell was a blue-black winged demon named Meroweiv, and that he had ruled for more than fifty thousand years.

A tugging sensation pulled deep in his bowels; drawn to a green vertical circle, casting its glow before him.

Thousands of rapid heartbeats played a quick cadence that reached into Sol Fierest. As with Pahlinsor, there were two forms of fear in Perahl'Glae. The citizens of the white city were afraid for their lives when they witnessed the approach of the Kasarin army.

There was something else among the fears of the people as well. The worrying fears of Solas of the Order of the Enlightened Sun reached out to him, unknowingly. Rylin stirred in response to this knowledge, and Naejestrisis wrestled him back into the inner darkness. Rylin was conflicted about this revelation. On one hand, he was grateful that any Solas still lived.

But he was irate that they remained hidden for so long. There was much more of Stratia to defend than this solitary city. Their knowledge and experience would have been invaluable to the Renegades. How could they crawl under cover and hide this way?

Rylin would not be permitted to voice his frustrations, now. Thoughts of judgement, as wielded by Naejestrisis, were at the forefront. These trifling emotions were little better than a nuisance.

Naejestrisis walked through the green rift of energy. The threshold was frigid. It scraped against his being like shards of jagged ice, pressing deep into his flesh as he passed. The barrier he crossed was crafted in ancient days. It was there to rend and disintegrate anything that tried to cross through. This only scratched at him as much as scrapes on a child's knee.

The Guilders and Ka'Rak were paralyzed with fear, as unmoving as the ivory statues that decorated the city. Many Perahli citizens were already cut down, bleeding into the myriad flower basins. The Kasarin long swords dripped with fresh blood, even as they remained poised to spill much more. Splatters of blood painted the ivory walls.

Naejestrisis's tiny black pupils scanned the beginning of the carnage with growing rage. Not even the children were spared the slaughter. Some of the bodies were barely old enough to walk, and their heads were severed with blood pooling around their open necks.

It was just as it had been in Tihl'Zen. It was the same bloodlust inflicted on the innocent and defenseless. The Aspect was right to be so critical of Rylin. These Kasarins were no more than diseased murderous animals. It was beyond time for these invaders to remember how to feel fear. It was time for them to remember how helpless they were during the Black Decade. It was also time for them to take their place in perdition.

"So, you wish to paint this white city red with blood," Naejestrisis observed, speaking Kasarin in his low quiet voice. "It shall be so."

Naejestrisis began to gather the Essence of Stillness. The Kasarins gathered their resolve to fight him. His magic was swifter and more brutal than their meager sense of defiance. He made a circling gesture with his hand, like coiling rope, before clenching his fist. He felt hundreds of soft veins in their necks break, pulled on intangible strings. The waves of Ka'Rak halted as their throats were ripped open in fountains of blood.

Naejestrisis made a pulling gesture with his other hand. The faces and helmets of the Ka'Rak were ripped to mangled visages as their teeth were yanked out of their jaws. They fell before he made a shoving gesture with both hands. The teeth floated in the air, then dashed in a deadly volley. They ripped through crimson scale armor, flesh, and bones with ease. The Kasarins were pelted with enough severity to rip their arms and legs to shreds. In seconds, the streets of Perahl'Glae were soaked with an inches-thick layer of Kasarin blood. Chunks of bone floated in the thick streams.

Naejestrisis deliberately aimed the volley below the necks so that he could yank new barrages of killing teeth. The result was a continual carnage shower of the city. Kasarin blood sprayed every which way, soaking everything.

Many of the severed limbs twitched and spurted fresh blood amid the flower beds. Blood ran from the statue fountains where it collected in pools of sickening red, littered with floating human bits.

Naejestrisis pulled from the dark ether of the alleyways and cellars, opening dozens of rifts into Sol Fierest. Cold black mists spilled out of the dark doors.

Then came the slithering, skulking black masses of hungry lesser predators that dwelled in the infinite dark world. They moved like oil on glass and skittered with the agility of spiders. They moved with unnaturally long and twisted limbs. If not for the darkness of the eclipse, the Perahli residents would have been exposed to the sight of the demonic intrusion.

Pairs of glowing red eyes flared with hate and

anticipation. They gathered armloads of the Kasarin remains. Frantic screams echoed from deep in the dark. The lesser Children of Nothing gathered Kasarin corpses and spirits, hauling them into the depths of Sol Fierest and the lightless eternity that awaited them.

The last of the denizens of Sol Fierest vanished through the rifts with Naejestrisis looking on. Though the walls and ground were still red with blood, every bit of flesh was removed. There was no trace left of the Kasarins in Perahl'Glae. The Stratian bodies were untouched.

Naejestrisis opened his being to the scouring flood of the Essence of Stillness. He climbed into a swift ascent in the black skies. Strobes of lightning, and shredding gales of wind embraced him.

He looked down, several miles to the east of the city, and saw the vast siege armies of the Kasarins gathered on the hills and rises. There were tens of thousands of them, a massive wave of swordsmen and magi, suitable for a city ten times as fortified as Perahl'Glae. If they were given a few moments more, the city would have been crushed. The city had no walls or gates, and no mentionable defenses for the expressive people. The last city of the Pearl Shine nation would have burned. The nation of scholars and artists would have been no more.

There would be cleansing fire, soon enough. But, for this moment, it was time for fear in its purest form. The Kasarins visited fear on the helpless people of Stratia long enough. It was time to return it to them.

Naejestrisis descended in a wind breaking dive, plummeting toward the front line of the Kasarin ranks. The wind shrieked around him at his approach. He curled his dive and lowered his feet at the last possible moment, slowing his descent. He allowed the Staff of the Abyss to remain floating beside him as he stretched out his arms.

There was a frenzied sensation of slimy wriggling in the sleeves of his black coat. Dozens of long gray strands, pulsing with jagged red veins, bolted free of his sleeves. They vaulted to the ground before they slithered with unerring speed towards the foremost of the Kasarins. As fast and deadly as an archer's volley, they bit deep into the eyes and throats of the first of the Ka'Rak. Their teeth sank deep, and the worms pulsed and throbbed. Their lengthy bodies undulated with lethal poison invading their victims.

Naejestrisis did not wait as he began another infernal sorcery. His inhuman voice was spotted with fits of mad cackling. The Guilders shaped their reactive sorceries. They panicked and acted with fearful haste.

The worm infected Ka'Rak fell into a brief death before they began to rise. The contagion in their blood reached for their souls before they departed from their mortal existence. They were forced to remain in their dead flesh. They stood; their weapons forgotten. They shambled and stalked toward their former comrades. Lightning flashed with increasing fervor, illuminating displays of carnage as the dead began to bite and tear into the living. They pulled heads from the shoulders, tore limbs away from the torsos, and yanked entire victims in two at the hips. Screams and dying gurgles sounded against peals of thunder. Entrails slicked the earth and masked the presence of the worms as they slithered to fresh victims. The living dead plundered and devoured the bloody aftermath. Their blank eyes rolled with momentary ecstasy as they consumed the mangled remains.

Naejestrisis continued his next shape. It was a lengthy summons, but it would be sufficient to reduce this Kasarin force to a fraction in a few minutes. The Havoc Magi were already pressed with fear as their forces began to tear each other apart in the darkness.

One of the sorcerers managed to make a ball of white light that floated high in the air. He regretted his choice to illuminate the full depth of their situation. Crayaht'En smirked at the center of the bloody rampage. Ignorance would have served the Kasarins better in their last moments. Dozens of shambling ghouls fell upon dozens more Ka'Rak. Some of the swordsmen managed to cut at the reanimated bodies, but they were slow to sever the heads. The bodies would fall, while the heads continued to move without effect. By the time more of the Kasarins discovered this, there were already far too many ghouls for these attempts to prove useful. They fell screaming as the ghouls weighed down in numbers and proceeded to devour them.

Naejestrisis finished shaping the summons. The conjured white light died. It was replaced with an omnipresent blood red glow. The ground began to tremble and groan before cracks began to split the earth. The living Ka'Rak began to break what disciplined formations they had left. They scattered and fled the battlefield in disarray.

They did not run far enough or fast enough. The cracks in the earth widened, creating a massive chasm. The blood red glow flared brighter from within the center of the opening. The reek of blood and sulfur assaulted everyone with the force of a blast. There was an infinite cacophony of fearful agonized cries sounding from men and women from within the blood pit.

The ground continued to quake as a large, round topped mound climbed from the dim red glow. It was slick with slime, ridged in places, and had the pink appearance of flesh. The agonized screams drew closer as the mound continued to rise from the red abyss. Two shining black domes came into view. This was no land mass, but a gigantic head, and the black domes were eyes.

The mouth of the beast opened wide, revealing the ability to swallow dozens of people at a time. Its long, wide, sharp teeth impaled scores of naked men and women as they dangled at odd, painful angles. Its exhaling breath roared out from a throat reeking of rot and death. The stench rolled out of its maw in a wave.

Its victims thrashed as though still alive. They were

weeping, moaning, and pleading for salvation from their eternal devouring. Their arms and legs tried, to no avail, to pull free from their tormentor. The smaller worms were present inside the mouth of the beast. They bit into the flesh of the would-be escapists, wrenching them back into the giant tongue and throat.

The upper half of the titanic beast cleared the edge of the hole. As it did, thousands more of the smaller worms shot out of its mouth. They sought out any Kasarin flesh they could. Many of the men and women screamed in sudden agony as they braced their hands against the fresh new wounds. There were too many worms to defend against. The worms tensed and dragged their fresh victims back into the mouth of the beast. The Kasarins thrashed and struggled, but the worms were relentless and inexorable.

Scores of Kasarins were dragged and hurled into the giant mouth. The struggling Kasarins frantically pulled at handfuls of blood-slick grass. They clawed at the earth until their fingernails snapped and their hands bled.

The worms ultimately accomplished their purpose and continued their pursuit of fresh Kasarin prey.

The Kasarin infantry fell into total chaos. The Havoc Magi focused their efforts on Naejestrisis. Around them, the Ka'Rak either fled and trampled each other to death, or futilely attempted to cut at the giant wyrm. The guilders stalked forward in smooth graceful steps. They projected a façade of killing intent while the Endless Current came to them in weak hiccups. They were trained to strain the Endless Current through their anger and rage. While they might have learned to channel their fear into anger, this fear was beyond them. The Prefect's Lashes were inconsequential, thin, and useless. The Emperor's Roses were no better than morning glory vines.

Naejestrisis answered with a cold smile. They might mask their feelings, but he saw their powers betray their lies. Their thundering heartbeats belied them. These men and women were already too sick and weak with their fear.

Two of the Havoc Sorcerer's were swept from underneath by several of the lesser gray worms. Their screams fell into silence as they were hurled into the mouth of the wyrm.

The other Havoc Magi closed within reach. Naejestrisis felt for their shifting anger and fear. When their anger sufficiently pressed down their fears, he moved first, and much faster than they expected.

A ball of red flame was snuffed out like a candle before it ever left a sorceress's hand, extinguished by a wide swing from his staff. In the same hell frost swing of the Staff of the Abyss, the staff lengthened and struck her head. Everything above her neck exploded in a shower of icy shards.

Naejestrisis made a yanking gesture with one hand. Tiny bits of jagged sharp bone ripped free of the flesh of twenty guilders. The bone shrapnel flew forward in a rending hail the cut down thirty more magi in front of him.

Lightning continued to flash with increasing fury, interrupting the blood red glow of Blot'K'Rark. Every flash created harsh illumination to the nightmare landscape that Naejestrisis fashioned from his enemies. The waist-high grasses were levelled flat, crushed down by trampling soldiers, maimed corpses, and gallons of blood.

Naejestrisis was the architect of a hell on earth for every Kasarin in Stratia.

-43-

Zenen'Rol sat cross-legged in his meditation tent. His attempts to maintain communication with his forces, via Scrying Sphere, were failing.

The last he heard from Ken'Tekira was just after Zenen activated the Seal of Stagnation. They struck at Pahlinsor from the inside. Then the unnatural eclipse began, followed by the chilling omnipresent chant. Then there was only silence from his Dragon.

Zenen'Rol might have been able to dismiss her lack of reply, but his field lieutenants among the Havoc Elite were also silent.

To make matters worse, Zenen'Rol's Scrying Spheres would only travel two hundred yards before they would black out. This was somehow the work of the enemy they hunted. Somehow, there was demon magic preventing Zenen'Rol from keeping informed. Somehow, this dark sorcery was at the center of this global phenomena.

The black storms that boiled in the skies in the wake of the eclipse were proof of it. Collaborative historical accounts all agreed that these night-like storms always accompanied the forbidden sorceries of the Void Hands. The constant frequent bright flashes of lightning only hinted at massive levels of Void Hand magic.

The howling winds ripped across the beaches and the

fields. Zenen's thick canvas tent fluttered and snapped, violently, in the ceaseless tempest. The usually musky scent of incense from his brass censer was sucked away into the winds that pressed into his private sanctuary. Along with the faint twinge of the sea breeze, there was the smell of sulfur and blood.

Though the Master Fist tried to ignore the sounds outside of his tent, he heard the nervous shifting of armor, and the furtive whispers of the Ka'Rak. His remaining Elite tried to quell the treacherous fear with angry threats, but the obedient silence they bought was fleeting.

Beyond the sounds of camp, ocean waves swelled and surged in the force of the wind. They crashed into the cliffs and bluffs, crushing down massive boulders. Whole precipices gave way, splashing thunderously into the water. Trees groaned and snapped as they were yanked away from their roots in the powerful tides.

Zenen was never in an event that felt so apocalyptic. While the giant sorcerer was not as prone to fears-and he was quick to convert it to rage-something about this felt unnerving to him. But if he acknowledged this, he would give satisfaction to the gleeful forewarnings of the possessed little girl.

Zenen could accept many truths, and he would always be humble enough to kneel before the Crimson Throne, but he already bested a powerful Chronomancer in a duel to the death. How could even a Void Hand, stand against his prowess?

The answer came in the form of sudden destruction. It came unbidden and absolute.

The wind stopped, stilled into perfect silence. The rancid stench of sulfur filled the air until it clung to the top of Zenen'Rol's mouth. A tremor quaked beneath his thick maroon rug. The distant horizon groaned with a rising peal like thunder.

For a moment, everything was illuminated in a bright green and purple mix of light. Then there was a heat, far beyond the testing fires of the Flesh of the Immortals. A roaring boom ripped away the tent and everything around it. Zenen shielded his face with both arms.

When it passed, Zenen'Rol still lived. He lowered his arms, feeling the tender singe of burns for the first time in years. It was nothing compared to what he saw in the ember illuminated landscape.

There was no base camp, no Ka'Rak, no Havoc Elite. The beaches were no more than black and red patches of sand, fused into glass. The tall fields and trees were scorched to a flat landscape of stirring ashes and clumps of dim embers. In the vague glow, and the flashes of lightning, the ocean waves continued their tides under clouds of steam. The surface was littered with chunky patches of slime. It was a moment before he realized it was fish, flash boiled to paste.

The sharp, choking reek of burning things and smoke was as strong as the rancid stench of sulfur.

Zenen'Rol squinted in the pressing dark, unable to see far. He was the only one left alive. Everyone and everything else were incinerated in an instant. This was hell fire. Of all magic fires ever recorded, only hell fire could burn so much so fast.

Zenen was alive only by purposeful design of the Void Hand who unleashed these fires.

"That is correct, Zenen'Rol. You live so that we may finish what we began, with justice."

The voice that came from above was a cold, quiet sound. How could such a sound travel so clear from so far. Yet this voice was also familiar.

Zenen looked up with eyes wide, grinding his teeth and knuckles. The flashes of lightning outlined the shape of the boy Chronomancer he left for dead in the far north. He had been left wounded, bleeding heavy, freezing, and helpless in the snow. How could he have returned?

But the startling question of it all: how was Rylin this Void Hand they had been hunting all along? The ancient history of the archives, gleaned at great lengths from Stratia, agreed on several points. The first was their ability to gather the Endless Current was severely limited. It burned them to try. The second was their appearance was forever altered, the more of the magic they mastered. Their dark order had to wipe away the memories of their fellows in the Mage Clans, so that no one would question their presence or appearance. This was especially true among the Emerald Specter Clan who were known for their short life span, and deathly sick yellow pallor.

When Rylin lowered from floating thirty feet in the air, the changes to his appearance revealed a person far different before Zenen'Rol. Gone was the blue farmer's tunic and brown pants. Gone was the deep green hooded long coat and emerald staff. His clothes were as black as the sky.

The luminous blue of his eyes was gone. Only the tiny black dots of his pupils were visible in the whites of his eyes. The lively color of his complexion paled. His cheeks were sunken, and his face and skin looked cold and clammy.

Around the boy, the ashes and embers cooled, replaced by a thin white layer of frost forming in a radius around him. Did the air chill in the presence of his malice? This was nothing at all like the Chronomancer he defeated.

"That is an accurate observation, Zenen'Rol." He was not Current Reading, but Zenen'Rol knew he could keep no secrets from this dark figure. "I am not Rylin. I am Naejestrisis."

Without warning, Zenen fell as the ground beneath him gave way. There was no landing, and the lightnings of the sky faded from his view.

After a great length of falling into the darkness, a strange heat climbed from below him. Perhaps it was the blood of Pravahs. Was he about to burn and dissolve in molten stone? But a cold crept, with subtlety, in his bowels. He knew that was not what waited for him. If Naejestrisis (as he called himself now) wanted to burn him, he would already be ashes.

His suspicions were soon confirmed. A faint, growing din of wailing and screams reached up from far below. Firelight cast dancing lights and shadows in the darkness of the chasm. The flames cast these shadows on the walls. It was a deranged play. It was a living mural of powerful inhuman figures looming, tall and menacing, before people on their knees in supplication for mercy.

Zenen'Rol's growing dread warped into fear and despair. After all his years serving the emperor with unwavering loyalty, expanding the empire in conquest, he had been cast alive into the burning eternity of hell. Though this judgment was passed by a boy, a voice whispered to Zenen'Rol from a forgotten recess within. It admonished him that this is where he should spend eternity.

Zenen'Rol fell flat, face down, against a hard surface. He coughed against a mouthful of ashes, gagging. It was a wonder that he still lived, again. It was miraculous that none of his bones were broken or sprained after such a monumental fall. The towers and fields of rainbow-hued flames burned at a distance away from where he fell.

Zenen stood up and brushed himself off. Large handfuls of soot and ash fell in showers. He looked down. The ashes formed a sporadic layer on glossy black stone. The piles of ashes reached above his toes. He looked around. He was on a wide stone platform, circled by a double length of thick rusty chains barbed in dagger-long razors. The chains were held up by four iron posts, set in the corners of the platform. Each post sported a skull the size of his torso, snouted, with protruding horns and long fangs. Their empty eye sockets were directed at the center of the platform.

The platform was suspended in the center of a chasm that fell far from view. It was much farther away, still, from the ledge of brimstone, fire, and ash.

Zenen looked up, hoping to see an opening out of the fiery domain. The multi-colored flames licked and roared far above, beyond the limits of his sight.

If the stench of sulfur could be called stifling on the surface, it was thick, saturating, and pervasive here. Its all-consuming heat dried his mouth and caused instant thirst.

Beyond the roaring inferno, the agonized cries of the dead and condemned were deafening. Demons spoke in their incomprehensible language, booming with laughter and shouting their tormenting jibes and taunts.

The demons pushed toward the platform, crowding and clustering at the ledge before the abyssal chasm. They watched in silent anticipation; their baleful glowing eyes filled with eternal hate. They stood still and waited.

"This is the Arena of Fury," Naejestrisis informed as he floated thirty feet above. "it is a coliseum for the Children of Nothing, and it is above the Mouth of Return. Only one of us will exist after today."

"Why? Why not leave me to this eternity?" Zenen's irritations stemmed from being looked down upon. It was only earlier in the day when he glared down on Rylin from high above. He was superior, then. Naejestrisis mocked their previous encounter.

"The Mouth of Return is one of the few places in creation that lead straight to Oblivion, to nothingness. First, one burns in hell fire, then they are no more," Naejestrisis continued the explanation emotionless. "Enough words. We end this now."

Naejestrisis slowly floated down to the brimstone arena. As he did, the denizens of hell raised their clawed fists and began a slow-building chant.

"Crayaht'En, Crayaht'En, Crayaht'En!"

Zenen'Rol hurled his anger against his despair at being cast into hell. He opened his being, with singular destructive purpose, gathering the Endless Current...

...and nothing came to him. There were no massive waves

of energy, radiating from all things in the universe. The Endless Current could not reach him in hell. He unsheathed his spell-cutting daggers and attempted to push his will into his arms and legs. He was relieved to find his will would answer him with power.

Was that surprising, though? He was only just cast down. Many theories claimed that hell's efforts were poised at breaking down a soul's will. He could have his will for as long as he could hang onto it.

Zenen's booted feet whispered in the layers of ashes as he stepped slow, circling Naejestrisis. The Void Hand floated several inches above the brimstone platform. His sickly cold skin radiated tiny tongues of black fire. He stood straight; his black semi-transparent staff held vertical in his left hand. His posture was completely prone. Zenen didn't see the need to circle and probe for openings. Naejestrisis stood in total invitation. Only his tiny black pupils followed the Master Fist.

Well, if the fool would ask for a dagger in his ribs, Zenen would oblige. He dashed forward, faking a cut for the eyes. Then he lunged, trying to get under his ribs with his other dagger.

Naejestrisis did not move for the incomplete high cut. He spun his staff in a swift arc and parried Zenen's stabbing forearm. The deflection forced Zenen to stumble to the side. The impact chilled his arm with a biting cold that threatened his grip. He slid in the ashes, and Naejestrisis rapped his lower back with a blistering strike.

Zenen straightened and turned, humiliated that his first exchange made him appear a novice. Naejestrisis did not use chronomancy to overwhelm him with unnatural speed as Rylin did. He read Zenen's movements with an uncanny clarity. But between their previous duel and this tiny exchange, it was far too soon to presume that Naejestrisis held some sort of fighting precognition.

Zenen launched into a flurry of high and low stabs and cuts. Naejestrisis matched every movement with a precise and ready defense. Every parry and hard deflection were so well placed that the duel began to appear choreographed. Naejestrisis allowed Zenen to move, to attack, as though he was toying with him.

Zenen wrenched himself free of the clash. His breathing burned against the inside of his throat. Sweat soaked and irritated his eyes and drenched his clothes. The intense heat of hell was eating away his stamina. Only his will kept him moving. While he wanted to risk a spell-shape on his will, he knew the effort would yield little reward against an opponent still so strong. It would be better to sustain his efforts and look for an opportunity.

In the inferno to Zenen's left, a creature of spines and hard leathery scales held up a mutilated figure by the throat. It wanted Zenen to see the prize. It was a woman in shape. She was missing a leg. Her two lowest ribs were snapped away like the ends of a wishbone, only to be gouged into her eyes. There was little left to identify the pathetic trophy. Her skin was peeled away and burned black. Her lips and nose were cooked, leaving her teeth exposed in a skull grin. The absence of her nose left an opening for her brains to melt and ooze free.

Her mouth moved in chattering soundless twitches for a moment before she screamed to the capacity of her weak body. Zenen recognized the voice in that blood curdling cry. She had never sounded so full of agony and despair.

Ken'Tekira had already been sent to hell. The demons were wasting little time in breaking what was left of her.

Many more of his subordinates were naked, burned black, and wailing pitifully as they were held aloft like trophies. Nameless men and women were now condemned for eternity. The demons wanted him to see them. They wanted him to know that he did this to them. He would soon join them.

Naejestrisis replied in his low cold voice. "No, Zenen'Rol. They want you to know what will become of your entire army after you cease to be."

Zenen'Roll ground his teeth and whitened his knuckles around his daggers. He whirled on the Void Hand, beginning a mad, howling barrage. His will was doubled with his heightened rage. He pushed his arms and legs to move faster, strike harder.

For all that Zenen was a whirling, spinning berserker, it did him little good. Naejestrisis side and back stepped with ease, using his weapon to block only when he needed to. Zenen was taught that only fools fought on defense, alone. But the only foolish one here was himself.

Zenen halted after ten minutes of sustaining a furious assault that led to nothing. He braced his hands against his knees. Sweat fell from his chin only to vaporize in the hot air. He glanced away for an instant, only to see the petite shape of the possessed demon child. She stood at the front of demons four times as large as her. Her smile was chilling and knowing, while her glowing red eyes conveyed her message.

I told you it would be this way.

Zenen tried to move, to strike again. This time, his arms and legs felt leaden and lethargic. He was weary. His lungs burned, though not as fiercely as the burn on his back. Everything he sailed in conquest to achieve seemed so far away and irrelevant, now. How did he feel this way, after less than an hour of fighting in hell? His resolve, the very core of his will, was eroding fast.

It was a relief when Naejestrisis smiled, cold, causing Zenen to succumb to an involuntary shudder. At last, the Void Hand would cease toying with him and end this. Looking at the demon child, at her smug smile, he was glad he would not exist anymore.

The blades of his daggers turned white with intense heat. They liquified and fell into puddles on the brimstone arena floor. Naejestrisis lunged forward. The point of his staff was unnaturally frigid. The point rammed hard into Zenen's sternum. There might have been more power to the strike. Perhaps Zenen was too broken to resist at all. He did not care to guess. The strike cracked his ribs and caused him to fly backwards, face up. He did not impact with the brimstone platform. He did not care that he was too high for the barbed chains to arrest his flight. He coughed up a spray of blood from the staff strike. His nerve endings seared and screamed into his brain.

Zenen'Rol, Master Fist of the Crimson Emperor, Patriarch of the Havoc Elite, fell into death and oblivion. He failed on multiple levels. He failed his emperor, and the edict to eradicate all Stratians. He failed his entire army, as they were now all dead and condemned. He failed to protect his people from the coming of the second Black Decade.

Every particle of his body seared away on the devouring hell fire, and Zenen knew he failed all Pravahs. There might be some truth to the giddy foretelling of dozens of demons. He was witness to the power of Naejestrisis. He knew Pravahs was in danger of being swallowed into nothingness.

-44-

Amorlic squatted against a corner of the outer wall, covering his head with both hands. The quaking from the explosive conflagration halted, leaving only the crackling sound of fire and the sizzle of steam.

The battle with the Kasarins was silence, now. It was tense and fearful. No one alive dared to move.

At the height of the fighting, nightmares were made real. Amorlic could not bring himself to think on it, would not give it words. If he did, he would begin to give it a shape and form.

Minutes passed, maybe more (Amorlic could only guess) as he huddled in still silence. He chanced a glance down to the mud at his feet. He trembled. Bits of burned and shredded carnage mixed into the wet earth. The sharp stench of urine reached his nose. He had wet himself.

Why was he so afraid? Amorlic had never been this afraid of anything his entire life. What, about this, was so terrifying? It was innate, raw, and primal. It was not the chaos that resulted from the long uncertain battle with the Kasarins. They were never so terrifying as this. Something occurred that plucked at every involuntary cord in his being.

Amorlic forced his hands down and his head up, willing away his fear. He was not the only one to have lost their dignity in the last few minutes. Some of his mother's finest mercenaries, including his own bodyguards, were lying in fetal positions, uncaring of the mud, and maimed corpses around them.

Many structures were levelled flat. Walls from the barracks collapsed, with two soldiers crushed in the debris. Their arms protruded from the rubble, clawed in a desperate unanswered plea for escape. Deep pits in the ground were forced wide, where the devastation blasted into the laboratories and forges below. Men were impaled, crushed flat, or torn limb from limb. Smaller fires continued to burn, absently licking at the wreckage.

Beyond the walls, the once drooping willows were reduced to blackened spikes protruding from the boiling swamp muck. The bodies of alligators and snakes floated, belly up, cooked to death. The iron spread of magic traps from the Blood Scathe Twins were melted to slag. The metal ooze still burned red beneath the swamp murk.

There was not a Kasarin corpse in sight. The cloud piercing pillars of green fire found their mark in every Kasarin, living or dead. There were the strange blood red pits and… Amorlic could not bring himself to remember the rest. It was better to think that the Kasarins were reduced to ashes and scattered.

But Amorlic wondered why only the Kasarins were cremated. This appeared to be the work of a sorcery of some kind. Wouldn't a sorcerer have to be close enough to see their targets? He thought to give the credit for their survival to the Blood Scathe Twins, but this kind of magic was not in their repertoire. Also, they were currently powerless.

Maybe they were dead and buried beneath the debris right now, or they were not. Their survival did not mean that much to him. For the time being, they would have to fend for themselves.

Amorlic inspected the situation further. He needed to focus, now, and ignore his own fears. The slave kennels were broken to bits. The half-naked bodies were buried in decimated cages or flung to land at contorted angles. Some of the explosive barrels, still above ground, were partly to blame for this. They were kept too close to the pens. He would have to reprimand the soldiers who did not think to move the remaining barrels out of harm's way.

Amorlic's mother lost her entire compound's wealth of slave stock. He could not imagine there was much left in the compound that could be salvaged. Only a detailed and thorough cleanup would reveal what remained of value.

"Get up!" Amorlic shouted, trying to avoid a pubescent sounding crack in his voice.

The answering movement was slow. Only their heads raised as they dared a timid, incredulous glance at him.

Amorlic lost his patience. "Get up, or I'll have the lot of you flogged with acid lashes."

"Begging your pardon, Lord Keeper," stammered a young sergeant of the darts. "but are you fates forsaken crazed? We don't know what just happened."

Amorlic stormed over to the hunched and squatting young soldier. He yanked his head back by his exposed long red hair before ramming a poisoned dagger into his throat. He let go and allowed him to fall and die.

"Would anyone else care to speak words of insubordination?" Amorlic's dare was in a shout, as he spread a challenging glance to everyone. "I'll tolerate no more whimpering in the mud. We need to sift through this. We need to find more able bodies as well as her majesty's merchandise. We need to set up a camp perimeter and a watch, and we need all of this now!"

Merahl did not dare to move until the lightning no longer flashed in the dark sky. He would not raise his head until the first of dawn's glow crested the eastern ridge. He needed reassurance. He needed the world he knew to place light on his shoulders, to let him know that all was well.

When he did raise his head to the morning light, he wiped away a trail of spit from the corner of his mouth. Merahl still could not look directly into the east, yet. What he saw in the night, in the revealing flashes of lightning, was more than just beyond logic. What the former Solas witnessed should have left him mad with terror. He looked around at Perahl'Glae. The ivory city held many plazas and by ways that were red and black, two stories up. Blood and ashes had changed much of the white city's color, bathing it in a half nightmare. He looked at the fallen bodies of the people, their white robes soaked in blood.

What happened to the people of the fair capitol was horrible; but Merahl could not bring himself to condone the gruesome, merciless nightmare unleashed on the Kasarins.

Merahl saw much more than anyone in the city. He knew this because people were already helping each other to their feet, holding and reassuring each other. Their faces, though quivering with tears, told him they would sleep again. Merahl was not sure when he would be well enough to close his eyes. Sleep was out of the question for him. He would always see the way the Kasarins ripped each other apart. He would always see the giant creature eating them alive.

Merahl would always hear the screams.

Merahl, the composed intellectual Archivist of the Enlightened Sun, fell to his hands and knees, weeping as he remembered. Beneath each body wracking sob, he blinked; and another horrifying image cast in the faint red glow played in his mind. He tilted his head back and screamed, howling with psychological agony.

Merahl felt hands on him, and he shoved them away, scrambling backwards until his back hit a wall. Though his vision was blurred with tears, he saw Nerilisse hunched low, approaching him slow.

"It is alright, Light Merahl." Nerilisse spoke soft, reaching for him slowly. "It's over, now; all of it."

Merahl shook his head with fervor, even as Nerilisse pulled him into her arms.

"No, it isn't over." Merahl's denial was sobbing and muffled against her. "I watched hell unleashed on our enemies. It can never be over, or alright."

"Then, for now, weep with me. We can stand another day," Nerilisse offered, allowing her own tears.

Maloric opened his deep brown eyes, warily. Though the eclipse was over, and the thunderous clouds were gone, night had come.

Tapestries fell to the ground to lay among piles of loose dust and chunks of marble. The explosions from within the palace shook and broke quite a bit, but that was merely the beginning of the chaos.

Maloric was certain, in an instant, that the 'prisoners' broke out of the dungeon. Marcelles did advise that they might try this. He also thought Lady Aemreen was correct to advise for Teranen's assistance. Even Maloric believed the Flame Witch of Dunell would be more than enough help.

Then pandemonium erupted all over Pahlinsor, for the next hour. It was too much for the king or any of his advisors to make sense of any of it. Then the skies went dark in an ominous unpredicted eclipse. The skies filled with the sound of a chant that made his blood run cold.

Maloric watched from the throne, through broken stained-glass windows. Strange fires burned to the edges of the city. Screams sounded from far beyond the palace walls, from more throats than there were people. Their chilling cries filled the broken darkness.

Maloric watched all this, even while his guards and Maesellen curled in a crouch, hiding in the shadows of the pillars. His disappointment was centered on his queen. Even though she was the most morally bankrupt person he knew (though he had no way of proving it) she also projected at least a façade of fearlessness. Today, even Maesellen cowered and trembled in terror.

With Marcelles still out and trying to rally the Phoenix Legion into a desperate defense, Maloric was alone. He directed his thoughts to what Yelisian would have done. He needed to draw an iota of courage from his deceased friend. Yelisian died facing down a darkness not unlike this one, remaining stalwart to the end. Maloric would have to do the same. He started by prying his hands away from the armrests of his throne and stood up.

Maloric's voice boomed in the cavernous silence. "I need a squad of thirty men, with cold compresses and splints, by the gates by the time I get there."

"You're a raving fool!" Maesellen hissed, not daring to raise her head. "You have no idea what transpired, yet you walk into it, brazenly."

Maloric's answering smile was sarcastic. "My queen, I did not know you worried for me."

"It is not worry you blundering idiot! Fates! Look behind your throne!"

Maloric turned and his brown eyes widened. In the darkness, what he saw should have been one of the first things he noticed.

The huge, wide, black sword, thought to be a replica and decoration, was lodged deep into the dais. It had hung on the wall, high above the throne, for as far back as Maloric could remember. His grandfather used to mystify him as a child by telling him it was there for two thousand years. Now, not only was it stabbed into the dais, but the blade hummed with a pulsing red glow. Its dim light filled half the throne room; and cast a tall shadow of Maloric and his throne.

In answer to this day's dark secrets, another part of history revealed itself. This was, in fact, the massive sword of Khalsis Moarenroak, first king of Malkanor, Magus student of Yaekrim, and a demon slayer since childhood.

It stood to reason that the sword was active now. It was a living weapon, and it felt the presence of its ancient enemies, the Void Hands.

That enigma would have to wait. There was nothing the sword could do to alleviate their current situation.

"Be that as it may," Maloric spoke steady, his eyes not removed from the glowing blade. "Right now, this bedlam will have ripped the certainty out from underneath the feet of our people. It is only right that we go to them, when fear grips them the most, and give them our support to stand again."

"Your idealism will murder you," Maesellen spat. "But, ah, go ahead fool. Go into that sulfurous stench and be torn asunder. I'll not stop your march into an unmarked grave of self-righteous heroism."

Maloric paid her warnings no mind as he strode out of the throne room. Two guards were quick to comply, rushing ahead in search of volunteers.

As Maloric shoved through the double doors, he was greeted with the wreckage of the explosions. The torches still burned in the iron sconces. They cast their glow on overturned tables, shattered porcelain, and crystal decorations. In the darkness, and broken aftermath, the palace was frightful and bleak.

Many of the palace servants showed no signs of seeing the cloud piercing towers of green light. They knew it was unnaturally dark, and they might have heard the inhuman chanting, but their fear did not stretch beyond that. Fortunate enough to be sheltered from the full magnitude, they held the presence of mind to see to other servants and soldiers who were crouched and cringing in the dark. They were quick to examine for head injuries from falling debris, and then other open wounds.

The stairwell that ran the height of the center of the palace was partially obstructed by corpses and piles of marble. Soldiers and servants worked, in tandem, to clear the stairwell, but there was only enough room to work in single file.

Maloric found an alternative way to the ground floor. He was met by Marcelles as the lord general ascended from the basement. Marcelles was accompanied by five soldiers while he supported Teranen as she leaned into his shoulder.

Teranen had two bleeding cuts on her head: one on her scalp, and another above her left temple. Her brown farmer's dress and gray robe were ripped, revealing many more cuts and angry dark bruises. Her left arm hung uselessly; covered in fresh blood mingled in a thick layer of dust. There were deep red welts that explained that the men had to reset her shoulder.

"She can't talk now, your majesty," Marcelles preemptively stopped the questions. "I think she may have been concussed. We had to free her from a large pile of rubble. She has no magic, and she needs a healer."

Maloric looked her over and nodded. "Very well, Lord General. See to her, then gather some men and join me in the city. We have much to do."

"I can help." Teranen protested even as her eyes drooped.

Maloric shook his head. "I'll have none of that now, Torch Teranen. Let us tend to your wounds; and, by the fates, stay awake!"

That bothered Maloric as he left them. Teranen had no magic, and he saw no one from the Enlightened Sun at work. The pillars of light were the last magic he saw.

How much work would have to be done by hand? How many people would die without sorcery to heal them?

-45-

Naejestrisis relinquished his control in a dense, cool forest, far north of Stratia's main nations. The trees were as wide as five men, and as tall as towers. The smell of forest earth and pine was thick and soothing, filling each breath with fresh invigoration.

Rylin needed that, now. The vibrancy of this forest fortified his will.

The black clothes were gone, and in their place was his normal green coat, blue tunic, and brown pants. His pallor and vision were normal, as well. The Aspect of Vengeance departed with all the tell-tale signs of the Void Triangle.

Rylin saw his emerald Displacement Staff was also returned to him. How and when did he retrieve it from the arctic?

But now he was weak and feverish. He leaned heavily on his emerald staff to keep from falling over.

Rylin inhaled the cool, pungent air and collected his thoughts. Looking at the massive trees, and the rocky outcroppings that broke through the forest foliage, he guessed he was about half-way between the nations and the arctic. That would place him in the heart of the Northern Wastes. He knew this because it wasn't hot or muggy like the nations would be in the summer, and it was not the endless winter of the arctic north.

Rylin squinted to look through the dense umbrella of forest branches, overhead. The sunlight that spilled through revealed the time to be mid-morning. To his left was an incline that descended far from view. If he tried to walk this downhill path, his legs would succumb to gravity. To his right, the climb was a steep ascent.

Why was it so much later in another day? Why was he in the Northern Wastes? His thoughts were fleeting and random the more he tried to concentrate. He placed the end of his staff ahead, pulling himself uphill with shaking and buckling legs. Between his inability to focus, and the weakness in his body, it was a grueling climb.

Sweat dripped from his brows and stung his eyes. His breathing labored in the thinner air and high elevation. A deep, subtle cold clashed with an uncomfortable warmth, seizing his head and back. Rylin had a growing fever. He needed to find a place to rest, soon.

Rylin closed his eyes against the strain and instantly regretted it. Ken'Tekira's blackened, maimed body filled his mind's eye, held up triumphantly by the neck. Her agonized cries blasted and rebounded deep in the recesses of his mind. The Aspect of Vengeance promised an all-encompassing solution; but Rylin did not expect it would be so horrifying.

"War is horrible, Rylin," came the Aspect's cold familiar voice in his mind. "When we are consumed by it, it forces us to do terrible things, and make terrible choices. The Kasarins knew this, and that is why they nearly killed us all."

"They were looking for you...for me...all along. It could have ended sooner," Rylin hissed between clenched teeth. Thinking and arguing was more difficult as the fever pressed on him.

The Aspect laughed. "Are you still thinking with altruistic simplicity? It is as foolish to believe one sacrificed martyr could have prevented so much, as it is to believe one display of power could accomplish the same thing. The appearance of the Void

Triangle made a valid reason for them to strike; but, in time, they would have done so anyway. If they executed us, they would have then justified genocide with the belief that any Stratian would become a Void Disciple."

"But you allied with those that started all this," Rylin accused, his voice rising. "They killed the leadership of the Enlightened Sun. You killed Martenen and gave the Kasarins reason to strike the Citadel without mercy. They murdered Yelisian!"

"That last is wrong. The Grand Illumination chose self-sacrifice to evade the inevitable; just as you suggested we do. It was met with the same result: failure."

The Aspect's point struck home, painfully.

"As Naejestrisis. I couldn't help but observe something valid," the Aspect continued. "I observed the same fear and pain in those Kasarin eyes that was present in the murdered people of Tihl'Zen. Just as the Kasarins were the nightmare existence to their peaceful lives, we were the ultimate nightmare of their entire history."

"I once held the chance to rid the world of the Void Triangle, forever. But they spoke a truth and potential I could not ignore. I saw this truth when we crushed the Kasarin army. The greater the fear an enforcer can impose, the more resilient will be the compliance to justice."

Rylin spat. "Those are the words of a tyrant."

"Think what you will. I can take ease with the knowledge that there will never be so much as a thought of a Kasarin invasion for more than ten millennia. Their histories record events very well."

"Condemning souls is no justice," Rylin shouted as the Aspect took visible shape in front of him.

"What of butchering children as they flee before you?" The Aspect snapped back, angrily. "By their ideology, their power granted them sufficient supremacy to dictate life and death. By that same ideology, I passed judgement, they were found guilty, and their sentence equals the lives and potential they ended. It is justice in perfect symmetrical form."

Rylin gritted his teeth, refusing to look at the Aspect. Perhaps he was too feverish, and his thoughts were too scattered, but the Aspect had a ready deflection for his every argument.

The real problem was that the Aspect was making sense. Rylin grudgingly admitted to himself that a tiny part of him agreed with the unforgiving rationale.

The Aspect turned and pointed uphill. "In about four hundred feet, you will see a place where you may rest, undisturbed. With your condition, you may arrive before evening if you go now. You may choose to thank me for transferring the Displacement Staff in place of the Staff of the Abyss. You will need it to climb in your weakened state."

Without farewell, the Aspect of Vengeance blurred and vanished like a thick wisp of smoke.

Rylin began his climb to a haven to rest for the next few days.

Four hundred feet sounded like a short distance to Rylin; but he was mistaken. Under ideal conditions, the footing on the peak was treacherous. The rocky, jagged protrusions were twice as tall as a man, or as small as the height of his shins and toes. The loose dust and redwood leavings created slippery surfaces in these rocky forests. The most promising paths were frequently obstructed by thickets of poison ivy and stinging nettle.

Rylin's fever and weak legs made the trek all but impossible. He fell, often, earning new bruises and aches. His pants and coat were opened with dozens of tears, even as rocks wore through the thick soles of his boots. The aid of his staff was the only reason he could continue the climb, at all. He had to lean heavily on it, often, when it was not used to assist him in traversing the difficult path.

Maybe it was his delirious mind, but Rylin began to see the travel pains as a penance for every life-costing mistake he made during the war. He would not allow himself to remain on his backside. He stood up, again and again, walking and allowing karma to exact its toll from him.

Rylin looked around, often, to appreciate the verdant landscape. The trees would not permit a view beyond the peak he climbed, but the wild, merciless growth reminded him of the uninhabited wild hills, many miles east of Pahlinsor. He wondered if this mountain range held similar dead-end canyons and labyrinthine caves.

The difference became obvious when the dense forests revealed a less wooded clearing and an abandoned modest gray stone cottage.

That anyone could have ever lived in such an inhospitable place was remarkable; but Rylin began to feel something strange as he drew closer.

It had a triangular wood roof that was rotting open in patches. A dusty stairway was piled with the remains of a long awning that decayed and succumbed to gravity. There were two windows at the front, but the glass was long since broken.

There was a cutting stump to the left, but moss claimed the wood and trapped a rusty axe inside it. Rylin knelt to find brittle pieces of a tanning rack that crumbled in his hands.

Still, the Aspect was right. It was a place to rest, undisturbed. Rylin stumbled up the steps and pushed his way through a thick wooden door. The hinges filled the air with a rusty scream of metal.

Inside was small, bordering claustrophobic. There were two empty thresholds, leading to cubby-sized bedchambers. The main room tried to provide everything in one tiny space. There was a stone hearth. Markings in the thick debris hinted at armchairs and a table that were either stolen or swallowed up in time and decay.

Rylin tried to imagine what this place must have been like before it was abandoned. His mind supplied him with an image that was not unlike the hovel Rylin called home for so many years.

The air would have been stale and moldy were it not for the broken windows and sagging roof. The openings brought in fresh forest drafts that stirred the layer of litter.

Close to the deep stone hearth, under a resistant patch of roof, there was a single bed and end table. The bed was little more than a crude stained mattress held by a rusty iron frame and posts. Rylin pushed down on the cold surface and found it would still support weight. He laid his emerald staff down beside the bed and took off his coat. He laid down and used the coat as a blanket.

He looked up through the gaps above. He began to drift into sleep while he watched the afternoon fade into dusk. Deep sleep came much easier than he thought the fever would permit.

Rylin opened his eyes in total darkness. He was covered in a layer of soft comfort much thicker and bigger than his coat. His shirt was off, and a cold damp cloth was folded and placed across his forehead. He scanned the darkness. His weak eyes shifted and searched for the unknown benefactor. He found no one.

The Aspect's voice broke a silence that was foreign for any forest at night.

"He comes with me now. He has rested enough," the Aspect of Vengeance demanded.

Rylin listened close, but if what he heard was an answer, he could not discern it. Low whispers, only a little louder than the rustle of leaves, held a defiant edge.

"Do not stand in our way. You do not possess enough strength," the Aspect warned, his threat low and chilling.

In retort, a howling gale blew through the small den, casting dust, leaves, and decayed bits into the air. The thick blanket, the damp cloth, and Rylin's belongings remained still.

This lasted for a few minutes before the deafening wind subsided.

"I should not have allowed him to stop us from travelling to the forgotten catacombs of Nerinmor," the Aspect grumbled with grudging frustration before Rylin felt his absence.

But this did not mean Rylin felt he was alone. He could not see anyone else, but he felt watched.

Rylin also felt safe.

Rylin was not afraid when the rim of a cold tin cup was placed gently against his lips. He looked for a hand or arm as the cup was lifted carefully. The liquid was slightly bitter, but the cool water soothed his parched throat.

Even as the cup lifted within sight, there were no hands.

Rylin thought to question his unseen caregiver, out loud, but his eyes became heavy with the renewed need for sleep.

Rylin dreamed of a forest glade, of towering red woods around a meadow of waist-high grasses, dappled with red and purple wildflowers. At the far end of the wide clearing, a shallow stream fed into a pond only deep enough to wade up to the hips.

Dragonflies hummed through the air beneath a sky mixed with light and dark gray clouds.

There was a vividly potent quality to the world around him. The forest and meadow were a fit for the mountains that harbored him. The air caressed his exposed skin with gentle breezes. The smell of the flowers, trees, and the water filled his nose and settled deep in his lungs.

Rylin was only surprised when he noticed the large boulder at one end of the pond. A woman sat on top of the stone, her hands wrapped around one knee, drawn up close.

She was a tall, middle-aged woman with long thick brown hair. The loose leather clothes made it difficult to define her shape beyond her height. Her deer skin tunic and pants were complimented with similar shoes. Her face was gentle and warm, adorned only with inviting laugh lines. There was something familiar about her narrow face and hard angled cheekbones. Her brown eyes were expressive, but they were focused and hard in contrast.

She looked up from the rippling surface of the water with an unreadable expression.

"I think this is the only way we could talk." She patted the surface of the boulder. "Please sit."

Rylin didn't know why he was quick to comply with the stranger. Maybe it was the sense of familiarity. He could trust her without understanding what formed such blind certainty.

"He would be here to talk, himself; but he has a lot of work. He always works too hard, even though he should rest, now."

Rylin nodded, masking his confusion. Her meaning was lost on him, now; but he knew she would help him to understand in her own due time.

"It was hard getting your attention, Rylin. You were so weak you barely felt my invitation. If your Aspect had its way, you would already be gone. You began to stir when you ended the war. That is what allowed you to pull apart."

Some of the woman's meaning began to filter into Rylin's understanding. "I pulled away, so you called to me to come to the Northern Wastes. Here I can rest and recover without slipping away, again."

She closed her eyes and shook her head. "It's not enough. I am giving you all I can, but I can only manage this for so long. I need you to fight and hang on to who you have always been. I will do everything I can to help. After all, we are all in grave danger if I don't."

She sighed. "He should not have simply left him in the Current. It wasn't enough. He needed to disperse him, entirely. The rules for such an existence are vastly different if you are strong enough to survive."

She laughed, a pleasant sound that filled the meadow. "But he does not listen. He never did, but they never listen to us, do they?"

That last was especially confusing, but there were layers of meaning shrouded deep.

"It's almost time for you to wake, Rylin. We must both hang on, together. Help will arrive. I am already sending the message. Remember all the good you have come to cherish, and let it burn bright within you."

With that, Rylin opened his eyes to the dark ruins of the cottage around him. As he lay staring up through the roof, he noticed two peculiar details.

There was warmth. Dim light filled the dark with a flickering orange glow. Rylin turned his head and saw a fire blazing in the hearth. The air was filled with the enticing aroma of seasoned meat. His stomach grumbled when he saw the tin plate of pulled rabbit bits. There was another cup of strange bitter liquid.

In the thick layer of dust on the table, a finger scrawled the words 'eat' and 'drink'. There was also the word 'fever' with a picture of an arrow pointing down.

Rylin sat up in bed, his body protesting with leaden weakness. His arms and legs trembled as he reached for the plate of food. He thought he would devour the meat with ravenous abandon, but his pace was lethargic and slow. He continued to feel the gaze on him while he ate. The hidden gaze did not hold the overwhelming piercing quality it did before. Whoever was watching him, they did not do so with ill-intent.

Rylin placed the empty plate down and drank the bitter water again. The water must have been laced with a concoction that brought his fever down and helped him sleep deep. So, it was not a surprise when his eyelids became heavy again.

As he drifted, Rylin absently accepted the idea that he was sleeping in a haunted cottage. It was not a horrifying concept. The spirit was doing everything possible to heal him.

Rylin sat on the boulder next to the pond, again. The woman was there. This time, there was a hunting bow beside her. Her gaze focused on sharpening an arrowhead against a flat stone.

Rylin looked at her hands. There was a wrinkled, aged frailty to them. Were her hands aging faster than the rest of her? She looked up at him with a wan smile and tired eyes.

"I'll be fine," she reassured. "Doing things, the way I did when I lived…it takes so much more out of me."

"You're the spirit! It was your home," Rylin gasped.

She chuckled, pointing the arrow at him. "I hope the fever is why it took you so long to figure that out; or he might be putting all his hopes in the wrong one."

The question from Rylin was a simple one. "Why?"

She sighed with exasperation. "Your fever must be up. You were quicker the last time we spoke." She put down the arrow and turned to look at him with a stern gaze. "Firstly: he puts so much of his hopes in you. He died, willing, and gave his spirit for you, which leads me to the second reason. What you did nearly rendered his sacrifice meaningless." Her voice held an angry edge, and the overcast skies began to darken. The air became colder. "Yes, I know you had no choice, then; but you made choices that led to that moment. It was almost enough to make me kill you when I had the chance. A part of me believes I still should; but while he worked for so much, he rarely hoped for anything. I won't take that from him, now. I will take my chances, even though you are a danger to all of us."

Rylin conformed to the tension of the silence, feeling awkward and nervous. He was not oblivious or asleep through Naejestrisis. He was aware of all of it. The dark and terrible knowledge Crayaht'En held was still in him. He found no fault in this spirit woman for wanting to kill him because of the danger he posed. But he could also conjure the mental image of what it would be like if she were determined to end him rather than aid him. Death, at the hands of a disembodied spirit, was a terrifying concept.

She sighed, and the sky lightened a little. She looked like she wanted to think about anything else.

"The young lady you love so much: Aemreen? I want you to close your eyes and think about her. See her in your mind as clearly as you can. Every detail."

Rylin held back the impulse to ask how she knew so much about him. He was living on borrowed generosity. Obedience was the best course of action. He closed his eyes, imagining Aemreen's almond complexion, the curves of her shape. He imagined her in the blue silk dress she favored when she wanted to entice his touch. He saw the warmth of her smile, and the compassion and curiosity in her green eyes. He imagined the tickle of her long dark hair against his arms while his hands clasped behind her back and waist. He felt the heat of her presence, and the press of her body against him. He imagined the heady smell of roses all about her. He felt and saw her so clear that it brought a pang of longing. Was she alright? Did Naejestrisis stop Ken'Tekira from killing her? Above all that he did, little mattered as much as saving her.

The spirit broke the silence. "Now, open your eyes."

Rylin complied. Aemreen stood in the grasses as vivid as his mind imagined. It was not truly her, though.

"Do not view it as illusion or deception. She is everything to you, and so you can see her here. That will help you remain who you are, Rylin. Seeing what you cherish will give your soul strength. It will remind you of why you fight."

Rylin nodded solemnly. He did need to ease the burden on the spirit woman. The strain was heavy on her, siphoning at her resolve in a fundamental way.

"How long since the Seal of Stagnation was broken?" Rylin managed, needing to take stock of his present situation.

She rolled her eyes, mulling the time in numbers. "Three days."

"What happens if this is too much for you?"

Her answering smile was sad. "If I am not strong enough, then I will never be with what I cherish, again."

"You do not have to do this."

"I only just told you that I would end your life with the hands of a ghost, and you worry that I miss my chance for eternal peace?" Her laugh was as weak and sad as her smile. "That is selfless and sweet, Rylin. That must be why he believes in you."

Her smile faded. "But I do have to do this. Your soul will not remain, on its own. You are not strong enough. Anyway, its only two more days. He had to bar the Aspect's way for more than a year. This is small in comparison."

Rylin sat in contemplative silence, looking at his boots. He pondered everything she said to him so far. There were clues in her words, things she said in a very indirect manner.

Then Rylin's eyes widened in a flash of realization. The

unnamed man she spoke of would have to be Yelisian.

The pieces of the puzzle came together in his mind: where he was, the cottage, and all her words. Rylin gasped as the truth dawned on him.

"You are Spark Yelisian's mother! He spent his childhood there!"

Her face lit up with a radiant infectious smile. The clouds broke, allowing a bright beam of sunlight to pour down on her. She tilted her head back, and closed her eyes, basking in the dream sun's warmth.

"It feels good to hear his name, again. When we cross, completely, it all comes back to us. In the space between life and death, we forget so much. I was always so proud of Yelisian. I loved and missed him, so much."

A single tear formed at the corner of her eye. Rylin watched as she struggled to contain it.

"His last thoughts were for you, Rylin. When he found out they were after you, it broke him. Do you know how it wounds a mother to watch her child's heart break? He was on his knees while those cruel fiends laughed. I could do nothing. But my darling, Yelisian, my brave, strong, baby boy, it meant so much to him that he offered his life and spirit. He did not regret or hesitate. It was not even a matter of debate for him."

The skies darkened, deeply, and a loud peal of thunder cracked across the skies as she looked at Rylin. "It is why I help you, now; and why we cannot fail. His father would be here, too, but Yelisian's sacrifice wounds him more than he can say. It falls to you and me. We must honor my son's wishes, Rylin. Naejestrisis must not happen again. You must make your soul strong enough to resist the emptiness that allows him to claim you."

She gripped Rylin's shoulders with cold hands as hard as iron, her fingers digging painfully into his flesh. Her face lost the warm visage of the middle-aged mother. The skin dried, pulling back against her skull while her eyes disappeared, leaving dark empty sockets.

When she spoke, her voice boomed across the meadow. "You believe he saved all that you hold dear. You believe he struck down all your enemies. You believe the war has come to an end, and you are mistaken. Your enemy stalks you, and he is relentless."

Rylin jolted up to a sitting position in bed, soaked in sweat. His breathing was rapid and heavy. New aches flared in his shoulders. He looked down at the bare skin. There were a multitude of dark angry bruises, with bleeding puncture marks in ten places.

Everything was illuminated in the pale glow of dawn. The sun had yet to climb high enough to reach down the slope.

Rylin looked around the den, and his fearful chill deepened.

On every surface, scrawled in the dust and debris thousands of times over, there were two words repeated with urgent fervor.

No fail!

-46-

The next day, Rylin's condition improved. He sat up and ate, drinking the medicine water, and he felt more lucid. He would sit cross-legged on the bed as the rays of sunlight spilled through the roof. He attempted a meditation that was common for Novices before the fall of the Mage Clans. It was a breathing exercise that improved blood flow and calmed the mind. It was designed to prepare the body to draw from the Endless Current.

Rylin could not attempt the meditation during the night. He already tried. The night before, as Rylin closed his eyes, he was greeted with visions of Naejestrisis. He looked into the dark pupils of his cold, colorless eyes. The looming black figure floated. Tendrils of cold flame licked and lashed from his pores.

"Enough! Rylin, withdraw!" Shouted the spirit of Yelisian's mother, Annahleth.

Rylin opened his eyes in a frightened gasp. There was no one in the darkness.

So, Rylin lay awake in bed, staring up at the view of the stars and pale half-moon. In the restless hours, he thought about everyone in Pahlinsor, and the Order. Aemreen occupied many of his thoughts. Where would their courtship go from this point on?

After all the chaos, Maesellen was certain to insist on Amorlic's return. The queen would also insist on rushing him into marriage with Aemreen. That would end their taboo courting.

Annahleth voiced her opinion in the next dream in the meadow.

It was the third night, and she was losing a lot of energy. Her hands were bony and transparent in places. Her thin hair hung in wispy, white, coarse threads. Her clothes were large and heavy, while her arms and legs were stick thin and brittle.

"What makes you believe you can be sure of any future, when it is a future of love?" Annahleth's hoarse voice croaked. "Need I remind you that if mortals could be so sure of fate, I would have killed you by now."

Rylin ignored the now frequent reminder that he survived on Annahleth's good graces. She was not doing it in the sense of posturing, but the threat was old and tired.

"If this all passes, as I believe it may, it is a matter between kings and queens. I have no voice, there." It sounded pessimistic and irrational even as he spoke.

"What you are truly being is a fool, Rylin," Annahleth bluntly chastised. "I did not believe my son would select one who would lie in submissive defeat with such ease. These matters have a way of escaping the hands of monarchs and rulers."

It was something for Rylin to ponder, and a reason to hold tight to what he cherished. Such downtrodden meanderings were little more than an effort to break him down from within.

On the fourth day, events took a turn for the worse.

A cold wind and grays skies brought a rain that turned to a heavy downpour within an hour. Lightning flashed in sporadic bursts around the cottage. Thunder rumbled with sufficient violence to quake the walls. Layers of dust and mold fell from above, mingling with the rain to become a chunky, wet mud.

Annahleth tried to bring down large branches to cover the holes above; but the decaying rooftop groaned in protest at the additional weight. There was little the spirit woman could do, and the rain tested her resolve as it continued to soak everything throughout the day.

With so much exposure to the cold, wet, mountain weather, a fresh wave of fatigue and aches assaulted Rylin. His fever returned, and there was little he or Annahleth could do for it. Nature was determined to test their determination, personally. Several times, Rylin opened his eyes and saw thin wisps of smoke in the hearth. They were failed attempts for even a strong spirit to start a fire.

The weather proved to be a harbinger of a long and terrible night.

Rylin opened his eyes to the dark and cold world after dusk. The Aspect of Vengeance returned, his voice dripping with contempt. The rain and lightning continued with more aggression than before, responding to the coming spirit confrontation. In the darkness of the woods, halted just outside the broken walls and windows, there were dozens of pairs of flickering red and green lights. They were lesser demons. Alone, each might be irrelevant for a strong spirit and an adept sorcerer; but they came in adequate numbers to aid the Aspect.

"Desist, ghost hag! He is dying of a different fever, entirely. His death, at this moment, would be too great a waste to accept." Rylin could not see the Aspect, but his anger was clear.

The howling winds and hard whispers that argued defiantly with the Aspect, before, were greatly subdued, now. Annahleth was much weaker than their first encounter. Rylin worried that she might not be able to bar the Aspect's approach, this time.

As weak as he was, Rylin felt dismissed and embarrassed. He hated being protected by the spirit of a woman who should be resting in peace. He thought about Ishell. She did not stand by idle, while children gave up their lives in battle.

He was far from the boy who resided in the outskirts, who

needed to be protected. He was a young man, and a sorcerer. If his fate was in question, it was his responsibility to make it his own, and fight.

"Your deception was as cowardly as it was abominable." Rylin sat up, directing his angry gaze into the darkness.

"I saved all of Stratia, everyone you love, fool," the Aspect retorted.

"And you believe this dark rescue entitles you to some sort of war prize? If you foresaw the potential actions and outcomes (as you claim you can with no spared repetition) then you are just as at fault as I am," Rylin shouted. "It means you knew the raw Displacement Cloak on the three Guilders would accomplish nothing. It would not cause them to reconsider and return to their empire. It means you knew about the Seal of Stagnation, even before the duel with Zenen'Rol. Fates! You may have known about the razing of Tihl'Zen, long before the Kasarins arrived. You say you seek justice, but I name you liar! I say you merely desired to become Naejestrisis and wield the power of a dark god. You wanted to preside in judgment over life, death, and eternity. Well, you may now judge and sentence yourself. Your undisclosed foreknowledge places the blood of thousands on your hands, as well. You knew, and you did nothing."

The Aspect spoke low and menacing. Rylin imagined the cruel, cold smile that played on its face. "Weak stupid Rylin. I brought many of the Children of Nothing. You are powerless, hiding behind the skirts of a frail shade. You are in no position to deny me. Allow you and I to be complete, once more."

"Ah!" Rylin wagged his finger. "Therein lies the truth of it all. I am not powerless. Our restored separation gave me the power of choice. You cannot have what I will not give. You may threaten with demons, as you barge in uninvited; but they, like you, can do nothing. Empty words, Aspect. All Empty words."

Silence and storm answered Rylin. He felt the Aspect staring with enraged consternation.

"I come offering to save your miserable life, so that you may return to the nations. I come offering a gift, and you hurl it in my face?" the Aspect hissed with venom. "So be it. You lack the will to do what needs to be done. May your mundane pathetic fever kill you, and may your spirit wander just out of reach of Aemreen's embrace."

A long series of lightning flashes filled the cottage. The glow of eyes vanished, and Rylin did not feel the cold presence of the Aspect for the rest of the night.

The night and the storm quieted after that confrontation. The rains decreased to a weak drizzle, while the thunder rumbled distant and low. Gentle fresh winds brushed the forest trees with cold whispers in the darkness.

Rylin passed in and out of dreams that bled into his delirious waking world. His head was heavy and stuffed when he woke. He was covered in a layer of mixed moisture of rain and sweat.

Rylin struggled against the crushing weight of his fever dreams. His mind wandered to his mother and father, and everyone he fought for. There were two ailments to battle, but he would not be found lacking now.

It was the longest night and struggle of his life. There was no way to measure the passing time. Every cool breath was long and grueling, stretching moments into years. Time drifted into an endless abyss. Insanity fashioned kaleidoscopes in his fevered perception. It was a mad limbo where crazed visions danced around him in ceaseless circles. Faces of the living and the dead played in a silent, vague maelstrom, dancing at the edge of shadows.

Rylin shut his eyes. In sleep, he returned to the greater insanity of his fitful dreams. Would these restless stirrings pass the time with greater mercy?

The bed shifted, many hours later.

"One for each element on every side. Hurry!" The urgent male voice was familiar.

At first, Rylin would not open his eyes. The glare of light, even with his eyes closed, caused his forehead to throb with insistent aches.

"How did he feed and care for himself? How did he last this long?" This last inquirer was a less familiar woman.

"The same spirit who called to me in a dream has been caring for him."

Rylin refused to remain locked in a helpless fever as he was during the Displaced Potential Reckoning. His awareness latched onto that sense of familiarity, forcing his memories to cooperate with him.

Rylin opened his eyes. Painful morning light flooded his vision.

"Light Merahl." Rylin's voice was a weak croak.

"Great work breaking his fever chill so quickly, Light Mathis," Merahl congratulated.

The dark-haired Katahni shook his head. "He is pushing through two diseases with his own will, Light Merahl. I am quite impressed. The physical fever should be enough to dull his mind, but this spirit malady should be crushing him."

"Where were all of you? Light Ishell…the Renegades, we all needed you," Rylin accused.

Merahl answered Rylin. "We settled in Perahl'Glae before the full onslaught began. When the Lancers were butchered, we knew the capitol would rely on us for survival."

"We had no word. We thought the rest of the Order perished."

Merahl looked away, his expression panged deeply. "I

know. When it was safe, I returned to the Citadel for information. We could no more rush to their defense than yours. We kept an illusion over Perahl'Glae to deceive the Kasarins. No one entered or left the city. It was the only way to keep the people safe."

Rylin gave a weak nod of acceptance, jarring the ache of his fever a little.

"Now, you need to rest. Your spirit is in a terrible state. Sleep." Merahl infused the order with a gentle push of the Endless Current.

Rylin was sound asleep in seconds.

-47-

Ishell and Solas Lauren arrived at the dilapidated forest cottage in the late morning. The air was thick with the smell of fresh rain and sweet forest growth. Birdsong chittered in the heights of the trees, at a tentative distance from the cottage.

The hum of the Endless Current was thick in this clearing.

A small crowd of Solas loitered about the outside of the ruined walls, speaking in hushed and nervous volumes. They were at ease in the cooler mountain air. The Endless Current bolstered their tolerance against the chill.

Ishell empathized. It was a great relief to gather those infinite vibrations. The past five days left her feeling useless as she walked the battle-ravaged streets. This was compounded as she listened to the cries of the sick and the injured. She watched the number of graves increase well after the burial of those who fell in battle.

Ishell was the daughter of a blacksmith, even before becoming a sorceress. Her father reminded her, every day she visited him, that her strength was more than her magic.

So, Ishell helped Aemreen and her troupe of healers, any way she could. She poured her frustrations into a shovel as she helped bury the dead.

Ishell halted her reminiscing and climbed the cluttered steps of the cottage. She stopped at the broken remains of the door to take stock of the situation. She relegated the signs of decay to obvious backdrop, focusing her attention on Merahl, Nerilisse, and three evokers Ishell only knew in passing.

Merahl held a book open in his lap while the four other Solas stood around a bed. They were concentrating on maintaining a complex series of spell-shapes.

The energies were bound to Rylin. He lay in the bed, sleeping, covered in sweat. His face was pale.

But it was enough to contradict the rumors that were passed between Legionnaires, villagers, and Renegades. They insisted they saw Rylin's shape in the darkness of the eclipse. They spread the impossible rumor that he was their terrifying rescuer, a Void Hand.

Ishell put those weighted suspicions down, angrily. Her friend was sick, and Merahl sent for her to help. She would not allow poorly placed fears to grip her in hesitation in front of Rylin, again.

After a moment, Merahl looked up to the front door, blinking in bewilderment.

"Ah, Light Ishell. It is good that you are here." Merahl put aside the large, leather book and stood up to embrace her in greeting. There was a trembling quality in his arms, and a trace of veins in his eyes that told her he was not sleeping well.

"My, but the war has made you formidable, hasn't it?" Merahl complimented.

There were many unpleasant things to say that came to Ishell's mind. She shoved it down, while she was just grateful to see any Solas still alive. She was concerned for Rylin.

"War only ever takes more than it will give, Light Merahl. Whatever strength I have gained is the smallest consolation when compared to the enormous loss of lives."

Merahl nodded. "Of course. Which is why I need your help to prevent the loss of one more."

Ishell looked over at Rylin, questioningly. "Displaced Potential Reckoning again? It is far from deadly, Light Merahl. He only needs rest."

The look on Merahl's face was as comical as it was dumbfounded. "Displaced Potential Reckoning? What tome mentions that?" Merahl shook his head, banishing a parade of questions for the moment. "Regardless, that is not what ails him. I assume his condition is much worse than what you are familiar with. His soul is barely tethered to his body."

"What?!" Ishell gasped, taking a steadying step back. "Are you sure? How can you be certain? No healer would know."

"Just as there are prerequisite skills for Solas, there are those for Ard Solas," Merahl explained. "A Solas must spend five to ten years in service to the world and the people; and must demonstrate adept knowledge of spirit spell-shapes. Martenen did not allow us to begin our service, so I took advantage of my abundant time in the archives to study."

Ishell looked at Rylin, then she looked at the interior of the ruined cottage. She thought about when he was last seen, and his acceptance of the duel with Zenen'Rol.

"How did he get here?" Ishell scrunched her brow in thought. "If he was in such a condition after fighting Zenen'Rol…"

Merahl gasped with interrupting alarm. "He fought the Crimson Emperor's Fist?! Fates, Light Ishell! That explains much. That one is a monster on the battlefield. He reclaimed and expanded the Kasarin Empire more in the past five decades than in the last eight centuries."

Ishell shrugged aside the accomplishments of the enemy leader. "That still leads me to ask how he got here from the arctic north. How has he lasted this long in such a state?"

Merahl smiled. "He had help. This is no ordinary cottage in the Northern Wastes. It is haunted by a most benevolent spirit. Light Rylin likely had help in getting here. The same spirit sent for me in my dreams. I was shown where to find this place, and when I could arrive. All the while, the host seems to have been focusing all their efforts on tending to his condition."

Ishell took in the surprising information with an ease she found unusual. She heard many stories about homes that were haunted, as a child. Much like the horrifying tales of the Void Hands, she spent years believing they were only so much nonsense. Recent events forced her to change her views about the evil sorcerers. Accepting spirits and haunted abodes was not much of a stretch from that perspective.

As a matter of curiosity, Ishell closed her eyes and quieted her mind. Now, she was not simply taking in the Endless Current. Her Elemental Affinity rekindled and resumed the sensitivity she had at the start of the war. The air shifted in response to the spell-shaping from the four Solas standing around Rylin. She felt the aggressive haste of the fire, the swiftness of the air, the implacable hardness of the earth, and the fluid coolness of the water. They were shaped into subtle forms as transparent as mist vapors. They converged and pooled into a protective humming dome over Rylin's body.

Ishell's senses drifted further into the cottage. There was a conflicted tension in the air. It felt both urgent and tired. It felt like walking into a long and senseless argument. Was it the result of the spirit's expended energy? She held no real knowledge of such things, but her intuition told her there was more to it.

Merahl interjected against her inner observations. "In any event, finding you was not simple. To be pointed: I need your help to save Light Rylin."

Ishell blinked, wondering why Merahl would begin to believe she would refuse.

Merahl was quick to raise a staying hand. He turned and opened the book he was reading, offering it to her. "Before you rush to agree, you should know what I am asking of you. Go on. The circumstances outweigh your curriculum and the Order's protocol."

Merahl was referring to the rule of the Order forbidding Torches and less advanced initiates from delving into Ard Solas knowledge. Ishell accepted the book and began reading.

Ishell read the intricate and ancient ritual Merahl intended to use to save Rylin. A moment later, her face warmed with an undeniable blush. After several detailed paragraphs, charts, and instructions, Ishell doubled over with an outburst of laughter that stole her breath.

Ishell felt Merahl's stare of confusion, but she needed to breathe before she could speak, let alone answer.

"Dear me, Light Merahl; but you appear to misunderstand the nature of my bond with him. I cannot assist you in this capacity."

Merahl's expression was plainly mortified. "His soul is in the balance. How can you speak so, and laugh?"

Ishell raised her hand, shaking her head as much to dismiss the laughter. "I will perform the ritual. But I have someone in mind who is better suited to help in the method you intend. Do you believe you can hold this spirit tether for several more hours?"

Merahl sighed, resigned, and slumped his shoulders. "It is a lot to ask of us, Light Ishell. The Four Element Spirit Cocoon is equally intricate and strenuous. The delicate balance of the four elements, and their constant shaping and weaving, can be very tenuous. We have to work in shifts of an hour, or we may exhaust, or worse."

Ishell nodded with solemn agreement. She was witness to several Current Dissolutions. She harbored no desire to see it occur to any other Light. "I will be as swift as I am able. Understand me when I say that I am about to attempt something nearly as delicate."

Merahl paused, inhaling deeply. Ishell was amazed that he could draw a refreshing breath here. The smell of mold and rotting wood was as thick as the rich, sharp musk of forest air outside.

"We will hold with all our strength," Merahl promised. "Waste no instant, Light Ishell."

Ishell's answering smile was bold and broad. "None, Light Merahl."

Ishell turned and left the cottage. She wanted to tell the men and women gathered here, that it warmed her to see so many Solas alive. Whatever the circumstances that allowed it, she felt a surge of hope. The Order of the Enlightened Sun would rise again, meeting the hard work Stratia demanded of them.

That, in turn, brought her a second piece of glad tidings. Ishell felt giddy to think about it. Nearly four years ago, Ishell made a silent pact with herself. Today, she believed she could fulfill that vow.

-48-

An eager predatory smile played on the deep red lips of Maesellen Moarenroak. Her stride was long and filled with purpose and energy. Her crimson velvet gown billowed in tandem with her long, braided, black hair.

She was flanked by two blonde handmaidens in pink silk dresses. They struggled to keep pace. Maesellen held no thought for them.

The Queen of Malkanor felt the tide of events turn in her favor as she approached the throne room. The invasion was a terrifying thing, and for a time it forced her to reconsider withholding her forces. But everything transpired better than she could have hoped for.

In the early morning, just as the sun crested the eastern rise, Maesellen sent a courier bird to the swamps in Nerinmor. A message was sent from a courier bird in her Nerinmor stronghold, telling her of Amorlic's collective successes. It was time for him to return to Pahlinsor. His ingenuity allowed only two hundred men to withstand repeated sieges against her compound. He developed new deadly weapons and toxins beyond even her own capacities. He safeguarded many workers and slaves, until the very end of the repeating sieges, losing them only to an all-out assault. Most of these triumphs he achieved with minimal supplies, and no reinforcements, even before she employed the assistance of the Blood Scathe Twins. He was far too talented, now, to be anywhere but the center of events.

Which brought Maesellen to the next wondrous news to reach her: most of the rulers of Stratia were unaccounted for.

Maesellen was aware of the plot between Lycendrik Derin and Delkit Mayzeneth to mercifully annex Malkanor. That was a decade ago. Lycednrik might be a peacock-brained lunatic, but Maesellen respected the unspoken element of his plan.

By taking control of both sides of the pacifist farmland of Teril, he could claim Talik's crown, as well. He would have controlled most of Stratia.

But fate favored Maesellen. Lycendrik had not been seen since the invasion was well underway. Delkit died in battle against the Kasarins. Talik ruled without military. If Lycendrik was gone, Behrain was too much of a brainless fool to resist the slightest aggression. King Kellman Forzen of Vodess was a worthless opium slave.

The greater boon of it all was that every known military was severely reduced by the invasion. Even the Order of the Enlightened Sun was numbering less than one hundred people.

With such a desperate need for soldiers and peacekeepers, Maesellen could begin the slowest and most critical part of her plan.

Then a frown straightened her lips and her brow furrowed. Could it really be so simple? Her enemies numbered far less than before, but enemies did not always require numbers to be dangerous. She would do well to remember that the Kasarins failed in the face of that very same truth.

Maesellen shuddered, involuntarily, as she remembered the black day that ended them. She was not a woman easily cowed by fears, but that day reduced her to a fearful cringing ball. It was humiliating to admit and remember, but that day was so raw and gigantic that it left her small and impotent.

When the skies allowed the light of the sun, again, there was not a single Kasarin corpse in all Malkanor. For all the screams, the fires, and the stench, it was though it never occurred. That detail haunted and chilled Maesellen.

In addition to it all: the giant black sword revealed it was no mere decoration. There was some sort of strange history about the unusual blade that was passed down between kings and princes of Malkanor.

That no longer mattered, now. The glowing weapon vanished in the night that followed the eclipse. Maesellen might have tried to discover how such a theft was executed, but the sword frightened her. She would have disposed of it, in time. This worked just as well.

At every corner and junction of the palace, the Phoenix Legions stood in stoic and statuesque pairs. After the dungeon break by the Havoc Guild, their vigil had become unwavering. They would not allow their capitol to be violated that way, again. It would be a long time before they relaxed their watch over the palace.

So, the throne room was no longer watched by the usual ceremonial honor guard. Two hard-faced corporals of the Phoenix Legions pulled the doors open with ease and stepped aside. The two guards were picked from the scarred veterans of the battle of Thriwald and Borkray.

The gathering at the cracked dais of the throne was a questionable surprise, drawing up one of Maesellen's eyebrows.

Maloric leaned forward in a hushed conversation with Marcelles. His expression flashed between dour and amused. They were standing close to the far corner of the throne room, just before one of the few red and dark blue stained-glass windows that remained intact.

It was conspiratorial, and that worried and angered her. She distrusted any instance where men might hold their secrets from her. They were, as a rule, too stupid to concoct a proper plan. Whenever their schemes were brought to fruition, it tended to be a disaster for everyone.

To the right stood Aemreen Tahkaer and the Order witch

girl...the daughter of that stubborn fool smith Errnik.

Whenever two young ladies of their age were together, Maesellen expected to see silks and frills with a lot of whispers and giggling. These girls were so far beyond that stage that Maesellen suppressed a wince, looking at them.

Aemreen no longer clattered around in that ridiculous suit of armor, and she no longer favored the blood and dirt-stained trousers and blouse. But her azure silk dress with its single thread embroidery was nothing more than plain. She was the daughter of the Lord General. She was betrothed to the future throne. Could her foolish righteous indignation not end?

Maesellen paid little heed to the Order witch. For all her bluster, and being permitted to hold sway among her betters, how much was it worth in the face of the eclipse? She was both powerless and worthless during the final Kasarin strategy. She wore the gray robe of the Order, likely hiding the brown peasant dress she would never rise above.

But what could the fool girl do now? The Order held no power.

Maesellen stepped with command to the dais and whirled to glare at the girl. "Will someone remove that filthy peasant girl before she spreads her stench in the palace?"

Maesellen did not look at Maloric; and did not see him pinch the bridge of his nose. She heard a nervous cough from Marcelles. She did see Aemreen cover her mouth to stifle a laugh.

The soldiers did not budge from their post. Maloric did not command his men to obey. The only noticeable result was a moment when the girl clenched her fists into white knuckles.

"I believe obeying that order would be foolish to anyone, your majesty." The girl spoke through clenched teeth, before calming herself with a deep breath.

"The palace and the throne tolerated your presence only at the behest of your successes and your power," Maesellen informed without betraying her irritation. "You are currently lacking both."

"I live, many of the people I cherish are still alive, and my homeland is not in ashes, your majesty. In these regards, success is mine. As for my power…" The girl raised her palm high overhead. A cloud of dust gathered over her palm, spinning, and congealing into a sphere of glossy obsidian. The ball rested in the center of her palm as she brought her arm down.

Maesellen quietly ground her teeth. She thought the days of pandering to the Enlightened Sun were over. Their loss of sorcery was only temporary.

"To what grace do we owe for your presence, Torch?" Maesellen feigned a smile and greeting that oozed condescension. Did the girl roll her eyes in disgust?

Maloric turned his attention back to Marcelles. "Are we in enough agreement to inform my queen, old friend?"

Marcelles answered with a somber nod. "I am resolute in this, your majesty. The condition has been met."

Maesellen knew she was not the only woman to don an expression of confusion.

"Forthwith, I, Maloric Moarenroak, lucidly possessed of the integrity of my word and honor, do hereby nullify the arranged agreement for my son, Amorlic Moarenroak, to wed Aemreen Tahkaer, daughter of Marcelles Tahkaer."

Maesellen was on her feet with livid outrage. "You cannot! The contract is binding."

Maloric nodded with infuriating patience. "It is, and so is the continuation that was drawn the same day. It was a condition agreed upon by Marcelles and myself, my lady. Without it, the contract would not have his signature."

And this was why Maesellen hated men creating their own schemes.

"And the conditions are?" Maesellen growled the question.

"Should Aemreen Tahkaer fall for a man whose integrity and good nature exceed the value of Malkanor's throne, the arrangement is nullified so that she may follow her heart's desire." The recitation seemed to be one Maloric memorized well.

"Whose greatness is beyond us?"

"Torch Rylin has won both my daughter's heart, and my approval, your majesty." The even and calm way in which Marcelles answered only angered Maesellen further. Did he think she would view this as any less of an insult?

"Torch Rylin? The one born of those filthy people of the Outskirts?" Maesellen clenched her fists, knowing this looked less than regal. "Perhaps the lord general will allow his daughter a tryst in the stables with one of the stable boys. Maybe he can pass her around his men like a tankard of mead."

It was Marcelles's turn to don an outraged and furious countenance. Both the girls looked ready to strike her. She welcomed the attempt. They would be in irons within an hour.

But it was Maloric who stepped forward, holding back Marcelles with one massive hand.

"My lady, on the honor of the throne passed to me by my ancestor, Khalsis Moarenroak, you will beg pardon for the strike upon the dignity of my guests." His brown eyes were flat with cold warning.

"I will not. All decrees and edicts of the nation are shared by the king and queen. There is no punishment you can serve me that I cannot nullify."

"Do not take this path, my queen." Maloric spoke more in warning than imploring. How much did the bear really know? His words hinted at far more, at knowing they had been in a deadly dance for many years now. Was he truly so aware? "We are all too weary and battered to cast ourselves into civil war."

The oaf was using a bold play of words that belied everything anyone ever believed of him. It did take her aback, but there was only one way to be sure of this gambit.

"Perhaps you and your men are, my king; but I have been safe and rested the whole time."

Maloric stared at Maesellen, quiet and unblinking. Maesellen would not stand down, and she matched his stare with her own icy gaze. They were at a royal impasse, a stand-off. She would force him to see that there was no test he endured that was not dwarfed by her own dark and hard experiences. Whatever he might bring to bear against her, it was small and irrelevant.

Aemreen cut into the silence. "How long do you imagine I will belong to his highness, your majesty?"

Maesellen answered without turning away from her stare-down with Maloric. "You will give him an heir, then he may do with you as he pleases."

"It is humorous that you believe I will tolerate nine months with that brute. Such a joyless world is no place for me, especially to shame the honor of my father by allowing our repeating rescuer to die."

Maesellen blinked and turned her eyes to the young noble woman.

"How does marriage have any relation to his life?"

"A good question, but I do not possess time enough to acquire the answer. Suffice it to say: if I do not do this (if I must turn away from Rylin to belong to your son) then the dishonor will be a deadly curse. It will end Amorlic's life or disgrace him. This, I vow."

So, the fool Tahkaer finally did it, did she? She found a way to best a far more experienced queen. Maesellen wished the steel in her veins, and the resulting victory, were present for any other matter. She measured the girl's resolve for murder or suicide and found no trace of bluffing. Now, she understood the heir of Malkanor would never be conceived by Aemreen Tahkaer. Her foolish altruism was a contradiction to any such futures.

This threat would not go unanswered, though. For this,

the girl and Rylin would die. It would take time, but she would make them both suffer.

"So be it, Tahkaer brat. Run along with your animal. May you birth a litter of worthless freaks."

There was a sharp sting and a jolting impact to the side of Maesellen's face. When she turned, she found Maloric standing before her, furious contempt burning on his dark bearded face.

"You disgrace us, my queen. I'll tolerate no more."

Maesellen paid no heed to the gaping expressions around her. She touched her cheek where Maloric's palm struck her, and then she shoved her way through him. She stormed her way to the throne room door. Consumed by such heated rage, the soldiers rushed to open the doors for her.

Before this day, Maesellen might have ordered her armies to graciously spare one or two of those fools. No more. This day, and its events, were a declaration of war. She promised herself she would mount their heads on spears at the four corners of her empire, no matter how many months or years she had to wait.

-49-

Merice walked a measured stroll down the ravaged road between the Zenith Citadel and Katahn. The boy Illumancer walked alone under a cheerful cloudless sky. It was a horrible contrast with the ruins and the blackened heaps of burned bodies from the citadel.

Merice hated being here, now. The ocean waves and the distant gulls filled the air with mournful cries and sighs, the only sound present. It was a bleak and sad monument to vibrant hopes, snuffed out and burned.

Not that new hopes could not be born from the ashes of the old. They would be, just as he knew he needed to be here. That was part of the mystery of Illumancy. It was infused with innate wisdom and the fickle appearance of foresight.

Those foresights drove Merice mad, now, because he did not know how far into the future these newborn hopes would persist.

Hopefully longer than the slab of white granite that was the monument to the fallen Lights of Katahn. It was nothing more than a deep black crater, peppered with tiny white chunks.

Merice sighed with deep sadness. Whatever came next for the survivors of the Order of the Enlightened Sun, and Katahn'Sha, it would not take shape here. This was a mournful ruin filled with ghosts of pain and loss.

Against such pain, Merice continued to descend the

broken incline.

There was not much time! Ishell read and re-read the ancient rite in the large leather book. It was thought that Merahl would shape the rite, as he was the most knowledgeable; but the rite called for the most powerful magi to shape it. Next to Rylin, that was her.

So, Ishell fastened down on her concentration. It was difficult as thoughts of a child's promise, and fate and irony paraded into her thoughts. Was it a coincidence that she was keeping her word, and standing at the head of this rite? She believed it was more.

Ishell sat alone on a boulder that overlooked a steep high bluff, far above a forested valley. It was the tenth time reading through the millennia old passage. The sun vividly defined the bright, gold-leaf words and colorful diagrams.

Half a mile up the treacherous rise behind her, the entirety of the living Order was gathered at the decrepit cottage. It was not the first time for her to wonder how Rylin (broken and beaten down to his spirit in a duel) managed the journey here with no magic. When he located the signature of Zenen'Rol's power, Rylin departed Pahlinsor with unstoppable haste.

But Ishell knew she was not the only one to mull that enigma over. It was an uneasy riddle, and it frequently conjured images of a dark and terrible shadow for many of them.

Be that as it may, Ishell could reassure herself that the Void Hand was not Rylin. Nothing of his appearance matched the old fireside stories.

So, Ishell turned her mind away from the unwanted paranoia. She brushed a stray lock of golden hair out of her eyes. Right now, Light Merahl was speaking with Aemreen, preparing her for her role in the rite. A tear of sympathy and admiration threatened to cloud Ishell's vision. The noble girl was so brave, so unflinching, when it came to Rylin. She loved him with every iota of her being. She was ready to give up everything for him. Titles, estates, luxury…these were nothing to Aemreen and her love for Rylin. She would offer her soul to save his life.

Which was why, just as Ishell vowed to protect their courtship, it was she who would personally oversee an unbreakable marriage between them.

So, Ishell read the rite again.

Merice halted twenty feet from the remains of the outermost structure. It was a series of perfectly preserved glossy black mounds. The trenches and molten remains created a grotesque black display, like heaps of frozen slime. Black timbers protruded, at random angles, like skeletal hands imploring for mercy.

This was the place where no being should be able to trespass. Life and energy would only meet sudden dissolution beyond this point. It was deadly to so much as touch the implacable Spirit Barrier.

Merice stood still for a long while, staring at the air in front of him, before raising his hand. He rested his palm on a cool, invisible surface rippling with watery blue light. It was like touching the surface of a still pond. It also felt refreshing to the touch, soothing his skin.

All at once, a cacophony of whispers filled his mind.

"I see." Merice appeared as though he was talking to himself. "So, a trespass has occurred."

Even before he learned more, Merice knew this could complicate things for a young Illumancer in training.

It was late afternoon when Ishell arrived at the littered clearing that surrounded the cottage. Sunlight poured through the thick patchwork of high forest branches before it gleamed faintly off the dull edge of the rusted wood axe.

It was a wide-open space; but it felt cramped with little less than one hundred Lights of the Order. Many of the Torches and Solas already looked exhausted. They already spent so much effort in maintaining the tether that kept Rylin's soul in his body.

Borvis approached Ishell first. His head was meekly bowed, and he rubbed a nervous hand through his short brown hair.

He chuckled, awkwardly. "So, marriage will save his life and spirit?"

"That is what Light Merahl believes. His musings are sound," Ishell answered.

Ishell felt awkward and fidgety herself. She stuffed her hands into the sleeves of her robe. The playful, skirt-chasing, former noble was intimately close to her in the time of war. She had her own cravings of him before then, but his presence grew to a comfort that bolstered her resolve. Now, she could not imagine returning to her studies and having him in a lesser capacity. She thought about it, and nerves tightened, because she hoped something like today waited in their own future.

"It is an awful lot, though; very restrictive," Borvis scoffed as his eyes shifted between her and the ground. "No secrets kept, no pains endured alone, no desire to hurt one another, ever. No lecherous thoughts."

"You sound as if that is awful."

Borvis stuttered, his eyes wide. Ishell wanted to laugh. This shy demeanor was unlike his usual bluster and wit. He was nervous about something, and she thought she knew what that might be. Watching him squirm still entertained her.

Her mirth must have revealed itself because his eyes

narrowed.

"I have also heard that such men cannot be frustrated with their wives. They cannot hunker down in a tavern and complain to other men over a heavy brew."

Ishell tapped her lips, feigning an expression of deep thought.

"It seems a proper way to get a man on his best behavior. Perhaps I should try it on you."

"You wouldn't dare force a man into matrimony." Borvis spread his arms high. "Think of the ladies of the world. The ladies, I say! They will forever mourn the loss of their premiere charmer. It is woe and lament, unbound!"

The thick rebuttal forced a peal of laughter out of Ishell. She didn't think she could laugh after the invasion.

"But a plain marriage with the right woman. I might be persuaded to stay my whining; and act a pretense of chastity."

It was indirect, but heat blossomed in her cheeks. With Borvis, a heartfelt admission was all but impossible. He favored his bravado and practical pessimism too much for that.

It was Ishell's turn to stutter.

"Such a thing would have to be overseen by fathers."

"Are you two going to promise, already? Or must I shove you into it?" The awkwardness of the moment shifted as Teranen approached.

"Is it not your turn?" Ishell asked.

The Pyromancer shook her head. "Light Merahl believes white Heart fire will be a potent aid in the coming rite."

Ishell knew the rite, forwards and back, and Merahl was right. The white fire was pure. It would reach and bind their spirits with greater ease.

It would also be reassuring to have Teranen's support. It was not just her power, Teranen was a treasured sister-in-arms, lending all her will in a steadfast presence. Beyond that, Teranen's loving nature reminded Ishell of other girl's stories of their favorite aunts. She also had a favored aunt's hot temper and fiery resolve.

Borvis tried to edge away. "I think I must attend the tether."

Teranen would not have it. She gripped his shoulder, yanking him back.

"Not this time, Light Borvis Len. I have watched you both about this for a long while. You are both the same age when I married. I will shame Borik's spirit if I do not set you, both, on course."

Teranen paused, looking to them at length.

"I don't need to Heat Read. I have spoken to both of you. Son of Len, hailing from northern Teril, boisterous Torch Polymancer of the Order of the Enlightened Sun, you have a query?"

At this point, any Light not aiding in the tether began to crowd close with undisguised interest.

Borvis was on the verge of panic. He licked his lips, nervously.

"Fates blight it all, Light Teranen!" Borvis grumbled as he bent to pick up a stone. "This is far less tactful than I imagined it would be. Let it never be claimed you possess a mastery of subtlety."

Teranen's answering grin was toothy. "I wouldn't dream of such a false boast, Light Borvis."

Borvis closed his eyes and closed the small stone in his fist. Ishell felt the Endless Current flow into him. She had to commend his self-control in these circumstances. Perhaps he should earn his silver staff before her. His mouth moved silently as his free hand traced circles around his closed fist.

When he finished, he opened his eyes and fist. Ishell saw a

gleaming gold band, sparkling with sapphires arranged to shape a tiny, jagged lightning bolt.

"Torch Evoker Ishell of the Order of the Enlightened Sun, daughter of the revered smith, Errnik, will you promise yourself to me, as I promise myself to you?"

Ishell accepted the tiny ring without looking away from the wiry polymancer's comical face. Borvis would always strive to comfort her; and make her smile. She imagined how a future like that would be. It made her inwardly happy to foresee it. A husband and wife, Lights of the Order in love, living and working side by side to better the world.

She thought about herself, in the days as a young girl, hoping to be discovered by the Order. She thought about her dreams and hopes of making the world better.

That dream could be made real, in greater ease, with Borvis by her side.

"I will, Borvis Len."

Merice stood, his eyes rolled back in his head. The spirits in the barrier conveyed everything to him. Being a child, and the next Illumancer, they trusted him to safeguard the knowledge they died with. And he felt them all. He felt the presence of those who died in the battle of Katahn.

His tears fell when he recognized the spirits of the Solas who remained in the Citadel after the departure of the Renegades. These were the brave Solas who stood isolated in battle against the Kasarins in their home. Their bravery was acknowledged, and they were beckoned into the barrier.

Merice saw events unfold from the perspective of an incorporeal bystander. He gained knowledge that was kept secret for two millennia by each Grand Illumination.

Merice, a child of ten, now knew more than almost anyone about the Order of the Void Triangle. He knew about their recent emergence as the blood-soaked Book of Worms. He knew about their role in the destruction of Katahn, after they allowed him to watch the battle take place.

The spirits passed the knowledge of what the book came to do. The scope and patience of their plan was enormous. Merice measured himself against it and felt small and helpless.

Worse still: the recent trespasses left reason to believe imprisoning the book was not enough. Something came and acquired all the dark instruction.

That something was the missing part of Light Rylin.

Merice was confused. How could anyone ever believe Rylin would align himself with a nihilistic demon agenda?

"I know enough about him to know he has a great heart. He seeks to save and protect, to help. Even if this Void Disciple was him, wiping out an exterminating army is not the same as ending creation."

The spirits answered. They were aware of this truth. It created a fog of uncertainty, rendering any action premature. There was no guarantee that Rylin would do as the Void Triangle hoped.

"Then why have me here, at all? Why tell me?"

The spirits explained that a great crossroads of fate had begun. Merice was called as a precaution. His first loyalty must be to them; to learning from and obeying the spirits, first and foremost."

Merice felt the immense gravity of the situation, but he held no doubts or hesitation.

"I vow, upon the fate of my soul, to serve as your student and vessel of your will."

◆ ◆ ◆

Ishell and Aemreen stood outside the clearing, and the prying ears of her fellow Lights. It wasn't that Ishell did not trust them. She believed that this moment should be shared by two ladies of the same age.

It was mid-sunset. The forest dimmed with the surreal glow that came with twilight's arrival.

"So, you believe Rylin will be adopted under the Tahkaer name?" Ishell inquired.

For a peasant born to any nation, marrying into nobility was not common. But while Aemreen was willing to sacrifice everything for Rylin, she believed her father would not ask anything of the sort of her. Marriage often involved taking the family name of a husband, but common born people were given no family name. That was a privilege reserved for highborn throughout Stratia. But a family name could not be removed unless the family disowned a person in disgrace. It was a rare circumstance.

"My father always liked Rylin, and his opinion has only grown. I think he will insist that he be taken in as a Tahkaer in marriage. He will be afforded some of the family respects and honors."

Ishell listened and smiled as a distant memory played in her mind. This truly was becoming a different world, full of changes. Here they were, all readying themselves to step forward.

Ishell shook the memory of fighting with Rylin in a Contest of the Magus. "Do you have jitters for what is to come?"

Aemreen looked thoughtful for a moment before shaking her head.

"Should it be strange? My body, my heart, mind, and spirit, all apart of him, and I only know I want it. It is more than I believed possible, but that only makes me wish for it, more."

"But he will be part of you, in the same manner." Ishell

broke the tension with laughter. "I have evaded Current Reading just so that I would not know what thoughts clutter him."

Aemreen's retorting smile was teasing. "Are you certain you do not avoid the clutter of your fiancée's mind?"

It was a light-hearted moment, and Ishell laughed with Aemreen. At that moment, Ishell felt like she knew what it must be like to have a sister. She was amazed that she would discover this feeling with a young woman born to aristocracy.

So, while there was still time, there was one thing left to do.

Ishell closed her eyes and stilled her thoughts. The Endless Current pulsed through her, filling the stillness. She thought about Aemreen, picturing her in her mind. As she did, she began to speak incomprehensible words. These words were only one sound melding into another. Her hands brushed the air in long wavy lines.

Ishell held an obvious weakness in transmutation. There was a difference in shaped elements; but making one object acquiesce to a desired change was far more complex. Borvis would argue that elemental work was harder. It really was a difference of opinion between the specialists.

Then there was a push of gentle blue light against her closed eyes. The shaped energy pushed out of her hands to wrap Aemreen in a cocoon of transformative light. She changed the color of her dress to a pale blue. Silver, flowery embroidery swirled in a snug silk bodice. Gossamer, white, lace work cascaded her arms and fell from the back of her hips. Two curling strands of her brown hair framed the sides of her face. The rest of her hair was gathered in a coiled braid on top of her head. Her hair was caught in a wreath of white morning glory vines, spotted with lilacs, irises, and lilies.

When Ishell stopped and opened her eyes, she was as speechless as Aemreen. The tear that fell from Aemreen's eye only added to her stunning radiance. Aemreen wasted no words in wrapping Ishell in a tight embrace.

"You are the dearest of friends, Torch Ishell."

Ishell found her own eyes beginning to water. "I could do no less for a bride and a friend."

Ishell waited before she led Aemreen back to her soon-to-be husband.

-50-

Aemreen imagined many ways of how it might be to marry Rylin; but this was the most unexpected. Ishell held her hand, guiding her through the rotted door frame and into the crowded den beyond. Ten Solas stood in stoic readiness. Four more Solas were seated in plain wooded chairs on each side of a bed where Rylin lay in feverish slumber.

The four Solas weaved their hands in various hard and gentle gestures. Their faces were furrowed and covered with a thin layer of sweat. The light of a full moon spilled through the roof, bathing Rylin's fitfully sleeping form in a pale halo. His breathing was labored and loud. His chest rose in rapid efforts to take in the air of mold and forest pungency.

Aemreen looked at Rylin and felt a pang in her chest that climbed her throat. Even though he was surrounded by his brothers and sisters of the Enlightened Sun, even though they concentrated all their energy on him, he still struggled to keep his life. He came back from fighting to save them all. Now, he needed to be rescued, himself.

Aemreen would be the key to saving his life. She would bind her soul to his, and his struggle would be shared. In the embrace of her spirit, she could pull him back from the precipice.

Beyond the whispered words of the Solas, the night was filled with the songs of night birds and cicadas. Tiny eldritch lights began to flare and fade around the cottage and forest. Fireflies had taken up residence in this unusual habitation. Were they drawn here for some reason? The combined night glow created a fluid, surreal sensation. With the cool subtle winds, it felt a little like being inside a reflective pool of water.

Teranen separated from the circling shadows of Solas and walked to the other side of Ishell.

Ishel turned to the Perahli Solas Merahl. "Any word about Light Merice? Though he is only a child, an Illumancer would be a great help."

Merahl shook his head.

"I see. I also would have appreciated the additional strength of Lights Layrienn and Kaysienn, but it can't be helped. Did you acquire Light Rylin's consent?"

"I needed to Spirit Walk in his fever dreams," Merahl shuddered at a memory, causing Ishell to quirk an eyebrow, "but he would give his entire being to her."

Aemreen was overcome with excitement as she heard those words from Light Merahl. This was truly happening! Rylin was the focus of her love from the deepest recesses of her being. She wanted him since the first day they met in the palace of Malkanor. This was a moment she wished for since before the day that led to their first kiss on the moonlit plains.

Ishell stepped aside, inviting Aemreen to take her place inside the circle.

It was an ancient custom that the couple should stand, side by side and hand in hand. The Lights of the Order were forced to improvise. They had to gain the permission before the Rite of Spirit Marriage, working with an unconscious man. It was especially brave of them since the Rite had not been performed in seven centuries.

Aemreen laid down in the small bed beside Rylin. She took his hand in her own and looked up into the sky, filled with the light of stars and fireflies. Potent energies hummed as they tethered Rylin when she laid down with him. Now those energies stopped.

The leaves and layer of decayed litter began to stir in a strange gust. The wind gained subtle intensity.

All at once, the night burst to blinding white life and crackling light. A ring of floating fire circled several feet above Rylin and herself. Inside the ring, there was a golden glowing aura. It formed a cocoon that soaked through her skin, permeating deep beyond her body before pausing. The glow cradled her with soothing warmth from within.

Ishell began to speak. Her words were loud enough to reach outside, to the edge of the clearing.

"In oath given, we gather in reverence, to bind thee, Light Rylin and Aemreen Tahkaer."

Every Light present intoned their response in unison. "Thy oath given, two shall be one."

"Since first the Endless Current was our ally, it was known that hearts in love continue beyond death's claim. To honor and celebrate this sacred truth, we deepen these bonds. We wed, not until the end of one life, but unto the end of eternity. We share all that we were, all that we are, and all that we ever shall be." Ishell paused.

"Thy oath given, two shall be one."

Ishell continued after the unified intonation. "And so, we shall bind thee. Thou shalt hold no secret; or shoulder any anguish in solitude."

Aemreen was also informed that this meant the death of one could mean the death of the other. There would always be the risk that she would be his mortal weakness.

"We bind thee in absolute loyalty. No pain can one inflict upon the other without receiving it as well. But, also, shall no end truly know thee. As one, thou shalt be forever." Ishell continued even as a slight tremor cracked her voice.

The infusing golden light moved anew. It reached deeper and deeper in Aemreen's essence. The white fire flared without growing hot. It created a circling wall around Aemreen and Rylin.

Aemreen turned her head to look at Rylin. She watched him and smiled as tears of joy filled her eyes. This moment was the start of an eternity together.

The voices of the Order filled the night, reaching beyond the clearing and deep into the woods. Their voices, united, were filled with the full potency of their passion and determination.

"Thy oath given, two shall be one."

When those words were spoken, a trickling seeped into Aemreen's mind. While the golden glow grew brighter, her brain was slowly infused with the tickling of memories and thoughts that were not her own.

There was an ache of thirst and a groan of a hungry belly as she toiled in relentless, sweltering heat. She fought the desire to drop the heavy straw basket and run for the shade of an apple tree. The bony, underfed torso of her father was a potent sight that morning. She would work at least as hard as him. She would help to return strength to his body.

A pang of guilt and sorrow swelled in Aemreen with Amorlic suspended in mid-air. Were Ard Solas Matisia any less powerful, she would have been executed as soldiers scoured the woods for pieces of the heir to the throne. She was torn between the relief that Ishell still lived, and the brooding remorse of being so nearly branded a murderer.

Then there was the unstoppable resolution to discover the source of an evil that would not allow its victims to speak of it in the presence of the Order. She reached backwards, through the emerald force of time, to discover its presence and raise a defense against its approach.

Rylin was a series of trials met with pain and determination. Everything he ever fought for, or endured, was for the people he cherished.

Aemreen was at the center of so many of his struggles.

She brought him back to himself, again and again, even while he lost himself just for her sake. It riddled her with shame and guilt that he should pay such a steep price for her.

So, Aemreen all but screamed as she watched his final moments of the arctic duel with the titan Zenen'Rol. Rylin was as amazing to behold as he was implacable in his desire to end the war for all Stratia.

But the Kasarin giant did not come to fight with honor. The deception was almost enough to kill Rylin, and all Stratia.

That was when Aemreen was greeted with the true secret of Rylin's predicament.

Deep in the darkest corners of Rylin's being, there slept a third presence. Aemreen already knew about the second presence. The predatory gaze of the resilient Aspect of Vengeance circled, even now. It was a cold judgmental force; but it was one of two parts needed to awaken the third presence.

Aemreen was overcome by an overwhelming pain deep in her middle as the memories around this third presence came forward.

Aemreen pleaded desperate cries that would not leave her mouth.

"No! No, please! I beg fates that this not be so!"

But there was no denying the terrible bloody memories she found. An icy resolve of killing intent settled over her. The darkness swallowed her whole. She was replaced with a being of maddening nightmares and darkest imaginings. She held the knowledge of secrets and methods no human should ever know, and she held the power to wield them. Demons rejoiced in her presence. Void Hands had given their lives, freely, so that she would become reality.

The third presence went by the name Naejestrisis. To all demons he was Crayaht'En…Creation's End.

Rylin came to this cottage at the summons of Yelisian's

mother. Together they were fighting against the darkness inside him. That by itself was alarming. They were not only fighting for his life. His spirit was weak from prolonged use of demonic sorcery. Aemreen gained the knowledge from Rylin that these arts scoured the soul.

Rylin would not die if his soul were scoured from his body. Naejestrisis would be the only remaining presence, then. Unleashed, he would begin the destiny the Order of the Void Triangle laid out for him.

Naejestrisis would first become a killer of worlds. Then he would wipe away every living and dead thing. There would be no spirits, no hell, and no silver fields of bliss. Everything would be swallowed up in nothingness.

Rylin, my love. What have you done? Would death for both of us have been so bad? Aemreen asked in the silence of her mind. *I never wanted you to pay such a price. It is far too much.*

Rylin's thoughts answered, defensively, surprising her.

I could not let you die.

A heavy fever soaked into her. Aemreen succumbed to a shared sleep to bring Rylin back. Sharing the fever, and the effort to sustain his spirit, he would wake in several hours. Ishell told her she would keep a watch over them until they could wake.

Aemreen steeled her heart with a resolve she reserved only for combat.

The war against extermination by the Kasarin Empire was over.

The war for Rylin's soul had only just begun.

-51-

What remains of home.

The survivors of the Order of the Enlightened Sun (heroes and saviors of all Stratia) climbed the broken road to the Zenith Citadel in silent shock. The hillside was pockmarked with charred craters. Heaps of blackened corpses lay closer to the collapsed entry. Among the burned, rotting bodies were the identifying patches of brown and gray robes.

The Kasarins did not get the chance to finish disposing of the remains of their enemies. There was no sign of Kasarin occupation. This hinted that the fighting in Malkanor might have drawn them in. Were they wiped away during the eclipse before they could finish their work here?

Errant early autumn leaves brushed the rise, caught in cold, soft winds born of the ocean. They added to the bleak surreal sensation, which was made worse by the light gray clouds that blocked the afternoon sun.

The Renegades walked in dragging steps. The sound of their scuffing boots was accompanied by the roar of the Maelstrom waves, and the cries of the gulls.

Teranen felt the same as her fellow Lights. No one spoke. Their breathing was labored and loud. Numb disbelief bore deep within them, dragging with unseen, and unbearable weight. Their eyes were blank as they stared at the black burns and the giant collapse. It was a testament to the tragedy that befell the pristine bastion, their home.

They were hollow, walking for the sole purpose of each step. They shared in the feeling of being broken and castoff. They were like restless spirits caught in a hazy netherworld.

Teranen recognized the feeling, very well. It was the same mind-shattering detachment she felt when she sat alone in a hut. Her self-preserving sanity could not accept her loss, then. It failed to do so now.

Then came the first intrusion on Teranen's fugue state. It was an insistent tug that ignored her body, reaching directly for the core of her being. There was a gentle warmth and invitation to the pull, a sense of a fond smile that urged her to follow.

So broken and weak, she would have accepted even if the pull were less friendly. She let it happen. She became a marionette on those intangible strings. What else was there to do, really?

Teranen stumbled, tripping, and sliding over the glossy and jagged heaps of debris. She mindlessly ignored the series of cuts and scrapes she recklessly earned as she began a downward climb.

The descent ended in the center of a smooth, black crater. Teranen looked about with a bewildered stupor. The bowl of the crater descended halfway into the basement. The floors above were shoved away from the crater from colossal force, hurled into the surrounding molten heaps.

Teranen looked down. There was a single large handprint in the epicenter, burning bright red with ceaseless heat.

Candle-sized blue fires danced and played in the print. Teranen knew those blue fires. It was Spark Barahn's Heart Fires! The blue was a sign of his love of drinking that kept him from achieving the pure expression of white fire.

Teranen knelt on both knees, reaching down, and cupping the blue flames in both hands. She pulled the fire close with slow reverence. She felt no fear or alarm as the fire absorbed into her skin.

Barahn's last moments found their way to Teranen. She fell forward onto her hands. A moment of numbing shock washed over her as he spoke his last words to her. He died smiling, proud of her; and she failed him. He was her teacher, her friend, and she could not wield enough fire to stave off his death.

And Barahn smiled, he smiled-brave, bold, and proud of Teranen. He fought against an enemy determined to kill the entire Order. He had no way to win or survive; still he smiled in a defiant end.

Teranen's tears came, then. They were futile and useless to her, now. She screamed her pain against the rubble, her tears falling on the-now cold-handprint.

She spent these last years studying in the Order, believing she was becoming powerful enough to prevent any more pain like losing her husband and son.

"My love, my treasured boy, and now my dearest friend. Why won't the fates show mercy and end me? I can't keep doing this. It is too much." Teranen's agonized cries faded, losing volume as she lowered her head.

Teranen felt a reassuring presence as Solas Nerilisse knelt and wrapped her arms around her, pulling her close.

"He passed his Pyromancer's legacy through you. It was more than he thought he would have. He must have known you battled with the full power and heart of his lessons in you. We all knew you were everything to Light Barahn. You were a hope he never dared believe he could have."

"He smiled and laughed as he died, Light Nerilisse." Teranen turned her tear-streaked eyes to the red-haired Solas.

"That means he faced death with no regret. That is only something we can do when we are certain we left the world better than when we came to it."

Barahn's last words reached through his heart-fire, coursing through Teranen's spirit.

I love you, my white Phoenix. What comes next for the Order, is in the hands of you brave Renegades.

The weight of those words settled on Teranen. Barahn never admitted to his deepest feelings before, even as she saw them, firsthand. He also left her no escape from picking up the pieces of the Order of the Enlightened Sun, and the arduous task of putting it back together.

This was true when Borik and Kaeden died. Teranen was left to press on without them.

Already, the Zenith Citadel seemed a place fit only for ghosts. The once ivory halls were cracked, and the floors and walls were scarred with deep, black gouges. The blood stains smeared large and dried to a brown crust.

There were no bodies. The Stratian corpses were piled outside in burned heaps. Maybe the same, or better, was afforded to the Kasarin fallen.

Ishell shuddered. Of course, there was the third possibility for the invader's remains.

Ishell walked the silent halls with Borvis, grateful for her fiancé's presence as she held his hand. Rylin Temporal Projected, just a couple of days ago, to discover more about the fate of the Citadel and those who fought and died there. The battle to protect the children had to have been fierce because the smell of burned things and smoke still lingered.

It was a hard moment. Some of the children were left behind in Malkanor to spare them the horror. Many refused to have any coddling of the sort. They were the survivors of hard battles. A good number of them survived the hours-long battle of Thriwald. Ishell knew better than to deny them in the face of all they endured.

Some were following Rylin, now. They were hoping to reunite with their close friends trapped in the Temporal Study.

It was two weeks passed since the marriage rite; and Rylin appeared to be in good health. He was physically able, and his powers were restored.

But there was something different about him. Rylin was quieter and more distant than usual. His eyes were frequently downcast and haunted.

Sometimes, Ishell caught glimpses of him wincing and grinding his teeth.

It was a matter for another day. Rylin was further along on the first floor, their paths diverged on his insistence. He told her to go to Spark Kera's chamber to her reading den. Ishell was not to go alone.

"I don't much agree with Light Rylin. I am certainly not as fond of him as you are." Borvis chose to break the depressing silence, but Ishell knew where he was going to go with it. She wished he would keep his thoughts to himself, just then.

"It is an ill-fitted moment for this, Borvis Len," Ishell growled. Since his proposal, Ishell took to using his full name when she felt displeased with him.

"Is it? We walk in the desolation of our beloved Order. They died knowing we would choose the new shape for all that we knew. For that to happen, we need a leader."

"I agree. Light Merahl seems like a logical and well-versed choice."

Borvis halted, and Ishell rolled her eyes as she stopped to face him.

"As an archivist, Light Merahl is fully aware that his abilities to lead are interim, at best. He would only do so because the best choice is not yet a Solas."

"If you know so much about leadership, then perhaps you

should lead. You are noble born. You should claim it."

Borvis shook his head and chuckled. "You lead a hundred Lights, who are not Solas capacity, against thousands of genocidal Kasarin Magi. You coordinate, you plan, and you inspire. You tuck away the burden of all your grief for the benefit of morale. Yet now, you fear taking the mantle we all agree is yours."

"Light Yelisian planned that role for Light Rylin."

"If Yelisian lived, his choice would be correct. He would have guided Light Rylin; and instructed him in wisdom." Borvis spoke heated, but he paused to breathe. "It is not Light Rylin's blame. I first accuse the Solas of cowardice. Left to learn by himself, he had no one to teach him as only a Spark can. It was all books, techniques, and practice for him."

"So, we further it by stamping him with the title of Solas and hurling him back into Malkanor, alone?" Ishell hissed, incredulous.

"No one is getting their title so quickly, Light Ishell. You know Light Merahl and the other Solas plan to spend the next while pressing the required knowledge onto us. Then they plan on putting us to trial."

Ishell seized the moment for a change of subject. She giggled and earned a sideways stare from the sharp-nosed polymancer.

"You know, they fear teaching you how to Current Read almost as much as they fear Light Rylin."

Borvis scoffed. "I don't need to read a lady's Current to know how to give her all she desires."

Ishell gave him a warning look.

Borvis rubbed the back of his neck. "Of course…I find it very simple," he stammered, nervously, "when I need know only one lady's desires…and I would never dare make a blacksmith's daughter very cross with me."

Ishell's meaningful stare intensified.

"...aaaannd..." Borvis dragged out the word.

Ishell said nothing, taking Borvis's hand and all but dragging him the rest of the way before stopping at Kera's chamber.

"Blacksmith's daughter, most powerful evoker, and far superior Light than I could ever hope to be," Ishell finished for him.

Borvis looked like he paused to swallow his pride before smiling. "Of course. That is precisely as I was about to say."

The levity departed as Ishell opened the door. What greeted her settled over her like a death shroud.

Kera's chamber was demolished. Her bed was smashed to pieces. The walls were gouged and broken with burgundy-hued vines from the Havoc Guilds. Pieces of her desk and end table were little more than slices and broken chunks of wood. Drifts of ashes stirred in errant breezes from the open window.

Ishell stepped forward, slow and shocked, her feet crunched against shards of broken glass. Seeing what was left of her mentor's bed chamber was as striking and final as seeing the body of Kera would have been. It was empty and violated, a telltale of a remorseless murder that occurred.

Her breath caught in her throat as she approached the door to her mentor's reading den. The door was closed. She held her breath, hoping that something of her friend and teacher was left intact to mark her presence in the world.

Ishell opened the door, her mind repeating silent prayers. The door did not creak, seemingly well-oiled. Maybe the Kasarins left her that much.

Books wore torn and burned on shreds of the thick rug. The four Current Sphere stands were broken and cast aside like twigs. The windows were broken, hanging on one bent hinge. The shelves and chairs were crushed to bits. The enchanted vials and daggers Kera displayed on the shelves were missing, likely the only objects stolen instead of destroyed.

"Look!" Borvis pointed across the room in a whisper.

At exactly the center of the far wall, one stone began to emit a low and quiet hum. Its surface radiated a pale blue glow. It was clear that it was set to react now, as Ishell walked in the room.

Ishell approached the wall in a numb trance. She lifted her hand and touched the stone. The small brick flared with azure light before vanishing.

In its place was an open alcove with an envelope sealed with red candle wax.

Ishell's name was scrawled on the unsealed face in gold-leaf.

Ishell broke the seal and opened the letter. Her knees buckled and her vision blurred while she read.

'Light Ishell, my dearest pupil,

If you are reading this, then I am no longer among the living.

Earlier this day, my Elemental Affinity sensed something very peculiar. Studying this, after allowing it to wash over me, I realized what it was.

I am so proud of you, my sister! You shaped the Song of the Thunder Gods! I never thought I would live to see it wielded by anyone. Only the most legendary of sorceresses have ever mastered it.

So, as I felt this, I knew you were in the heat of battle. The Kasarins are likely angered, and it is only a matter of time before they come here. For reasons I am forbidden to divulge, I cannot leave.

I really wish it were otherwise. A spell-shape like that is worthy of a Solas. I would join you, grant you your silver staff, regardless of protocol, and we would face this enemy as equals.

Already, you have walked an extraordinary path. It has filled me with joy to watch as you matured. All along your journey, I have been proud to watch you embody the spirit of the Order of the Enlightened Sun.

But I can see that this is when the fates decree that teacher and student must walk different paths. As we do, I depart happy in the knowledge that I left all that I was in expert hands. You will honor every evoker sorceress that has ever been.

Watching with pride,

Solas Evoker Kera of the Order of the Enlightened Sun

Ishell clutched the letter close, the final thoughts of her mentor. Borvis saw the great hiccupping sobs wrack her body. He rushed to hold her, keeping her from falling.

"It is alright, Ishell. It is time for all your tears," Borvis reassured as he stroked her hair.

Months of pent-up grief, congealed within from ceaseless war, filled the air with her cries. Her screams rang off the walls as the pain pierced deep.

She saw Kera in her mind. She replayed the first moment she approached her and her father. They knelt in the rain and debris of a decimated outskirts.

"My good man," Kera addressed, politely, "If you would trust her to my care, I believe I can show the world the wonder that we both know she is."

Ishell's father always trusted in the wisdom of the Order of the Enlightened Sun. He needed no further convincing. Ishell never forgot the gentle warmth of Kera's smile, that night. Even in her mentor's most stern moments, Ishell always saw traces of the caring Vodessian woman.

Ishell thought about all the hard training duels Kera forced upon her, at the end. Looking back, Ishell realized her mentor struck with a twinge of sadness in her eyes. Kera must have understood, even then, that their time together was about to end. Kera's all-consuming thoughts were driven to prepare

Ishell for a hard future without her.

Rylin walked through the halls with an agility that belied his current sense of awareness. He was vaguely aware of over a dozen battle-hardened children following him. They were freshly raised to the level of Candle. He tuned out all sounds, and so did not pay heed to the sound of their footfalls.

His eyes were lowered, shadowed, and concealed by the hood of his coat. His emerald staff 'clacked' against the ground with every other step.

Rylin was in an introverted frame of mind for over a week now. He spent his time sorting through a new variety of feelings as he experienced an onslaught of new thoughts and memories. They belonged to Aemreen, now his wife in both body and spirit. He needed to organize these new additions. He needed to separate what was her from what was himself.

But there was more than this compartmentalizing. The only reason Rylin could function at all was Aemreen's added strength. They fought side by side against a hungry pulling vortex, a cold hollow place inside himself that sought to swallow him whole. It was always there, as implacable as any force of nature. So, they stood close in battle, even though they were miles apart.

Remember what Solas Merahl advised. Aemreen's thoughts projected into the spirit bond. *The good you do in service to the world, will impart greater strength to your spirit. Rescue those children, my love. Honor the sacrifice of those who fell in the Citadel.*

Rylin answered with the image of an accepting nod to her. Aemreen projected a memory of a long, heated kiss with perfect clarity. Rylin tripped over his feet as he walked.

I love you, Torch Rylin. Do pay heed to the world and the moment.

Rylin chose to follow her advice, allowing the sounds and sights to wash into his mind, anew. He heard the quiet murmurs of the Candles in the tentative entourage. They sounded depressed and doubtful. What words he made out told him they believed their fellow Lights were forever lost.

Rylin straightened his posture, trying to convey his certainty. He was not skilled at speeches, like Ishell, but he believed his actions would say more. These children walked broken hallways of an empty ruined home they cherished. They believed they would be the last of the Enlightened Sun.

This despair could not be allowed to consume them. The Order was not on its deathbed, it was at a moment of rebirth; just as it had been two millennia ago. The Mage Clans passed only for the Order of the Enlightened Sun to rise in its place.

The tears of his fellow Lights were warranted. Rylin understood that need from the loss of Yelisian. But they would have to believe and have faith in the virtues and purpose of their teacher's sacrifice. They needed to realize their strength and rebuild the Order in far greater glory. They needed a sign for their hope to breathe again.

Rylin stopped at the dark oak remains of the door of his Temporal Study. He admitted that it seemed plain and undecorated compared to the grandeur he saw at the Temporal Sanctum. He would have changed that, perhaps emulating his forebears by aspiring to their designs. But Rylin was not planning on staying among the Order for much longer. He would study for his trial, pass, and then return to Malkanor to begin his service. One day, he would become an Ard Solas. He would return to the Order only when it was mandatory.

The Candles behind Rylin stopped short with trepidation, giving him adequate space among the broken remains of the door. Silence settled over them after several anxious whispers.

Rylin closed his eyes. Breath by breath, his mind lulled into the silence of the single moment. He would start with Temporal Projection; but he needed to do much more. He needed to reach and pull.

Time moved backwards, deep into the immutable cold blue of the past. For long moments, there was nothing. After more than a month back, he watched the crimson and gold armored Ka'Rak walking backwards, unperforming their tasks.

He quieted the reactive sense of anger and killing resolve as he watched them. They were dead, now. All of this was the past. He watched as the bodies of the Solas were placed back in their last moments of life.

The cold of the past deepened to a biting chill in Rylin's brain.

Rylin watched as a brown trail of blood turned red, telling the tale of the Kasarins as they removed Solas Kera's body for burning. A pang of deep gut-wrenching sadness struck him as he looked at her, knowing he was about to watch her die. The door to the Temporal Study reformed, and a blast of orange fire returned to her hand as she died in Zenen'Rol's merciless grip.

Rylin ended the reverse progression of moments abruptly.

Now came the more difficult task. He only ever managed this once, and that was by accident. Both in the present and the past, Rylin grasped the doorknob to his Temporal Study. The last time he tried something like this, he copied a mind that was dead for two millennia.

The Temporal Current disapproved. This was not something as ephemeral as a mind grafted onto his own. Rylin was attempting to pull a solid object out of time. Worse still: the object created a path to a future that no longer existed. When the door was destroyed, the Temporal Current began dissolving the wayward space and time.

Rylin grabbed that space, in the moment before dissolution, and reconnected it with the present.

Rylin felt the stones at his feet tremble. A heavy suffocating presence filled the air, groaning and growling like a threatened animal. Green light pressed, angrily, against his closed eyes. The Candles talked fearfully as the Temporal Current protested his efforts.

Chronomancy was about pressing the limits of acceptable manipulation. This time, Rylin pressed the limits much farther.

The slivers and bits of broken wood from the door whipped around him, darting into place at his command; rushing to where they should be.

Rylin's lungs squeezed, forcing the air, and straining each breath. Gravity crushed down on his body, forcing him to lock his knees and brace against the intensifying force.

Though time tried to shatter his efforts, Rylin stood and defied. At last, his Chronomancy could save lives as he always wanted. Today, he would honor Yelisian's teachings. Today, he would live up to the hopes of the Temporal Arbiter and the Supreme Magus.

Rylin pushed against time, and his spirit flared to life with unyielding resolve. The vortex of Naejestrisis pulled, time pushed, but Rylin found the iron within to stand against both. Aemreen smiled with pride for him.

Triumph over it, my love.

"We can make this right again, dearest heart." Rylin spoke out loud.

In that moment, the Temporal Current could no longer defy Rylin. The smell of burned wood filled the hall for an instant. The pieces snapped and cracked, immediately taking rectangular shape. The pressure in the air burst with a loud pop and the ground stilled. The green light faded.

Rylin looked down to see a brass knob in his hand. The dark oak door was intact.

Rylin opened the door while the Candles held a collective breath.

Over thirty children in brown robes sat expectantly in the room around his meditation circle. Their eyes were fearful, glistening, and wet. Time had not passed for them. They believed the Kasarins still lived.

The Candles cheered as they rushed to their friends. Rylin would allow them to explain everything that happened.

Rylin watched the Candles, embracing the Flames, and he smiled.

His spirit surged with the added strength of doing his best to do what was right.

Yes, the Order of the Enlightened Sun will stand again.

Return for more of Destiny of the Void Triangle in 'The Chronomancer and Creation's End'

Made in the USA
Columbia, SC
07 August 2022

64558383R00252